More Praise for *Lifelike Creatures*

"Rebecca Baum's writing is honest and concise. She can conjure our humanity in a sentence, deftly revealing a humble decency or an utter depravity. *Lifelike Creatures* unapologetically displays our ability to abuse and our capacity to love. The perspectives of a daughter who is so easy to love and a mother who is so hard to forgive, are raw and wrenching. I could feel the fear and shame and rage of vibrant and resilient Tara Saint-Romain. I think every daughter will recognize the precipice of that age, and the tug of war of wanting both the protection of our mother and the freedom from her. I look forward to clearing more space for Rebecca Baum on my book shelf."

— Téa Leoni

"There is something thrilling about reading a first novel such as Rebecca Baum's. The experience gives you the feeling of being in on something special. A story wonderfully told, with vivid description and characters, *Lifelike Creatures* is at once a smash debut and undoubtedly the launch of a bright literary career. Buy this book, it will be something you can brag about in years to come."

— Brian McDonald, author of *My Father's Gun* and *Last Call at Elaine's*

"One of the many appealing things about Rebecca Baum's telling of this story is that it is both familiar, in a ripped-from-the-headlines sort of way—i.e. corporate malfeasance, white and black hats, environmental destruction, illicit drugs, class warfare, situational ethics—and surprisingly personal…This isn't a story about an individual who comes to symbolize something larger; it's a story about individuals caught in extraordinary circumstances and how they respond. Their responses demonstrate how complex, nuanced and personal human drama is. *Lifelike Creatures* is a plainspoken story that deftly avoids polemics and convenient heroes and villains."

— David Roth, author of *The Femme Fatale Hypothesis*

"Raw, sensual, and unapologetic, *Lifelike Creatures* exquisitely examines corporate greed, regional disaster, addiction, and one girl's journey to find solid ground in an unreliable, unforgiving reality. An impressive debut."

— Heather Siegel, author of *Out From the Underworld*

"With beautiful and incisive prose, enjoyable characters, and dynamic narration, Rebecca Baum carries the reader deep into the quest of an unusual teenager who struggles to shore up her difficult mother as a sudden industrial disaster throws her rural Louisiana town, and her world, into chaos."

— Susana Aikin, author of *We Shall See the Sky Sparkling*

"You can practically feel the murky heat and smell the swamp-water air off the Louisiana bayous in Rebecca Baum's gripping tale of toxic Americana. Be prepared for whiplash plot twists and feral rage. Be prepared, as well, to shed tears for the winsome and resourceful young Tara Saint-Romain as she struggles to make sense of the noxious world around her; she's like a twenty-first-century female Oliver Twist, and just as unforgettable."

— Jan Alexander, author of *Ms. Ming's Guide to Civilization*

Lifelike Creatures

Rebecca Baum

Regal House Publishing

Published by
Regal House Publishing, LLC
Raleigh, NC 27612
All rights reserved

ISBN -13 (paperback): 9781646030163
ISBN -13 (epub): 9781646030439
Library of Congress Control Number: 2020930420

Interior and cover design by Lafayette & Greene
lafayetteandgreene.com
Cover art from the Biodiversity Heritage Library.
Digitized by Smithsonian Libraries. | www.biodiversitylibrary.org

Regal House Publishing, LLC
https://regalhousepublishing.com

Printed in the United States of America

To my mother, Linda, who taught me to cherish
creativity and the arts.

Tara

1.

The secret of cigarette smoking revealed itself to Tara Saint-Romain a few weeks before she turned fourteen. She was crouched on the roof of the cavernous old house she shared with her mother, woozy and raw-throated from hacking her way through her first Winston Reds, swiped from the pocket of her mother's bathrobe.

It had taken all her stubbornness, and a flood of acrid tears, to get it right. But now, as she gazed at the luminous drift of night sky, with a chemical hum in her veins, she finally understood her mother's pack-a-day devotion.

Her eyes landed on a single bright star, floating at the fringe of her tangle of dark curls. As she exhaled, sending smoke spiraling up and out, she imagined some trace of her left with her breath, even as her body stayed firmly rooted to this place, and the heavy, familiar earth of Terrefine, Louisiana.

"Tara?" Her mother's voice seeped into her awareness.

"Coming!" She skimmed the night sky once more, then ducked through her bedroom window.

Her mother was downstairs in the kitchen, her eyes locked on the TV, where a fleshy, tentacled mass quivered on the face of a doomed space traveler.

"You watching that again?" Tara asked, stepping into the sweltering room. "Must be the hundredth time." The oven door hung open, belching heat across the worn linoleum. She switched off the knob and flung open the back door, then propped the box fan in the window above the sink.

"Don't, Tara. I'll catch cold." Her mother clutched at her robe, drawing it closer.

"If I'm going to make us something to eat then the oven has to be off. Unless you want me to die of heat exhaustion."

"I don't want you to die." Her mother's rheumy gaze found Tara.

"Well, then…" Tara examined a can of red beans while resting her slender frame against the counter. "You don't realize it's broiling in here 'cause you're stewing in it."

Tara ladled beans and pork sausage over rice and carried two plates to the table. She studied her mother between bites, wondering if she was starting to resurface through the murk of whiskey and pills. Tara had become skilled at ferrying the two of them across these times, intuiting whatever was needed to keep this shadow of her mother from harm until they were safely on the other side. She made sure the bills got paid or put off, and that they didn't starve. She chased away the Pentecostals and the insurance salesmen, gassed up the lawn mower, and flipped the overpowered breaker switch. Invariably, her mother reemerged. It was just a matter of waiting it out.

They ate in silence, with the night air winding though the kitchen, until the alien beast was ejected from the ship. "Do you ever think about traveling to outer space?" Tara asked, as the credits rolled.

"And get my face sucked off? No, thank you. If there are aliens, you can bet they're just as twisted up as people. Better to stick to the demons you know." Her mother rattled the ice in her pink cup. "Can I get my bedtime drink? I'm ready to go upstairs."

Tara splashed Jim Beam into the cup and topped it with root beer. "Thank you, baby." Her mother wrapped her in a flimsy hug and Tara tried not to recoil at her sharp, unwashed smell. She watched her mother climb the stairs, pale fingers gripping the railing, her lank hair a spill of muddied gold down her back.

"The window," her mother called from the top step.

"I know, Mama. I'll shut it."

The road slipped beneath Tara's bike tires in an unending pattern of asphalt pancakes and potholes. To her right, the bayou plodded along, flashing sunlight at each lazy curve. She'd arisen early, ahead of the pounding August heat, intent on exploring a pile of furniture and appliances that someone had illegally dumped a mile away in a barren field. She had her eye out for a working toaster. As she swerved to avoid the crushed remains of a turtle, the road and the earth beneath it seemed to shudder.

Startled, Tara skidded to a stop. She became aware of a vigorous gurgling and traced the sound to a curious pocket of bubbling brown water just off the bayou bank. As she considered investigating, a shock of moving air and color blew past—accompanied by an ear-shattering whistle—almost toppling her and the bike. She steadied her bike and sighted two fast-moving bicycles on the road ahead, beneath a pair of unknown boys. The two didn't even bother to look back.

Tara hammered down on her pedals, quickly overtaking the smaller boy and entering into a neck-and-neck sprint with the other. When she was near enough to note his crooked grin and how it faltered as she closed in on him, a cramp seized her hamstring. Her leg shot outward and the seat slammed into her crotch. She steered the speeding bike onto a strip of soft dirt and managed to maneuver a controlled wreck.

"You're a son of a bitch," she growled at the older boy. He'd circled back and was now eyeing her, his forearms resting on his handlebars. His head was overly big, capped in short waves that nearly matched the deep honey of his eyes.

"You're a badass," he replied, admiring the whorl of fiery scrapes on her calf. "And almost as fast as me."

Tara kept her face frozen, masking the throbbing between her legs, as she righted her bicycle and hobbled toward the road.

"Why are you limping?" the younger boy asked. He was small and wiry, with shell-pink lips and glaring dark eyes. "You hurt?"

"Go to hell," she said, pedaling one-legged while her hamstring unwound.

"Girls shouldn't curse," he called after her.

Bike tires crackled on the sunbaked road as the boys fell in behind her. "You live in that old house back there, right?" the older one asked, catching up to her. "I'm Gerard, and that's my brother Louis. We're your new neighbors."

Tara ignored the boys, pedaling until she reached the barren field and the pile of abandoned junk. As she moved through the refuse, inspecting power cords and chipped furniture, Gerard peppered her with questions. She maintained her wall of silence until he approached her with a nearly new blender. Her frown softened as she took it from him. When he again asked her name, she relented.

Each day for the next two weeks, Tara met up with the boys. She learned that Gerard was fourteen, heading into tenth grade, and Louis was twelve. They'd moved to Terrefine because their father worked for Mid-South Petroleum, a company that also employed a good portion of the town. They'd lived in four other places, relocating whenever their father was reassigned.

Gradually, she began to crave the curt compliments that Gerard occasionally tossed her way, often at the expense of Louis.

"You're way more mechanical than him," Gerard remarked when she quickly identified the reason for the scraping on Louis's bike. When she yanked an inch-long splinter from the pad of her big toe, he laughed. "No way Louis could do that himself." She looked away to hide her smile.

Tara managed to avoid any mention of her mother until the end of the second week, when she took the boys crawfishing in a flooded field. She and Gerard were alone, harvesting the wire and cloth nets, while Louis sulked nearby. She'd snickered when Gerard first arrived wearing brushed white cotton shorts. Now they hung low on his waist, soaked and muddy.

"How'd you learn all this stuff?" he asked as she dumped the squirming haul into his bucket. "Crawfishing, fixing bikes, knowing what's poison ivy and what's poison oak. I don't know any of that."

"My mom," Tara answered proudly, then remembered her mother's robe-clad figure, still asleep when she'd left the house at noon. Warmth crept into her cheeks as she drove a stick into the bucket and flicked a small snake back into the water. She began to prattle, her too-eager words spilling out. "She taught me to drive too. Lets me take the truck to the Buy-U-Mart. Once she killed a rattler. Cut him in two. We still have the skull. And she's an expert camper. She'll take us all one day soon," she promised before she could stop herself.

She hurriedly reached for Gerard's bucket. "Four pounds!" she announced, joggling the handle. "Not enough for a boil. But maybe you can make a crawfish étouffée." With her heart thudding, she renewed her vow to keep the boys away from her house until her mother was well again.

"Louis!" Gerard yelled.

Louis tossed aside the stick he'd been using to hack at a nest of fire ants and hurried over.

"Take it home," Gerard said, threading his brother's thin arm through the handle of the bucket.

"You take it home!" Louis shot back, letting the bucket with its writhing contents fall to the ground. He pulled his collared shirt taut, examining the front. "You better not have gotten mud on me."

"Beat it, Louis. I mean it. Don't make me hit you."

"Let her take it. She caught 'em."

"Go." Gerard loomed over his brother, whose face narrowed with fear even as his dark eyes sparked with hostility. "And take the bucket with you."

"I hate you," Louis hissed before trudging off, the bucket banging against his shins.

"He'll be all right," Gerard said, meeting Tara's gaze. He dropped to a fallen log and began stripping the bark from a small, wayward branch. The afternoon sun cast a silken glow on his short wavy hair.

"Why you'd run him off?"

He shrugged. "Sometimes I don't feel like hanging out with a little kid, you know?"

The heat pressed down. Moisture gathered between Tara's shoulder blades and slid, tickling, down her spine. She remembered the orange juice drip on her T-shirt and crossed her arms before scooting next to Gerard.

"You have the greenest eyes I've ever seen," Gerard said. "Like Sprite-green."

"Yours are nice too," Tara muttered as a rose-tinged static enveloped her senses. Gerard leaned over to kiss her and she stiffened, wanting to give him something strong from which to push off. She felt the soft click of teeth and the timid glance of his tongue.

"I know a place we can go," he said. Tara hesitated, then nodded her assent.

He led her beneath two towering pines, at the edge of his backyard, where the low branches formed a shaded cavern. He was gentle even in his awkwardness, easing off her T-shirt in silence, swatting away the gnats, spreading out his own shirt for her to lie on. She was surprised by the pleasure of his touch and how, with her eyes closed, her body felt limitless. She liked how he trembled when she ran her fingers along his skin and how her long bones curved into his.

"Don't," she said, when he pressed himself against her still-bruised groin and tugged at her shorts. He retreated, nuzzling against her side, his quick breath captured in the crook of her neck.

When his father yelled from the back door, Gerard leapt up and shoved her T-shirt at her. "Stay," he whispered. "Until you hear me go in." As she left the cover of the pines, he reappeared and slipped his prized cube of iron pyrite into her outstretched hand.

The next day, Gerard and Louis departed for a week-long trip to visit relatives. Tara was left to pedal the streets alone, endlessly replaying the kiss, the touching, the smell of dry pine needles. The air in her house felt stagnant, and her habitual patience with her mother grew thin. "What's got up into your craw and died?" her mother asked, after Tara banged her way through the dinner preparation.

On the day of the boys' return, she hurried to what had become their meeting place—a clearing in the field midway between their houses, fringed by a semicircle of trees. As she tramped across the rows of turned earth, she noticed dark jags of smoke and wondered if Louis had finally agreed to light the bottle rockets he'd been hoarding.

As she drew closer, she caught sight of Gerard splashing lighter fluid over a smoldering hunk of metal, sparking the flames anew. Louis stood nearby, shirtless in the heat, his small chest thrust forward. When he noticed Tara, his eyes narrowed and he nudged his brother.

She raised her hand in greeting, prepared to welcome them home, but when her gaze fell on the smoking heap, she felt her heart jerk and shudder, like a fish thrown ashore. The blackened matter at the heart of Gerard's fire belonged to her. Though thoroughly singed, there was no mistaking the bent-tipped antenna and sloped handlebars of her bicycle.

For a moment, she clung to the ridiculous notion that the charred bones of her bicycle would resurrect itself, that the brothers would wave her over so they could explain their clever prank. *Aha! We got you!* But there was no prank revealed and no resurrected bike, only the boys' razor-thin smirks and bright, expectant eyes as they watched her, waiting for the fruit of their labor to fall.

Tara returned for the bike at sunset, when the heat began to lift and a band of golden haze fused land to sky. The metal was still hot, but she could bear it. When the rims stuck in the mud, she slung the frame on one shoulder and trudged down to the bayou. She eased the bike far into the still brown water, ignoring the creatures that brushed against her legs, then forced the frame below the surface.

As the bike sunk into the bayou's soft slime, releasing trails of effervescence, she parsed through her days with the brothers, roaming the woods of Terrefine, fording storm-swollen ditch waters, and raiding the cane fields to chew the sugary stalks. The whole time, the boys had been bound to each other, letting her scrape along after them like a hungry stray, knowing full well that when the time came, they would cut her loose.

She slammed her palm full force against the water. As a hot sting entered her fingers, a swarm of fresh bubbles surrounded her. She thought it was her bike, sending up its last gasp, but the bubbling intensified and with it, a noxious stink. The mellow hum of insects and frogs exploded into a throbbing chorus.

She sloshed through the gurgling water and scrambled up to the road where mosquitos fell on her, spiking her calves. Headlights flared on a faraway bridge, bouncing crazily, and a peal of manic laughter split the night. As she hurried toward the burning square of her kitchen window, her mother's face appeared, a dark oval sealed behind the glass, beckoning Tara, drawing her home.

2

A lifeless squirrel lay on the counter below the window, its ash-brown fur glossy even in death. "Food or taxidermy?" Tara asked Mrs. Honoré, the squirrel's killer, in whose kitchen they were standing.

"Gumbo." Mrs. Honoré turned from her kitchen sink to smile at Tara, her lined cheeks drawing back from sturdy, coffee-stained teeth. The light from the window cast a ruddy glow on her dark brown skin. Her wiry black hair was neatly clipped above the collar and touched with gray. "Not many folks care to mount a squirrel. Too humble. Unless they're doing it themselves, to learn."

In search of the chores her friend often paid her to do, Tara arrived just as Mrs. Honoré returned from hunting. Tara needed the distraction. All morning she'd been plagued by leering visions of the brothers and her torched bike. She glanced across the kitchen toward the dining room where a swell of white feathers shone through the half-open door. She'd known Mrs. Honoré all her life yet had never seen the dining room, or its long table of dark oak, used for anything other than taxidermy.

Local hunters paid Mrs. Honoré for trophy mounts of ducks, quails, and turkeys. She also supplied birds and small animals to minor museums and the occasional state university. These were creatures who'd died from natural causes, discovered by Mrs. Honoré as she hunted on her property or fished the bayou. There were also those hardscrabble townsfolk who plucked dead animals from the roadside in exchange for a few dollars. Mrs. Honoré had come by one of her proudest pieces that way—a magnificent red fox that now graced the LSU Museum of Natural Science.

Mrs. Honoré removed a large Tupperware from the icebox and popped off the lid. "You got a few minutes to shell?"

Tara nodded, accepting the Tupperware and settling on a cypress bench near the back screen door. Mrs. Honoré followed with a skinning knife and two squirrels in a battered metal bowl. As her fingers split the pea pods, Tara's eyes slid to the wall opposite, where a pattern of roses crept to all corners of the room. She let her vision grow soft and the flowers morphed into a multitude of grinning Gerards and Louises, sly-eyed and taunting. "What?" Tara asked, catching Mrs. Honoré's stare.

"People survive worse than what you've got to deal with, Tara." She dangled a squirrel by the tail and thumbed its rear claws.

"I didn't say anything." Tara cracked open a pea pod and four crisp green orbs dropped into the bowl.

"You don't have to say anything. Your long-suffering face says it all." Mrs. Honoré peeled back the squirrel hide to reveal baby-pink tissue, lacy with pale cartilage and ligament. "And don't think after shelling you're gonna mope around under my feet all day. You have a mama and a house. And I have to work on her this afternoon." She nodded toward the dining room.

"The pelican?" Tara asked.

"Egret. For a museum at Tulane, in New Orleans. They have an artist, a lady, who puts birds in the art somehow."

"I'll come to New Orleans when you drop it off, if you want."

"We'll see." Mrs. Honoré rose, carrying the metal bowl to the faucet to rinse the skinned squirrels. "What about those Ledroit boys?"

Tara studied the shiny clump on the newspaper in front of Mrs. Honoré's stool, pinpointing the heart in the pile of tiny organs. "What about 'em?"

"I've hardly seen you this past couple weeks, except for flying by on your bicycle with those two. Looked like you might've been having fun for a change." The knife flashed bright as Mrs. Honoré flicked clean water from the tip.

"You're better company."

"Well, I thank you. But nothing wrong with having friends your own age."

Gerard and Louis had been fascinated by Tara's friendship with Mrs. Honoré, always nagging her for details about whether Mrs. Honoré really was a witch, or a devil-worshiper, or if she had a taxidermied man hidden in the attic—ideas floating in the ether of Terrefine for as long as Tara could remember. But the boys were never so bold as to broach the most outlandish rumor: that Mrs. Honoré had purposefully poisoned her only son.

Tara had never joined the brothers in making fun of her friend, but she hadn't defended her either. She'd kept quiet, pedaling faster when she cycled past the tall windows of Mrs. Honoré's front porch. "Anyway, we're not friends anymore," Tara said. She set the peas on the counter and folded the squish of squirrel parts into a triangle of newspaper.

Mrs. Honoré chopped the small, slippery bodies into quarters, then retrieved an onion from a hanging wire basket. Tara could feel her waiting, leaving a space for her to say more, but she kept quiet. Leaning on Mrs. Honoré now would only deepen the betrayal.

At the edge of Mrs. Honoré's backyard, Tara flung the squirrel offal into the woods. As she crumbled the newspaper, her eyes fell on the red-smeared headline, "Hottest Year on Record." That's when she got the idea.

Stealing Gerard's bike was easy. He'd complained that his father dragged him and his brother to The Crab House on Sundays, so when Tara rolled the bike from the carport at midday the house was empty. It seemed natural to burn it where they'd burned hers. The scorched earth had been prepared. She doused the frame with gasoline, siphoned from their lawn mower, and tossed a lit match. As the flames erupted, an acid flood of satisfaction washed through her, and the knowledge that by her own power, she'd restored the balance of things.

She spent the rest of the afternoon in her backyard, sorting through the clutter of her mother's half-finished projects: the potter's wheel, the rusting husk of the wine fermenter, the busted brass cash register. As she peered into the belly of an antique cast-iron stove, she heard the dusty pop of car tires on the shell driveway. A door slammed, followed by a boy's voice, plaintive and thin. "I told you, I don't know! She just did."

A man's voice, edged with anger, shot back. "She 'just did'? Son, nobody just steals a bike and burns it."

Tara crept to the edge of the carport where she sighted a shiny, black double-cab pick-up truck in her driveway, parked behind an almost unrecognizable Gerard. Gone was his usual swagger. Instead, he slouched behind his father, his arms hanging long. His father wore a button-down shirt and dark jeans, his clean-shaven face unsmiling beneath a Mid-South Petroleum cap. She'd never met him, but she'd seen his truck pass her house many times.

"What are we even doing here?" Gerard asked.

The man swung around and Gerard wilted beneath his furious gaze. "We can leave any minute. All I need is the truth. Your choice."

Tara was stunned to see Gerard so cowed and disgusted that he hadn't been able to keep their secret, either because he was stupid or gutless. She would've liked to remain hidden, to witness his further unraveling, but the thought of her mother shuffling to the front door, half-asleep, sent her sprinting through the carport to intercept them.

As she ran toward Gerard, she felt her outrage rising, sounding a steady thrum throughout her body. Her skin remembered his eager hands. By the time she reached him, she wanted only to bury his face in the dirt. She barreled into him, sending him sprawling.

"Simmer down!" his father cried as he dragged her off Gerard.

"You got no say over me!" she yelled, swinging wildly.

"Stay!" the man barked at Gerard, who'd risen to one knee. "Until you tell me what the hell is going on. You too." He glared at Tara. "I caught Louis dragging what's left of Gerard's bike from the field. Did you burn it, like he says?"

Tara narrowed her eyes, then nodded, enjoying the clean feel of the confession.

"Why? Tara, that's your name, right? Why would you destroy somebody's property? It's against the law."

Tara remained silent, her unblinking gaze fixed on Gerard.

The man leaned closer. "I asked you a question, Tara. Why?"

Still, she refused to speak, her eyes boring into Gerard's, until finally the boy blurted out, "Because I burned her bike first. Okay? Are you happy?"

The man grabbed Gerard by the shirt and jerked him to his feet. "What has gotten into you?" The man's eyes screwed shut as a red tide rushed across his face. "Your mother…"

"My mother what?" Gerard's voice rose to a jagged screech, like a prehistoric bird.

Gerard's father herded him back to the truck, shoving him into the cab and slamming the door. He pressed his palms on the hood, staring skyward until his breath calmed, then strode back to Tara.

"I apologize for my son's behavior," he said. "It's inexcusable." He flipped open his wallet, extracting two hundred-dollar bills. "It's all I have right now." He flashed a small white card and handed it to her. "If a new bike costs more, call me. Or have your mama call me. I'm Eddy Ledroit."

Tara was up in time to catch the early morning mist and feel the spray of dew on her bare shins as she made the short, weedy descent from the road in front of her house to the bayou's edge. She squatted on the shore as the mist burned off the broad shallow stillness, revealing the knobby knees of cypress trees and branches draped in silvery Spanish moss. A half-collapsed pier glowed with milky-green fungus.

The turtles were out, their dark heads breaking the silky, brown water before again disappearing. A small alligator followed, its ridged snout cutting a delicate line through the glassy surface, until it emerged, minutes later, on the far bank to hunker glistening atop a log.

She'd awoken thinking of the money and buying a new bike, of how she would have to get to Walmart in Leittville, a half-hour away. But her thoughts kept returning to her own bike, now encased under-water in cool mud. It had been a good-enough bike. Maybe she could get it working again, with tires and parts from the dump, then pocket the cash. She and her mother had made good money at the flea market more than once, restoring objects others had left for trash.

Tara found a long, sturdy stick bobbing at the bayou's edge, then chopped the surface of the water, scattering any curious creatures be-fore wading in. She probed the area where she thought the bike should be but turned up nothing. She widened her search, keeping parallel with the shore, until a loud burbling erupted behind her. Spinning around, she discovered another of the strange bubbling pools. A foul whiff burned her nostrils and she recognized the odor that had sprung up the night she'd buried her bike. She sloshed to the shore as a second cluster erupted nearby and a third beyond that. She'd counted a total of seven churning pools when she felt the earth tremble.

Tara dropped low, her fingers clutching the grass, and searched above for thunderheads. Aside from the wispy remnants of morning fog, the sky was clear. She remained frozen, wondering if the ground would shift again, perhaps more violently.

The murmur of slowing vehicles drifted from the road above and moments later, a bearded man in a Mid-South Petroleum cap clambered down the bank, away from Tara, and toward the dilapidated pier. He was followed closely by Eddy Ledroit and a squat man shouldering some kind of equipment. None of the men noticed her.

The squat man traveled to the end of the pier and positioned a metal box at his feet. He extended a long pole with a funnel at the end above a section of the water where roiling bubbles disturbed the surface. Eddy Ledroit mumbled something to the bearded man, and Tara crept closer, straining to hear.

"That don't make sense, Eddy," said the bearded man. "The pipeline runs straight across. If it was leaking, gas should only escape right above it. Not higgledy-piggledy all over the water."

"Exactly, Byron. It's not the pipeline. It's swamp gas. Naturally occurring."

"Since when does swamp gas cause a tremor?" Byron asked as he filmed the bayou with his phone.

Eddy cupped his hands to his mouth. "What you got, Wayne?"

The man at the end of the pier dropped to one knee and squinted at the metal box. "Natural gas!" he yelled. "From someplace deep."

"Shit." Byron pocketed his phone and spat into the bayou.

"Might be a good idea to fly a drone over the area for the next week or so." Wayne's voice echoed across the water. "See if the gas patterns remain consistent."

"We need to call the state," Byron said.

"Slow down," Eddy said. "There are still 101 things that could be happening."

"'Course they might call us first," Byron continued. "That little seismic was enough to get noticed."

Eddy flashed his open palms. "Fine if they do. We've got nothing to hide. Who's to say the bubbling and these little tremors are even related? Hell, McCann thinks the vibrations are from those heavy eighteen-wheelers on Highway 80, driving through for the construction on that new cement plant. It's an old highway, and close by." He slid a walkie-talkie from his pocket. "Now calm yourself. I'm going to let HQ know the chance of subsidence is slim." As he spoke into the radio, Eddy glanced backwards and caught sight of Tara crouched among the weeds. At first he seemed not to recognize her, but then he waved. She rose, frowning, then climbed to the road and jogged home.

As Tara lugged a watering can across her front yard, she mulled over Eddy's remarks. He seemed to believe his own words, but she wasn't so sure about the other two, especially the whiny one with the beard.

"Tara!"

She looked up from dousing a scrawny apple tree. Eddy strode toward her as two Mid-South trucks pulled away, his face half-shadowed by the brim of his cap.

"Okay if I come onto your property?" he asked. "I'd appreciate a word."

"You were here before, weren't you?"

He leapt across the ditch into the yard, his long-toed boots plowing through the grass. When he drew closer, she noted the smooth tuck of his shirt in his jeans.

"It sounds like my boys really trashed your bike." As he spoke, his eyes scanned the patchwork of scars on her legs and the thigh-high watermark imprinted on her by the bayou. She felt her face flush and released the metal handle of the watering can, splashing water on his boots and the front of his jeans.

"Gerard's bike doesn't look so good either," she said.

He snorted softly. "No. It's wrecked. Same as yours." He lifted his gaze to the house. "Your mother home?"

"Yeah, but she's not seeing anyone. She's got a migraine." Tara was glad for the easy access to this half-truth. Occasionally, her mother suffered from crippling headaches, though it had been almost a year since her last. She held Eddy's gaze, silently daring him to call her bluff; for the first time, she recognized Gerard's honey-dark eyes.

"Y'all felt that tremor in the ground earlier?" Eddy asked.

"You saw me down there," she replied, glancing into the watering can where the silhouette of her skull gently rocked. "What's subsidence?"

"Fancy word for *cave-in* or *sinkhole*. You know Mid-South?"

"Everybody does."

"We have the equipment to figure out what exactly happened, which is probably not much. You can tell your mama not to worry."

"My mama's not worried."

"And we may need to get into your backyard to take some readings."

Eddy tipped his hat before turning to go.

"Doubt she'll let you!" Tara called as he hopped the ditch.

"We'll be in touch."

3.

Tara woke to the gurgle of water filling the old claw-foot tub. She lay in bed until she heard the creak of the faucet knob, then a rhythmic drip. She slipped from the covers and padded to the bathroom to peek through a gap in the bowed doorframe.

The steaming water was just below the lip of the tub. Her mother was completely submerged, her hair drifting around her petal-white breasts like golden seaweed. A bubble had formed on her nostril, as if she'd grown a pearl. Her eyes flew open and she rose through the water, rivulets streaming from her fine-boned shoulders. A rainbow drop glinted in the delicate hollow of her collarbone, caught in the sunlight from the window above the sink.

Her mother hadn't asked for her bedtime drink since the quake, three days before. The pill bottles were gone from the bedside table. But first they'd had to endure two long nights of her twisting and groaning in sweat-soaked sheets, a big metal pot on the floor next to the bed.

"Tara." She wiped the water from her eyes. "Don't spy."

Tara nudged open the door. "I just wanted to make sure it was you."

Her mother laughed and turned her glistening face to Tara. "When's the last time *you* took a bath?"

"It's summer," Tara said, covering one foot with the other to hide the dried mud between her toes. She held her mother's clear gaze, then backed into the hallway, feeling suddenly small. "I'm gonna have some cereal."

"If you can hold your horses, I'll make pain perdu."

"With what? We don't have eggs." The words came out harder than she'd meant. Her mother dropped her eyes to the warm pink islands of her knees. "I can make you cereal too." Tara crowded her words into the silence. "We have Frosted Flakes. I'll cut you a banana."

"Let's go by the Buy-U-Mart for groceries. You can drive."

"It's too early for them to be open."

"Tammy'll open the store for us. Lemme give her a ring." Her mother pulled the plug and water rushed to the drain. Tara turned away, just glimpsing the snakehead tattoo at the base of her mother's spine, forked tongue splitting at the top of her buttocks, red eyes peering over the taut curve of her bottom.

Tara waited in the truck, keys in the ignition, until her mother appeared on the front porch in a white T-shirt and cut-off shorts, her wet hair wound into a thick knot. She slid into the cab, parking her flip-flop in the crook of the open window as Tara revved the engine.

"Hit it," her mother said, lighting a cigarette. She monitored the truck's proximity to the ditch as Tara maneuvered out of the driveway.

"Can I have one?" Tara asked, once they were on the road. She glanced down at the bayou. Aside from the gentle ruffles from the morning breeze, the water was serene.

Her mother blew smoke out the window. "I can't stand being around other smokers unless I'm drinking."

"Does that mean no?"

"For as long as me telling you 'no' means anything." She pointed to the road ahead. "Pothole."

At the Buy-U-Mart, Tara bought eggs and a loaf of Bunny bread while her mother gassed up the truck. On the way home, her mother read the *Terrefine Journal* aloud. "'Seismic activity appears isolated.' Isolated from what?" she mused. "Not our living room."

"You felt it?" Tara asked.

"Yep." She stretched her arms and yawned. "We used to get those little quakes in East Texas."

"Is that why you left?" Tara turned into their driveway. "The quakes?"

Her mother tucked the newspaper under one arm, as Tara killed the engine. "You mean was it fear of earthquakes that landed me in Terrefine with a man old enough to be my grandpa?"

Tara winced. She preferred not to think of the man who'd fathered her. His coal-black eyes and loose-jowled face had startled her more than once, staring out from the old photos that seemed to materialize in the corners of her dresser drawers or beneath her bed. She'd made it her mission to destroy any evidence of him, or his kin.

"I wish I could blame it on something other than being young and ignorant, but I can't." She ruffled Tara's hair. "But we got each other, didn't we? And this house, as long as it doesn't fall down on our heads and kill us."

Tara coughed, trying not to laugh. Her mother reached over and drummed her fingertips along the nape of her neck, as she used to do when Tara was a tiny girl. "Stop!" Tara swung open the truck door to escape the pleasure of her mother's touch.

"The lawn is a jungle. Let's mow after breakfast," her mother said, wedging one long leg in the screen door while reaching down to toss stray branches from the porch to the yard.

Tara set the eggs and bread on the kitchen counter and grabbed milk and butter from the icebox. "Ready!" she called to her mother, who'd gone upstairs.

"Peeing!" her mother called down. She flushed and a cascade of watery whispers flowed though the wall.

"I'm starting without you!" Tara yelled, surrendering to her growling stomach. She dipped the bread in egg, then laid four viscous slices on the hot skillet.

"Tara." Her mother was suddenly in the kitchen doorway, the iron pyrite in one hand and the two hundred dollars, folded with Eddy's business card, in the other. "Where did this cash come from? Who the hell is Eddy Ledroit?"

Tara's shoulders stiffened. "He's the one who moved into the Gremillion's old house."

"He give you this?"

"He owed me."

"Owed you? For what?"

Tara didn't answer. Instead she turned back to the skillet and flipped the blackening bread. Her mother's concern felt ill-timed and intrusive. It had been Tara's battle, already fought and won. She slid the pain perdu onto plates and carried them to the table.

Her mother stepped into the kitchen and brandished the money. "Well?" she demanded.

"Can we just eat? It's no big deal. Don't worry about it." Tara felt hollow with hunger. A flush of saliva filled her mouth as she dropped into a chair.

Her mother planted the pyrite in the center of the table. "I guess Eddy Ledroit is going to have to tell me himself." She started for the front door.

"What do you care?" Tara jumped up. "Where were you when it happened?"

"When *what* happened?"

Her mother's alarm almost melted Tara, almost had her unburden herself of the hurt and rage of those two days, but her tongue had turned to lead, and her words sank before she could speak them. From the kitchen window, she watched her mother fishtail out of the driveway, a shovel thwacking against the metal walls of the truck bed.

Tara was oiling the cast-iron skillet when the earth moved again. The windowpanes rattled and the house moaned. A fine dusting of plaster fell across the remains of her pain perdu, and the can of Steins cane syrup slipped from the edge of the table and thudded on the floor. It lasted only seconds, but some impulse propelled her to her feet and out of house. As she stepped from the porch to the yard, she was hit with an acrid smell, like the fumes of a gas station. She detected a low, insistent sound, a kind of prolonged gurgle, which at first she imagined was an approaching car. But the road in front of her house was empty. She followed the sound, hurrying along the road to the curve where the Mid-South trucks had parked the day before. She took a few steps down the bayou bank, her throat burning, and was confronted by a landscape that had reorganized itself.

The shallow body of water that streamed gently past overgrown banks and around cypress trees was gone. It's river-like boundaries had sloughed off and widened into a restless, churning lake, the length of a football field in all directions. Directly across the water, the banks continued to cave, crashing down into the oily pinks and blues that undulated on the water's surface. The pier where Eddy had taken measurements had vanished.

Tara picked her way down the bank to examine a stand of a dozen tall, slender cypress trees clinging to the periphery of the rumbling water. The feathery leaves shuddered against the clean-swept sky, and with a sound like breaking bones, the cluster of trees plummeted underwater, as if a rug had been yanked out from beneath them. She stood stock-still, transfixed by the seething cross-currents. Her mind raced through all the memories of her short life, trying to anchor this moment to some experience she'd had before, something that had already been named—the flash flood the previous year that had swollen the bayou to twice its size; the world spinning out of control when her mother passed out at the wheel; the locomotive howl of the tornado that ripped past her third-grade classroom. But nothing landed.

Tara stepped back and slipped on the raw, wet earth, sending her sliding down the crumbling bank. She clutched at an exposed root but it slipped from her grasp, slicing open her palm as she hit the water. She swam hard until she realized she was only drifting further away from the bank.

"Help!" she called to the empty shore. She let herself be carried by the current to save her breath, then tried again. "Help me!"

She coughed, choking on the harsh fumes blanketing the water. From the bank, the churning water had seemed random, even at odds with itself, but beneath the surface a steady drag spiraled her toward the center. The water had turned thick and chill. She flipped onto her back, gasping for fresh air. An oily wave slapped against her face and slipped down her throat. She panicked, flapping her arms and gulping more water. She tried to yell again, but no sound made it through the water pressing on her lungs. She thrust her arms above her head, her open palms shooting out of the water, but the weight of her own body dragged her down.

A red band of oxygen deprivation had encircled Tara's brain, tightening to the point of oblivion, when her wrists were yanked skyward and she was hauled into a motorboat. Eddy Ledroit, one eye newly blackened, moved to press his mouth onto hers, but her fist flew to the side of his head. She felt a violent upwelling and vomited into his face.

"She's alive!" he yelled. "Let's go!" He pulled a crumpled bandana from his jeans pocket and wiped his face.

As her vision cleared, she recognized the driver as Wayne, the stocky Mid-South man who'd been with Eddy on the pier. "The motor is tapped out in this current!" he yelled.

"We got to take it at an angle," Eddy said, waving Wayne aside.

Tara's lungs pumped furiously, restoring her breath, as the boat escaped the watery vortex and gunned for the shore. Eddy ran the boat aground and slipped an arm around her, guiding her up to the road, where her mother rushed to meet them. The siren of Terrefine's lone fire truck wailed in the distance.

"Joan! Take my truck. Tara needs medical attention."

"I do not!" Tara wrenched herself from Eddy's arms, forcing herself to walk a steady line to her mother. "I'm fine."

"You sure, baby?" Her mother glanced toward the seething water.

"I said I'm fine," Tara croaked through her burning throat. "Please, let's just go."

As her mother walked her to the truck, Tara overheard Wayne speaking to Eddy. "The live video feed from my drone might give us some idea of the initial point of collapse. At least from the surface. I've got fly-by footage from the boat starting from early this morning."

"Thank god you were out there, Wayne. This could have been bad." Eddy clapped his hand on Wayne's shoulder as Joan slammed the truck door.

They wove through the growing confusion of cars and emergency vehicles crowding the narrow road. The truck's interior felt suffocating. Tara rolled down her window, only to take in the corrupted air drifting up from the water. She closed the window and slumped in her seat, agitated by the sight of her mother's hands on the unfamiliar steering wheel.

"Where's our truck?" Tara asked, shivering despite the heat.

"We're going to it now, hon," her mother replied, speeding up as the road cleared.

Minutes later, Eddy Ledroit's white-columned house came into view. The little white truck was parked on the neat front lawn, with the driver's door left open. The shovel lay in the grass nearby. On the front porch, Gerard and Louis stood shoulder to shoulder, their wide eyes tracking their father's truck as it turned into the driveway.

"No." Tara gripped the dashboard.

"Eddy told me what happened between you and those boys. Right after I gave him a black eye. Trust me, they are straightened out but good. Eddy's got 'em on lock down. They can't even leave the yard. There's nothing to be afraid of."

"Ha." Tara forced her lips apart as her shivering intensified. "I'm not afraid of those little shitzzz."

"Jesus, you're shaking all over." Her mother braked abruptly and killed the engine. She hurried to the passenger door, but Tara hit the lock. "Hey!" her mother called through the glass. "I promise we won't be here long! We..." Tara flipped on the radio and cranked the volume, burying her mother's voice beneath a cheerful announcement for two-for-one fryers at the Piggly Wiggly. Her mother brought her face closer to the window. Two sharp creases deepened between her eyebrows. Her concern had given way to annoyance.

I'm not coming out, Tara mouthed. *Sorry.*

"Suit yourself!" her mother yelled. She smacked her palm against the glass then marched back to the house.

Tara considered sneaking to the little white truck and driving off, perhaps to Mrs. Honoré's, perhaps to the Dairy Queen on the far side of town, but the memory of the bayou split wide open made her hesitate. What if the road crumbled while she was driving? She could be buried alive.

As Willie Nelson's twang drifted from the radio, she turned from the window and flopped across the front seat. Cocooned in the heat of the cab, she felt her muscles soften and her shivering subside. She examined her skin, taut and itchy from the drying bayou slurry.

Tara was inspecting the cut on her hand when a voice cut through the radio music: "KFIV's got some breaking news, folks. We received a report that what appears to be a sinkhole opened up beneath a section of Bayou Reve owned by Mid-South Petroleum on the west side of rural Route 19. Mid-South says they're aware of the sinkhole, have people onsite, and are communicating with the state regarding emergency measures. The sinkhole is estimated to be 350 feet wide, depth unknown. That's a huge hole, folks. No cause has yet been identified."

Tara frowned. She'd never thought of the bayou as belonging to anyone, certainly not Mid-South. If anything, she'd considered it an extension of her front yard, the same way she'd always thought of the fields and woods surrounding their house as hers to explore freely.

The DJ continued. "The Mid-South rep says it's possible some quantities of methane gas and petroleum were released in the collapse, and that the company has taken it upon itself to determine if this poses any danger to the community."

With her head propped against the driver's side door, Tara watched

Gerard's reflection in the side-view mirror, creeping toward the truck. When he was close enough, she flung open the door, knocking him to the ground.

"Wait, I come in peace! Sandwich!" He waved the bread at her, trying to ward her off.

She flew at him, and the sandwich took flight. They rolled across the packed earth beneath the oak tree, locked in a tight embrace. Steadily, Tara gained control until she'd pinned Gerard facedown. She wrenched his elbow behind his back. In the background, the radio announcer droned on. "One resident who called in claims that the odor from the sinkhole smells, and I quote, 'like a sick giant's fart.'"

A giggle escaped Tara. She released Gerard's arm and slid off him, rocking with laughter. He soon joined her, the two of them rolling in the dirt as if possessed.

When Tara finally regained her breath, she crawled to her knees and gathered the remains of the sandwich. She shook the dusty remnants at Gerard, whose menacing face had morphed into that of a mere boy. "No mustard?"

4.

From the rocking chairs on Gerard's front porch, Tara, her mother, and the boys watched a parade of emergency vehicles rumble past. Her mother, in her restlessness, had emptied the freezer of every imaginable meat and staged a huge barbeque on the back patio. A plate of ribs grown cold sat on the end table next to Tara, the blackened bones barely visible in the shadows.

Tara kept nodding off. After the fight with Gerard, she'd crashed, her body hardly able to carry itself. "You're gamey like meat from a spooked deer," her mother remarked, thrusting her remedy of raw egg mixed with Tabasco at Tara.

Her mother sat next to her now, creating her own night breeze with the vigor of her rocking. A faint hooting came from Louis as he blew across the top of his Coke can.

"Eddy, it's Joan Saint-Romain again." Her mother spoke into her cellphone, red-lit in the lights of a passing police car. "Nobody's paying me to babysit over here." She leaned forward and winked at Gerard and Louis as red flashed to blue. "An update on what the hell is happening would be nice." She clacked the phone shut and sighed. "Think your daddy'll come home tonight?"

"Dunno," said Gerard. "When the plant in Lake Charles caught fire last year he stayed gone for two whole days."

"Lake Charles. Is that where your mama is?" As her mother posed the question, Tara realized that she'd never stopped to consider it. She'd been too consumed with what the boys might think of her mother to wonder about their lack of one.

Gerard remained silent. Louis slid from his rocking chair, still hooting, and disappeared into the house. Her mother's chair became still as she struck a match and her cigarette glowed to life. "She left y'all?" The soft words drifted past Tara.

"She died," Gerard said, his voice tightening. "Cancer."

"Damn." Her mother's breathy whistle lingered in the porch shadows. "It's a terrible thing, Gerard. No fairness to it."

"I don't really think about it much." His last word stumbled, becoming a stifled hiccup. Tara could feel his grief spreading, like ink in water. She was glad for his sake that the porch was dark.

A blade of light fell across Tara's lap and she twisted to face the living room window. Louis was hunched on the sofa, his thumbs striking the buttons of a handheld video game. He seemed younger than his twelve years, a frail bird of a boy.

Her mother clucked her tongue as she followed Tara's gaze. "That one of them miniature arcade games? I'm gonna do y'all a favor and teach you to play a real game." Her cigarette traced an arc through the darkness. "Gerard, you got a pack of cards?"

Tara lowered her cards and dropped a mini Snickers on the pile of candy at the center of the kitchen table. "Raise."

They'd been playing for an hour and her lids felt heavy. But she refused to fall asleep anywhere but her own bed, surrounded by the whispers and creaks of the old house. She shoved a gooey square in her mouth, nursing the shot of sweetness to stay awake.

Her mother sang along with a string of oldies served up by the late night DJ. Earlier, Gerard had tuned the radio to the local station hoping for updates on the sinkhole. But the same announcement looped again and again, with no new information. Finally, her mother threw down her cards and found an oldies station.

Tara glanced at the display of cut glass liquor bottles on the shelf above the radio. Her mother had lingered only briefly before the warm ambers and deep burgundies, and she still nursed the Coke that Tara slipped in front of her at the start of the game.

"Man..." Gerard grumbled. "I fold."

"What about you, big Lou?" her mother asked. She'd donned a golf visor that she found hanging near the back door. A cigarette dangled from her lips.

Louis furrowed his brow. "Wait...what is the five cards with five hearts?"

"A flush," said a voice from the doorway.

They all turned to see Eddy, filthy with grime. His eyes met Tara's as he removed his cap and cleared the small step down to the kitchen.

She immediately pictured his face wet with her vomit and dropped her gaze to the poker game.

"Dad. Hey." Gerard rose from the table, his hands in his pockets.

"Son." Eddy nodded, drawing closer. "I'm sorry I couldn't call you back, Joan. It's been nonstop."

"Don't worry about it," her mother replied, a yawn underpinning her words. She tossed the visor aside and unfurled her slender arms, stretching wide. "Y'all got everything under control? Seems like half the construction vehicles in Louisiana are down there."

"We're getting a bead on it. How you feeling, Tara?"

As Eddy awaited Tara's answer, the dull throb beneath her arms where he'd hoisted her into the boat seemed to sharpen, and the faint burn of bayou water arose in her throat. The reality of her near-drowning hit her with stark clarity. She felt embarrassed that she'd almost died and humiliated that she'd needed saving. She felt a sob welling up and clawed her short nails into her thighs. "I'm fine," she replied, lifting her gaze to Eddy's. "Thank you for pulling me out."

"Just promise you'll stay away from that water."

"Yes, sir. I'll keep to the house and the yard."

His eyes cut away for an instant, like a stray dog hiding its sickness.

"Eddy, there's burgers and ribs in the fridge. Plenty for tomorrow," her mother said, gathering candy wrappers and wiping the table in a few swift strokes.

"You're not leaving? It's past one in the morning. Y'all stay in the extra bedroom tonight. Please."

"Oh, no. We've worn out our welcome." As her mother attacked the dishes, her hair loosened from its bun, spilling down her back in pin-straight lengths of gold.

"I insist, Joan." Eddy's voice was friendly, but his eyes were grim, almost cold.

"Mama…" Tara said, unease prickling the length of her spine.

Her mother glanced back and Tara flicked her eyes to Eddy's haggard face.

"What?" her mother asked, letting a fork clatter to the sink. She spun around to face Eddy, her shorts and T-shirt still imprinted with the dirt of Tara's body. "Tell me what's wrong. Now."

"I'm afraid you can't go home. It's not safe." Eddy's fingers tore through his matted hair. Louis drifted from behind the table toward his father, his poker cards clutched in one hand.

"Says who?" her mother asked.

"For now, just me. But by tomorrow, your home will be part of a mandatory evacuation area."

Her lips grew thin with derision as she absorbed Eddy's words. "Like hell! What gives you the right to put me out of my home?"

"It's not my right, it's the state's right. But it is my responsibility, and Mid-South's, to recommend evacuation. The sinkhole has slowed, but it's still collapsing. You don't want to be there."

Tara's mother swatted the air. "I know you're new to town, but nobody gives a rat's ass about me or my home. They may say something different to your face, or mine. But trust me, it's the truth."

Eddy clasped his fists and held them out to Joan. "Stay here for tonight. Please. Methane gas may be leaching into the bayou and the surrounding land. Methane is flammable."

Her mother rolled her eyes and fluttered her pale-tipped lashes. "I may be country but I'm not ignorant. I know what methane is."

"Then you should know to take this seriously." A bead of sweat raced from Eddy's temple, sweeping through the grime and slipping beneath his jaw. His burnt-gold eyes shone with urgency.

Tara felt behind her for a chair, then collapsed with a dramatic gasp. "Cramp," she hissed, gripping her hamstring.

Her mother broke from Eddy and dropped to Tara's side. "You okay?" she asked, kneading the back of Tara's leg. Tara grimaced, then carefully got to her feet, limping from behind the table.

"She gets those a lot," Louis remarked.

"Come on, baby. We better stay here tonight and figure out what to do in the morning." Her mother paused in front of Eddy and gave him a pointed look. "This is a real shit show."

"It is." He nodded.

Gerard led them through the carpeted hush of the hallway to a guest bedroom. Tara maintained her limp until she was in bed, under the covers. For tonight at least, they were better off here.

Tara awoke to a frigid blast of stale air, pouring from the ceiling vent. Her mother was gone. She threw off the covers and hurried through the empty house to the front yard. There was no sign of the little white pickup, or Eddy's truck.

The cut on her hand throbbed, her bladder was ready to burst, and her stomach was an empty, ravenous sack. "Where is she?" Tara demanded of Gerard as he dragged empty garbage cans from the end of the driveway.

"She went back to your house with my dad. To get your stuff."

"I thought it was off limits," Tara snarled, rubbing her eyes and feeling the sting of crust breaking off her lids. "They should have waited for me!"

"Don't yell at me. It's not my fault."

He returned to the garbage cans, leaving her to glare across the road and down a grassy slope where the bayou crept, dark and glistening. The only sign of the destruction a half-mile away was the oily rainbow slicks that occasionally shimmered past. Tara thought briefly of Mrs. Honoré, and whether the water flowing near her house was also tainted. She went inside to pee, curling her lip at the peach-colored seahorse soaps on the bathroom counter and the matching hand towels, then hunted through the refrigerator in search of last night's meat. As she warmed two patties in a skillet, Louis padded past in search of a glass of water.

"Why didn't you just use the microwave?" he asked, pushing his cup beneath the ice dispenser.

"I hate the microwave." She wasn't about to admit that she and her mother didn't own one; or that she'd used the skillet only after punching all the buttons on this one and then cursing it.

"Why is it blinking all crazy like that?" Louis asked, squinting at the microwave's touchpad.

Tara carried her burgers and a Coke to the back patio. Gerard was shooting baskets on the packed dirt near the edge of the yard. Louis soon wandered outside to join him, swiping the ball as it rebounded. Wind rippled through the trees where she'd hidden with Gerard. She stabbed at the last hunk of burger and considered hiding out there today, alone with the bugs and the shadows. She drained half her Coke, then waited for her burp to ripen, opening her mouth wide for the full eruption.

Gerard and Louis halted their game to gawk at her. She got to her

feet and emptied the rest of the can. The second burp, wet and reso-
nate, was louder.

"Sick." Louis cocked his head and bared his tongue.

She slammed the can on the table. "I'm going by my house."

Gerard tugged at the front of his shorts. "You can't. You heard my
dad. It's dangerous."

"Then why's my mama over there? It must not be that bad. Besides
I'll walk the back way, along the sugarcane fields. That's nowhere near
the water." She left the patio and started across the backyard.

"He told me not to let you leave!" Gerard's voice faltered as she
threw him a vicious pair of eyes.

"You forgot to clean up your dishes!" Louis yelled as she stepped
from the shady yard into the blistering heat.

The earth bristled with tall stalks of sugarcane, the sharp, papery
leaves seeming to chatter at her as Tara tromped past the rows. The
stretch of vacant land between the cane field and the road was clotted
with Kudzu vines and the voracious green tendrils had nearly engulfed
a lone telephone pole. The heat seemed to intensify with each step,
falling in scalding eddies down her shoulders and back.

When an oily stink arrived on the breeze, she dug her toes into the
dirt, feeling uncertain. She considered turning back, but there was no
way she could sit there watching Gerard and Louis bounce a ball while
her mother and her house were unprotected. And she couldn't let the
boys think she'd chickened out.

The cane field fell away, revealing the distant huddle of trees where
her bike, and Gerard's, had been burned. A pair of bulbous Mid-South
refinery tanks blotted the horizon. The gassy stench grew heavier.

Soon, the back of her house rose from the tall grass of the adjacent
empty lot. Her yard came into view and she spied her bedroom window on the second floor, propped open with a water-logged Yellow
Pages. Her mother's window, which had resisted Tara's many attempts
to unstick it, was thrown open as well.

Eddy Ledroit stood near a snarl of blackberry bushes that bordered the backyard, a walkie-talkie to his ear. She guessed he'd been
up all night, but he must have managed a shower at some point. His
long-toed boots were fringed with mud, but his light blue polo seemed
fresh. As he spoke, his eyes swept the ground incessantly and he failed

to notice her slip into the yard. Through the carport, she spotted the little white truck in the driveway and beyond it, the fat tires of Eddy's truck filling the ditch in front of her house. She eased open the back screen door and entered.

Tara blinked at the unexpected flood of light which left her living room almost unrecognizable. The dusty curtains had been twisted aside, and no dark corner escaped the reach of sunshine. She saw faded patches of the original fabric wallpaper. A water stain blossomed along the side of the sagging couch. The carcass of a forgotten houseplant hunkered in a corner.

Above the stairs, dust motes boiled in the glare from a high window. As Tara ascended, she discovered a miniature oval-framed photo, over-looked during her purge of the Saint-Romain family gallery. Her father stared at her from beneath raven-black brows in a distant, sepia-toned world. *Jackson Saint-Romain, age thirteen years* was scratched into the photo paper. She palmed the picture, marking it for destruction, and continued to climb, winding a dark spiral of her hair tight around her finger. She soundlessly crested the stairs and peered into her mother's bedroom.

Drawers hung open and clothes littered the floor. Her mother had her back to the door and was locked in a gaze with her own nude reflection in a flimsy mirror propped against the wall. Her eyes, sunlit and cornflower blue, flitted across the smooth curve of her abdomen, climbed to her slender waist, then swept along the trim flare of her ribcage, coming to hover at her pale, full breasts. She frowned.

Tara had started to back away, embarrassed, when her mother's fingers shot up, twisting the flesh of her belly and breasts, leaving a trail of splotches. "Mama!"

"Jesus, Tara." Joan spun around. "You are about the stealthiest thing I know."

"What are you doing?"

"I'm changing. I smell like a dead animal." She pulled a tank top from a nearby drawer.

"I saw you pinching yourself." Tara gestured at the splotches. "It was weird."

"Trying to wake my dog-tired self up. I couldn't sleep a wink with you donkey-kicking all night long." She scooped a pair of cutoffs from the floor. "Besides, who's the weird one? You're sneaking up on me."

"You left without me."

Joan jerked the shorts up and zipped the fly. "I had to. You were dead to the world and I was ready to go. You snooze, you get left."

As her mother turned away, Tara spied a muddy boot print on the carpet beneath the window, like the prow of a small boat. Nearby lay a clipboard emblazoned with the Mid-South logo. "You got the window opened."

"Not me. Eddy. He kept hounding me to air the place out. I said fine, except my window doesn't open. So he generously took a half-hour away from getting us kicked out of here to go at it with a hammer."

"I would have done it if you had waited for me," she said, smearing the print into the carpet with her toe.

Joan jabbed a cigarette in her lips and shoved a cardboard box at Tara. "Put your stuff in here."

"We really leaving?" Tara asked, staring into the empty box. "Where will we go?"

"Please don't ask me questions I can't answer." Joan spun in a slow circle until she spotted her cellphone beside a moldy sandwich. She pocketed the phone and headed downstairs. Tara fingered the soft pack of Winston's, nabbing one for herself, then ducked through her bedroom window and onto the roof.

She was seated cross-legged, half-way through her cigarette, when Eddy appeared in the backyard, squeezing between an antique sweet potato harvester and a cement pagoda. Byron, the bearded Mid-South man who'd been with Eddy on the pier, shuffled after him, tortoise-like beneath the heavy equipment strapped to his back.

The two wandered through her backyard until Eddy reached a pool of standing water. As Byron tottered forward, waving a black wand above the puddle, he smashed into a mangled strip of wrought iron.

"Shit!" Byron exclaimed. "This would be a easier if we didn't have to work in a junkyard. What is she? Some kind of hoarder?"

"You shut your mouth!" Tara yelled down.

Byron's head snapped up. Eddy shielded his eyes, searching the roof until he spotted her. "Tara! Where'd you come from?"

"This is my home." She aimed her smoke at the upturned faces. "Remember?"

"She's going to blow us up!" Byron cried, executing a bumbling crabwalk toward the front of the house. "I'm out of here."

"You're *kicked* out of here!" Tara yelled as Byron disappeared beneath the carport.

"Byron can be an ass, but he's right about the smoking," Eddy called up to her, craning his neck.

Tara crushed the butt, flicked it into the gutter, then gripped the window frame so she could lean over the roof's edge and look him full in the face. "The other day you said not to worry. You said Mid-South would figure it out. Now you're telling us to leave our home."

"It's just a temporary measure. Until we can get a handle on things."

"It was nice of you let us stay over last night. And I'd be dead if it weren't for you. But the rest is bull crap. You don't seem to know what you're talking about. Or else you're a liar." Before Eddy could answer, she swung back through her bedroom window.

She began a sullen examination of her dresser drawers, tossing T-shirts and shorts into the cardboard box her mother had given her. She swaddled the rattler skull in layers of socks, nestling it on top. As she ferreted through the knots of clothing on her mother's bedroom floor, a faraway thwacking grew steadily louder, until it thundered through the sky above the house. She raced downstairs, covering her ears, to search for her mother, then bolted out the house to the front yard.

Her mother and Eddy were in the driveway, facing the empty lot. The tall grasses twitched and bobbed as a helicopter maneuvered to the ground. When Tara appeared at Eddy's side, he turned to her and mouthed, "Wanna take a ride?"

5.

The earth heaved and fell away as the helicopter took flight. Tara was strapped up front, next to Eddy, her ears shielded from the noise of the blades by a chunky headset. She'd almost missed the moment when they left the ground, riveted as she was by Eddy's cool command of the aircraft, the precision of his fingers over the toggles and gauges of black steel, and how he seemed at once both vigilant and at ease.

The pilot who'd delivered the helicopter now occupied the rear with her mother, who kept grasping reflexively for her cigarettes. Tara was surprised that she'd accepted Eddy's invitation. Her mother hated heights and wouldn't even brave the tiny Ferris wheel at the annual church fair.

"No smoking," the pilot politely reminded her mother as she brandished a cigarette. "It's against federal law."

"Joan," Eddy chided her through his headset, "I had to pull a few strings to get y'all up here. Don't get me in trouble for it."

"You'll be in more trouble if I keel over and die from nerves," she replied, her light ash brows peaked with agitation. "Besides, I ain't gonna light it."

Eddy maneuvered the craft above their house. The rotor beat the air and a flock of plastic grocery bags blew from beneath the carport and sailed across the yard. As the helicopter pivoted to the south with dragonfly quickness, an electric hum infused Tara's skin, her cells, her whole body. Soon they were above the fields, ruffling the trees that surrounded the blackened earth where the bikes had been burned and sending small dark birds darting from their branches.

They rose higher, still tracing a lazy half-circle as they re-approached Terrefine. Bayou Reve glistened below, cleaving the town into the simple shacks and trailer homes on the north; and the nicer residences of tumbled pink brick and wide sloping roofs to the south, trimmed with bright azalea and palm trees. Charming piers and boat launches fringed the bayou on the south side, as well as her old school, plain and squat, which housed the K-8 classrooms.

Tara craned forward and spotted Mrs. Honoré's house, with its hulking barn and ancient live oaks. Her property marked the eastern flank of Terrefine. Beyond her woods lived the swamp, thick with the burnt emeralds and mossy greens of cypress, maple, and black gum trees. Abruptly, the shadow of a swift-moving cloud engulfed the swamp forest, dousing the land in faded blue. A sigh filled Tara's headset. Eddy chuckled and she realized the sigh had been her own.

"Different from an airplane, isn't it?" His voice through the headset had a thin insectile quality.

"I wouldn't know." She wiped her exhale from the cockpit window.

"Really? First time flying?" His lips were obscured by the mouth-piece, but his eyes held no trace of mockery.

"Uh-huh."

"What about you, Joan?" he asked, as he angled the copter south.

"Bus is good enough for me, thank you very much. Better yet, my own truck." Her mother's voice was calmer, and she'd settled into her seat, the unlit cigarette resting between her curled fingers.

Tara touched the altimeter. Fifteen hundred feet above the earth, above Terrefine, above all she'd ever known and done, her life played out on a plot of dirt that Eddy in his helicopter could break free of in a heartbeat. She lifted her gaze to her left, and the farthest point on the horizon, where a spill of gold melted into the sapphire sky.

"What's that?" The glass was cool against her fingertip.

"The Gulf of Mexico."

"And after that?"

"Let's see. You have the Yucatan Peninsula, that's Mexico. Then Central America, countries like Guatemala, Nicaragua, Costa Rica. Then South America, so Brazil, Chile, Peru, a bunch of other coun-tries. And after about 8,000 miles you'll hit…"

"Antarctica and the south pole," Tara finished. The ends of the earth.

"That's right." This time she could see his smile. "I wish we could make it a longer ride…"

"Then you'd better hand me an ashtray now," her mother interrupt-ed. "Or a gun."

"Speaking hypothetically, Joan!" His eyes crinkled as he met Tara's gaze. "Even if your mom was up for it, Davis back there is scheduled to take up a survey team."

"I know," Tara replied, not because she did, but to distract from the ache she felt as the helicopter gently tilted and the Gulf slid from view.

As Eddy brought them lower, a curdled blight appeared on the lush surroundings of field and forest. "That's it," he said. "The sinkhole." The whirlpool of yesterday had subsided, leaving in its place a huge cratered pit filled with a vomitous slurry. Slimy gobbets of earth mingled with hairy mats of strange vegetation floating atop water tinged the color of sickness. Tara looked away, remembering her mouth filled with that noxious brew.

"Crowded up here." Davis's voice crackled in her ears. "Chopper at eight o'clock."

Tara strained to see the other helicopter and found herself staring into the flat eye of a TV camera.

"Our pals from the press," Eddy said. He flipped a toggle on the console. "Aircraft 1245 withdraw, please. You're obstructing an emergency survey. Over."

"Acknowledge 3730. Over."

"Let's see how long that lasts," said Davis.

"They got a job to do, just like us," Eddy said.

"If you call inciting the good folk of Terrefine a job. I'm sure they'll have plenty to say about the exploratory well."

"That's enough, Davis."

He banked the helicopter toward a swath of land west of the sinkhole that had been scraped flat to create a staging area for the army of Caterpillars, dump trucks, and emergency vehicles. Dozens of workers scurried to and from the sinkhole. A speck of a man wielding bright orange flags guided three newly arrived tankers through the commotion.

"Tara," Eddy began, "earlier when you were on the roof, you said either I don't know what I'm talking about, or I'm a liar. I've been thinking about it, and I'll have to go with I don't know what I'm talking about."

"Huh?"

"I don't know what I'm talking about. Actually, *we* don't know what we're talking about. We've never seen anything like this. We could never have predicted it, not in a million years. Otherwise we would have been prepared." He paused to glance at her. "We would have had more than a drone down there when the collapse occurred. And we would have never let you, or anyone else, have access to the area."

Sunlight ignited the dull water of the sinkhole, then snuffed out as the helicopter banked. "I brought you and your mom up here," Eddy continued, "because I want to show you that we're throwing everything we've got at this." His thumbs reared up from the steering mechanism. "We've determined we need to drill an exploratory well 3500 feet down into the Terrefine salt dome to assess whether or not it's been compromised. You know about the salt dome?"

She did. Though she couldn't have said when or where she'd first learned that her town had been built atop one. Before fifth grade, when her class had studied salt domes, she'd pictured the New Orleans Superdome made out of salt, buried a few feet below her front yard. But the teacher had explained that the domes were more like underground mountains, formed when an ancient seabed buckled up over millions of years through the surrounding crush of earth. The salt behaved almost like lava, flowing upwards until it capped near the surface. For a time afterwards, whenever Tara salted her food, she imagined tiny flecks of bizarre prehistoric sea creatures mixed in with it.

"The sooner we can get that well drilled, the sooner we can get a handle on this so you and your mom can get back home. You getting this, Joan?" he called back. Her mother nodded, though her eyes were shut.

"She's got it," said Tara, letting her eyes fall again to the shiny ribbon of Bayou Reve, following its twists and turns all the way to Eddy's house. She wanted to believe that this huge undertaking was all for her and her mother, but it seemed too fantastic. Whenever they lost power during tornados, it took the electric company days to reconnect them. Once, they'd gone half a year with a downed telephone pole in the front yard.

"Goddamn, that's foul," her mother spat.

Tara's eyes filled as the now-familiar toxic stench flooded the cabin. She turned to Eddy, stretching the collar of her T-shirt over her nose. "Why does it smell like a gas station everywhere?"

Within seconds, he brought them higher and the smell dissipated.

"Where there's salt domes, there's oil and gas," he replied. "Little reserves develop during the dome formation. We think some of that is probably getting released because of the sinkhole. But we'll be able to tell you for sure when we drill that well and finish our radiography." Eddy's thumbs again twitched away from the steering mechanism. It seemed to Tara that he hadn't finished, that he'd tucked the rest of his words away, like a wad of chew. She waited, but he said nothing else as the horizon tipped and her house came into view.

"Any questions before we land?" Eddy's fingers performed a graceful sequence over the dashboard, his eyes never straying from the approaching ground.

"How can I learn to fly?" She waited for him to laugh, or brush her off, but instead he seemed eager to offer the information.

"Mid-South sent me to flight school. They're my lifelong employer and they've put me through a bunch of different trainings. Davis back there learned in the army."

"Free rent, food, and flying lessons if you don't mind wearing green for a few years," Davis added.

"Yeah, and having somebody order you around from morning to night," her mother said.

"True," Davis said. "But you get used to it pretty quick. And we were airborne less than a year after basic. It's worth looking into."

"No, thank you," her mother scoffed.

Eddy eased the helicopter onto the flattened spiral at the edge of the grassy lot. With the blades still whirring, he motioned for Tara and her mother to unstrap. He helped them out, sheltering them beneath his outstretched arms until they'd cleared the blades and were safely back in the front yard.

They stood watching as Davis brought the helicopter to full power and lifted off, Eddy's arms still draped over them. Joan's hair rippled in the gusts from the departing helicopter, forming a halo of white-gold around Eddy's head.

With the helicopter gone, the heat barreled in, heavy and insistent. Eddy cleared his throat and slid his arms from their shoulders. He approached the little truck and gripped the sidewall while eyeing their beat-up cardboard boxes. "This all you got?"

Her mother slammed the tailgate and propped her flip-flop on the rear bumper. "We don't need much. My kin in Texas has everything."

Tara shot her mother an incredulous look. Texas? They'd never been there together, not once. Nor had her mother ever shown any interest in taking her.

Eddy nodded, drifting to the front of the truck where he straightened the hood ornament. "There's one other piece here to consider about the drilling..." For a split second, Tara saw it again, the look of a sick dog she'd seen last night in his kitchen, hiding its hurt. But his eyes jumped to the road behind her, and his brow darkened.

Tara followed his gaze. Through a curtain of heat, a straight-backed figure on horseback was approaching. She recognized the sturdy build immediately.

"He's trespassing in a restricted area," Eddy said.

"She. And she's not trespassing, she's my friend," Tara said, feeling a surge of the loyalty she'd denied so many times before when the brothers had teased her about Mrs. Honoré.

"I'm sorry, Tara. It's for her own safety."

"She knows what's safe, more than anybody." Tara waved as Mrs. Honoré drew closer, rocking gently astride Lightning, whose coat appeared copper in the midday sun.

"How y'all doing?" Mrs. Honoré clasped the saddle horn and swung down to the grass. The horse nipped at the overgrown lawn while she looped the reins around the trunk of the apple tree. She pulled Tara to her in a rough hug and Tara breathed in the scent of horse and saddle, and something deeper, almost peppery, that was Mrs. Honoré.

"Been waiting for that helicopter to clear out so Lightning wouldn't get spooked," Mrs. Honoré said as she gave a final squeeze, then let Tara go. "Smells strong here, stronger than at my place."

"Naturally occurring reserves of gas and oil are being released from the sinkhole. It's most likely a compromise of the salt dome," said Tara, experimenting with the new information.

"Is that right?" Mrs. Honoré smiled and a web of wrinkles grew from the corners of her eyes to the deep brown of her weathered cheeks. "I hear you went for a swim?"

"Ugh." Tara stuck out her tongue. "It was stupid of me."

"I wouldn't say that. You okay now?"

"She's healthy as your horse, Loretta." Her mother didn't bother to smile. Her long-standing resentment toward the older woman was no secret, to Mrs. Honoré or Tara. It had become part of the natural grain of things. "It's nice of you to always be checking up on us. But believe it or not we're doing okay on our own."

"No one's said otherwise, Joan."

Eddy extended his hand to Mrs. Honoré. "Eddy—"

"Eddy Ledroit, Mid-South Petroleum," Mrs. Honoré finished. "I've been leaving messages for you all morning."

"My apologies." He pulled his phone from his hip holster and glanced at it. "My cell coverage is spotty in this area."

"Mine too. That's why I thought I'd better drop by."

"Yes, ma'am. Though you really shouldn't be here. How'd you get past the roadblock?"

"Roadblock? Son, I pulled Blake Brouillette from his mother's loins when he came early. No roadblock he's manning will ever impede me."

"Duly noted," said Eddy, letting his arms fall to his sides. Tara felt a twinge of pity. She'd been on the wrong side of Mrs. Honoré a few times. It had been devastating.

"We were on that helicopter that just left," said Tara, thinking she'd let Mrs. Honoré know that Eddy wasn't all bad. "I wish you'd been there. Eddy took us up."

"Did he?" She removed her battered leather hat and swabbed her forehead, before settling it back on her skull. "I'd say that's the least Mid-South can do for you and your mama."

"Loretta." Her mother tossed her chin at Mrs. Honoré. "No need to break the man's head for doing a kindness."

"A kindness? Destroying your property to clean up their mess is a kindness?"

Eddy's jaw clenched, and Tara felt her stomach go sour. Her mother sliced through the heat with her open palm. "What in God's name are you talking about?"

Mrs. Honoré shook her head at Eddy. "You mean you haven't told them?"

"How would you have access to that information?" he asked. "And of course, we intend to review the impact of the subsidence mitigation with Mrs. Saint-Romain and her daughter. I was about to walk them through the ten point plan…"

"If you can't speak plain English, Mr. Ledroit, then allow me." She turned her back to him and faced Tara and her mother. "You're being evicted by the state so Mid-South can drill a well straight through the heart of your backyard."

6.

The house, the yard, the whole world wavered in the heat, as if struggling to remain upright beneath the white-hot glower of the sun. The clang of heavy machinery rang out from the direction of the sinkhole.

"Easy girl," Mrs. Honoré murmured, stroking Lightning's powerful, sleek neck.

Tara's mother scooped a twig from the grass and skewered a dense knot of her hair. "The state? Evicting people? Sounds like you were up too late listening to trucker gossip on your CB radio, Loretta."

But Tara saw the truth of Mrs. Honoré's claim in the needle-thin creases falling from the corners of Eddy's mouth. He pawed the earth with his boots. "She's right, Joan. One hundred percent."

"You shittin' me?" Her mother's teeth flashed bright through her half-smile, as if she were holding out for the joke. "Since when?"

"Since this morning. I planned to tell you while we were in the helicopter, when I could give you an aerial of the operation, but your nerves…" His fingers left his waist to stir the air. "And Tara's first flight. It didn't seem like the right time. See." He brandished his phone like a small shield. An orange slide with the Mid-South logo flashed on the screen. "I loaded up a whole presentation to show you."

"How nice," her mother said, "that you made a little video game, or commercial, or whatever that is. But I'd rather you keep that thing in your pants and talk to my face."

"Of course." Eddy cast a sheepish glance at his phone before returning it to its holster. "It's a pretty straightforward strategy. We'll need to appropriate the whole backyard, which will require the temporary relocation of your…antique collection. We'll construct a platform, bring in the drilling equipment, and dig the well. Shouldn't take more than two or three weeks, probably less. Our findings will help the appropriate parties design a remediation plan for the sinkhole. We'll also get a sense of when you can return to your home."

41

"Any reason you can't use the giant empty lot right next door?" Tara's mother asked. "Or somebody else's property? I don't guess you volunteered your own home."

"He can't," Mrs. Honoré cut in. "Mid-South doesn't want to pay what it costs to drill anywhere else. They've got to protect their bottom line."

"And more importantly," Eddy said, his words gliding around Mrs. Honoré's. "You're just off the top of the dome, uniquely situated to optimize the exploratory well. The most recent geo survey shows the land is stable enough to support the equipment. We really couldn't ask for a better site."

Her mother slipped a hand beneath her tank top, exposing the smooth concave between her ribs and belly. "Well, I guess that settles it," she said, idly scratching her skin, as if she were absorbing a foregone conclusion.

"I'm glad you understand," Eddy said, his shoulders relaxing. "Good news is that Mid-South can put you up in their company suite in Baton Rouge."

Joan glanced briefly skyward, as if searching for an end to the swollen August heat. When she spoke again, she sounded almost amused. "You are smooth as a pair of silk drawers, Eddy Ledroit. Clucking around the backyard like a mama hen, talking about safety and airing out the house. Even offering to jimmy my stuck window while giving me that farm boy grin." Her mother dug a cigarette from her pocket and scrutinized the filter and the tip.

Eddy stiffened. "Probably best not to smoke till we get a better handle on the methane concentration."

"I knew oil and gas men like you growing up in Texas." Joan gestured toward Eddy with her cigarette. "Y'all made all the rules. Who gets to stay on their land and who doesn't. Where the roads get built. Who works. My daddy pissed off the boss once and never worked again. Rained hell at home."

Her mother struck a match one-handed, a trick that was a favorite of Tara's, then casually touched the flame to her cigarette. She dragged deeply, her gaze traveling from Eddy's face to his groin and back up again, until her eyes, limpid and cool, came to rest on his. "I trust my gut a helluva lot more than your words," she said. "And my gut tells me that if I leave my house to you and your buddies, I'll never see it again. You need to find yourself another piece of land. And another sucker. 'Cause I ain't it."

She plucked the twig from her bun and her hair fell, a screen of bright silk that kept time with her hips as she strode to the house.

"Please reconsider, Joan," Eddy yelled after her. "Mrs. Saint-Romain! We're dealing with an industrial emergency!"

She ignored him, her long legs scissoring through the grass until she reached the porch. Seconds later, they witnessed a cascade of falling windows as she sealed herself in.

Eddy parked his hands on his leather belt. His fresh blue polo shirt was now sodden. He glanced at Mrs. Honoré, who stood nearby, her rose-brown lips pursed as she studied the house. "Can you talk some sense into her?" he asked. "Convince her that nobody's trying to grab her land or take her home?"

"I can't assure her of what I don't know," Mrs. Honoré replied. "She's got every right to be suspicious. And you weren't exactly straight with her."

"There's no playbook for this. Or time," Eddy blurted, then catching himself, softened his tone. "Things are bound to get messy. I'm sorry for that. But she's got to understand what's at stake here."

The upstairs windows slammed shut in quick succession. Her mother's was the last to fall, but not before her voice rang out. "You forgot something!" Eddy's clipboard shot out the window, skittered down the roof, and wedged in the leaf-choked gutter.

He turned to Mrs. Honoré, his tanned forehead rumpled with concern. "The state of Louisiana has ordered Joan and Tara to vacate the property for the duration of the drill. The marshal will deliver the notice within the hour." He released a long sigh. "If she won't cooperate, they can force her. Please. Will you talk to her?"

Mrs. Honoré exchanged glances with Tara, her dark irises floating on cloudy white. "Think she'll hear me out?"

Tara shrugged. "I can ask."

Tara expected to find her mother darting through the house securing windows. Instead, she was perched on the bottom step, dust glittering high above her head in the light from the stairwell window. Her fingers clutched the framed photograph of Tara's father as a boy.

"I meant to get rid of that, Mama," Tara said.

Her mother tore her eyes from the picture, her face drained of the bravado she'd launched at Eddy. She held out the photo to Tara who stuffed it deep in the belly of a Hefty bag, slumped just inside the kitchen doorway.

"Seeing him as a boy…." Air hissed through her mother's teeth. "I always think of him just appearing one day. *Poof.*" Her fingers fanned. "Full-grown, black heart thumpin'. Not born like the rest of us." Her eyes raked across the fissured ceiling, the faded, stifling living room, and the worn wooden slats extending from the foot of the stairs. "My one regret is that he died of a heart attack and not by my hands."

"Come on, Mama. You ain't a killer."

"Everybody's a killer for the right reasons, baby."

Tara frowned, shifting her weight to one hip, as she studied the tender strip of scalp on her mother's bowed head. She was surprised by the jagged heat of her mother's words. Her rare mentions of the old man were typically matter-of-fact, almost devoid of feeling, such as yesterday's casual remark in the truck about the "ignorance and youth" that lead to her marriage in the first place. She could recall once or twice when her mother had called him an old buzzard, but never anything harsher than that. In no way did she think her mother's feelings came close to her own gut-aversion to the old man. Instead, she took it for granted that her mother had shrugged off that part of her life the way she shrugged off most things that had turned out badly over the years.

"I promise you," her mother breathed, her eyes cutting jerky, fugitive circles on the floor. "He's toasting blood with the devil right now, celebrating me getting thrown out of here. He'd love knowing I ended up on the street. Bastard."

"Maybe marrying that old buzzard wasn't the best choice you ever made." Tara purposefully used her mother's past insult, hoping to reawaken her usual indifference toward the old man and break up the dark mood that had descended on her. "But who cares? He's dead as a doornail now. Nobody's toasting anything."

"Choice?" Her bitter laugh startled Tara. "I guess you would think that. I never told you any different."

"Told me what different?" Tara asked, a sudden chill in her belly.

Her mother's lips contorted, as if struggling to contain a mounting pressure from within. Then her words burst forth, scattershot, almost too quick for Tara to follow. "That we married because he won me in a poker game. From my own daddy, to save my daddy's land. That I was sixteen and too stupid!" She slammed her palm on the tattered fabric covering the stair. "Too stupid to spot the shit storm that was coming my way. That there was no getting out of it once he got me here." Her sapphire eyes glowed with an animal sheen. "When the sheriff came to say they found him dead in his truck, I screamed myself hoarse. He thought it was grieving and having a belly ripe with you. But it was joy. For being let out of hell."

Her mother's words hung in the air, amidst the swirling dust. Tara hid one trembling leg behind the other as her mind stalled, short-circuited with shock and dismay. "If I saw him nowadays…sometimes I play it out, him trying to get up on me. I'd snap his neck." Her hands jerked into fists. "I don't care if he had a whip, or a knife, or a gun. You got to know that about me, Tara." Her voice broke into a guttural sob.

As Tara felt the rage pulsing off her mother, her trembling legs quieted. Her own emotions fled to some far corner of her being. She recognized this fury. She'd felt its current all her life, speeding and slowing her through her days, orienting her directions and decisions; so much a part of her existence that she'd never stopped to consider its origins.

Yet here it was, the monstrous truth. Tara's life had been wrenched from her mother's, a girl only two years older than she was now, passed off as poker spoils by her own father, forced to share the bed of someone who could rightfully be her grandfather. Kidnapped, really. A prisoner.

The revulsion she'd always felt toward her father now made sense, and she was glad for it, glad that she'd never built a fairy tale around him the way some fatherless kids at her school had done.

Her mother raised her red-rimmed eyes to Tara's. "I bought this house with my misery. I'll be damned if I'm gonna give it up without a fight."

Tara joined her mother on the stairs, shoulder to shoulder, her dark locks brushing against her mother's light ones. She felt the weight of her debt to her mother, and the stain that she would always bear, half-formed as she was of that man, of his cruelty and meanness.

The front porch creaked, and Tara remembered Mrs. Honoré, and the impending eviction notice. It dawned on her that it wasn't Mrs. Honoré who needed to talk to her mother. It was her daughter.

"Mama, I'm proud of you."

"Proud? For what?" A glob dripped from her nose and Tara sprinted upstairs to the bathroom. She returned with a wad of toilet paper.

"For being strong," Tara continued as her mother blew into the bouquet of tissue. "Most people would give up. Even give up their child, after what you went through. But you didn't."

Her mother threw the damp ball of tissues against the wall where it plopped into a cardboard box filled with clothes. "I'd never give you up, baby. You're all I got. Plus you were such a skinny little frog. Too ugly for anybody else to want you."

Tara's lips drew into a soft smile. "And you did a good job ripping Eddy a new one out there."

"You think so?" She slung an arm over Tara's shoulder. "I meant what I said. They're going to have to pry me out of here to drill our land. I'm not gonna just roll over."

"But what about the house blowing up?"

"Hasn't yet. Probably a lie to scare me out of here."

"They could arrest you."

"I'm not afraid of being arrested. The sheriff and me are on friendly terms."

Tara stared at the ceiling, its rafters slung with cobwebs and thick with dust. She thought of the windows that rattled in a strong breeze, the warped back door that gaped at the bottom even when closed. The house barely kept out the wind and rain. She and her mother had their work cut out for them if they were going to resist the eviction and burrow in. Right now a lazy man's kick to the front door would bring it down. She touched her mother's knee. "We should nail the windows shut. Maybe push the couch in front of the door. I can keep watch from the roof tonight."

"Tara, you're my pardner and all, but maybe you shouldn't be here, in the middle of all the hoopla. I hate to give Loretta Honoré another reason why I'm not worth a flip as a mother."

"She doesn't think that. She wants to help." Tara straightened. "She asked if she could talk to you."

Her mother rose from the stairs and padded to the kitchen. "Tell her no thanks," she called through the doorway. Water gurgled from the faucet. "I got nothing more to say."

Tara welcomed the breeze sweeping through the front yard, dispelling the sinkhole's lingering odor. Mrs. Honoré was nowhere in sight, but Eddy was there, pacing out figure eights on the shell driveway as he spoke on his phone. He noticed her and gestured to the side of the house where she found Mrs. Honoré watering Lightning. The horse swished her tail along her russet flanks as Mrs. Honoré held the hose near her muzzle.

"She won't talk to you," Tara said, in response to Mrs. Honoré's raised eyebrows. "Her mind is made up."

"Doesn't surprise me. When your mama is up for air, she's the most headstrong person I know."

A dull sedan with a dashboard siren turned into the driveway. The "marshal" turned out to be Eugene Billets, who Tara knew as a bag boy from the Piggly Wiggly. She was surprised when her mother answered his knock, smiling and gracious. Eugene's face blossomed with splotches as he presented her with a manila envelope.

"Good afternoon, Mrs. Saint-Romain. If you wouldn't mind, please consider yourself served this notice of eviction, effective immediately." His voice broke on the word *eviction*. "But the sheriff says to tell you to take up to twenty-four hours if you need it. He would have served you himself, but he's spread thin with all this sinkhole business."

Eugene's blush deepened as her mother touched his forearm. "You tell Sherriff Grady howdy from me and good luck with this mess," she said.

As Eugene left the front porch, her mother shook the notice at Eddy and ripped it in half, leaving the pieces to float to the ground.

Mrs. Honoré nudged Tara. "You save that paper. You'll want to know what it says. I'm going to make some calls, see what I can find out about your rights." She tugged Lightning's reins, leading her toward the road. "Why don't you stay with me tonight?"

"Thank you, ma'am. But I'm staying put," Tara said, strengthening her stride as she thought of shoring up the house with her mother.

There was the tiny voice, too, whispering of her mother alone in the house, her rage winding her tighter and tighter as the old man crept through her consciousness. It was easy to imagine her unearthing one of the bottles stashed around the house or cajoling the greasy teenager who sometimes brought her "medicine" to find a way past the road-block. She could hurt herself messing with tools or moving furniture.

"You're not scared of anything are you?" Mrs. Honoré frowned. "It's wise to be scared of a few things here and there."

Tara forced a smile, dismissing the impulse to ask about the potential dangers of a sinkhole. There was no need, she reasoned. Hadn't the sheriff given them a whole day to leave? If there was any real risk, he probably would have raced over here himself with his sirens flashing or ordered Eugene to pack them up right away and hurry them out of the area. And knowing her mother, twenty-four hours from now she'd likely talk the sheriff into giving them even more time.

When they reached Eddy, his face was flushed. His cap lay nearby on the grass. "Let me finish up here," he said into the phone. "I'll see you at the site in ten minutes. Bye."

"Any luck?" he asked Mrs. Honoré, who was adjusting the reins. "I didn't see you go in."

"Joan isn't interested in talking to me." She clasped the saddle horn and swung onto Lightning. "But I'll keep trying. I'll call her when I get home."

"I feel for her. I do. But the delay won't make a bit of difference in the long run." He stepped toward his truck. "And if I fail to get her to cooperate, they'll probably replace me as the liaison. I really didn't want that."

Tara escorted Mrs. Honoré and Lightning as far as the grassy lot. Her friend dug into the saddle bag and withdrew a pint Tupperware container. "At least you two can have a good dinner tonight," she said. "Squirrel gumbo."

Tara clutched the food to her chest, watching Mrs. Honoré until she was out of sight. Evening fell, as slow and gentle as any other night. The chirping of the ditch frogs cycled against the hum of cicadas.

She would not abandon her mother.

7.

Her mother breathed smoke into the blue hush of the evening. Her long hair, wheat-colored in the fading light, brushed against the small of her back. Her forehead glistened, and wet half-moons darkened her tank top beneath her arms. A hammer dangled from one hand, a cigarette from the other.

Nearby, Tara examined an overturned refrigerator, its interior bristling with wooden boards of various sizes harvested from the backyard. She nodded at two of the longest pieces. "Those'll cover the front door, easy."

Her mother whacked the old lumber with her hammer, testing its sturdiness. "What you got for the living room windows? And the side door?"

"I was thinking these pieces from the old mantel for the door. And that plywood for the windows."

"We can always just fire up the flame thrower." Her mother grinned and slid the hammer through the belt loop of her cutoffs. She stretched her arm, lean muscles flexing, to the tall tip of the lumber and jerked two pieces level with her waist. "Grab the other end," she ordered, tucking the planks beneath her arm.

Tara trotted behind her, hauling the wood across the yard and through the backdoor. Inside, she held the planks steady as her mother sunk nails into the front door and the frame. The radio hummed with eighties rock-n-roll, piped from a station too far away to care about the sinkhole.

"Damn. Pounding shit feels good," her mother mumbled through the two nails tucked between her lips. She paused to gather the sweat-darkened strands from her neck and swirled her hair into a rubber band. "You wanna grab me a cold one, baby?"

Tara loitered in the cool of the open fridge, regarding the shiny Bud Light cans as her mother's hammering reverberated throughout the house. Her mother held that light beer didn't count as drinking, which was true. It was right there on the label, only 4.2 percent alcohol content. Her usual Jim Beam was 37 percent. But part of her wished her mother would take a break from even light beer for a while.

"You gone by way of Kalamazoo?" her mother called through a pause in her hammering. Tara popped open the can and rejoined her. The front door was now secured with two wide planks in an X shape.

"Should I look for another long one?" Tara asked, handing her mother the beer.

Her mother took a long swig then slid the chilled can across her forehead. "Couple more boards ain't gonna make a difference. None of this is gonna keep out a soul really wants to get in. We're just buying ourselves a little time to think."

"Then what?"

Her mother shuffled backwards, the hammer crammed head first into her back pocket, and eyed the living room windows. She glanced at Tara and flared her eyes dramatically. "I don't know. Depends on who shows up." She stuck out her tongue.

"This is serious, Ma! We need a plan." But Tara grinned through her protest. It was hard to resist her mother's playfulness. It had been months since they'd worked on a project together, restoring sec-ond-hands, or changing the oil on the truck. Even with the drama of the past two days, building something together made things feel almost normal.

"You're right. But I gotta be honest. More I think about it, more this seems like one giant bluff. Yeah, a big hole opened up and filled with stinky water. But now?" She gestured toward the stairwell window where the first timid lights peeked through the purpling sky. "Nothing out there but stars. I'll bet my left cheek they're just looking for an excuse to stick their big, old man-drill in our land." She let the hammer swing briefly at her crotch.

"Gross, Mama."

"Just calling it like I see it." She pointed at the windows above the sofa. "Wanna grab that plywood? For there?"

Outside, Tara eyed the remaining boards and predicted a shortfall. She combed through the backyard, searching the lengthening shadows for overlooked scraps.

"You hungry?" her mother called from inside.

"I'll make something later!" Tara hollered back. "After I find a couple more pieces."

Light filled the kitchen windows and her mother flashed into view. She rooted through the refrigerator, emerging with her favorite snack, Philadelphia cream cheese doused in Worcestershire sauce and black pepper. Tara was relieved to note the absence of a second beer.

She continued to rummage through the backyard, until the hollow in her own belly sounded. She retrieved the gumbo from where she'd left it in the carport and plunked down on a lawn chair. She hadn't bothered to mention Mrs. Honoré's offering to her mother, who made a show of never eating Mrs. Honoré's food.

Tara gulped straight from the Tupperware, savoring the stringy squirrel, as darkness gathered and a faint sliver of moon appeared. She was halfway through the container when a thunderous boom split the air. She jumped to her feet, sniffing the wet night for fumes, but smelled only honeysuckle and everyday bayou rot.

"You heard that?" her mother called from inside.

"Yep!" Tara yelled. "I think it was just some machinery. Down at the hole!"

She burped softly into the crease of her elbow and ducked through the carport to scout the front yard. The garish blaze of the emergency staging area dominated the western sky, obscuring the lights from town. The narrow country road stretched flat and empty in both directions. The rest of the world seemed to have winked out of existence, leaving only Tara, her mother, and the throbbing sinkhole. As she listened to the mechanical echoes disrupting the night, Tara remembered the torn eviction notice and Mrs. Honoré's instruction to retrieve the pieces.

After groping her way along the darkened porch floor in vain, Tara decided to fetch a flashlight from the carport. As she descended the steps, she bumped a stack of clay pots. A loud crash ensued and feet thudded down the inside stairs, pounded through the living room and out the side door. The carport light switched on.

"Tara?" Her mother's eyes were blazing lanterns as she stepped from the carport and glared into the darkness. A ribbon of white paste trimmed her upper lip. "Any of you Mid-South motherfuckers out there, I gotta a hammer with your skull's name on it!"

"It's me." Tara stepped from the shadows. "What's on your face?"

"You about gave me a heart attack." She patted the goopy moustache. "Bleach cream. I found three black hairs. What was all that racket?"

"I broke those." Tara gestured to the clay slivers trailing down the stairs. "Sorry."

From the road beyond the house an engine roared to life and the headlights of an SUV burned bright. It slid through the pitch darkness before braking in front of the house. A glossy image of her mother, bare-legged, the unguarded white of her neck rising from her tank top, was reflected in the back window.

"Get over here, Tara." The edge had returned to her mother's voice.

Tara strode toward the carport, then spun around and blasted a full-throated yell. "Beat it!" The SUV lingered a few seconds longer before revving the engine and pulling away.

"Should we call the sheriff?" Tara asked.

"Naw," her mother replied, though her voice was strained. "It was probably some of those shitheads from the hole. Getting their kicks while they're on break."

Tara awoke to the watery dawn light creeping through the boarded windows of the living room. Her eyes stung. She squeezed them shut, determined to fall back asleep, and squirmed deeper into the couch.

A choked whisper prodded her back to awareness and her eyes fluttered open. Her mother sat hunched on the far end of the sofa, her head in her hands. The TV flickered with muted gospel singers in purple robes. On the coffee table, potato chips trailed from a gaping Lays bag. A saucer streaked with Worstershire sauce sat next to the cellphone.

"Migraine," her mother croaked. She lifted a trembling hand from her scalp. "Excedrin. Kitchen cabinet." She fell silent, overtaken by a dry heave.

Tara was wide awake now, coughing as she hurried to the kitchen. The sinkhole fumes had returned, as bitter and penetrating as the day the earth first opened. She flung open cabinets, riffling through seasonings, canned food, and Wesson oil. She overturned the wire basket on the kitchen table but found only jar lids and loose pennies. "Not here," she yelled across the kitchen. She listened for a response as she sifted through a row of drawers, then returned to the living room with a cool cloth to place on her mother's neck.

"You got me something?" Her mother's voice was barely audible. Her head was between her knees, her breathing ragged.

"I'll bet it's upstairs," Tara said, keeping her voice soft as she backed out of the room.

She ransacked her mother's bedside table, then the bathroom, squinting to keep her burning eyes free of tears. There was no Excedrin or even aspirin. She tore through the medicine cabinet, tossing a crusty Pepto Bismol bottle, eye drops, and a bottle of Tums in the sink. A throat lozenge fell from the cabinet and bounced to the floor. Tara narrowed her eyes and dropped to one knee. Two identical white pills peeked from beneath the back edge of the grimy toilet rug. She examined them, recognizing the medication the clinic had prescribed for her mother's last migraine. The pills had worked miracles. She had been back on her feet in a couple of hours.

After the migraine was gone, her mother continued taking the pills, at first "just to make sure," then for a broken pinky toe, then for no reason at all, often with a whiskey chaser. When Tara caught her snorting the crushed tablets, her mother invented a phone call with a doctor, claiming he'd prescribed the method for quicker relief. When the clinic had refused to give her more, she found them elsewhere. The months-long slide had left her mother a zombie. At times, Tara worried her mind had gone. And last week's detox had been one of the worst. Tara pocketed the pills, then combed through her own room, even though she knew she'd find nothing. She never took medicine, not even aspirin.

The day had grown brighter, revealing her unmade bed and the drawers left open during yesterday's hurried packing. She tucked a loose cigarette behind her ear, realizing she'd have to drive to the Buy-U-Mart to find relief for her mother.

As she descended the stairs, she heard the squeal of brakes and the rattle of a large motor. She peered through the glass oval of the front door, visible in the cross section of their makeshift blockade. Tatters of morning fog drifted along the road where a flatbed laden with enormous lumber planks slowly maneuvered behind a parked Mid-South truck. A police cruiser was close behind, not Sheriff Grady's aging vehicle, but a dark gray squad car, like the ones that lay in wait off the interstate between Terrefine and New Orleans.

Her mother's moans pulled Tara from the glass. She huddled at her mother's side, rubbing her back as her torso undulated with empty retches. Her mother snaked an arm free and held her open palm out to Tara.

"I'll get something for you, Mama. I promise."

Tara grabbed the cellphone and checked the front yard again. The state troopers had left the squad car to approach the Mid-South truck. The taller of the two gestured toward the house, his fingers mapping the air as he spoke to the driver. She dialed Mrs. Honoré, but the call went straight to voicemail. She tried again, knowing the spotty cell coverage could revive at any moment, but after a third try she was forced to leave a message. She lowered the phone and studied the Mid-South truck. Eddy Ledroit was a liar, but he had pulled her from the water. And right now there was no one else.

Tara plucked the hammer from the floor and set to work levering the planks from the door. She strained against her mother's handiwork, repeatedly throwing all her weight on the hammer handle until the semi-rotted wood broke free. She emerged, panting, on the front porch and paused to gather the torn eviction notice before descending the steps. A fire truck sped past, lights flashing, the siren ripping through the dawn quiet.

The troopers jerked their heads toward Tara when she appeared. The taller one clapped the hood of the Mid-South truck and started toward the house. Despite the fumes invading her lungs, she quickened her pace, determined to intercept them. She met them at the ditch. Up close, with their mirrored glasses and domed hats, they looked identical. The taller one removed his glasses and fixed his gray eyes on her. "Louisiana state police. Where's your mama, young lady?"

"I'm looking for Eddy Ledroit," she said, glancing past him at the Mid-South truck.

"Don't know him." He turned to his partner, who plumped his bottom lip and gave a terse shake of the head.

"He's there, driving," Tara insisted. But as she said it she could see that Eddy wasn't in the truck. The only man she recognized was Byron, who she'd screamed at from the roof for calling her mother a hoarder. His eyes connected briefly with hers, but he made no sign of recognition.

"We need to escort you and your mama to safety immediately. Orders of the state," said the taller trooper.

"No, sir," she replied, panic tearing through her chest. "We were supposed to have twenty-four hours." She held the trembling pieces of the eviction notice together for the trooper to read. "See, that's this afternoon."

"The emergency's escalated. There was a new cave-in an hour ago."

"Look, we'll explain all this to your mama," the smaller trooper interrupted. He strode past her and his partner followed.

Tara's mind raced as the two men marched past the little apple tree. Yesterday, her mother had pledged to stand her ground for as long as she was able. If they had more time, even a few hours, her mother could recover, and they could figure out a plan. But right now her mother was a puddle of pain. All their stuff was still in the back yard. She glanced at the mud-spattered bulldozer that had joined the flatbed truck. They would probably just plow everything under.

"Wait!" she called after the troopers, charging through the grass to block their path. "My mother can't talk to you now."

Annoyance flooded the smaller trooper's face. "We're in a state of emergency. No time for your mother to powder her nose."

"She's not powdering her nose." Tara bristled. "She's…" Her mind ranged wildly until she remembered a story overheard at the Piggly Wiggly checkout. "She's got lots of blood this month from her endometriosis. The doctor said it's blood enough to kill two men, but not my mama. She just needs a few minutes to swab up the bathroom. You got a problem with fifteen minutes?"

The trooper's mouth twisted into a bow of distaste. "You got fifteen. That's it." He popped his sunglasses back on.

Tara ran back to the house, not caring if the men saw her rush. Her mother was curled on the sofa, clutching her skull. Tara replaced the fallen cloth on her neck. "Mama, what should I do?" she whispered, falling to her knees. "They're all out there—Mid-South, the police— crawling all over our property."

Her mother raised her pain-drenched eyes to Tara's. Her mouth remained slack and wordless. A pack of men's voices sounded from the driveway and Tara frantically peered outside. A cluster of Mid-South workers surrounded a man aiming a gun-shaped sensor at the house. He exchanged words briefly with the troopers, then tromped through the carport and into the backyard. The rest of the workers trailed behind him.

Tara found the hammer. She withdrew the two pills and arranged them on the coffee table. "I got something for you, Mama."

Her mother's eyes fluttered open. Tara lowered the cold metal onto the tablets, crushing them until only powder remained. She scooped the dust into her palm and held it beneath her mother's nose. "You can do it, Mama. I know you can. I need you to."

8.

The pills worked quickly. Within minutes, her mother was upright on the sofa, sipping the day-old coffee that Tara had warmed for her. Her face, which had been buckled with pain, was now merely puffy.

"Another." Her mother held out her cup.

Tara poured coffee from a saucepan while peering through the wooden boards nailed over the kitchen window. The troopers eyed the house from the squad car. The taller one spoke into the radio while his partner rapped his knuckles against the car door. Emergency work crews came and went through the front yard, their fluorescent vests shocking in the early morning light.

"Good and strong," her mother murmured, after Tara returned with the thick chicory brew.

"Drink it all, Mama. They're coming back soon." Her mother gave her a frowzy quizzical look over the top of the cup. "The state troopers," Tara added. Her mother's pupils shrank to pinpricks as she nodded her understanding. Tara had hurriedly described her encounter with the troopers while the pills were taking effect.

From outside, the blunt slam of a car door was followed by another. Tara knelt on the sofa beneath the living room windows to watch the troopers march toward the house, expressionless behind their sunglasses.

Warm breath grazed the back of Tara's neck as her mother knelt behind her. "I swear that little one got me last summer for going five miles over the speed limit."

"It's probably just the uniform, Mama. They all look the same." Tara stole a glance at her mother's profile, the now-bright eyes, the flared nostrils, the restless jaw.

The troopers clomped onto the porch and tried the broken doorbell. When the knocking began, Tara stayed put, waiting as her mother drained the last of her coffee. Her mother was in no hurry, pausing between sips to stretch her legs and roll her ankles, nudging her body awake.

"Open up. State police. We have an order for your evacuation."

The knocking intensified and Tara cast an anxious look at her mother.

"Go ahead, baby," her mother said, stretching one last time. "I'll talk to 'em on the porch."

Tara unlatched the door, but before she could speak, the smaller trooper had ducked beneath the remaining piece of wood and shouldered his way past her. His partner followed.

"Mama, they're inside!"

"State police!" the trooper called, his gaze sweeping around the hallway and up the stairs.

Her mother's sing-song voice sounded from the living room. "Howdy, state police. Joan Saint-Romain."

The smaller trooper sprang to the living room door where he stopped short, taking in the languid figure of Joan, with her bare feet and dirt-smudged tank top, her nipples discernable beneath the thin fabric.

From behind Tara, the taller trooper raised his voice, "I'm Officer Hall. My partner, Officer Gaffin, has a notice of emergency evacuation for your review. But frankly we should have had you out of here a half hour ago." Tara slid into the room, past the shorter trooper as he stepped toward her mother with the notice in hand.

"Officer Gaffin." The name fell like ice chips from her mother's mouth. She leaned forward with her hands on her knees. "You remember me from last summer? I-10?"

"No, ma'am. But how about we reminisce in the car. You got sixty seconds to grab your purse before we have to forcibly remove you, for your own safety. And your daughter's."

Her mother's face darkened. "You said we had an understanding, you little twerp. Why did my license get suspended? You know how hard it is to pay them insurance rates when you're a single mother?" She snatched the lighter and a cigarette from atop the TV and flicked on the flame.

"Put it out!" Officer Gaffin barked. When instead, her mother fired a plume of smoke his way, he lunged, knocking Tara to the ground.

"Hands off my daughter, you little shit!" her mother yelled, seizing a lamp and thrusting it at Officer Gaffin.

"Drop it!" he barked, ducking and circling until he'd seized the lamp and wrenched her arms behind her back.

"Leave her alone!" Tara screamed as she regained her feet. The taller officer looped an arm around her and hauled her from the room.

Officer Gaffin dragged her mother into the front hallway, tightening his grip as she struggled to free herself. "Goddamn it, be still and you won't get hurt," he grunted.

"Make him quit it!" Tara yelled. She twisted in Officer Hall's embrace, craning to see his face. "She's sick, I already told you." But the officer's gaze remained fixed on the tussling figures, and he made no move to separate them. Tara's hand shot up. She ripped the radio microphone from his shoulder, crushing her fingers around the buttons. "Help! The cops are hurting my mother!"

Pain sliced through her wrist as the officer squeezed her hand. She dropped the device, yelping as he pinned her arms against her body and hugged her to his chest, blocking her mother from sight.

"Dispatch. This is Officer Hall. Disregard prior signal. We have a distressed minor in custody. Arrest of the parent in progress. Over."

She heard the rasp of the handcuffs, then Gaffin's labored breathing as he spoke to her mother. "You have the right to remain silent. Anything you say can and will be used against you in a court of law..."

He hustled her mother to the front door. They scuffled again briefly as he forced her headfirst under the remnants of the barricade, then scrambled after her while still gripping her arms.

"You little pissant!" her mother screamed as she stumbled through the front yard. "You weren't so tough when you were asking to see my titties on I-10! What d'ya think the judge will have to say about that?"

The entire assemblage of workers and machine operators froze in the midst of their emergency operation, gawking as they witnessed Tara and Joan's removal.

"Get out of my yard, motherfuckers!" her mother shrieked at the curious faces. "This is my land! You hear me?"

As Gaffin shoved Joan into the back seat of the squad car, her eyes met Officer Hall's and her voice evened. "Take my daughter to Loretta Honoré's, across the bayou."

"Tara. Here." Officer Hall opened the opposite car door and her mother's screams erupted once again.

"Loretta Honoré's, on Pecoke Lane. You bastards!"

The door slammed and her mother rammed her bare foot into the partition shielding the front seat. On the other side of the bulletproof glass, the officers stared rigidly forward as the car swung away from the house.

"You okay, Mama?' Her mother nodded, but she was trembling, her rage leaking slowly from her body. "You're bleeding," Tara said, noticing a bright trickle from her cheek bone. She bellowed through the partition, "She's cut! My mother's hurt!" Neither of the officers took notice. Tara licked her thumb, then touched it to her mother's face. "It's just a little one. Soap and water is all you need."

"Is that all?" Her mother gave Tara a thin smile, before drawing her cuffed wrists to her chest and turning her face to the window. As the squad car slid past the train of construction and emergency vehicles, Tara searched in vain for Eddy. A woman in a dark T-shirt with Louisiana Disaster Response written across the back in stark yellow letters waved them through a road block. Sunlight flared off a low-flying helicopter and Tara pressed her face against the glass, hoping to catch sight of the pilot.

Through the back windows of the squad car, the passing landscape of Terrefine seemed unfamiliar, even after they'd left the chaos of the evacuation area. The sluggish bayou, the rustling rows of sugarcane, the pockmarked country road, all filtered strangely through the impossibility of sharing the backseat of a police cruiser with her mother. When at last they pulled into Mrs. Honoré's driveway, it took Tara a full breath to recognize the house.

Officer Hall swung open Tara's door. She hesitated, locking eyes with her mother. "Let's go, young lady," he said "We can't wait."

Her mother grunted, rage flickering across her face. "Yeah. Don't wanna be late for your appointment to throw an innocent woman in jail."

He tugged Tara from the backseat and slammed the door, cutting her mother's *fuck you* in half.

"I'm going to get you out, Mama," Tara yelled as the officer ushered her to the house.

The front door flew open as they reached the porch. Mrs. Honoré loomed from the top step, glowering at the officer. "What's going on here?"

"Mrs. Loretta Honoré?" Mrs. Honoré nodded and the officer nudged Tara forward. "Her mama's been arrested. She asked that you keep Tara."

"Of course I will." Mrs. Honoré's eyes leapt to the police cruiser. "What can I do for Joan?"

The officer flicked a card at Mrs. Honoré. "Call this number after three p.m."

Tara cast a final glance at the retreating squad car, then climbed the steps to the porch. She ducked beneath Mrs. Honoré's arm and through the open screen door, careful to avoid her friend's gaze. As she dragged her feet down the unlit front hall, she shuddered beneath the weight of her guilt. This was all her fault. If she hadn't given her mother those pills, she would have never been arrested. She should have just let her mother be. Or given the pills one at a time, the way you were supposed to. What she had done was wrong. She slumped at the kitchen table, shredding a paper napkin until Mrs. Honoré set a can of Coke in front of her.

"Thanks," she said, though she couldn't fathom anything slipping past the bony knot in her throat.

"Want to tell me what happened?" Mrs. Honoré asked softly.

"It's all my fault," Tara said, the words barely escaping.

"Who told you that? Your mama?" Tara shook her head. "Then why would you think that?"

Tara peeked at Mrs. Honoré's face, at the spray of lines between her brows and her soft frown of concern. She imagined the gentle eyes widening with shock and the kind mouth curling with scorn, after hearing that Tara had shoved drugs up her mother's nose. She dropped her gaze to her fisted hands.

"I've known you long enough." Mrs. Honoré placed a wide hand, fingers spread, on the checked tablecloth. "I know what things are like. Your mama doesn't make it easy for you."

"She's a good person." *She kept me*, Tara added silently.

"She loves you. But she lets you take on troubles that are not your own, troubles that you're too young to deal with."

"I'm not too young. I'm smart as most adults I know."

"You are. But it's not just about smart." The chair squeaked as Mrs. Honoré parked her elbows on the table. "My son, William, was like her."

Tara's head shot up. In all the years she'd known Mrs. Honoré, her friend had never spoken her son's name aloud. Tara had sketched an idea of him through artifacts—a pair of size eleven boots, stiff with mud, inhabiting shelf space in the barn; a child's chemistry set tucked away in a cabinet; a high-school graduation announcement clipped from the *Terrefine Journal* that listed his name among the graduating class of 1985.

"How?" Tara asked, not sure she wanted to know.

"Hardheaded. Willful. Liked to do things his own way." Her fingers trembled and then closed around the saltshaker. "But they're most alike in how they drink."

Tara's face flamed. "What do you mean? Lots of people drink."

"Yes, but not like they do. Like he did. I'm worried she's going down the same road." Tara dropped her gaze to the worn tablecloth, silently willing Mrs. Honoré to shut up. "It killed him, Tara. And I helped. Every time I bailed him out, made excuses for him, cleaned him up so he could start all over again. I put at least half the nails in his coffin."

"He's your family," Tara said, pity striking her heart. "You're supposed to help him."

"That's not how you help people like William. Or your mama. I know that now. They're alcoholics."

"That's a lie." Tara shoved back her chair and stood. "You hate her. Everybody knows."

"I don't hate her," Mrs. Honoré called as Tara fled upstairs. "But she's sick!"

Tara ducked into the nearest room and locked herself in. She flattened her palms against the door, breathing heavily as shame and outrage coursed through her. How could Mrs. Honoré say such horrible things?

When her breath calmed, she turned from the door and almost shrieked. Dozens of shining eyes peered at her from feather-tufted faces of all shades, shapes, and sizes. A knobby-kneed spoonbill stretched its rose-flamed wings toward the ceiling. A brown pelican in profile, its body soft and sleek, watched her from one gray-green eye. A row of stuffed owls, some with heads spun backwards, tracked her as she moved toward the wrought-iron bed. She realized she was in William's old room, converted after his death into storage for Mrs. Honoré's taxidermy projects.

Tara plopped on the bed, puffing dust from the quilt, and reclined against the wrought-iron headboard. *Alcoholic.* The word throbbed inside her skull. Mrs. Honoré must be crazy. Alcoholics were smelly men in shabby clothes, like the toothless man who sometimes begged leftovers outside the Buy-U-Mart. Her mother was nothing like that. She pushed aside the memories of her mother wrapped in her ragged robe in August, nursing her pink plastic cup. "That's different," she blurted, addressing the gallery of birds.

Most of the time her mother was her normal self—strong, and beautiful, and fun. Hadn't Gerard and Louis laughed at her jokes and wolfed down her barbeque? Gerard had been in awe of the things her mother had taught her. He and Louis were useless in comparison. Their own daddy, with his big job at Mid-South, had managed to teach them nothing.

She clutched a handful of quilt, coaxing more dust from the fabric. Today was not her mother's fault. It was hers. There were a million points along the way where she could have made a better choice or done things differently. If Mrs. Honoré had been there, she'd have understood who was to blame.

The stairs creaked dryly as Mrs. Honoré ascended. Her light knock went unanswered. Tara hugged her knees, sealing her lips against her skin. "Cheese grits and orange juice out here if you want them," Mrs. Honoré said, sliding a tray on the floor outside the door. Tara stayed quiet, her eyes fixed on a faded photo of young man on a horse. "I'm sorry if I upset you, girl. What I was trying to say is that I'll help however I can. I guess I didn't do such a good job of it." The wooden floor murmured beneath her solid frame. "What I said about your mama. I was wrong. She's got a lot going for her that William didn't have. The most important thing is you." After waiting for another moment, she left.

Tara blew a dark curl from her eyes, listening as Mrs. Honoré moved about the kitchen. When Mrs. Honoré made a phone call, Tara pressed her ear to the door, straining to make out the words. She heard her mother's name, but the rest was garbled. She straightened her T-shirt and met the collective gaze of the curious flock. What the hell was she doing pouting up here like a little kid? She was needed downstairs, working alongside Mrs. Honoré to get her mother home. She touched a mallard's leathery foot before unlocking the door.

Tara was forcing down a bite of grits at the kitchen table when Mrs. Honoré found her. As she slid into the chair opposite Tara, a softening at the corners of her mouth betrayed only the smallest hint of relief. She flashed Tara the card from Officer Hall. "All they did was confirm that we need to call after three. But at least someone answered."

"Yes, ma'am." Tara lowered her spoon. "I appreciate your help. My mother needs it. I need it. But she is not an alcoholic. And I beg your pardon, but she's not like your son." Tara held her friend's gaze. "Okay?"

9.

Tara pinched the longest of the sharp pins lining a metal taxidermy tray and passed it to Mrs. Honoré. Before them, on the plastic-covered dining room table, perched an elegant snowy egret, forever on the verge of capturing its prey.

"Keep your eye on what you're doing. You're gonna poke a hole in me," said Mrs. Honoré, checking Tara's arm and gently sliding the pin from her fingers.

"Sorry." Tara tore her gaze from the far side of the room, where an antique clock sat on the mantel above a tiny fireplace. It was two o'clock, five minutes past the last time she'd looked.

"You want me to call again?" Mrs. Honoré ran the pin against the grain of the egret's feathers, plumping the bird's face and neck. She had already dialed the number on Officer Hall's card three times, always with the same result—call back after three p.m.

After each call, Tara ordered herself to be patient, to stop bothering Mrs. Honoré. But then the ruminations would start up—her mother in a cold, dark cell with rats crawling all over her; her mother being menaced by her cellmate, the ax murderer; her mother in shackles on a chain gang. Tara shared these fears with Mrs. Honoré, who assured her that her mother was most likely still being processed and booked. When she was finally "locked up," she would probably be put in a large holding cell with a few other unfortunate women. She might encounter a few roaches but probably no rats.

"No, ma'am. I can wait," Tara replied, resolving to hold out for another hour.

Mrs. Honoré spun the egret on its stand, making minute adjustments to tail and wing feathers. She used only her fingers for this final stage of preening. When she'd scrutinized every inch of the bird, she reached for a rag and stepped away from the table. "What do you think?"

Tara glanced at the clock, then took her place beside Mrs. Honoré to study the egret. This bird had a brilliant wild mohawk. Its wings were crooked, as if it were at a hoedown. At the end of its long, shaggy neck, a black beak thrust earthward, aiming for a mosquito hawk or a minnow. It was one of Mrs. Honoré's most beautiful pieces, and yet... Tara's gaze lingered on the bird's upper half. "He's beautiful. But a little too high up in the wings."

Mrs. Honoré snapped a picture with a small silver camera. "That's right. I let my glue set a minute too long and I couldn't force that last degree on the wings, especially the left one." She rounded the table to capture the rear of the bird, for a moment obscuring the clock face. "But luckily most folks don't have your eye, not even my fella at LSU. Of course, I'll point it out to him. And knock down my price. He'll still be happy to have it." She shot one last photo, then gingerly carried the fresh mount to a side table.

"How did he die?" Tara asked as she gathered the plastic sheeting from the table.

"Got ahold of some poison or pesticide." Mrs. Honoré scooped up the tray, rattling the instruments as she walked them to the kitchen. "Ted Ducote found him at his crawfish pond." She lowered the tray into the sink and turned to face Tara, who clutched the plastic to her chest. "You can leave that in the yard, near the shed." She glanced at her wristwatch. "There's corn to shuck if you're up for it."

From a wicker stool on the back porch, Tara shucked green sleeves and ripped golden tassels. She dropped the shiny cobs into a high silver pot at her knees, keeping a clear view of the wall clock through the screen door.

At a quarter till, Mrs. Honoré came out with the cordless phone, a yellow legal pad and a pen. She eyed the pot of gleaming corn. "That should be enough." But Tara kept shucking, and Mrs. Honoré soon joined her.

At 2:55, Tara could no longer tolerate the anxiety whipsawing through her gut. She dropped a half-peeled cob to the ground and mashed her thumbs together, staring at the planks beneath her feet. Mrs. Honoré finished up her last ear of corn and placed the legal pad on her knees. The clock struck three.

"Let's wait till a couple minutes after. No reason to waste our time or theirs."

"Okay…" Tara felt her face contort. "But now it's almost 3:01, so it really is after three."

Mrs. Honoré started to reply but instead pulled the card from her pocket and dialed the number. She pressed the phone to her ear, her pen poised over the pad. "Good afternoon." Her voice was calm, her words precise. "Loretta Honoré again, calling for arrestee Joan Saint-Romain. Has she been booked?"

Mrs. Honoré began scribbling. *Booking number—340875. Resisting arrest. Assault. Unpaid traffic tickets.* The pen was still for a moment, and Mrs. Honoré stiffened. *20k* appeared beneath the rest of the writing. "What about a personal security bond? She does have property." She jabbed the pen top into the pad as she listened. "I see," she replied, her voice flat. She jotted down a phone number at the bottom of the page and then hung up.

"Bureaucratic bs…" Mrs. Honoré mumbled as she began dialing another number.

"Wait! What did they say?" Tara pointed to the *20k*. "What does this mean?"

"That means that some full-of-himself judge set the bail for your mother at $20,000." Mrs. Honoré shook her head as she waited for the call to connect. "It's disgusting. They let that man in Monroe out on personal recognizance and he nearly beat his wife to death."

Tara's panicked thoughts piled one atop the other. Twenty-thousand dollars? It was an otherworldly amount. She thought of the drawer in her mother's bedroom where $600 remained until the end of the month. Plus the $200 that Eddy had given her for her bike. That left $19,200. Her mouth went dry.

Mrs. Honoré's voice grew crisp as she again spoke into the receiver. "Yes, ma'am. How late are you open? And where can I find y'all?"

Minutes later Tara scrambled into the dusty cab of Mrs. Honoré's Chevy. Her bare feet were now clad in thong sandals from Mrs. Honoré's hall closet. The legal pad lay on the seat between them. The truck's great engine roared to life, jiggling the rubber coil from the CB radio.

As Mrs. Honoré pulled onto the road, Tara glanced through the rear window gun rack, in the direction of her house, but immediately turned back around. Her house didn't matter now. Her mother wasn't there.

The wind whistled though the half-open windows as they merged onto the main highway toward New Orleans.

"How far away is the jail?" Tara asked.

"Half hour. But we're not going there. At least not yet. First, the bail bondsman." She lowered the sun visor. "The real twist is that since the state took over your house, I'm not even sure your mama can use it as collateral to secure her release. Typical Louisiana."

Tara felt her stomach grind as she thought again of the twenty thousand dollars; she wanted to pretend it didn't exist, to keep driving with Mrs. Honoré through the shimmering afternoon heat toward her mother, hoping for some miracle between now and then. But hope, and waiting for miracles, always blew up in her face. She fixed her eyes on the yellow centerline dashes and forced herself to speak. "Mrs. Honoré, we don't have that money."

A burst of static erupted from the CB radio, then voices filling the cab with news of the sinkhole and that day's fresh cave-in. Mrs. Honoré lowered the volume to a faint chatter. "I know y'all don't, Tara. That's what the bail bondsman is for. I should have explained sooner. All we need is ten percent of the money, and the bail bondsman will put up the rest."

Tara hung her head. "But we don't even have that."

"Yes, we do. I can spare the money for a while. I know y'all are good for it." Mrs. Honoré kept her eyes on the tractor she was passing, giving it a wide berth before returning to the right lane.

"That's a lot," Tara whispered, terrified that her friend would change her mind and equally terrified to be in Mrs. Honoré's, or anyone's, debt.

"I wouldn't offer it if I couldn't afford it. It's been a good year for my taxidermy." Her eyes left the road and found Tara's. "It's just a loan. That's what friends do."

They drove the next several miles in silence, with Tara struggling to act normal. She pretended to read the legal pad, asked permission to find a station on the radio, and became absorbed in adjusting her sandals. Her discomfort with Mrs. Honoré's generosity, and her weak-kneed gratitude, made her want to jump out of her skin.

The Chevy slowed, and Mrs. Honoré pulled into the gravel parking lot of a low cinder-block building that was dwarfed by its own neon sign, Little's Bail Bond and Pawn. It was the only building in sight, with the land on all sides stretching flat and empty and the highway running dead into the horizon.

The parking lot was crowded, and once they got inside they had to wait almost an hour before they made it to the counter. Tara picked out one other kid, a scrawny girl with a scratch across her face who glared at her with open hostility.

When at last they made it to the window, the clerk, a doughy-faced young woman whose breath was heavy with garlic and tobacco, eyed them with indifference. "Who was arrested?" Her plump fingers hung above the keyboard.

Mrs. Honoré slid a piece of paper across the buckled vinyl counter. "Joan Saint-Romain. All her info is here."

The clerk sucked the inside of her cheek as the keyboard clattered. Tara maneuvered to Mrs. Honoré's side, angling for a glimpse of the computer screen.

"No Joan Saint-Romain," the clerk reported.

"You mean she's not eligible for bail?" Mrs. Honoré asked.

"I mean there's no prisoner named Joan Saint-Romain on the bail blotter. Either she's been released or she was never arrested."

"She was too arrested." Tara spoke across Mrs. Honoré. "I was there."

"Well, lucky you," the clerk said as she stuffed a square of gum in her mouth. "I'm just telling you what the database says."

Tara heard a snicker and she spun around to find the scrawny girl laughing into her fist. Tara lunged toward the girl, stopping just short of an attack, sending her cowering against the jean shirt of a thin goateed man.

"Hey! Muzzle up your girl," the man barked at Mrs. Honoré. The rest of the waiting room tittered, and from the corner someone yelled, "Cat fight!"

"Calm yourself." Mrs. Honoré pulled Tara to her side as she addressed the clerk. "Are you sure that machine is accurate? We're talking about a person's liberty here."

"All I'm sure of is what I see on my screen. If you don't trust me then you can try Easy Bond on I-80. Or call the station yourself." She looked past Mrs. Honoré. "Eighty-nine!" An ashen-faced elderly man shuffled to the counter clutching a heavy gold watch.

From the parking lot outside, Mrs. Honoré dialed the police station and confirmed the clerk's claim. Bail had been posted and Joan Saint-Romain released.

"Your mama must have called someone," Mrs. Honoré said as she revved the engine and threw the truck into reverse. "Any idea who?"

"Maybe Mrs. Tammy at the Buy-U-Mart. But I kind of doubt it. Or somebody from the casino?" Tara added, referring to the gambling venue run by the Chitimacha tribe where her mother occasionally subbed as a cocktail waitress.

"Let's just be happy she's out, however it happened. Here, try her." Mrs. Honoré held out her cellphone to Tara as the Chevy sped down the highway, leaving Little's Bail Bond and Pawn behind.

"We didn't have time to bring the phone or anything," Tara said, flashing back to the ugly moments before her mother's arrest. The truck shuddered in the backdraft of a passing eighteen-wheeler.

Mrs. Honoré slipped the phone back into her pocket. "We're almost to the jail. We'll stop in and see if someone can tell us who she left with."

The highway was a straight shot to the parish police station from the bail bondsman. The five o'clock heat poured in through the open windows and the back of Tara's legs melded to the vinyl seat. She alternated between scrutinizing each oncoming car and scanning the side of the road. After some minutes, she bolted upright in her seat. "Look!"

The figure was little more than a pinprick far ahead on the shoulder of the opposite lane. Tara was uncertain of herself even as she raised the alarm. But as the Chevy drew closer, it became clear that the solitary person standing in a clump of dusty weeds with her thumb extended was her mother.

As Mrs. Honoré slowed and U-turned, her mother withdrew her thumb and plucked a cigarette butt from her lips. Tara threw open her door almost before the truck came to a full stop. Fumes from the baking blacktop engulfed her as she rounded the front of the truck and jogged along the shoulder.

Joan waded through the roadside weeds to meet Tara. Her legs were filthy and scraped. She'd been given a flimsy pair of cloth shoes. She flicked her cigarette away and pulled Tara into a rough hug.

"We were on our way to get you, I swear," Tara said, surrounded by the odor of her mother's night in jail. "Who bailed you out?"

"Like you don't know." Her mother's eyes jumped to Mrs. Honoré, perched behind the wheel of the Chevy. "Thanks, Loretta. I'll get you back," she called.

"Nothing to thank me for, Joan," Mrs. Honoré replied, leaning her head through the window. A gas tanker sped past, blaring its horn and sending up a cloud of stinging dust. "Y'all better get in before you get run over!"

"Will you come with us?" Tara backed away to inspect her mother's face.

Her eyes were almost unbearably blue against her heat-flushed skin. Her bottom lip was split, but still full and crimson. A neat line of butterfly stitches spanned the cut on her cheek. She smiled crookedly, revealing a bright line of teeth. "Got nothing else on my dance card right now."

When they reached the truck, Mrs. Honoré squinted at Joan from the cab. "You all right? You need a doctor?"

"I'm fine. Look worse than I feel."

"Good. Y'all hop in."

Tara felt a squeeze on her shoulder. "I'll ride back here," her mother said, nodding at the truck bed. "No offense, but I can't look at you right now, Loretta."

"None taken."

Her mother clambered into the back of the truck. When Tara started to follow, her mother raised her hand. "Do me a favor and ride up front, hon. I need to be alone. Catch my breath."

Tara nodded and ducked into the cab. Mrs. Honoré rummaged behind her seat and pulled out a plastic water bottle. "It's warm, but it's better than nothing."

Tara rapped on the glass, then thrust the water through the window. As Mrs. Honoré sped back on to the highway, her mother tipped the bottle high and drained it.

The upstairs toilet flushed and shortly afterwards Joan appeared in the doorway of Mrs. Honoré's kitchen, creases from the bed sheets mapped into her face. "You could have woken me, Tara."

"Tried twice," Tara answered through a mouthful of baked beans. "You were dead to the world." She took the plate of roast beef that Mrs. Honoré held out to her. "You hungry, Mama?"

Mrs. Honoré gestured to an empty chair. "I hope so, Joan. There's way too much to eat here."

"Thanks but no thanks, Loretta," she said, though Tara could plainly see her mother's eyes roving over the steaming plates. "What I'd really like is to wash up." Her mother threw back her shoulders. "The yard hose and some soap will do fine."

"Yard hose? Something wrong with my shower?"

"Rather not put you out," her mother answered gruffly.

"Suit yourself. There's Palmolive at the kitchen sink and a hose at the bottom of the back steps."

Joan went outside and soon the splash of water mingling with the whir of insects drifted through the screen door. Tara caught Mrs. Honoré's gaze. "She just being proud."

"Oh, I know," Mrs. Honoré replied, rising from her chair, a dish in each hand. She rinsed the plates, then settled at a small table near the screen door where she kept her indoor CB radio. She fiddled with the dials until she tuned into a stream of local voices. The sinkhole was still the leading topic, with "Coon Dog" and "Red" trading volleys over who was more responsible, the state or Mid-South.

Tara paled when minutes into their debate, Coon Dog spoke of her mother's arrest. She glanced nervously toward the screen door. "How do they know?" she asked, in a low voice.

Mrs. Honoré raised a finger to her lips and cocked an ear toward the radio.

They havin' a community meetin' tomorrow at the CYO. Mayor said. Over.
Copy that Dog. I heard the same. Mid-South and DEQ will be there. Over.
Yeah. And a lotta pissed off Cajuns. Over.

"Y'all need to be at that meeting," Mrs. Honoré said, lowering the volume. "You and your mama. To let everybody know what's happening to y'all, and your house."

"You damn right we're gonna be there." The screen door swung open and Joan stepped from the dark porch into the warm kitchen light. "I doubt anyone gives two shits about our house, but I'm bound to get another shot at Eddy Ledroit."

10.

The morning of the community meeting, Tara, her mother, and Mrs. Honoré strategized at the kitchen table, a mound of bacon and eggs between them. It was a first for Tara. For all of them really. There was a sense of alliance, a shared resolve. Instead of bridling at Mrs. Honoré's advice about the community meeting, her mother listened, sometimes agreeing, sometimes not. But never responding with sarcasm or resentment. For her part, Mrs. Honoré expressed her anger at how Joan had been treated and promised to offer whatever help she could.

When it was time to leave, Tara wedged between her mother and Mrs. Honoré in the Chevy's dusty cab. On any other day, she might have felt something close to happiness. Instead, a cloying dread crept over her as she thought of the meeting, which was probably already roiling with news of her mother's arrest.

The CYO came into view, a white-washed miniature of the Catholic church to which it belonged, with a columned porch and biblical images molded above the arched doorways. The parking lot was full, so Mrs. Honoré hopped the curb and parked half off the sidewalk. She killed the engine, and the three of them sat listening to the ping and hiss of the settling motor while the rest of Terrefine streamed into the building.

Tara recognized her eighth-grade science teacher, Mrs. Thevenot, and her husband the pharmacist ascending the cement steps. Mrs. Thevenot was a passable teacher, but Tara was put off by her overbearing kindness. She felt lucky to have spotted the teacher first. She'd have a better chance of avoiding her.

"I bet this is the first time Mrs. Adelaide's left home in a decade." Mrs. Honoré pointed to a tiny silver-haired woman escorted by a homecare aide.

Tara frowned, remembering the day she'd plucked a fig from the old woman's tree. She'd caught sight of a rifle nosing through the flowered curtains. "I wouldn't mind if she stayed home for another ten."

Mrs. Honoré chuckled, then shoved her legal pad into her armpit. "You ready, Joan?"

"Yep," Tara's mother replied, looking into her open palms. At Tara's prodding, she'd changed into one of Mrs. Honoré's short-sleeved flannel shirts. Tara had also run their clothes through the wash. She guessed the two of them would look no worse than most of the folks in the meeting.

As Mrs. Honoré stepped out, her mother reached for her door handle. Tara grabbed her wrist. "People were talking about your arrest on Mrs. Honoré's CB last night."

Her mother cocked an eyebrow. "Of course, they were. People must be wearing out their tongues between me and that damn sinkhole." She swung wide the truck door and dangled her foot above the ground. "Truth is, I'd probably be doing the same. Big news on our little bayou."

Mrs. Honoré was waiting for them next to the entrance. *Here we go,* she mouthed and threw open the door. It took a moment for Tara's eyes to adjust to the fluorescent-lit room. But gradually she made out the townsfolk standing against the walls and seated in rows of metal folding chairs arranged along the old basketball court. Everyone's attention was on a small stage framed by a threadbare velvet curtain where a man in rumpled khaki fiddled with a standing microphone.

Eugene Billets, the gawky deputy who'd served her mother the notice of eviction, manned the table near the entrance. He nodded at Tara and Mrs. Honoré and stared at Joan until she met his eyes and grinned. He was quick to return her smile, but only after a strange expression flitted across his face. Shock? Anger? Eugene waved them past before Tara could decipher it.

The ancient speakers crackled and the man in khaki introduced himself as Ned Elder of the Louisiana Department of Natural Resources, "DNR for short." Behind him stood the mayor, who Tara recognized from a faded election poster in the window of the Buy-U-Mart. Sheriff Grady stood to his left.

Eddy was also on the stage, his back to the audience as he unfurled a projector screen. Byron was there, too, slapping a roll of papers against his thigh. When he caught sight of Tara slipping into the last row of chairs, he leaned over and whispered to Eddy.

Joan filed in behind Tara. As she slid back her folding chair, it snapped shut and clattered to the ground. The noise echoed off the high ceilings and bare walls. The entire assemblage whipped around to face her mother. Murmurs erupted, with one clearly audible, "My god, that's Joan Saint-Romain." Tara cringed as she caught sight of Mrs. Thevenot, her eager face brimming with pity.

"Take a picture, it'll last longer," Tara blurted out as she scrambled to right the chair.

"I got it," her mother said, scooping the chair from the floor in one fluid motion. She offered a half-smile to the gawkers as she settled into her seat and crossed her legs.

Ned Elder hadn't paused during the disruption and gradually the inquisitive faces turned back to the stage. Tara flashed her middle finger at a boy from her class and her mother rolled her eyes comically. But the skin above Joan's collar was flushed, and two bright dots flared on her cheeks. Tara felt her own face burning, but she trained her attention on Ned, who gestured toward the projector screen where a map of Terrefine had appeared. A large oval had been superimposed on the town and the surrounding farmland and swamp forest. Bayou Reve was a mild curve down the middle.

"As y'all know, almost all of Terrefine sits on top of a salt dome." Ned traced the oval with his finger. "The very base of the dome is a little over two miles down. It's about five miles at its widest point." He thumbed a smaller circle, positioned inside of the oval. "They call this the cap rock. Think of the cap rock as the peak of the salt dome. It's about two miles across and lies 350 feet below the ground. You with me so far?"

As the heads in front of her bobbed, Tara perked up, noticing a small triangle near the middle of the map labeled *32 Horseshoe Lane*. Her home address. A red circular blot hovered nearby.

"The initial collapse happened here." Ned stabbed the red blot with his pinky. "It's as if, three days ago, the bottom dropped out from under this section of Bayou Reve. A second collapse happened at 5:30 a.m. yesterday at the same location, widening the sinkhole to over 1,000 feet in diameter."

"Tell us something we don't know!" a voice demanded.

"What none of us knows, is why. Not yet." Ned removed his cap and flicked it toward Eddy and Byron. "For years, Mid-South Petroleum has used the domes to store hydrocarbons, carving out dozens of caverns and pumping in propane, butane, and natural gas. They've been ordered by the state to drill an investigatory well to test the integrity of the cavern closest to the sinkhole. We hope to have a better idea of what caused this once that's happened."

Murmurs rippled through the crowd. Tara studied Eddy's face as he listened to Ned, arms crossed, long-toed boots forward-facing. When he'd shown her the sinkhole from the helicopter, he'd spoken as if Mid-South was conducting the clean-up and investigation on its own, as if the sole motivation was helping the community and getting her and her mom back home. He'd never mentioned anything about being ordered by the state. She looked away, disgusted.

Ned raised his voice until the chattering subsided. "Before Mid-South gives you their update, let's get to the question that's on everybody's mind. How dangerous is this thing? One of you stopped me by the front door to ask if he has to be worried about getting sucked into the earth like that poor lady in Florida. While that particular scenario is unlikely, a mandatory evacuation has been extended to all of Terrefine."

A low roar filled the room, and a hail of protests were directed at the stage. "Now wait a minute!" Ned raised a hand above his head. "Quiet please!" The grumbling petered out and he continued. "We are not in a police state, and no one's going to throw you in jail if you stay home. But if you stay, you stay at your own risk, and that risk includes the release of methane—"

A voice rang out, cutting across Ned's words. "What about Joan Saint-Romain? She got thrown in jail for trying to stay in her home!"

Tara scanned the crowd. Many of the faces registered agitation. Some even looked hostile. She was stunned when Mrs. Thevenot's husband jumped up, his face puckered with anger. "That sounds like a police state to me!"

A chorus of agreement sounded, and someone else yelled, "And look what they done to her face!"

Ned Elder faltered. "I am aware of that incident, but I don't have all the details." He turned toward the other men on the stage. "Can anybody add anything here?"

Sheriff Grady started forward, but Eddy had already sprung into action. In two long strides, he was front and center. He waved his arms, trying to contain the uproar.

"I'm Eddy Ledroit, field safety engineer for Mid-South." He projected his voice across the room, ignoring the microphone. "And acting community liaison. My understanding, which includes speaking to eyewitnesses, is that there was a miscommunication in the middle of an extremely heightened emergency situation. This resulted in Mrs. Saint-Romain's unfortunate arrest."

"That's what happens!" Mrs. Thevenot's husband interrupted. "The minute they say 'emergency' you lose all your rights!"

A man in front of Tara muttered to his neighbor, "Everybody knows the state's on Mid-South's payroll anyway."

It suddenly dawned on Tara that the looks her mother had received might have been filled with outrage *for* her, rather than scorn. People were angered by her mother's arrest and afraid that it could happen to them too. She glanced at her mother. Her face was serene. She seemed poised and observant, a still point in the midst of the tumultuous room.

Eddy grabbed the microphone from Ned. "This is a difficult situation for everyone, but I urge everyone to stick to the facts." Amplified, his voice had a forceful calm.

"Mid-South wouldn't know a fact if it hit 'em in the face!" someone shouted from the back wall.

"Let's hear from Joan!" another voice called.

"That's right! Tell us what happened, Joan!"

Once more, the townsfolk spun around in their chairs, but this time their weathered faces were staunch with encouragement, earnestly beckoning Joan to speak her piece. To Tara's astonishment, her mother started to stand.

"Mama!" Tara clamped down on her mother's forearm. "What are you gonna say?"

"Simple. The truth."

Tara looked to Mrs. Honoré for help, but her friend's eyes were on her mother, alight with the same eager anticipation as everyone else's.

"Please don't," Tara pleaded, but her mother seemed not to hear her. She shook Tara's arm loose and rose to her feet. The room fell silent, except for a feeble remark from Ned regarding the Q&A at the end of the meeting, which Eddy waved into silence.

Joan

11.

Her daughter's eyes sparked with panic, but there was no cause for alarm. Joan had always been good with a crowd. Anyone at the casino lounge would tell you that. Especially a crowd like this one, riled up on its own juices, needing some place to land its anger. She was happy to oblige.

"The facts. Like the man says." Her words felt gritty in her burned-out throat. "Fact number one, I ain't no saint, but I think most of you know that already."

Joan paused to let the laughter burble through the small sea of faces, faces which over the years had greeted her with everything from disgust, to desire, to contempt, to affection. Even love. In the thirteen years since the old man had died—praise whatever, whoever—these people had mostly left her alone to live out her life as she pleased. An outbreak of nasty gossip and cold shoulders was as bad as it ever got. They'd also been as predictable as the sun and moon in their orbits. Their anger today surprised her.

"I've had my fair share of brushes with the law," she continued, when the laughter subsided.

"Me too, Joan," an older man called, his face craggy above a full white beard.

"Thanks, Lew," she said, with a smile. "Fact number two, I didn't ask to have a front row seat to this sinkhole, but I've done my best to cooperate. Hell, I even babysat that one's boys the night after it happened." Her easy tone tightened as she pointed to Eddy with the same hand she'd used to clasp his shoulder and trace the length of his spine as he pried her bedroom window from its swollen frame the morning after the sinkhole.

It had been a moment of raw, uncontainable longing. A yearning to crash against this steady-seeming man, with all his clear purpose and precision. But he'd refused her, plucking her hand from his waist and retreating from her attempted kiss.

She'd made a crude joke about owing him for the window, but his rejection rattled her. Men never, ever said no to her. House on fire, or hurricane. God's men, or the Devil's. It was the one enduring truth of her life.

A story had then infected her mind that Eddy's refusal was high-minded and respectful. She'd overlaid other events to reinforce this mistaken notion—the cash he gave Tara for her bike, his insistence that they stay at his house the night of the sinkhole, and of course pulling Tara from the water. Her mouth turned sour thinking of the foolishness of it now.

He'd kept up the show, right until after the helicopter ride when Loretta Honoré had unmasked him for what he was, one of Mid-South's best fix-it men.

The CYO's AC unit groaned to life and a chill flowed down her neck. "Fact number three," she continued. "Yesterday morning I was dragged from my home, in handcuffs, by the state police. This happened in front of my daughter and half the employees of Mid-South. Not a one of those workers said squat while it was happening, by the way. I spent the day in lockdown."

As she spoke, she gauged their expressions, careful not to pile anything on too thick. Her memory of the arrest was hazy, the gaps filled in by Tara's reluctant retelling and Loretta's prodding about what should be said today.

"Did they have a warrant, Joan?" Mrs. Thevenot's husband called out.

She bowed her head, as if to gather her thoughts, then slid her eyes to meet the white-hot gaze of her daughter, who shook her head imperceptibly.

"No." Joan's head snapped up. "They did not. Fact number four—"

"Let me butt in here real quick." Eddy advanced to the edge of the stage. "For the sake of accuracy, I'll just add that there was a notice of emergency evacuation—"

"That's still not a warrant!" Mr. Thevenot cried.

"Why is Mid-South speaking on behalf of the state police?" a voice rang out.

"Let her finish!" Lew glared around the room as he twirled his snowy beard.

"Fact number four. They evacuated us, all right. My daughter and me have nothing but the clothes on our backs. The state of Louisiana's got my home and my land." Joan turned a steely gaze to Eddy. His quiet countenance pissed her off, knowing as she did that beneath it he was weighing outcomes and hedging Mid-South's bets. Loretta had laid the whole thing out for her this morning.

"Mid-South has free range to do what they want, drill that exploratory well or drill to China. Nothing I can say or do about it," she finished. "I never thought I'd see the day."

The hall exploded with a decade's worth of unvoiced grievances. Fingers jabbed the air, people whipped their arms at the stage and each other, a band of agitators shouldered forward demanding the microphone.

"Now wait a minute!" Ned Elder reclaimed the mike. Dark patches had appeared beneath his arms. "We're on your side! The DNR was the first state agency on the scene!" His voice rose to a whine as the chaos grew.

Sheriff Grady strode to the front of the stage, his barrel-chested build eclipsing Ned and Eddy. Joan knew him as a patient and fair man who'd banked a lifetime of goodwill with everyone in Terrefine, her included. "There's a lot that needs to be said here." The room settled as his voice boomed through the mike. "I'm all for that. But let's take it one at a time so everybody gets heard. We'll start here." He passed the mike to a petite woman with a tearstained toddler on her hip.

"I'm Jessica Juneau and I'm shocked at y'all." She swept her gaze around the room. "All us Juneaus work for Mid-South. Going back forty years. They're like family." She shook her head. "Half this town would be out of work if it wasn't for them. Rose, they buy gas from your station. Ed, they eat at your restaurant. They built the baseball field where our children play Little League. I'm sorry for what you went through, Joan. Truly. But Mid-South is a part of this community and they wouldn't lie to us about this hole...or anything."

Applause peppered the room as Jessica surrendered the mike to Lew. "Let's talk about the right to bear arms—" he began.

"Thanks, Lew, but we all know your views on gun ownership,"

Sheriff Grady interrupted. "And if anybody doesn't, they can grab you after the meeting. For now, let's stick to the matter at hand."

"All right then. I'm with Joan," Lew said.

Clara Baker and Martha Stowe, devout widows who organized fundraising events for the church, spoke next. Clara's forehead was a cross-stitch of indignation as she surveyed the men on stage. "I felt those tremors two months ago, Mr. Elder. I called DNR twice and they insinuated it was my hearing, or my mind. How come nobody did anything?"

"Unfortunately, two months ago would have been on the watch of my predecessor, so I can't really speak to how things were being handled then," Ned answered, rocking back on his heels. "But if you have a name, I'll be happy to look into it. The important thing is that DNR is on top of this now. Our survey drones are gathering important data. We're sharing all that info with the USGS and Mid-South to mount an effective response."

"That's another thing!" Jessica Juneau shot up from the front row where she'd reclaimed her seat. Her baby's eyes widened with the sudden movement. "Wasn't it a Mid-South drone that spotted Tara Saint-Romain drowning? Right before Eddy Ledroit rescued her?"

A cascade of expectant faces turned to catch Joan's reaction.

"Well, my god," Joan breathed as her fists slid to her hips. "Of course, I'm thankful that he saved my daughter. But it doesn't give anybody a lifetime pass to roll me over."

"If I may!" Loretta Honoré's voice rang through the speakers. "I think Joan, and all of us, could be forgiven for being less than impressed by Eddy's gracious act if it turns out that Mid-South is responsible for the hole and the child's near-drowning in the first place."

For the first time, Byron, the other Mid-South representative on stage, spoke up. "That's an outrageous claim!" he sputtered, pointing at Eddy. "This man saved the girl's life!"

The room erupted in a din of competing stories. Cellphones were passed to and fro as, in heated tones, people analyzed the images on the tiny screens.

"What's everybody looking at?" Joan asked Tara, who seemed to be sinking into her seat as she stared over a woman's shoulder at a cellphone video.

"Me," Tara said in a small voice. "Someone posted the drone footage."

Opinions about Tara's near-drowning and Mid-South's credit or culpability flew scattershot around the room. Her daughter's face darkened with anger, or shame, or both.

"You want to step outside?" Joan asked.

Tara released a burst of held breath and rose from her chair. They quietly slipped from the back row and headed for the exit. Outside, Joan found a spot on the steps and patted the cement next to her, but Tara remained standing, her arm encircling one of the flaking columns. "I've got to pee," she said. "But not in there. I'll go around back."

After Tara left, Joan studied the empty space where she'd been, sticky tendrils of remorse grabbing at her. She sighed, then slipped off her jail slippers, spreading her toes, and picking debris from her nails.

The CYO doors creaked open and a tall navy-suited woman clacked past. She paused at the bottom of the steps and dug a lighter and cigarette from her handbag. "Can I bum one of those?" Joan called. The woman looked up, her lips ripe berries against her too-white teeth, and extended the pack. "Thanks," Joan said, extracting a cigarette and leaning toward the woman's flickering lighter. Her eyes fell on a bulging leather briefcase. "You visiting family?"

"Work," the woman replied as smoke coiled around her. Her gaze swept around the parking lot and up the CYO steps. "You did an outstanding job of communicating your message in there."

"Is that what I was doing?" Joan asked. "Thought I was just telling everybody what happened."

"Come on. That couldn't have been a cold delivery." The woman's lips widened and a streak of scarlet appeared on her eye tooth.

"What're you saying?" Joan narrowed her eyes.

"Just that you're persuasive and charismatic. A natural leader. And smart."

"Ha!" Joan raked her fingers through a tangled length of hair. She thought of the old man's mockery of her tenth-grade education, of her reliance on Tara for anything math-related outside of poker. *Smart* was not a word she used to describe herself.

"I am sorry for what you've gone through," the woman continued. Her eyes flickered briefly across Joan's bruised cheek.

"It'll turn out," Joan said. "Where're you from? You talk like some-body on TV."

"Occupational hazard. School up north, followed by a few corpo-rate gigs, washed my southern accent right out of me."

"You with the state?" Joan nodded toward the building.

The woman shook her head. "I was called in by some members of the community who are concerned about the situation with Mid-South."

Joan felt her daughter before she saw her, a shadow reaching from behind. "Hey, baby." She twisted around. High above, a crop duster droned through the baked blue sky.

"You're Tara." The woman's smile stretched. "Taking a play break back there?"

"Pissing." Her daughter's eyes locked on to Lydia's clean-lined face and tracked her close proximity to Joan. "Mama, we should go back in. They might say something you need to hear."

Joan shrugged. "So far it's been nothing but a hot air contest."

"I peeked in. The questions are done. They're not talking about… what happened to me anymore. The DNR guy is on stage. The sweaty one."

The woman reached a hand toward Tara who looked uneasily at the short red nails. "If it's any help, my colleague Justin is in there, taking notes and recording everything."

"Who are you?" Tara asked.

The high wooden doors swung wide, disgorging the meeting-goers who flowed down the steps. Mrs. Thevenot and her husband caught sight of Joan and bee-lined toward her. "You met Lydia! I hope you'll be joining us in the lawsuit."

"No introductions have been made." Lydia offered a crisp smile. "Or discussion of any pending suits."

"Oh," Mrs. Thevenot said. "Then allow me. Joan Saint-Romain, this is Lydia Desaurus. She's a marvelous class-action attorney. And she's here to help us."

Mr. Thevenot wedged himself between his wife and Lydia as the crowd continued to stream past.

"We got to get on top of this, Joan," he said. "Bring these boys to task. There's some nasty stuff that's gone on here." He leaned in closer and clasped Joan's hands in his. "Sharon and I are with you and Tara. Lydia is too. You need to talk to her."

"I'll be sure to do that," Joan replied, taken aback by his earnestness. "Thank you. Both of you." Her eyes found Lydia's. "You want to grab a beer? I bet Cee-Cee's is open. I didn't see him in the meeting."

"Sure," Lydia replied. "You need a ride?"

Before Joan could answer, a frail hand encircled her wrist. Tiny Mrs. Adelaide, her homecare aide shielding her from the crowd, pulled Joan's ear to her lips. "Don't let the bastards get away with it," she whispered with talc-scented breath. "I'll say a rosary for you," she added, before departing.

Joan remained on the steps, with Tara and Lydia nearby, shaking hands with well-wishers and ignoring the few scowls that were directed her way. When the parking lot was almost empty, Sheriff Grady ambled over. He removed his hat and raised his doleful eyes to hers. "Joan, I really dropped the ball on this one. I should have been in communication with the state police. Making sure this got handled properly. I got so tied up with all the sinkhole activity and the crews coming in. It just got away from me."

"Not your fault, Robert. You've always done right by me."

As the sheriff turned to Tara, offering her an apology as well, Joan remembered the brief period years ago, after his wife's death, when they'd meet at Rudy's, a motel on the outskirts of town. His gales of sorrow always followed their lovemaking. They'd stopped meeting when the darkest days of his grief were done.

"Joan!" Loretta was descending the steps with a pudgy, disheveled man, his bald pate shiny above tiny penetrating eyes. "This is Ricky Delray. He's been following the shenanigans of Mid-South for a long time. I asked him to meet us here."

"It's a pleasure, Mrs. Saint-Romain." He wiped his hand on his pants before clasping Joan's. "I was really impressed by you in there."

"Thanks. You can call me, Joan."

"Ricky. What a surprise." Lydia broke from her conversation with Sheriff Grady.

"You know each other?" Joan asked.

"There's a lot of…overlap in the work we do," Ricky said.

"Ricky often subcontracts for our firm," Lydia added. "We

sometimes need people like him for background work. Pulling records. That sort of thing."

"He also happens to have single-handedly collected the most extensive archive of research pertaining to Mid-South in the world," Loretta added.

"It's been a pet project of mine," he admitted, with a smile, pulling his gaze from Lydia back to Joan. "Ever since my grad school thesis on industry's environmental impact on the Gulf region."

"Ricky has some time now and would be willing to share what he knows with you," Loretta said.

"We were actually headed to Cee-Cee's for a beer." Joan hooked a thumb at Lydia. "She's got a bone to pick with Mid-South too."

"Good idea." Loretta nodded. "They've got those round tables. Room enough for us all."

12

Joan chuckled as Ricky Delray plumbed a boiled crawfish head with his index finger and brought forth a glob of yellowish head fat. After inspecting his fingertip, he plunged it into his mouth and tossed the head onto a pile of ravished crawfish shells at his side.

"Best part," Joan said.

"That's right." Ricky smiled. He dragged his hand down his napkin-covered chest, leaving a greasy slash, then brought the dark neck of his Budweiser to his lips.

Joan waved her own empty bottle at the waitress. "Sandra? Please?"

Next to Joan, Tara murmured, "Mama, you're up to twenty dollars of food and beer already." She pushed away her own shallow bowl, scraped clean of a muddy étouffée.

From her seat on the other side of Joan, Lydia leaned forward and caught Tara's eye. "Not to worry, Tara. My firm is picking up the tab for this one."

"Why?" Tara asked.

"It's what they expect me to do when I'm assessing a lawsuit. I'm just obeying orders."

Joan nodded at the empty plastic cup in Tara's hand. "You should get you another Coke."

"One is plenty." Tara rattled the ice, sucked noisily on the straw, and pushed the cup away.

"Suit yourself," Joan said as the waitress placed another Bud in front of her. She would have preferred whisky, but she thought it better to stick with beer for now. At least until she had a handle on what these people really wanted. Or until the sun went down.

Joan drained her bottle in long, delicious swigs. She felt relaxed for the first time all day in the cool familiar darkness of Cee-Cee's, with stale booze perfuming every corner. She liked having Lydia at her side, with her silk shirt peeking through the dark wool jacket and a diamond glinting at her neck. Normally Joan would disregard a woman like Lydia, who was wealthy, well-maintained, life coming at her on a silver platter. She occasionally crossed paths with women like that at the casino; if they were with their man, they stared at her, openly taking stock of her legs, her breasts, her backside, their gawking as intrusive as any man's. Or else they were working women who pegged her for a whore and a dummy after the briefest of glances. They proceeded to stare through her, denying her existence until they needed a cocktail.

Joan wasn't above provoking these women for a laugh, or stealing their men for a few hours, but she'd never had a real conversation, woman-to-woman the way she had with Lydia today. The woman clearly had an angle, but Joan was okay with that. Everybody did. At least, Lydia hung it out in the open.

Joan inched her toes along the crusty floor in search of her shoe. "Let's get this show on the road," she said, her toes latching onto something warm. "Whoops! Sorry!"

"That's okay," Lydia laughed.

Joan turned to Tara. "Where's Loretta?"

Tara craned her neck to look through an archway into the next room, where a pool table and a row of winking slot machines were visible. "She's still on the phone."

"Seems like everybody's on the phone all of a sudden," Joan said, gesturing to the far end of the table where a boy with shiny blue-black curls pecked away at his phone. What had Lydia called him earlier? Her assistant?

"Justin's not being rude," Lydia said. "He's actually uploading his notes from the meeting to our database." Justin flashed Joan a bright smile before returning to his work.

"Mrs. Honoré's not being rude," Tara said.

"That's not what I was inferring," Lydia said. "She strikes me as an honest and loyal person. And a good friend to both you and your mom. That kind of person is rare."

Joan almost let slip a smart-assed remark to coax a laugh out of Lydia but, at the sight of the tiny softening in her daughter's face, she plugged her mouth with her beer.

"Here she comes." Ricky tore the napkin from his chest and burped softly into his sleeve.

"My apologies," Loretta said, taking her seat behind an oyster po-boy.

"Anything new?" Joan asked, hailing the waitress with her empty bottle.

"Taxidermy call," Loretta replied.

"Joan, you seem eager to get going," Lydia said. Joan toasted her assent. "Then why don't I explain the class-action process and similar cases handled by Paxton, Myers, Hicks, and Simms. Our firm—"

"Miss Dasaurus," Loretta interrupted, "I think it would make more sense for Ricky to give us some background on Mid-South before you introduce your firm. Some of the stuff he mentioned to me will hit really close to home for Joan and Tara."

"Of course. Ricky's certainly done some valuable back-end research over the years." Lydia twirled her phone on the placemat and glanced at Justin. "That could prove helpful here."

"All right," Ricky began, fishing the last bit of food from his teeth. "It's pretty straightforward, Mrs. Saint-Romain."

Lydia's phone buzzed loudly. "I have to take this. Sorry. Our firm is wrapping up a two hundred million dollar settlement this afternoon. Similar circumstances." She nodded at Joan. "But trust me, there's nothing Ricky will say that's new to me." She squeezed Justin's shoulder as she walked past. "Full transcript, please."

Ricky briefly followed Lydia's narrow back as she disappeared into the pool room. "As I was saying, Mrs. Saint-Romain, I've been around the oil and petrochemical industry for a long time. What happened to you and your daughter, and your home, and what is happening to the town of Terrefine is part of a long-time pattern of willful neglect and regulatory disregard by Mid-South. Since the family-owned company was absorbed by their now parent company, Global Petrol, in the seventies, they've been accountable only to shareholder interest in a cut-throat pursuit of profit."

Ricky paused as the waitress dropped a fresh beer in front of Joan. At his side, Justin's thumbs seesawed furiously, his face blue-haloed from his phone. Joan tipped back her beer and met Ricky's beady gaze.

"In the past forty years," he continued, "Mid-South, and Global Petrol, have been responsible for on- and off-shore explosions that have killed and maimed their own employees, the poisoning of acres of farmland, the decimation and abandonment of small communities due to waste runoff from their refineries and plants, and—pardon my strong language here—the rape of the wetlands by ignoring their contractual obligation to restore the land to its original condition. And that's just the shortlist." Ricky paused to take a breath. His voice had grown steadily louder and his cheek mounds and the tip of his nose had grown bright pink.

"Most outrageous of all," he continued, a slight wheeze underpinning his words, "they've been encouraged. They've basically had carte blanche to pillage this area because the state of Louisiana throws open its arms to the oil and gas industry. I'm sure you've heard the saying, 'the flag of Texaco flies over the state capitol'?"

"No," said Joan. "But I believe it. Probably a few other flags up there too. But that's how they do it in government. There's no changing that."

Ricky straightened in his chair. "That's where I respectfully disagree with you. It may be too little too late, but things are starting to turn. Ordinary people aren't so quick to defend industry the way they used to. You saw it in that meeting today. Climate change is at our doorsteps and the land is shifting before our very eyes. A football field an hour to coastal erosion, Mrs. Saint-Romain. A football field."

"That's a lot of dirt," Joan agreed. "But what does that have to do with me?"

"Good question," Lydia called from the archway to the dining room.

She placed her phone on the table but remained standing, one hand on her navy-clad waist. Joan could easily picture her striding up and down the courtroom, grilling some poor witness to the brink.

"I know this is what you do best, Ricky, but I fear you're losing sight of Joan's interest in the pursuit of some environmental witch hunt that could take years. What we're proposing is a straightforward class action on behalf of everyone who's been affected by Mid-South's negligence. There is plenty of precedent to support this approach and the probability for success and substantial compensation is high."

Ricky shook his head and gave a curt laugh. "What good is a fat settlement when Louisiana is melting into the Gulf? This thing is much bigger than any of us. And yet it has everything to do with people like Joan and Tara."

A cowbell jangled, and a beanpole of a young man entered Cee-Cee's. Joan recognized him as the teenager who often fished the bridge near her house. He'd once squirmed his tongue obscenely between his two fingers as she drove past. She'd returned the favor, which had cracked him up.

He was accompanied by a younger boy, with the same yellowish skin and bulbous eyes. Two teenaged girls were there as well, both in cut-off shorts, dollops of rear-end visible below the frayed hem. Each of the four lugged boxes of empty beer bottles which they heaved up to the bar top.

As they waited for the bartender to count out their bills, the young man removed his cap, airbrushed with a leaping bass, and flashed the peace sign. "St. Joan!"

"See what I mean," Ricky said, as the cowbell jangled and the teenagers left. "These are the disenfranchised, the forgotten. Joan is already inspiring them, just by being herself." He dropped a fist on the table. "We have a chance to make a real difference here, with Joan Saint-Romain as the face of this long-overdue reparation to the land and people of Louisiana. And, yes, the chances for just compensation are good. But more important is the chance to send a message to big industry. And to alter the way this broken system is run, so that your daughter's children can still fish these bayous and live on this land."

Ricky snatched a soiled napkin from the table, mopped his brow, and then gazed at Joan expectantly.

"Disenfranchised?" Joan caught the waitress's sleeve as she swooped past. "One last beer, Sandra," she whispered, then raised her voice. "Is that what they're calling us these days? Used to be white trash. Or rednecks."

The impassioned look on Ricky's face flickered.

Joan stripped the label from her bottle. "I know everyone is here to help, including you, Ricky. I can tell this stuff turns you inside out. But when you talk about me being the face of what's-it—"

"This long-overdue reparation," Justin quoted.

"That's it," Joan nodded. "That's where you lost me. Look, I'm pissed off. I'd like Mid-South to feel some pain, Eddy Ledroit in particular. Maybe those cops, too. But all them other things you mentioned...why should I care? You're asking me to stick my neck out there for a bunch of stuff that's not my problem, when I already got a whole mess of my own."

"If you'll just step back. Look at the bigger picture," Ricky said.

"Those kids that were in here. They called me St. Joan. You know who St. Joan of Arc is?"

"Of course," Ricky replied.

"Then you know they burnt her up. Alive. Her own people let it happen. Even after she saved them from the English. What?" she asked, catching Tara's raised eyebrows. "You're not the only one who watches PBS."

"That's true, Joan, but I didn't make that comparison. That boy did. He probably didn't know the full history of Joan of Arc."

"Right," Joan said. "'Cause he's disenfranchised."

Ricky started to speak, but Joan barreled on. "What good is it to me or my daughter to put my face on some big protest against the powers that be?" She swung her beer high, then banged it down on the table. "And where will you be, Mr. Delray, when the flames are frying my backside?"

She tossed a bottle cap into the arrangement of artificial flowers at the table center, then glanced at Tara. Her daughter's eyes were unreadable in the murky light of Cee-Cee's. Her hair was a nest of tangles. The girl needed a combing out.

Lydia broke the silence. "Well, Joan, you seem pretty clear about your goals here."

"I guess I am." Joan searched the table for a pack of matches before remembering that she didn't have cigarettes.

"I hope I didn't offend you or seem insensitive to your life here, Joan. And I'd still like to offer whatever help I can," Ricky said.

Lydia smiled. "Thank you, Ricky. We'll let you know if there's anything you can help with along the lines of your usual research role."

"Did I miss something?" Loretta Honoré asked. "I didn't hear Joan say that she was interested in your representation."

"I am," Joan said, pushing back from the table.

As Joan made her way to the bar in search of cigarettes, resisting the urge to sway, she could hear Loretta chiming in. "Joan probably needs a day or two before she makes any final decisions about anything."

That woman always knew better.

"Sandra, you got a cigarette I can bum while they're over there talking about how I should live my life?"

"Sure, Joan, but you know you gotta smoke outside now. We went smoke-free."

"Well, good for y'all." Joan pursed her lips and nodded before accepting a cigarette and heading outside.

After the darkness of Cee-Cee's, the glare of the overcast sky stabbed her eyes. For a moment, she worried about another migraine. She scrunched her lids closed and pinched the bridge of her nose, waiting for the bright pain to pass. As the burn in her sockets drained away, she heard a car pull in and park nearby. The door slammed, followed by quickening steps.

"Joan? You okay?"

She cracked open her lids. Eddy's face was pinched with concern. She took in his mud-caked boots and his T-shirt, a damp membrane against his chest. Her truck was parked behind him.

"You got possession of my vehicle now too?"

"I was bringing it to you."

She took the keys from his outstretched hand and moved to pocket them, but they slipped from her grasp.

"Whoops." Eddy's hand shot out. He snatched the keys from the air, then tucked them in her palm.

"Thanks," she said, eyeing the pulsing vein above his grimy collar.

The rage that had fueled her during the meeting was still alive, but there was also something else creeping cat-like up the back of her calves and hamstrings and tickling the length of her spine.

"I should get in that truck and run you down right now." She cupped her elbow in her hand and blew smoke above Eddy's head.

"Jesus. I would handle so much of this whole fiasco differently. In retrospect." He studied the gravel at his feet. When he looked up, his eyes were sorrowed, lost. She recognized a kind of heavy regret and the powerlessness to change course. She greeted many mornings the same way.

Thunder trembled at the fringes of the sky. Joan took a long drag from her cigarette, her lips pressing against her fingers. Maybe she'd have a whiskey when she went back in.

"Where's Tara?" he asked. "The boys won't stop asking about her."

"You still got 'em here?"

"No. They're in Lafayette with my wife's folks. My wife who passed."

The cowbell clanged and Joan turned to find Lydia emerging from the restaurant with Tara trailing behind.

Tara didn't return Eddy's greeting but remained silent, her gangly arms pressed to her sides.

"Mr. Ledroit," Lydia said, brandishing a business card. "Lydia Desaurus."

Eddy scanned the card then glanced at Joan. "What's this?"

"It's my contact info," Lydia replied. "I'm heading up a class action for victims of the sinkhole against the responsible party." She nudged a piece of gravel with her sharp-nosed pump. "When that party is identified, that is."

Eddy returned the card to Lydia, a seam closing over his face. "Not two days gone by and the legal eagles are circling."

"Joan and Tara, and folks like them, don't have the resources your company has," Lydia stated evenly. "Or the state. The sooner they get organized the better."

A truck bearing the Mid-South logo slowed in front of the restaurant and honked.

"Back to the grind." He tipped his hat to Joan, nodded at Tara, then strode across the parking lot.

"This whole thing could take a year or more, you know," Lydia said, folding her arms as the truck pulled off. "You're going have to figure out a way to stay mad, murder-mad, that whole time. At him. At all of them."

"Ain't gonna be a problem," Joan replied. "My blood turns to fire ever time I see that man."

13.

Joan slipped her palm beneath the baggy Saints T-shirt that had belonged to Mrs. Honoré's son, smoothing the gathering moisture on her belly. The rusted Coca Cola thermostat on Mrs. Honoré's back porch read ninety degrees. And only 8:30 a.m. She tipped the wooden swing into motion, hoping to create a breeze.

Footsteps sounded and the screen door bounced open as Tara's slim butt nudged through, her hands taken up with a cup of coffee and two of Mrs. Honoré's legal pads. She spun around, two pencils gripped between her teeth, and passed the coffee to Joan. Tara shook the heat from her fingers, then plopped down on the swing.

Joan brought the coffee to her lips, sending little gusts across its surface before swallowing the scalding liquid. The bitter darkness of it cut through the cotton of her hangover. She felt cozy in the aftermath of what had been a good drunk—fully remembered, no harm inflicted, no sulking from Tara this morning.

"What you writing, baby?" Joan asked.

Tara shoved a pad and pencil at Joan. "The homework Lydia gave us. To write a timeline for the day of the sinkhole. And whatever we remember about your arrest. Plus anything Eddy had to say about any of it."

"I don't think she meant we had to do it right away." Joan yawned.

"Yes, she did. Don't you remember her saying so last night at Cee-Cee's?"

Joan felt the prick of doubt in her daughter's gaze. "Of course I do. I can't have ten seconds to relax first? Besides, I thought you didn't like Lydia. You had your hackles up the minute you met her."

"I guess my mind changed when I saw how she was with Eddy. I could tell she was on your side."

Tara gnawed briefly on her pencil eraser. Soon, a trail of shiny script appeared on the pad. Half the page was filled before Joan had her third sip of coffee. Joan tried to think of something to write, but her mind was a wide, empty sky, uninterested in cluttering itself with timelines and details. She'd always hated this kind of shit, pinning down black-and -white specifics, cramming life up against a ruler. Filling out job applications or welfare forms was a special kind of torture. She leaned over to read Tara's words. *When the sinkhole happened, I was home alone.* A hot drop of coffee blotched the yellow paper.

"You're smearing it." Tara slapped her palm on the pad.

"Excuse me, Miss Priss."

"Uck…you need to gargle, Mama. Your breath stinks."

"Well, aren't you a bag of sunshine."

Tara stood up from the swing, clutching the pad to her chest. "Lydia says it has to be our own separate recollections. To try and see what we each remember and then compare." She descended the porch steps and swept her gaze across the backyard. She headed for the vegetable garden, taking a seat on an overturned bucket beneath the fuzzy stalks of a monstrous summer squash. Her bare feet were hidden in a spasm of weeds, her curls shoved behind her ears. Today, she looked like Junior's child. The full lips that barely contained her teeth; her skin, mellowed and browned by the summer; the kudzu-green of her eyes—they all reminded Joan of the rangy boy in East Texas who had been her first.

But tomorrow, or next week, Joan knew she would be equally sure that Tara belonged to the old man. Because her daughter shared his widow's peak, and sometimes his meanness, and because the worst of two things generally won out. She'd gone around and around with it since the day the lady doctor at the clinic informed her that she was six months pregnant. Forty-eight hours and two men. That was one timeline she'd never forget. It was burned into her.

Joan scowled at the empty porch and the unwelcome memory of that day with its brief joy devoured. It was a day that saw the end of one small hell in Texas and the beginning of a greater one in Terrefine. She set the coffee cup on the swing beside her and took up the pad and pencil. She flicked a gnat from the page and wrote, *Junior Chenier.*

A mixed-race boy, friendless like her, banished to a few acres of lifeless dirt, also like her. They'd quietly sighted each other throughout childhood, passing on the dusty road or hunkered at opposite ends of the school bus, morphing slowly into almost-adults, until finally, the day before the old man came for her, Junior spoke. *Bonjou.* He breathed a Creole hello through a gap in the shelf of powdered milk at the grocery store.

Joan found an hour to escape housework and nursing her mother, who'd been removed to a cot in the laundry room because her husband couldn't take the smell of her dying. She met Junior at the tallest pine tree for miles. His arms were long enough to embrace both her and the tree trunk. Pine bark nipped at her spine and her blood christened the roots. He pressed a honeysuckle flower into her hand when they parted, a sweet sag to his smile.

When Joan returned home, her father smacked her in the head for being gone. It was from the floor, sprawled on all fours, that she made the acquaintance of her future husband, Jackson Saint-Romain. It was partly spite that made her leave with the old man so readily. And partly fear. More and more, her father's looks were not the looks a man gives his daughter.

A gunshot split the morning silence, mushrooming across the field behind the house, then swallowing itself. Mrs. Honoré, killing Lord knows what with her rifles back there. At least she and Tara had the house to themselves for a while. Joan crumpled the paper and threw it across the porch.

"What day did the hole happen?" she yelled to her daughter.

"Friday," Tara replied, without looking up. "Four days ago."

Four days, four weeks, four months. Joan threw her coffee dregs over the porch railing. What good were dates and facts when they didn't lead you to the truth? When the doctor told her how far along she was, she hoped it was Junior's, but she wasn't able to give it much thought. She was mainly occupied with devising ways to escape, or kill herself, or murder the old man.

And yet that whole time, Tara had the audacity to continue to come into being, to keep growing inside the soft shell of human skin, despite the misery on the other side.

"Anybody home?" a voice called from the side of Mrs. Honoré's house. Joan and Tara exchanged glances.

"Justin," Tara said.

"Who?"

"The guy that works for Lydia."

Justin turned the corner, fully suited and cradling a white cardboard box. "There you are. Morning!"

"Morning," Joan called. "Where's your boss?"

"She's finishing up a conference call with the partners to discuss the logistics of the suit. She asked me to bring you these before she gets here." He held the box aloft. "Donuts from the Fry Palace. According to my research, they're the best."

He ambled over to Tara, hot dew spraying the cuffs of his pants, and held the box open for her. She stared at him, unsmiling, before choosing a glazed.

"Good?" he asked, as she polished off half of it in one bite, her eyes never leaving his. "You know what. Don't answer that. I know how important the first donut of the morning is. I'll leave you in peace." Justin approached the porch, his dark eyes friendly beneath tousled curls.

"You want some coffee?" Joan asked, suddenly remembering Tara's complaint about her breath. She jumped up from the swing to head inside, too late forgetting the Saints T-shirt was all she wore.

"That would be great, Mrs. Saint-Romain. Thank you," Justin answered, his eyes widening with the effort to keep his gaze confined to her face. She spun around, a sliver of her bare bottom peeking out, and disappeared into the house.

Upstairs, she searched the bedroom floor until she found the cut-offs and flannel shirt she'd worn yesterday. The fact that Eddy hadn't brought their clothes along with the truck was beyond irritating. The garbage bags filled with their stuff had been left in the carport. Maybe Lydia could do some lawyer thing and get them access to the house, Joan thought. She wanted to grab the cigar box with her cash and check between the mattress for any pills she might have stashed and forgotten. Assuming those fuckers from Mid-South hadn't ransacked it already.

In the tiny hall bathroom, she loaded her finger with toothpaste and rubbed her teeth, then gargled with a crusty old bottle of Scope.

Downstairs, she rummaged through the kitchen cabinets and drawers, grumbling to herself, until she discovered the coffee canister in plain sight on the counter. She set the dented aluminum pot on the stove top and turned up the gas flame. Laughter sounded from the backyard, and it took Joan a moment to realize it was Tara. Her daughter wasn't given to bursts of laughter. She peered through the screen door, following Justin as he waltzed through the grass, balancing an upside-down broom in the palm of his hand. Tara, still seated on the bucket, followed his every move. The legal pad had slipped to the grass, forgotten.

Behind Joan, the stove sizzled and hissed. "Damn it!" She crossed the kitchen and lowered the flame. Mrs. Honoré's half-assed coffeepot was spewing water and grounds. Why couldn't she have a plug-in coffee maker like a normal person? She managed to clear most of the grounds from Justin's coffee and carried it out to the porch. Mrs. Honoré had returned from the fields and sat astride Lightning in the middle of the yard. Justin and Tara were next to each other staring up at the woman like both she and the horse were made of gold.

"Her name is Lightning," Tara said to Justin, as Mrs. Honoré dismounted.

He took a slow step toward the animal. "May I?"

Mrs. Honoré nodded and Justin stroked the caramel coat. "She's beautiful. Quarter horse?"

"That's right," Mrs. Honoré answered as she unbuckled the rifle holster and slid her gun from its sheath. "Used to have three of 'em. But it got to be too much. Now it's just me and Lightning." She gripped the gun, pointing the barrel to the ground, and walked it to a small shed attached to the barn.

"Do you know how old she is?" Justin asked Tara.

"Fourteen. My age. Actually, my age in a couple of weeks. And fifteen hands high."

"Libra?"

Tara wrinkled her nose. "You don't believe in that stuff, do you?"

"Sometimes. For fun."

Mrs. Honoré returned to remove the saddle, patiently instructing Tara and Justin so they could help. Watching the three of them, Joan felt something sour snake through her gut.

"Justin," Joan barked, interrupting his question about a scar on Lightning's leg. She held up the coffee cup. "For you."

"Excuse me." He left Tara and Mrs. Honoré and mounted the

porch steps. "Thank you, Mrs. Saint-Romain," he said, taking the cup with a smile.

"Please. It's Joan. I'm only just pushing thirty."

"Joan it is." His eyes flicked to Tara as she took the saddle blanket from Mrs. Honoré.

"Can I ask you a question?" Joan blurted, wanting to keep him on the porch.

"Of course." He picked a coffee ground from his tongue.

"You ever tried to find somebody?" she asked, her eyes lighting on the crumpled ball of paper at the far end of the porch.

"You mean file a missing person's report with the police? Or the FBI?"

"No. On your own."

"Like a private detective?"

"Yeah."

"I haven't personally, but I know our firm uses private detectives, or research detectives as we call them." He paused, his brow wrinkling. "You lose someone?"

She looked beyond his earnestness to the yard, where Tara led Lightning to the barn. Mrs. Honoré followed, a hunting sack, bulging with the small bodies of her kill, bouncing against her camo-pants. Their words were indistinct, but the ease between the two was unmistakable.

"Yes." She returned to the cool melt of Justin's eyes. "Me. I'm the missing person."

"How do you mean?"

"I don't." She drew her lips to one side and lowered her lashes. "I don't mean nothing. Just messing with you." She forced a laugh, then dropped onto the swing, jangling the chains. She stretched first one ivory leg, then the other, aiming her toes at Justin. "What I really want to do is file a complaint." She flung her arms across the back of the swing and nodded at the legal pad beside her. "This writing stuff. I can't do it. Y'all gotta figure out something better."

He swiped the air and grinned. "Don't even worry about that. When Lydia gets here, we're going to record you. The writing was just to jog your memory. But our primary source material will be the recording. On this." He brandished a matchbox-sized device.

"That lil' thing?"

"Yup." He grinned. "Spy-worthy, huh?"

The front doorbell buzzed, and Justin slipped the recorder into his blazer pocket. "I'll bet that's Lydia," he said.

"How many cars y'all brought out here?" Joan asked, rising from the porch swing.

"We drove Lydia's Lexus from her New Orleans house. Then I rented a car from Zachery's on Highway 1."

"That man's a cheat," Joan called over her shoulder as she flung open the screen door and strode to the front hall. "You better keep a tow truck number on you."

"How you holding up?" Lydia asked as Joan ushered her in. Lydia wore a steel-gray tailored suit and her hair was swept into a glossy twist. Her measured steps echoed through the house as she followed Joan to the kitchen, taking in the dark wood staircase, the stuffed fox on the hall mantel, and the snowy egret, visible through the open door to the dining room.

"Okay," Joan replied. "It would be nice to get some clothes though. And some cash. You think you can get us into our house for a little while?"

"I'm so sorry." Lydia pivoted to face Joan, but her eyes were fastened on her phone. "This needs an immediate response." Her mouth twitched with half-words as she typed. When she was done, she touched Joan's shoulder. "Okay. Accessing your home for your clothes. That's a reasonable request. But starting now, we need to control the narrative. Every step of the way. You've already gotten us off to a tremendous start with your performance in the meeting. But we can't rest on our laurels. Appearances matter." She smoothed invisible wrinkles from her slacks. "How would it look to a judge, and all the potential jurors following news, if we felt so confident in the goodwill of Mid-South and the state that we would work with them to gain access to your home? Or, worse yet, if they granted that access. We can't create any opportunities for them to seem like the good guys."

Joan shrugged. "All right. But my cash is in the house too. $600. I have the truck, so I could hit the dump and do some flea marketing. But that takes time. And gas."

"Not to worry. My firm has a relationship with a kind of...bank that can offer advances to plaintiffs in cases like this. Let me make some calls. In the meantime." She reached into her purse and rifled though her wallet, then handed over a few bills. "It's not much. But it should get you through the next few days. We'll settle up when all this is done."

Joan studied Lydia's face. "Thanks." She squared her shoulders as she took the bills, rolling them tightly before tucking them in the coin pocket of her cutoffs. "I'm usually not big on borrowing. But I'm kinda screwed here."

"I know," Lydia said. "And you shouldn't have to worry about money on top of everything else. But I'm certain that when this is all settled, you'll end up with just compensation for the wrongs you've endured." She paused and looked out the kitchen window. "As will the rest of the people of Terrefine who've been affected."

"They'll have their own lawyers though, right?"

"There will be a team of us assembled down here soon. I'll be coordinating everyone."

"But you'll be my lawyer. Specifically. Right?" Joan tugged at the seam of her coin pocket.

"Joan." Lydia lowered her chin. "You will have full access to me. But this will be a team effort. Several teams, in fact. My position at the firm requires that I be the driver of those teams."

"I'm not sure if I would have signed those papers last night if I knew you were going to be spreading yourself so thin. I mean the Thevenot's are okay. But the whole town?"

"Listen to me." Lydia tented her fingers on the kitchen counter and crossed her ankles. "Your story is what's going to help make this whole thing a PR nightmare for Mid-South and prompt them to settle before we ever get to court. You're our star. Ricky Delray was right about the swell of support and interest that you've generated. You've got fire in your eyes. We're gonna use that. Not in the way Ricky was envisioning but as added leverage to resolve this whole thing as quickly, and for as much money, as possible. Which reminds me." She glanced at her rose- gold watch. "Chase Robichaux will be here in a couple of hours."

"Who's he?"

"A reporter. We've booked your first interview."

14.

Lydia doled out her words like crisp dollar bills. "Joan, walk me through it again so I can better understand the flow of events on the day of your arrest."

"You mean like I already did ten times? I'm trying not to get aggravated, Lydia, but you got me feeling like I'm the guilty one here."

They were seated at Mrs. Honoré's kitchen table, the tiny recorder in the center, red eye flashing. Across from Joan, Justin tapped away at his cellphone, taking notes. Tara sat apart on a stool, her back against the wallpaper of writhing roses. Mrs. Honoré hovered at the sink, packing away the day's kill. Or at least pretending to, Joan thought. More likely, she was listening in on every word.

"Anyway," Joan added. "Tara already gave you what she wrote. She's got a better head for details than I do."

"Tara has been a tremendous help," Lydia said. "But we've got to reconcile your version of events. If we can't pin that down between us, then we won't have a leg to stand on when we file our suit. Not to mention keeping our facts straight when you're giving interviews, like the one today with Chase. The media is where the real battle will be fought and won." She glanced at the open folder in her hand. "There are just a few details I need you to fill in. That's all. I'm on your side."

Joan fluttered her lips, releasing a heavy sigh. "Fine. But I'm taking a smoke break in ten minutes."

"Deal," Lydia said, tapping the folder's edge on the table. "Let's pick up right before your arrest. You're in your living room and the police show up. What time?"

"Crack of dawn. Smelled like a gas station, like it did the first time the hole opened up. My head felt like a split-open melon."

"The migraine."

Joan nodded, remembering the blade of bright pain that had awakened her, magnified by the choking, oily stink.

"You said Tara answered the door?"

"Yes!" Tara leapt on the question before Joan could answer. "That was after I'd already been outside once."

"Thank you, Tara. But again, let's hear what your mom remembers."

Tara slumped against the wall, gnawing her lower lip, her face winding tighter. Joan wondered what the girl was so worked up about. As usual, she looked like the smart one, while Joan came across as a stone-cold dummy.

"Go on, Joan," Lydia coaxed.

"After Tara pumped me up on coffee and Excedrin so I could see straight, the cops barged into the house. Two of 'em."

"What was the first thing either of them said?"

Joan struggled to keep her eyes from Tara as she confronted the jumble of mental images from that morning, many of them vivid but still resistant to her mind's attempts to organize them. She decided to jump to the part of the story that was easiest, connected as it was to another ugly-as-hell memory that was clear as day.

"What happened was I recognized one of the police. The littler one. He stopped me a couple of months ago for speeding. He said he'd let me go if I'd show him my tits."

"And did you?"

"To avoid a two-hundred-dollar ticket? Goddamn right. But the little shit gave me one any way, supposedly through the mail. I never saw it until it had all kinds of late fees tacked on."

"And you're sure it was the same cop?"

"Pretty sure." Beneath the table, Joan tugged at her cutoffs, freeing the inseam from her crack. "I'd have to find the ticket. Seems like I was sure that morning."

"And that's why you went after him with the lamp?"

"No. Tara says he knocked her down. That sounds more like it."

Lydia's brows peaked. "Is that what you remember? Or is that what Tara told you?"

Tara, who'd grown increasingly restless, now gripped the seat of her stool and leaned forward, nearly tipping over.

"Do you mind not breaking my furniture?" Mrs. Honoré called, pulling her head from the deep freezer.

"Sorry," Tara said, planting the stool legs on the linoleum.

"Joan." Lydia stroked her chin, her red nails flaring. "Were you impaired that morning?"

"Like on drugs?"

"Yes. Or alcohol."

"I had a couple of Bud Lites the night before. Otherwise, all I took was the Excedrin Tara gave me. Right, hon?"

Tara's face narrowed. She knotted her arms around her ribs.

"I only ask because of your difficulties with recall," Lydia added. "It seems unusual."

"You get dragged from your house by the cops and see if you don't take a few wrong turns strolling down memory lane!"

Lydia set the folder aside and perched her elbows on the table, weaving together the fingers of each hand. "If you were impaired, it would be important for you to tell us now. Before we got too far along."

"I thought I did just tell you," Joan replied, a swarm of tiny hooks sinking into her mood. "Or am I just sitting here talking to myself?"

"Mama!" Tara blurted. "I need to talk to you."

"I'm done talking," Joan said, plucking the cigarette from behind her ear and shoving her chair from the table. "I've been chasing my own tail for an hour and people don't even believe what I got to say."

"Wait!" Tara popped off the stool. "I didn't want to tell our business in front of everybody, because you're gonna be pissed." Her gaze darted to Justin and Lydia, then to Mrs. Honoré, who'd emerged from the deep freezer to join them.

"It's my fault you got arrested," Tara continued. "The pills I gave you. They weren't Excedrin. They were that really strong stuff you took for your last migraine. The Vicodin." Her eyes shifted to Lydia. "I knew you wouldn't wanna take it, but there was nothing else. And you were nearly passed out from pain." Her voice lowered to a near-whisper. "I crushed them so they'd work quicker."

The deep freeze motor rattled to life, its hum invading the kitchen.

"I messed up all of this. I'm sorry," Tara whispered as she slipped from beneath the comforting hand Mrs. Honoré had placed on her shoulder. She wrapped one lanky leg behind the other and fixed her gaze on the worn linoleum, her unkempt curls veiling her eyes.

"That's bull crap," Joan said. "My arrest had nothing to do with you.

Whatever bad happened was because of those cops. And Mid-South. Not 'cause you gave me any pills."

"Joan, did you have a prescription for the Vicodin?" Lydia asked.

"Yep," Joan replied. *At some point*, she added silently.

The tablecloth quivered as Lydia jiggled her crossed leg. She seemed to be staring at Justin, but Joan could tell she'd merely parked her gaze on the boy's face as her wheels spun round and round. She was probably gearing up to ditch them. Fine, Joan thought. Let her head over to the Thevenot's and torture *them* with a million and one questions. She rose from the table, squeezed her daughter's sharp-boned shoulders, and started toward the back porch. "Smoke break."

"One second more please, Joan." Lydia perked up. "So what you are saying is that a thirteen-year-old girl was trying to resurrect her mother from a crippling condition when the cops showed up to clear the property. Instead of proper medical attention, she was treated to handcuffs and harassment while a host of Mid-South's finest looked on." She raised her brows at Justin, who was typing furiously. "Looks pretty bad, wouldn't you say?"

"I would say."

"Tara, you wrote down that you told the police officers they had to wait before coming in. Was that because your mother was suffering?"

"I, well, I told them she was sick, yes, but not exactly with what."

"But they knew she was physically compromised in some way. That's what's important." She looked at her watch. "It's noon. Chase will be here at five with a photographer. Justin, draft some simple talking points that Joan can keep coming back to during the interview, drawing on what we've discovered here. Joan, enjoy your smoke. We've got more than we need for today."

"And, Tara," Lydia said, switching off the recorder. "I commend you. You were incredibly brave and resourceful in a terrible situation."

Joan straightened as Tara snapped the strand of pearls, dredged from some corner of Mrs. Honoré's attic, around her neck. She smoothed her braid and fingered the necklace as she glanced at Lydia, stationed near the bedroom door.

"Pearls and a work shirt." Lydia nodded. "Perfect. And nice braid, Tara."

"They really need to take pictures for this interview?" Joan asked.

"Absolutely. 90 percent of a story is conveyed visually these days, especially on social media."

"Whatever you say. So, keep the plaid shirt. What about the jeans?"

Earlier, in the kitchen, Joan had guffawed when Justin presented her with the clothes he'd picked out at the Walmart in Leittville. She was surprised to discover that he'd actually done a good job.

"Keep the jeans," Lydia said. "You're the only woman I know who has ever looked good in a pair of Lees. I actually thought the brand was dead. Good call, Justin."

"Thank my four older sisters," he replied from the hallway. "And buying three sizes of everything."

"You can come in, by the way. Let us know what you think," Lydia said.

Justin propped his lean frame inside the doorway as he scrutinized Joan's outfit. "Do you mind if I try something?" he asked, his hands reaching for her waist.

Joan winked at Lydia and smirked. "They don't usually bother asking."

Justin timidly untucked her shirt. He reached for the open collar of her blouse, then halted, fingers trembling. "Maybe you should do it." He tapped the neck of his own shirt. "One less button."

"Whatever you say, cowboy," Joan purred, readily exposing her collar bones. Her skin glowed beneath the pearls.

"Too much?" Justin asked as he retreated to Lydia's side.

"Just enough," Lydia nodded.

"Enough what?" Tara asked.

"Great question. Enough to emphasize your mother's strength and beauty so readers won't see her as a victim. People will avoid a story if it makes them feel too uncomfortable. Nobody wants to be made to feel sorry for you. What works is when they actually identify with you and, even subconsciously, think that they're the ones who are being wronged."

"What about shoes?" Joan held up Justin's picks—blue Converse sneakers and low-heeled mules. "Actually, there's no way I'm wearing these maw-maw sandals. Sorry, Justin."

"What about those Carhartt boots on the back porch?" asked Lydia.

"Mrs. Honoré's," Tara said.

"You mind asking if we can use them? They'll help us hit the roll-up-your-sleeves note that we want for the full-length shot."

"I told you. She's a genius," Justin said, handing Joan a small paper bag. "One final touch. Makeup."

"Tara, you gotta do this. I'll poke my eye out."

"Me? I don't know anything about makeup."

"You've seen the commercials. All you need is a steady hand."

Tara's breath tickled Joan's cheeks as she methodically applied lipstick and mascara. Joan laughed, a sweetness surfacing beneath Tara's precise, gentle motions. "Keep still," Tara said as she pressed her fingers to Joan's temples and gave her lashes a final stroke. She backed away, then glanced expectantly at Lydia and Justin.

"Excellent," Lydia said, tugging her cuffs over her wrists. Justin flashed a thumbs-up.

Joan scrutinized her image in the mirror above the bureau. "Tara, move that owl will you." She had to admit, she looked good. The jeans fit perfectly, drawing attention to her long legs and slender waist. The ruddy tones of the work shirt warmed her complexion and set the blue of her eyes alight. She twirled to admire the snug cling of the jeans on her ass—still high and tight, thank god. She felt a small, rare gush of pleasure at her own beauty. "Y'all, I'm about to jump in the truck and drive to Cee-Cee's to shoot pool. Who's coming?"

"Slow down," Lydia said, with a smile. "First, let's nail this interview with Chase. He's a critical first step in getting our story out there. And he's great at what he does. He even won some awards way back when, reporting overseas. We've worked together a few times."

"You're in the newspaper business too?" Joan asked. "You get around, woman."

"Not exactly. Chase has a knack for covering industrial disasters and corporate malfeasance. He's interviewed several of my high-profile cases over the years. I've benefited from the public interest he's generated. It's sort of a reciprocal relationship."

"I get it. Back-scratching."

"Right. Although, we'd never call it that. And you shouldn't either. It's important that he appear independent." She smiled brightly. "Which, of course, he is."

"Tara!" Mrs. Honoré's husky voice called from downstairs. "You wanna help me curry Lightning?"

"You go, baby," Joan said in response to her daughter's questioning look. "I'm just gonna sit on my butt until this fella shows up. Don't wanna mess my new clothes."

Joan had just settled on the porch swing with a fresh smoke when Justin poked his head out the screen door. "Talking points!" he said, waving a piece of paper. "For the interview."

"Jesus. You people never stop."

"I promise this won't take long." He slid next to her on the swing, his suit pants brushing against her new jeans.

"I'm glad you didn't get me the stretchy kind." She ran her hand down the length of her thigh. "I hate those."

"Me too. Give me the old-school original blue jeans any day."

"Honestly, it's the first time a man's bought me anything in a long while."

Justin's swallow was audible. "That seems hard to believe." He thrust the paper between them. "So. In terms of our target audience, Lydia thinks you should really emphasize the themes of self-determination and personal liberty."

"Help!" The scream shattered the muggy afternoon. Joan leapt from the swing and ran to the porch railing. Tara was rounding the far side of the barn, sprinting toward the house. "It's Mrs. Honoré!" Joan flew down the porch steps with Justin behind her. They charged after Tara until the barn's wide entrance came into view.

Mrs. Honoré was on her back, her head and torso outside the barn and her legs within. Just beyond her, in the shadowy interior, was a large, dark mass. When Joan's eyes adjusted, she recognized Lightning, collapsed on her side.

"She was like this when I got here." Tara spoke rapidly. "I tried to wake her, then I started to feel dizzy and fell down. I crawled out and ran to get you. We gotta help her!"

"I know CPR," Justin said, sprinting toward the barn. When he reached Mrs. Honoré, he wobbled then staggered backwards. He dropped to his knees. "Whoa!" He squinted toward Joan. "Woozy."

"Get back here." Joan snatched his arm, dragging him away from the barn.

"Let him go back, Mama! Or I'll go."

With her free hand, Joan shoved her daughter to the ground. "I said, wait, damn it! Listen. The horse and Loretta passed out. You and Justin got dizzy. There's got to be something poison in the barn."

"We need an ambulance," Justin whispered, falling back onto the grass.

"Call Sheriff Grady!" Joan ordered and Tara bolted toward the house.

In the square of sunlight across Mrs. Honoré's body, Joan could see the rise and fall of her chest. She took a deep breath and held it, then darted forward. She grabbed Mrs. Honoré by the wrists, then heaved her backward until she was clear of the doorway and in the fresh air.

As Joan lay on the ground, gasping, Tara and Lydia rounded the building. Lydia's phone preceded her, dagger-like, as she captured Mrs. Honoré's prone figure, Joan and Justin struggling to their feet, and the half-visible horse in the barn.

A far away siren wailed as Tara dropped to her knees at Mrs. Honoré's side. Joan crouched opposite. Mrs. Honoré moaned and her eyes opened. Her gaze met Tara's, and she whispered, "Lightning's dead."

15.

The Saints and the Cowboys silently collided on the muted TV in the hospital waiting room. Brightly lit vending machines hummed in the corner behind a row of vinyl couches and plastic plants. Joan and Tara were alone except for an orderly on the far side of the room who'd snuck in to watch the preseason game. He was sunk low in the couch, neck craned to the shifting screen, feet propped on the rim of the planter in front of him.

"Five dollars the shoes come off," Joan whispered.

Tara smiled, a smear of tangerine Cheetos dust on her chin. She offered the snack bag to Joan as she licked each fingertip clean.

Again, Joan registered the strange expression on her daughter's face, lips lightly pursed, eyes probing and bright. Joan first noticed it on the ride to the hospital, in the back seat of Lydia's Lexus. She'd assumed it was worry for Mrs. Honoré, but now they knew she would be fine. The doctor said the damage to her lungs would heal in just a couple of weeks.

Maybe Tara was ruminating on the next big fish they had to fry—where they were going to sleep now that Mrs. Honoré's property was poisoned. She glanced through the plate glass at the parking lot where Lydia was ensconced in her car, backlit by the interior dome light. She gripped the steering wheel as she fielded an endless stream of calls through the phone in her dashboard. Next to her, Justin hunched over his laptop, his finger scrolling across the screen.

Every half hour, Lydia popped into the waiting room with updates. Her latest news was that the gas in the barn was 99 percent likely related to the sinkhole. Methane was bubbling up all over town—through puddles in people's backyards, trapped beneath the low ceilings of homes and sheds, even in faraway areas of the bayou. There was a report of someone fainting while doing the dishes with the kitchen faucet running, suggesting that methane had invaded the freshwater aquifer. People who'd initially scoffed at the mandatory evacuation order were leaving town in droves.

Lydia kept using the words "industrial disaster." Joan glanced down the empty hospital hallway. Must be the quietest disaster in history then, she thought. The doctor who'd admitted Mrs. Honoré hadn't even heard of what was happening two towns away in Terrefine.

The orderly glanced around, gave Joan and Tara a small smile, then bent forward and loosened his laces. He slid off the heels of each shoe but stopped short of removing them altogether. Joan raised her eyebrows at Tara, expecting a chuckle, but again she was confronted by her daughter's curious look.

"Don't worry, Tara. We ain't sleeping outside tonight. I have some cash. We'll get a room at Rudy's. Tomorrow, we'll make a plan."

"I'm not worried," Tara said. "Not at all."

"Uh-uh!' the orderly yelled. A close up of a referee filled the screen. The orderly glanced over his shoulder with a sheepish grin. "Sorry." He turned back to the TV, shaking his head, as he laced up his shoes. He began a slow-motion exit, backing toward the door, his eyes lingering on the game until he'd crossed the threshold. "All right, y'all," he said, waving to them before disappearing down the hallway.

"Who dat!" Joan called after him. She reached for the Cheetos. "What is it, Tara? You've been staring at me like I have another arm coming out my head."

Tara twirled a knobby cheese puff before answering. "I guess I'm getting used to you being a hero."

"What are you talking about?"

"I heard Lydia saying it on the phone to that guy, Chase. Actually she called you a folk hero. I don't know what the folk part is about. But I know that anyone who saves a life is a hero."

"Oh my god," Joan said, crunching a mouthful of puffs. "What are they putting in your head?"

"My head is my own." Tara reached for the Mountain Dew balanced between her knees and swigged. "You saved Mrs. Honoré. That makes you a hero. A + B = C."

"If that's what you want to believe, fine. Just quit your gawking," Joan said, snatching a *People* magazine from a nearby chair.

Tara drained the rest of the soda, then placed it upright on the floor. "You reminded me of Officer Ripley. The way you pulled Mrs. Honoré out of the barn and kept me and Justin from running around like headless chickens."

"I hope you don't mean the first *Alien*," Joan said. "She cried her head off in that one."

Tara stood, resting one flip-flop atop the soda. She wobbled as she glanced sideways at Joan. "Sheriff Grady said you could have keeled over on top of Mrs. Honoré trying to save her." She sprung upward, balancing all her weight on the can. For a moment, the aluminum withstood the pressure, and Tara remained frozen in mid-pounce, then the metal collapsed into a neat puck. Tara grunted with satisfaction, scooped up the flattened can ,and tossed it in the wastebasket.

Joan frowned, considering Tara's words. She hadn't stopped to think about saving crotchety old Mrs. Honoré, which was probably a good thing. Nor had she felt afraid. Something had driven her to the barn, a sense that it was the natural next step in a flurried sequence of events, regardless of who was lying there. Is that what made you a hero these days?

Joan pretended to read the magazine while watching Tara from the corner of her eye. The day before Joan was arrested, when Tara found her on the stairs clutching the picture of the old man, Tara had been all dewy-eyed and pitying, listening as Joan confessed her first hellish year in Terrefine. It had turned Joan's stomach to see her damaged self reflected in her daughter's eyes. Tara wasn't pitying now. Her observations were matter-of-fact, respectful even. As if the woman who'd dragged Mrs. Honoré from that barn was the real Joan Saint-Romain. Someone who was the source of help, instead of the one who needed it.

Tara glanced at the waiting room clock behind its wire grid. "Mrs. Honoré should be out of her treatment now." She passed Joan the bag of Cheetos. "You can have the rest."

Truth was, Joan had never put her mind to anything but surviving. Even holing up in the house against the evacuation order had been a reflex, triggered more by her hatred of the old man than her desire to stay.

"I'm coming," Joan said, surprising herself, as she'd already had a sufficient eyeful of Mrs. Honoré hooked up to her machines. She tipped the bag, rattling the crumbs into her mouth, then crumpled the packaging and arced it over Tara's head into the garbage.

Mrs. Honoré, upright and rigid in her mechanized bed, chest puffed with outrage, brought to mind one of her great stuffed owls. A thin plastic cannula fed oxygen into her flared nostrils. Joan almost pitied the young doctor at the foot of the bed, stuttering through the reasons Mrs. Honoré needed to stay in the hospital overnight.

Tara rapped on the doorframe.

"I need a minute more with the patient before she has visitors," the doctor said, pressing a clipboard to his chest.

"I'll say when my guests come and go, Dale." Mrs. Honoré waved them in. When Tara hesitated, she barked, "Get in here, Tara. You too, Joan."

"Dr. Brand." The doctor frowned. "Dale is my first name."

"I don't need a doctor to tell me how I feel. I also don't need to stay in this hospital overnight so you can rack up another five thousand dollars."

The doctor pulled at the lapel of his starched coat. "You're a lucky woman. This could have been far worse. But you're a senior. You're at risk for developing pneumonia. It's my professional opinion that you should stay the night." He cast a pleading look at Joan. "Perhaps your friends can help you understand."

"Sorry, Dale, you're on your own," Joan said.

A nurse entered the room and began palpating IV bags and checking various monitors. He whipped out a thermometer and tucked it into Mrs. Honoré's mouth. "Fact is," the nurse said, "you've already been admitted. In-patient. Your Medicare will cover the night."

"There now," the doctor said. "It's all taken care of. Nurse, let's administer another albuterol treatment, continue the azithromycin."

Mrs. Honoré jerked the thermometer from her mouth. "I will not be drugged and held captive."

"Ma'am, if we wanted to drug you, we'd have done it already," the nurse said. "Be a lot more peaceful in here."

"Nurse Donato is, of course, making a joke," the doctor said. "As unprofessional as that is."

"New guy," the nurse said under his breath as the doctor was leaving.

"Mostly knows what he's doing." He winked at Joan and Tara. "Mrs. Honoré, it sucks here. I concur. So unless you want to prolong your stay, you'll finish up the course of antibiotics." Mrs. Honoré grumbled but took the pills. "Well done," the nurse called as he left the room.

Tara gravitated to the room's sole window, reaching for the cord from the venetian blinds and winding it tight around her forearm, the dark forests of her eyes tinged with sadness as she regarded Mrs. Honoré.

"Loretta, you may as well stay here," Joan said. She swung her legs up on the empty bed next to Mrs. Honoré's and crossed her arms behind her head. "We're all wandering gypsies now, what with that gas leaking out on your property. Hell, maybe we'll join you in here."

Mrs. Honoré chuckled, her face softening. "I know what you did for me today, Joan. Thank you. I won't ever forget it."

"Thank Tara," Joan stammered, feeling the warmth rising to her face. "She's the one that found you."

"I know Tara did her part." Mrs. Honoré glanced at the girl. "But you risked your life. I'm deeply grateful." She reached her hand across the gap between the beds. Joan stared at the open palm, a hectic map of callouses and creases, then gripped it in her own.

"You and Tara have always got a place with me, regardless of where we end up."

"Beautiful." A deep, resonant voice drifted through the doorway. Joan released Mrs. Honoré's hand and peered across the room through the doorway.

A tall man wearing creased linen stood in the hallway, his gray-streaked hair combed back from his hawkish face, his eyes underscored by dark half-moons. "I'm so sorry to intrude," he said, lowering the cellphone he'd aimed at them. "But the authenticity of this moment was just breathtaking. I had to capture it. I've run a million different endings to today's story through my mind. I couldn't land on anything. But this…"—his eyes drifted skyward as he searched for words—"… was sublime."

"You're that reporter," Joan said. "But how can you already be at the end of the article when you haven't even talked to me?" She glanced at her filthy Lee jeans, remembering the day's preparation for the interview.

"This story is writing itself." Chase smiled. "Though I do hope you'll still give me some of your time. After all, you're the belle of this ball."

"Ha!" Joan slid her knuckle beneath the strand of pearls and tugged. "You're full of it."

"On the contrary, I'm quite serious."

"I hope your story can write itself some other ending," Mrs. Honoré said, settling back into her pillows. "Since you won't be using my private conversation. You haven't even done the courtesy of introducing yourself."

"I do apologize, Mrs. Honoré. And I hope you're on the mend." He started to enter the room, then paused, lowering his chin to reveal cheeks surfaced with faint acne scars. "May I?"

Mrs. Honoré nodded curtly and Chase advanced, his thin fingers extended in greeting. "Chase Robichaux. It's my pleasure to make your acquaintance. And it's my hope that you'll realize this isn't my story. It's Joan's." He bowed to Joan. "And Miss Tara's." He clicked his heels and smiled at Tara. "And everyone in Terrefine, including you, Mrs. Honoré."

"When will the story come out?" Tara asked.

"It's out. At least the teaser version. We'll have a much longer feature in the Sunday edition." He glanced at his phone, buffed the screen on his leg, and dropped it into his blazer pocket. "That's what I need the ending for."

"You're shitting me!" Joan said. "Why did Lydia have me go through that whole rigmarole like we were going to sit down and have an interview? And how did you print up the papers so fast?"

"A sit-down interview, built around your personal story was the original idea, and we'd still like that to happen. But I'd be no kind of reporter if I hadn't covered a life-threatening event that is a direct result of this sinkhole."

Joan and Tara exchanged glances, expecting an eruption from Mrs. Honoré about Chase airing her business to the world, but when they glanced back at the hospital bed, Mrs. Honoré's eyes were closed. She'd sunk further into the pillows, her head canted to one side. Asleep, her puffy flesh registered the day's trauma. Dr. Brand's senior comment suddenly seemed fitting.

"You're lucky she's asleep," Tara said, lowering her voice. It was dusk outside and the glass reflected the hospital room's dull florescence. "She won't like being in your paper. Or Lightning."

"It's news, Tara," Chase said. "If I hadn't reported it, rest assured someone else would have. And it's always preferable to be covered by a friend." He reached into his shoulder bag and pulled out a thin black laptop. "Why don't you see for yourself?" He flipped up the screen and balanced the computer on his forearm. Joan and Tara gathered on each side. The webpage was already open, crowned with the headline: *Near-Fatal Methane Poisoning Leaves One Badly Injured. Salt Dome Sinkhole to Blame.* Directly beneath the headline, the image of the sinkhole with its rainbow slick of crude oil loomed above two short paragraphs.

"There's hardly any words," Joan said, fingerprinting the screen.

"That's right," said Chase. "Breaking news is mostly conveyed in photos with short descriptions. But you'd be surprised what a photo can accomplish." He clicked on the sinkhole image and Joan appeared, dragging Mrs. Honoré from the barn, Lightning's corpse visible behind them. "Images drive straight to the heart, bypassing the conscious mind altogether. Though, of course, my extended article will be the real coup de grace."

"Is that picture from Lydia's phone?" Tara asked.

"No," Chase answered. "My photographer took these from the road with a telephoto lens. We'd just arrived when Joan reached the barn."

"No better than a peeping Tom," Joan said.

Chase grinned. "I've been called worse. But that's how the news is captured. Rights of the press. How do you think all those movie stars end up with their bulging bellies all over the web?"

"Yuck," Tara said. "Who wants to see that?"

"Mostly their own fans," Chase replied. He clicked his track pad and a close up of Joan's face appeared, her sharp cheekbones slick with sweat, her eyes enormous and fierce, mud smeared across her chest.

Joan touched her skin above her open collar. The mud was still there.

The scroll of photos advanced—Joan and Tara kneeling over Mrs. Honoré; the ambulance arriving, the yellow tape cordoning off Mrs. Honoré's property; Joan and Tara embracing, bright figures against the knobby hide of a live oak. A shot of Mrs. Honoré being loaded into the ambulance was followed by one of Lightning, collapsed on the ground, framed in the barn doorway.

"It's sad," Joan breathed, engrossed in the images. "Mrs. Honoré loved that horse more than any human. Except maybe Tara."

Tara nodded. "Lightning was her family."

The final shot was of the sinkhole, a wider angle that included the surrounding land. Joan and Tara's house was visible, with the giant derrick for the exploratory well erected and operational. The contents of their backyard were now in a pell-mell heap in the grassy lot next door.

The sinkhole had collapsed further, bringing it closer to the house. It was also encroaching upon the service road that gave access to the staging area for the emergency and construction vehicles.

"Hold up." Joan leaned in closer. She yanked the laptop from Chase. "My house…"

The southwestern corner of the house looked as if it had been chewed away, destroying much of Tara's room and the kitchen below.

"Mother fucker," Joan spat, shoving the computer at Chase. "Not even a word from them that they destroyed my house." She retreated to the window and confronted her own pinched reflection.

"Joan?" Chase called in a soft voice.

She spun around to face his camera. A tiny green light shone at the top of the lens.

"Tell us what you're feeling right this minute. About the destruction of your home."

16.

The late afternoon light, mottled with shadows from the restless tree outside, had long ago breached the flimsy blinds of room nineteen at Rudy's Hotel-Motel. Joan hocked a wet glob into the plastic cup at her bedside table and propped herself up on one trembling arm. It was her third attempt to wake up. As of yet, she'd been unable to break through the cement slab of her hangover.

The coffee milk brought in earlier by Tara sat untouched, a travel packet of Advil tucked in the handle. Joan felt the nip of remorse and defended herself to the empty room. "I'm full grown. I can drink however I wanna drink."

No one could blame her for throwing back a few after finding out a hunk of her house was gone. In fact, it was Justin who'd bought her the first sympathy shot at T-Rudy's, the tiny lounge attached to the motel. She dry-heaved, remembering the Jagermeister.

Many more shots and beers followed as the lounge filled with other lodgers, mostly townsfolk uprooted by the sinkhole. Everybody was banking on FEMA, or Mid-South, or the state of Louisiana to foot the bill, including Rudy whose grin never left his face as he liquored up the crowd.

At first, Joan lingered near the booth where Lydia, Chase Robichaux, and Justin were huddled around Chase's laptop. She chuckled listening to their intricate debate over her video in Loretta's hospital room. The three of them split the hair of a hair over every detail: if the lighting was okay, if Joan's waist length hair which had escaped Tara's braid made her look too young or too pretty, how Loretta's foot sticking out of the blanket in the background would "read."

The biggest to-do was over the part where Joan said she wanted to burn down the Mid-South plant so they'd know how she felt. Lydia pleaded with Chase to cut it, afraid that people might lump Joan with terrorists. But Chase refused, insisting that it was the highlight and "a thrilling display of Joan's outrage."

When no one asked her opinion, Joan offered it anyway. Why not shoot the whole thing over, with a new outfit, minus Loretta's foot, maybe at the casino, or someplace equally nice? But she was soon drowned out by a stream of lesser plaintiffs crowding around the booth to yammer their questions at Lydia.

Later, when Chase found her on a bar stool, she knew that the video had made it to the newspaper webpage or wherever it was supposed to go. "Bombs away," he'd murmured into her neck, making himself heard above the racket.

The booze flowed all night, as did the sinkhole war stories. Cajuns knew how to party through any disaster—hurricanes, funerals, and now the earth caving in. There were a few emergency workers staying at Rudy's and at one point a fight broke out, with a couple of locals mistaking the workers for Mid-South reps. By midnight they were staggering through the bar, arms slung over each other's shoulders.

Tara spent the evening by the dry weed-bottomed pool, mesmerized by Justin's electronic tablet. Joan was glad to be free of her daughter's searchlight eyes for a few hours. She should get her hands on one of those machines for the girl. Maybe Justin would leave it with her. He probably had a bunch of them.

A gush of sour filled her mouth and Joan dragged herself to the bathroom. She lunged for the toilet, knocking the forgotten shaving kit of a past guest from the counter. She hung her head above the bowl, mucus trailing from her lips, and eyed the straw-colored wisps between her legs. She lifted one hand from the seat and probed herself until she concluded she'd most likely come back to the room alone last night.

After a cold shower, she stood dripping in front of the AC, shuddering to alertness. She threw back the Advil, chasing it with a near-full Miller that she found perched atop the black and white TV. She felt almost normal by the time she slipped into the aqua-green scrubs she'd lifted from the hospital.

A murmur of voices outside her window grew steadily louder. She peered through the blinds on the poolside wall of her room. It looked like the entire motel was out there. People filled the rusting patio furniture and picnic tables, looking on as Lydia spoke and Justin passed out booklets. Tara was near the front, squatting on a cinder block.

She let the drapes fall. How could they have a meeting without her? She was the one in the papers and the video. The one with firsthand experience of that damn hole. She thought of Chase, Lydia, and Justin ignoring her suggestions last night, arguing about her "too young," "too pretty" hair.

She yanked her hair into a thick rope and whipped it into a coil at the base of her neck, flinging drops of shower water across the dull wall mirror. She studied her reflection. The Miller had reactivated last night's booze, flushing her cheeks and sending a lush gleam to her eyes. The scrubs hung low on her hips, exposing a strip of belly. With her hair pulled back, she could have been one of those karate people in the posters that used to hang in the Buy-U-Mart before they replaced the video rentals with slot machines. She delivered a chop to the mirror then slipped on Tara's flip-flops. As she turned to go, her eyes fell on the shaving kit and its contents strewn on the bathroom floor.

Lydia was in mid-sentence as Joan pushed open the chain-link gate to the pool area. At the creak of the hinges, a half-dozen heads jerked her way. She grinned, feeling the warm afternoon breeze sizzle across her scalp.

"That's Joan!" a reporter exclaimed from where he sat with the handful of press who'd turned out for the meeting. He narrowed his eyes. "Isn't it?"

"What happened to her hair?" Lew's craggy voice sounded from a picnic table on the outskirts of the gathering.

Joan winked at Lydia and immediately knew her decision to buzz cut her hair had been a good one. Lydia stalled in the midst of her presentation, for once at a loss for words.

"Hey, y'all." Joan smoothed her close-cropped head with one hand, discovering a stray piece that had escaped the clippers. She'd have to ask Tara to neaten things up later.

A flash exploded and a bright starburst flooded her vision, almost causing her to stumble. The reporters, armed with phones, recorders, and note pads, rushed to meet her. The sound of running footsteps on gravel preceded the arrival of a squat woman shouldering a TV camera.

"Mrs. Saint-Romain!" The cry came from a wiry woman in a khaki vest who seemed to be partnered with the camerawoman. "I'm from the *Houston Remark*. Your hair. Is it a gesture of protest?"

"Yeah. I'm protesting anybody who thinks they got me figured out."

"Was it part of planning your next video?" the reporter continued. "Your current one is getting national coverage and putting this disaster on the map. Does that give you any consolation?"

"I'll get my consolation when my daughter and me are under our own roof again."

"Joan!" A dark-eyed man sporting a five-o'clock shadow aimed his phone at her. "You were exposed to poisonous gases when you saved Mrs. Honoré's life. Are the gases affecting you as well? Is that why you've been laid up all day?"

Joan wet her lips and flattened her stomach so her scrubs slipped lower, past her hip bones. Before she could assure the man that she was feeling just fine, Lydia's dark-suited arm windmilled between them. "I'm sorry, Joan," she said in a low voice as she planted her blood-red nails on Joan's bicep. "Justin was supposed to intercept you before you got here. Let me handle this."

"Do me a favor, guys," Lydia called out. "Help us stay focused on the meeting agenda. We'll hold a Q&A with Mrs. Saint-Romain, and the plaintiff's team in good time. Remember, we are talking about an entire community that's been affected here, a mass displacement of families who have no greater wish than to go back to their normal lives, just like Mrs. Saint-Romain."

The dark-eyed reporter glanced at the meeting-goers then frowned at Lydia. "My editor had me drive three hours to talk to Joan."

"Same here," said the woman from the *Houston Remark*, tipping her head toward the camerawoman. "We've been on the road since dawn." She aimed her pen at Joan. "For her."

After the remaining reporters expressed their overriding interest in Joan's story, Lydia released her arm. "Of course," she said, her eyes boring into Joan's. "Mrs. Saint-Romain's experience is an important bellwether of the overall response to this disaster. I'm sure she'll offer some valuable insight."

Joan squared her shoulders as the reporters crowded around her once again. She caught sight of Chase slouching against the trunk of a sprawling tree that threw tiny rotten pecans over most of the pool area. He looked up briefly, scanning Joan from head to foot, fingers dancing across his scarred cheeks, then dropped his gaze to his notebook where his pen moved unhurriedly.

At Lydia's instruction, Justin invited the rest of the meeting-goers to take a break, but everyone remained seated, their attention on Joan. "Do you blame Mid-South for what happened here, Joan?" the dark-eyed reporter asked as he brandished a newspaper with a photo of Joan dragging Loretta from the barn splashed across the front page.

As the question hovered in the sticky air, Joan caught Lydia's eye. The lawyer's poised smile sharpened. What had she said that first day at Mrs. Honoré's preparing for Chase's interview? About nobody wanting to feel sorry for you? And yet, Joan could feel the smug expectation of the reporters, waiting for her to point every finger and toe at Mid-South, the state, and God above.

Earlier, Justin had thrust an icy bottle of water at Joan and now she clutched it to her chest. "This ain't about blame. This is about responsibility. That's a different thing."

"Then you think it's Mid-South's responsibility?"

"Put it to you this way. My daughter, Tara, has been cleaning up after herself since she could barely walk, without me saying squat. Here we got a bunch of grown-ups, educated up and down the wazoo, with their computers and their heavy equipment. They been punching into that dome for years. Yet, somehow, they don't seem to know how to clean up their own mess." She hooked a thumb in her waistband and leaned into one hip. "I'd be happy to pitch in. I think we all would. But we ain't the so-called experts, are we? What about you, Rudy? You got a pretty nice motel here. You think you can figure out how to fill that hole?"

Rudy donned a rueful smile as he brushed his steel gray hair from his forehead. "No, ma'am."

"Me, neither. That's why we left it to the boys in charge. Anybody here happen to see pictures of my house lately?"

Grumbles of protest on Joan's behalf erupted as the dark-eyed reporter waved his notepad in the air. "I got a statement from Eddy Ledroit at Mid-South who claims the damage had nothing to do with their sinkhole strategy. A wayward crane clipped the wall while they were erecting the derrick."

"That's a comfort," Joan said, shaking her head. "Like I said, their mess keeps getting messier. Meanwhile, the rest of us just want to get back to living our lives."

"Joan!" A voice fought through the next jumble of shouted questions. "When should we expect another video update from you? I'm following you on Twitter."

"Better not follow me. I ain't on that thing."

"That was stellar." Lydia pursed her lips as Joan flopped down on the bed and wrapped one leg around the other.

They were in Lydia's motel room, which was twice the size of Joan and Tara's, but equally ramshackle. The TV had disappeared and the space reclaimed for stacks of papers and a computer. The cheap laminated dresser was covered with manila folders and thick research binders. Three cellphones were jammed into a power strip at the base of the wood-paneled wall. Tara perched on a corner of the bed and Justin sat in a wooden chair near the door.

"I could not have scripted a better statement," Lydia continued. "You are a natural off the cuff."

"Really?" Joan asked, scrunching her nose to keep her smile in check.

"Really," Lydia replied, pointing to a copy of the *Baton Rouge Herald* that lay on the bed. "The article came out well, too. You're hitting all your marks. I'm very pleased."

"I'll autograph one for you if you want," Joan said, riffling the front page.

"Save the autographs for all the people you've inspired. But, Joan," she said, leveling her gaze and adopting a serious tone, "from here on out, we've got to stay in communication about every detail. You have the right to do whatever you want to with your appearance under ordinary circumstances. But right now, such a drastic alteration could be interpreted as impulsive, or worse, unbalanced."

"You mean my hair? They loved it!"

"They did. In fact, Chase stopped me to say he thought it was brilliant and would ratchet up the positive media attention. But I'd still like to request that you run your ideas by me before executing them. Deal?"

"I'll do my best."

"I'd appreciate it. As for you," Lydia said, turning to Justin who sank lower in his chair. "Let's put aside the fact that you failed to buffer Joan from the reporters at the pool. Who authorized you to roll out a social media platform for her? Are you out of your mind?"

"I was just showing Tara how Twitter and Facebook work," he stammered. "She's too young to create a profile so I thought I'd set one up for Joan."

"I told him he could," Tara said.

"I'm not paying for that," Joan said, cracking the window and fishing her cigarettes from her pocket.

"It's free, Mama."

Joan shook the pack, counting the remaining cigarettes. "Tara, you taking from me?"

As Tara shook her head, Lydia crossed her arms and faced Justin. "You are out of line," she said, her tone only slightly deviating from the one she'd used when singing Joan's praises. Even so, Justin blanched. "Does Joan even have an email address?"

"She does now," Tara said. "Joanstromain@gmail.com." She extended the tablet to Lydia. "And she already has 2,000 Twitter followers."

Lydia was silent as she examined the screen. "You only set this up last night?" she asked, swiping the glass then looking up. "You tweeted the video."

"I thought I'd show Tara how to attach a piece of media." Justin's voice quavered. "You said to get it out everywhere we could."

Joan blew smoke through the window screen and watched Rudy's daughter lug a white plastic bucket up the steps to the lounge's walk-up window. Inside, a silver daiquiri machine tumbled a florescent pink slush. T-Rudy's door swung open and the din of voices, bucking and rolling, blared forth. The reporter from the *Houston Remark* stepped outside with Chase, the two of them deep in a conversation which they continued on the bumper of a news van topped with a satellite dish.

Joan glanced over her shoulder, leaking smoke into the motel room. "What about those other pictures of me Chase said he was gonna take? Or should we let that lady reporter do it?"

Lydia subjected Justin to a final withering glance, then checked her wristwatch. "You're meeting Chase in a hour. I agreed to his request for location shots, maybe even some video, as close to the evacuated area as possible."

Joan flicked her cigarette butt out the window just as a white sedan pulled up to the far end of the motel. One of the room doors swung open and an emergency worker emerged cradling a large cardboard cylinder. He approached the car, tipped his hat, and slid the cylinder through the driver's side window. The worker chatted with the driver as Rudy's scruffy dog ambled over to sniff one of the sedan's front tires. Soon, the driver stretched out a hand to scratch the animal's head.

"I'll be right back," Joan said, speaking over Lydia's minutely detailed instructions on how Justin was to handle the social media strategy moving forward.

Joan quietly shut the door behind her and crossed the few feet to the van where Chase and the reporter were still engrossed in discussion.

"You might want to get your butts into gear," Joan said, interrupting them. "Find out why Eddy Ledroit is over there in somebody else's car. My guess is that he's spying on me."

17.

Twilight arced above the motel and the surrounding woods, tamping down the day's heat and pooling shadows between the low cinder-block buildings. At the far end of the parking lot, the brake lights of Eddy's car cast a cherry glow.

"Joan, if Eddy's here for you, then it should be you who approaches him, *non?*" Chase asked, his eyes wide, his pupils spilling into ink-black irises. "We reporters are merely here to record your triumphs."

"You're right." Joan flared her arms, pumping the stale air from her lungs and inhaling the evening cool. "It's me that needs to handle Eddy."

"*Hasta siempre.*" Chase's words faded as she stepped into the darkness beneath the oaks overhanging the parking lot. Eddy shook hands with the emergency worker through the driver's side window then backed the car away from the concrete riser, U-turning into a vacant slip of gravel. As he flicked on the headlights, Joan stepped from the trees.

His car jerked to a stop. She remained motionless, illuminated in the high beams. It was impossible for her to see beyond the burn of the headlights, and for a moment she had the sense that she was utterly alone, that the rest of it—Rudy's, the sinkhole, even Tara—had vanished.

Eddy threw the car into park and dimmed the lights. "Joan!" The disembodied voice could have belonged to the evening breeze. "I almost didn't recognize you."

She strode toward the passenger side and perched her forearms in the open window, feeling the chill of the AC snake between her breasts. "Got a minute?" Before Eddy could answer, she jerked the handle and ducked inside.

Under the flood of the dome light, Eddy loosened his grip on the wheel and watched her slide in. His sharp jaw was rough and unshaven. Beneath a layer of fine grit, sunburn darkened his cheeks and forehead.

His lashes hung low over sleepless amber eyes as he took in her shaved head and the newly revealed contours of her skull.

She slammed the door, leaving them in near darkness. Outside, the light from T-Rudy's lounge shone on the truck bumper where Chase and the reporter were no longer sitting. She rolled up her window and motioned with her chin for Eddy to do the same. He obliged, then killed the headlights and lowered the volume on the fifties music drifting from the radio. "We on speaking terms now?" he asked.

She ignored the question, tapping her fingernail on a plastic cup in the center console half-filled with the chewed remnants of sunflower seeds. "How come you don't spit 'em outside?"

"Habit." He placed his hand over the cup and removed it to the back seat. "A wife who wouldn't tolerate me spitting anything out the car window."

The light of a nearby room flicked on and a child's head bobbed past the curtained window. "I guess you were minutes from knocking on my motel door to tell me about my house. Am I right?" she asked.

"No. I didn't know you were here." He shifted toward her, his face murky in the muted light of the dashboard. "Anyway, I'm no longer the community point person. You should have gotten a call from Carville, the guy who replaced me. Did you?"

"Not before I saw a picture of my tore-up home on the computer."

"I'll be damned." His fist bounced off the steering wheel. "He swore you would be notified immediately."

"You could have called yourself. It was shitty of you not to."

"You're right. It was." Eddy fell silent as a dark oblong insect scuttled across the windshield. "I'm sorry. Once again." He dragged his hand roughly across his eyes and let his head fall back on the seat. Joan felt the stirrings of satisfaction as a dense frustration crept into his face.

"You see my article in the Sunday paper?" she asked.

"I did," he answered, straightening up.

She pulled her T-shirt taut across her belly. "And?"

"Setting aside the fact that me and my company look terrible, it was a fine story."

"You wouldn't believe those reporters, how they come after me—" Joan started, but the harsh buzz of Eddy's cellphone interrupted her.

"Excuse me." Eddy's muscled shoulder pressed into her as he reached across the dashboard. "Hello?...no...absolutely not...tell him to meet me onsite in a half hour." He dropped the phone into the cup holder where the sunflower seeds had been. "Sorry. You were saying something about the reporters."

"Just that they're all over me."

"Of course, they are. You're a force to be reckoned with."

"Too much of a force for some." Her body softened as she turned toward him in the darkness, silently urging him to pick up on her hint. When he remained quiet, she blurted, "That morning in my—"

"In your bedroom," he interrupted, reaching down to switch off the radio. "Joan, we were in the middle of a crisis."

"I saw you looking at me. When we were at your house. And at mine."

On the far side of the parking lot, the door of T-Rudy's opened, releasing a burst of voices and light. She pressed her toes into the floorboard, awaiting Eddy's second denial of her, bracing herself to shove him or kick open the car door. His seat creaked gently.

"How could any man not look at you, Joan?"

She felt his calloused fingers tracing the length of her neck. A rupture of warmth gushed through her. She gripped a handful of his shirt.

"Wait." He clasped her wrist. Alongside the car, the crush of gravel underfoot grew louder. Eddy uncurled her fingers and returned her hands to her lap just as a rap shook the window.

"You all right, Joan?" A flashlight flicked on, revealing Lew's haggard, white-bearded face at the passenger side window. He squinted past her into the car, then aimed the light at Eddy.

"What the hell, Lew? You gonna blind me for life." Joan shielded her eyes as she lowered the window.

Lew snapped off the beam. "Sorry. You been in there a while. Thought I should check on you."

"That's sweet. But I'm fine. Just wanted to hear from the horse's mouth what went down with my home."

Lew nodded, his tongue darting out as he backed into the darkness. "You holler if you need us. We'll be right here."

"We?" Eddy asked as Joan rolled up the window.

He clicked on the headlights. A semicircle of humorless faces stood squinting against the brightness, forming a barrier between his car and the motel exit. Lew was front and center, a pistol bulging from his waistband.

"Jesus. Did you plan this, Joan?"

She chuckled. "I didn't, Eddy. I swear to you." She swung open her door and rose from the car, resting a foot on the running board as she addressed the gathering. "Hey, y'all! I appreciate the back up, but I'm all right. I'll be at the bar in five minutes, anyone wants to buy me a drink."

The crowd shuffled toward T-Rudy's, disappearing into the lounge except for a few stragglers, including Chase and Lew, who eyed Eddy's car between sips of beer. Joan draped one arm on the car roof and the other on the open door, one hip jutting forward as she held Eddy's gaze.

"Afraid I have to get going," he said, throwing the car into gear. "Still on the clock."

"Why don't you come back later? Finish our talk. I could meet you up the road."

He looked away, half-smiling, before cutting his eyes back to her. "I wish I could, Mrs. Saint-Romain. I really do. But like I said before, we're in the middle of an emergency."

She slammed the door and he started to pull away. "Hey!" she called, slapping the car trunk. Eddy braked and she hurried to his window. "When the hell do I get back in my house?"

"When the hole stops growing, the engineers and geologists can determine if and when it will be safe for you to return. They say we're maybe halfway there."

"Horseshit."

"Horseshit." Eddy nodded, fatigue creeping back into his face.

"This is so cool!" Justin breathed as he splashed through the watery field, flanked by Tara and Joan. A bulky camera bag slammed into his thigh with each step. Traces of oily stink scented the air.

"Please don't let your joi de vivre endanger Daniel's equipment," Chase murmured as he scanned the white-hot horizon. "Though that middling cameraman deserves a little damage for nearly derailing our adventure with his food poisoning."

"He's missing out on some incredible shots," Justin said.

"What's the big deal? It's just a big mud puddle," Joan said. "Good for nothing but a few crawfish and maybe some snakes."

"Snakes?" Justin froze, clamping down on Tara's shoulder.

Tara nodded, her unkempt curls casting wild shadows on her cheeks. "I could have baited a crawfish net with chicken gizzards if I'd known you wanted to see a snake." She rested a bare foot on her shin and glanced back at Chase's SUV, parked on the dirt road that bordered the field. "Rudy probably has nets. We could go back."

Justin released Tara's shoulder, his Adam's apple bobbing as he searched the brown gruel overtopping his galoshes. "Thanks, but we'd better get the shoot done. Lydia's expecting me back in a couple of hours."

"We're almost there," Tara said, pointing to a narrow band of woods. A break in the trees revealed a distant convergence of heavy machinery and construction vehicles. "Twenty more minutes and we'll have a clear view of the hole."

"Well done, Pocahontas," Chase said. "Several of Rudy's patrons owe me a meal. I'll remember to always put my money on you, my dear."

"Are we done standing around?" Joan asked, fingering the belt loop of her cutoffs and flicking water with her toes. She was agitated. Since last night, torrid thoughts of Eddy roiled endlessly through her mind, pleasurable at first but now a torment. Her whole being was racked with a hollow yearning. She felt trapped between the noon day sun and its blinding reflection on the flooded field, and the urge to fill herself was strong, with mud, with sticks, with her own fist, anything to quell her animal longing.

They continued the slog across the field in single file, with Tara in the lead. At one point, Justin asked if anyone had sunscreen. Only Tara bothered to answer. "Never used it," she said shortly. When at last, they reached the stingy shade of the trees, Justin, sodden and panting, offered his water bottle to Tara and Joan before emptying most of it himself.

"And now to strike up my one-man journalist band," Chase said. "Reporter, cameraman, and videographer at your service. Not a word to anyone. What remains of my reputation will be shot." He took the shoulder bag from Justin and withdrew a video camera. A long, soft-tipped microphone was mounted on the top.

"You gonna film me or fuck me with that thing?" Joan asked, then glanced back at Justin whose eyes were bolted to the ground as he fumbled for his cellphone.

"My, my," Chase said, panning the landscape. "Someone's feeling feverish from the heat."

"I'm just playing. Anyway, I bet if a man said the same thing you wouldn't think twice. You'd laugh."

"You're right. I wouldn't think twice." Chase lowered the camera to adjust a loose strap. "But I wouldn't laugh."

"How many of those tweets I got now, Justin?"

"You mean followers, Mama," Tara said.

"Yesterday it was about two thousand," Justin started. "Now," he said, showing the screen to Tara, "it's 10,643."

Tara let her gaze fall briefly to her mud-caked feet. "A 532 percent increase," she said.

Justin gave Tara a curious look, then tapped his fingers on his leg. "That's right," he said, his fingers coming to stillness. "Wow."

"Wow is right," said Joan. "Don't they have anything better to do than play on a phone all day?"

"They can't help it. You're contagious," Chase said, ushering Joan from the shade to a patch of earth in the blazing sun. She narrowed her eyes at Chase. "*Contagious* is a social media concept. It means you're popular, spreading like wildfire."

Chase brought the camera to his face and focused on Joan. Behind her, the whole commotion of the sinkhole was visible in miniature, a blur of activity against the heat-stunned landscape. A ghostly shimmer, far beyond the site was the only hint of her house.

"Wardrobe," Chase murmured as he angled Joan's shoulders and widened the V-neck of her T-shirt. His eyes roved across her face and neck, lingered at her breasts, and slid along her legs, coming to rest at her bare feet. "The feet might not work."

"Too bad. They're the only ones I got."

Chase turned to Justin, the corners of his mouth curling. "Would you kindly loan her your boots? Just for the shoot."

Justin wordlessly complied, his black-socked toes sinking in the mud as he carried the boots to Joan. As she slipped them on, he hurried to a nearby mound of dry earth and withdrew a sheaf of paper from his waistband. "I'll be here, cueing you with the notes Lydia reviewed at breakfast." He flashed the first rumpled sheet which bore the smeared phrase: *Grateful for support.*

"No need for your cues," Chase said. "This is an interview, remember? I'm not Lydia's PR man."

"Whatever," Joan said. "Let's get this show on the road."

Chase began filming. "Tell us who you are, dear. And where we're standing."

Joan delivered a wooden greeting into the camera's dark eye then awkwardly indicated the sinkhole by paddling her arms behind her.

"Cut!" Chase lowered the camera. "Joan, forget the camera is here. See if you can place yourself, in your imagination, at T-Rudy's. You're just telling a story to some of your comrades over a drink. Close your eyes and try it."

Joan shut her eyes and saw Eddy lowering himself onto her, a gold chain dangling from his neck, his unshaven face raking her skin. Her lids flew open. "That ain't gonna work."

"Tell us what it's like living at Rudy's then. All your possessions were left behind, weren't they? Nothing but the clothes on your back?" Chase pointed the camera at Joan, who twisted around to face the sinkhole. "Face the camera, please."

"Somebody's coming," she said. A fast-moving speck seemed to have broken off from the main operation and was headed in their direction. "On a four-wheeler," she added as the putter of the motor became audible.

"We're not trespassing, right?" Justin raised his eyebrows at Joan.

"Nah. Rudy's brother, Clyston, owns this land. He don't care."

The four-wheeler was now close enough to make out the tall, rail-thin rider. "It's Bible-beater Billy," Joan said. "Before he found Jesus last year, he was Wife-beater Billy."

They waited in silence until Billy rolled to a stop a few feet from Joan and killed the engine. Chase, who'd been filming the four-wheeler's approach, lowered the camera to his side, while keeping the lens trained on Billy.

"How's it hanging, Billy?" Joan asked.

"Y'all need to quit nosing around and clear outta here," Billy said, ignoring Joan and addressing Chase as he adjusted the brim of his Mid-South cap.

"And from whom do you get your authority?" Chase asked.

"Fifteen years of my heart and soul at Mid-South." His hand moved to his waist where a nightstick dangled. "And the God-given courage to do what's right."

"Mid-South don't own a stick of this land," Joan said. "God neither."

"This area is well outside of the evacuation zone," Justin said. "I checked this morning."

"Look," Billy said, leaning back on his seat and resting his hands on the nightstick. "I know you're out-of-towners, so you can't be expected to know certain things, but you can't believe anything that comes out of the mouth of a woman like that." His upper lip curled as his eyes fell on Joan.

"Mama." Tara pointed toward the sinkhole. Two more four-wheelers and their black-capped riders were ripping across the field toward them.

18.

The four-wheelers swooped past Billy and skidded to a stop on either side of Joan, Tara, Justin, and Chase. The drivers remained mounted, their engines idling.

"I take it these gentlemen are with you?" Chase asked, his camera tucked against his side, discretely capturing Billy and the two other Mid-South employees.

"That's right. And they're under orders to keep the emergency area secure," Billy said, his lower lip glistening. "By whatever means necessary."

"It's fortunate then that Justin, our legal beagle, confirmed that this land is well outside the condemned area."

"I spoke with Mid-South's community liaison." Justin's chipper tone wavered as Billy brandished a nightstick. "Mr. Carville."

"I bet the farm you didn't tell him you meant to come out here and spy. You got papers authorizing you to take pictures on this land?"

Justin's eyes bulged as he glanced at Joan, who was busy crushing a mosquito against her leg and wiping the blood on her cutoffs.

"We have presumptive authorization from the landowner," Chase said.

"Sounds like a fancy way of saying no." Billy thrust the nightstick toward the camera and growled, "You need to put that back in your purse. You think I don't know what that little blinking light means?" He rose from his seat, balancing on the struts of the ATV, a black-clad skeleton against an empty sky. "You think you're smarter than me, don't you? That I'm too stupid to notice you taking spy pictures right under my nose."

"You far overestimate the power of my camera. Anything I shoot from here will show the emergency site in the distance as it appears now. No different from the multitude of images that have already appeared in the press. And my subject of interest is Joan Saint-Romain, not the sinkhole." Chase drew his lips into a thin smile. "I hope that puts your fears to rest."

"My fears?" Billy said, his voice twisting. "This ain't about my fears. I got no fears. This is about you disrespecting the men risking their lives trying to stabilize that hole. And as far as *that*." He jerked his gaze toward Joan. "Any video Joan Saint-Romain's in better have three *X*s at the end of it."

Joan pulled herself from a heated rumination about Eddy and his hands to glare at Billy's sneering face. The bony bastard would bully you out of your own thoughts. Her words formed even as she registered the twitchy fingers, the whip-ready arms, the spinning nightstick. "Hey, scarecrow! How's Pris?"

The stick froze in its revolutions. Billy's bottom lip fell, exposing a dingy canine.

"Pris is his wife," Joan said, addressing the other Mid-South guards. "He ever mention her to y'all?" She fondled the hollow at the base of her neck. "Good lady. Haven't seen her in a while. Did she ever get back full use of that arm? I hear her teeth turned out pretty good."

Billy's face was a mask of purple-veined rage as he jumped to the ground. "Don't you ever!" He whacked the stick on the ATV's metal rack. "Ever! Speak of my family again."

"Billy," one of the guards called as he slid off his machine. "Why don't we just let them film? It's way out here. Who cares?"

"I care," he said, through clenched teeth. "Someone's got to care." His eyes returned to Joan. "You and me both know that God sent that hole to suck up that den of iniquity you call a home. He's going to purge you from this town."

"Maybe we should come back at a more convenient time," Justin said, checking his phone. "Friday looks good. Chase? Joan? Thoughts?"

Joan filled her lungs as she faced off with Billy, invigorated by the rage she'd sparked in him. She caught his dank smell, like rotten leather. "You can hide behind your Bible talk all you want Billy-boy. But that don't change the truth." She gave a serpentine twist to her neck as she leaned closer. "A man who hits a woman is a small man. A tiny man." She extended her pinky finger and wiggled it near her crotch.

"You're a damned whore!" Billy roared, dropping his nightstick as he lunged for her throat. The Mid-South men scrambled to restrain him, but not before Joan rammed a knee in his groin and Tara snatched the nightstick and slammed it across his back.

"I'm calling the police!" Justin yelled. "Where are we? Chase! Help me out here!"

But Chase had fallen to one knee, enthralled, his camera devouring the slumping figure of Billy and the sun-lit form of Joan, her shorts torn where Billy had gripped them on his way to his knees, exposing a bright curve of Joan's flesh.

Lydia dropped her phone into the mauve leather handbag resting on the bar at T-Rudy's and clinked bottles with Joan. "Mid-South says Billy Fontaine was acting on his own volition. His two underlings were following his lead."

"Bull crap," Joan said, aiming her cigarette smoke above Lydia.

"Probably. Regardless, our messaging of the event will point to Mid-South's responsibility." She raised her brows at Justin, who whipped out his phone and started typing. "Our narrative will describe an aggressive company culture of regulatory disregard that precipitates this kind of violent behavior in its employees. It's easy to understand how an industrial disaster like the sinkhole could occur under the watch of such a willfully negligent organization."

On the other side of Justin, Chase perched on a barstool, finalizing his article and reviewing the day's footage while Tara looked on.

Lydia hooked the heel of her pump on Joan's stool and crossed her arms. "You missed an opportunity by not letting Sheriff Grady photograph those contusions. Or going to the hospital to get yourself checked out."

"What for? They're scratches." Joan gestured toward the angry streaks from Billy's fingernails on her outer thigh, just below the series of safety pins securing her ripped shorts. "And I don't want people thinking that dick-lick got anything on me."

"Once we've posted my article and the video there'll be no question as to who had the upper hand." Chase pivoted the laptop toward Joan. "Or whether good triumphs over evil. Luckily, Daniel was able to work his video-editing magic between bouts of vomiting. Care to have a look?"

Joan leaned forward, dousing the screen with cigarette smoke. The video opened with Billy professing his loyalty to God and Mid-South while the two other Mid-South men closed in on their four wheelers. Most of Chase's exchange with Billy had been omitted, leaving only Billy's threats to halt the filming and his menacing gestures with the nightstick. By the thirty-five second mark, Billy was celebrating God's purging of Joan's home with the sinkhole. At forty-five seconds, he was lunging for her throat.

"Pure gold," Lydia said, breaking into a rare, full-toothed smile when the video was done. "The ending is almost too on the nose. Amazing."

Joan wiggled her pinky at Chase. "He left out my best cut-down."

"Time constraints. Though Lydia's probably glad. Best not to cast you as a provocateur, despite how true to life your gesture may have been."

Joan poked her daughter in the gut. "You didn't think I could take that bag of bones? And you, Justin." Joan gave him a long look, then burst out laughing.

"What?" Justin asked, crimson splotches overtaking his face.

Lydia shot him a questioning look. "Did I miss something?"

"Justin got Sheriff Grady to come," Tara said, her voice rising above her mother's laughter.

"Justin played his part perfectly." Chase's dark eyes flashed. "Now let's inject this meme into the world. It just posted to the *Tribune*'s website. Joan, how about a tweet for all your adoring fans."

Joan stuffed her cigarette in her beer bottle and squinted at the laptop. The video had been replaced by a screen full of tiny photos and cryptic phrases and symbols. "I hate that computer shit," she said, bristling. She pushed the laptop away. "Let Tara do it."

"Are you willing to be your mother's proxy?" Chase lifted Tara's fingers and drew her closer.

"Shot of whiskey and a beer, Angel!" Joan called to Rudy's daughter, who was bartending. "Put it on Lydia's tab and give yourself a good tip."

"It's done," Tara said, pulling her hand from Chase's.

"Good job, baby." Joan swiveled on her stool. "Hey, Lydia, I could use a phone. Mine's somewhere back at the house. Probably stolen by those Mid-South crooks by now. Can't do my business." She needed to reach out to Eddy. Who knows how many times he'd tried to call her by now? She'd suggest they meet in the woods or off the highway between the motel and Terrefine.

Lydia jerked her head at Justin. "Get her number ported to a new cellphone and ship it here."

"And I want a normal phone," Joan said, eyeing Justin. "Nothing with Twitter or Facebook or any of that crap."

"She means a flip phone," Tara said. "We had an LD580 from AT&T."

"I'm on it," Justin said.

Red light rolled across Justin's face as he gathered his things. He craned his neck to peer through the row of dirty windowpanes that faced the parking lot. "It's an ambulance," he said. The rest of the bar-goers crowded around the glass.

"They got Loretta Honoré," someone murmured. Tara sprung from her stool and flew past Justin. Joan hooked her beer neck between her fingers and followed her daughter outside.

The ambulance was really a hospital transport van. The sliding door was open, revealing a robust and rested Mrs. Honoré. She rebuffed the helping hand offered her by the medical aide as she stepped from the vehicle.

Tara bounded up to the van. "I tried to call you at the hospital this morning. They wouldn't tell me anything."

"Doesn't surprise me. That place is almost empty and it's still a mess of disorganization." Mrs. Honoré's work boots crunched gravel as she touched down. "Why aren't you in school?"

"We're in a state of emergency."

"The students from Terrafine have been relocated to the Leittville school system for over a week now."

"I'm too busy helping the legal team with Mama's case. I'm learning more than they can teach me in a year at school." She flicked a stray bottle cap aside with her flip-flop.

Mrs. Honoré's eyes narrowed. "Where's your mama?"

"Hey, Loretta," Joan called from the lounge doorway. She stifled the urge to hide her beer bottle. "How you feeling?"

"I got a cough. And I want to be back in my home, same as you." She paused as Lydia emerged from the lounge, her cellphone glued to her face. "You didn't hear about school being relocated, Joan?"

"How? I got no phone."

"She's been busy too," Tara said. "She's gotten a tremendous swell of support on social media."

"A swell of support. That's something."

"Lydia thinks I'm basically solving the case for everybody." Joan took a swig of her beer. "Including you."

"Mrs. Honoré!" Lydia pocketed her phone as she swept past Joan. "It's great to see you up and about. We were all so worried. Did you get the flowers?"

"I did. Thought the lady down the hall would do better with them. Throat cancer."

Lydia clicked the top of the ballpoint pen protruding from her fist. "After you've had some rest, I'd be happy to brief you on some of the conversations we've had with the community. A lot has happened in the past couple of days. We're getting some real traction with Mid-South."

"By community, do you mean the folks of Terrefine that you are representing?"

"For the most part, yes."

"What about the children of the community?" Mrs. Honoré's eyes lit on Tara. "Are their parents getting briefed on the relocation of Terrefine's students?"

"That's more of a municipal communication, but I believe so. I would imagine that some parents might decide to keep their children with them until the situation stabilizes. No one can fault them for that."

Mrs. Honoré flicked a june bug from her sleeve. "Unless school happens to be a stabilizing factor for that child. A bus will be stopping out front of Rudy's starting tomorrow at seven a.m. Any parents, or anyone who might be interested in the welfare of Terrefine's children, you let them know."

"That's wonderful news," Lydia said. "I'll have Justin add a line to our next email update."

"Where's Rudy?" Mrs. Honoré asked Tara as she studied the rows of warped wooden doors.

"In the back," Tara said. "Frying fish."

As Mrs. Honoré turned to follow Tara, Lydia called after them. "One quick item. Justin hasn't received your paperwork. Not at all a problem. You've been in the hospital, after all. But it would be good to tie that up."

"Nothing to tie up," Mrs. Honoré replied over her shoulder. "I'm working with Ricky Delray."

"Got it," Lydia said, her voice taut. "The important thing is that you have representation."

Joan threw back her beer then swiped the back of her hand across her lips. "You know who told me to go to school when I was a kid?" she asked, her eyes resting on the corner of the building where Tara and Mrs. Honoré had disappeared. "Nobody."

"Self-sufficiency is way undervalued in parenting today," Lydia said, while composing a text. "In my opinion."

Joan secured a fresh beer from the bar and drifted to the pool area. Rudy was stooped over a huge metal pot balanced on a spindly burner. Checkered tablecloths covered the rusted patio tables. Stacks of paper plates and plastic cups rested on a nearby picnic table next to an explosion of plastic utensils.

"Fried catfish in a half hour, Joan," Rudy called.

"You seen Tara?"

"She took Loretta Honoré to her room."

"You didn't stick her next to me did you?"

As Joan turned away from Rudy's laughter, tiny shards of old resentments resurrected and began to whirl in her chest. Tara had called Joan a hero for pulling the old woman from the barn. But even that wasn't enough. In Mrs. Honoré's eyes, Joan would only ever be a fuck-up. Her truce of the past week with Mrs. Honoré snapped as soundlessly as a spider's web.

In the green shadow of the ancient poolside pecan tree, three men were starting a poker game—Chase, an emergency worker, and the sallow young man who fished the bridge near her house.

"You play?" Chase called when he caught sight of her.

"When I got cash."

"We're playing for change," Chase said. "I'll gift you your first five dollars. A reward for today's brilliant performance."

The smell of fried catfish wafted over the players as they dealt several hands. Evening deepened. Twice the young man left the table and came back sniffing and wide-eyed.

"Taking your vitamins?" Joan asked, the second time he returned.

"Yep."

"Got any extra?"

The boy remained standing as he motioned for Joan to follow him.

"Y'all freshen up the drinks." She winked at Chase and the other players. "I'll be right back."

She let the boy drape his arm around her as he held his clenched fist to her nostrils, a bump of sickly yellow powder balanced near the bottom knuckle of his thumb. She snorted twice, feeling fire spread through her sinuses and throat. "Meth?" she asked, sliding from beneath his arm.

"That's right, St. Joan," he said, his eyes straying to her breasts.

The meth held her for the remainder of the night, arresting the collapse of her new self, a self fed by Lydia's assurances and Chase's reporting, a self that flickered in the light of Tara's admiration.

Sometime near midnight, she followed Justin and Tara to the roof, watching as they fired off a pack of roman candles left over from the Fourth of July. She left the two of them up there, then stumbled through T-Rudy's in search of Lew, who she'd coaxed the sallow boy into admitting was his dealer. When she failed to find Lew, she carried a beer and a shot to her room and passed out watching infomercials.

The next day, around noon, she shuffled from her room, clutching the coffee milk that Tara left for her. The door to Lydia's room was open. Lydia was staring intently at her laptop, with Justin hovering above.

"Hey!" Joan called, her voice husky. "Did Tara go to school?"

Lydia and Justin looked up, faces bright with excitement. Lydia brought her palms together and drew a deep breath. "Half a million views, Joan," she said. "And counting."

19.

The SUV swerved, sending Joan crashing into Tara. Justin smacked the steering wheel and his eyes, pained and dark, appeared in the rearview mirror. Lydia, in the midst of a phone call, intensified her even tone while baring her teeth at him.

Tara leaned across her mother to stare at the flattened armadillo until it was engulfed by an eighteen-wheeler. "Too bad we can't stop," Joan said. "We could of had 'dillo fricassee. I know y'all eat that in Texas." Justin slumped lower until his brown curls disappeared behind the headrest.

"He died quick, Justin," Tara said.

On each side of the two-lane highway, acres of broken earth stretched to the horizon, ravaged by the recent soybean harvest. Overhead, the morning sky boiled orange and gray with an approaching thunderstorm.

They were driving to Leittville for the second community meeting with Mid-South and the Louisiana Department of Natural Resources. A larger venue was needed so the town's high school auditorium had been secured. The number of reporters at Rudy's had doubled in the two days since Joan and Billy's video had gone viral. Lydia was besieged with phone calls for statements and requests to interview Joan.

"Why didn't Mrs. Honoré ride with us?" Tara asked, when Lydia was off the phone.

"It's more appropriate for her to ride with her own counsel," Lydia replied, pursing her lips. "You getting enough air back there, Joan?"

"Yeah, if I was a package of ground round in the Piggly Wiggly meat department."

"Justin, manage the AC please," Lydia said.

"Global Petrol is down 13 percent at market open," Chase reported from the seat behind Joan and Tara where he was ensconced with his laptop. "Not an insignificant drop, and certainly not a coincidence."

"Who's Global Petrol?" Tara asked.

"The parent company of Mid-South. They've managed to elude the spotlight thus far, but if their precious shareholders are impacted, the great beast will no doubt awaken."

Lydia stroked her pearls as she twisted around to study Joan. She was wearing the navy suit she'd worn the first day they'd met on the steps of the CYO. Joan was begrudgingly wearing her own suit now, a dove-gray tailored jacket and slacks. She'd been tickled at first by the novelty, and by Tara's astonishment, but now she felt constricted by the stiff cloth and biting leather pumps.

"Can I help you?" Joan asked, when Lydia continued to stare without speaking.

"Sorry, I'm just considering our strategy for today. Your spontaneity has been a real asset, Joan, but today when the press approaches you, I'd like you to voice your sympathy for your fellow plaintiffs, then refer the reporters to me. And during the meeting itself, let's maintain a dignified silence."

"Silence? You mean you dressed me up like an undertaker just so I can keep my mouth shut? I have about a hundred messages I'm supposed to pass on from everybody and their cousin about how the hole messed 'em up." She arced her thumb at Tara. "She's got the list."

"It does seem foolhardy," Chase said, hooking his elbows over the seat, "to squander the momentum my reporting has built. The press doesn't care a whit for the rest of the class. They're hungry for Joan. I say feed them while they're snapping." He relaxed back, his gaze still on Lydia. "Saving the tastiest tidbits for *moi*, of course."

"We must maintain the momentum, yes, but with control," Lydia replied. "We're at a critical moment here. Mid-South hasn't officially claimed responsibility for the sinkhole, nor has the state pressured them to do so. They can't without tangible proof." She glanced at the eighteen-wheeler now passing dangerously close, black smoke streaking from its stack. "Plus, we didn't anticipate Global Petrol's active involvement. Once they step into the fray, it's a whole new ball game."

"You mean once they've been *pulled* into the fray…by Joan," Chase said.

"Exactly. And, Chase, it goes without saying that this is all off the record."

Chase nodded. "Should I assume you aren't interested in the three messages Harrison Cole left me this morning?"

"From GQ? You know him?"

"We stumbled out of the same graduate program. The magazine's doing some kind of environmental issue. He'd like to feature her on the cover." He pulled a thread from Joan's lapel. "And not in a suit."

"We'll consider it. Justin, contact Cole's assistant and set up a call." Lydia returned her gaze to the road ahead. "If we decide to move forward, we can script multiple versions of the interview so we're ready no matter how things play out."

They passed Walmart, then a used-car dealership, as they entered the town of Leittville. "Can we stop?" Tara asked, pointing to an approaching McDonald's. "We don't have one in Terrefine."

"Good idea," Joan said. "I'm getting my appetite back."

Justin wordlessly caught Lydia's eye. "Make it quick," she said, after checking the time.

They hurriedly ordered at the McDonald's drive-thru and were soon back on Leittville's main street, with the aroma of fast food permeating the car. But in that short time, traffic had ballooned. As they inched forward, a burst of pings sounded from Justin and Lydia's phones.

"Mid-South's going to announce an addition to their remediation plan," Lydia said, reading her messages. "We say nothing, neither support nor reject, until our people give us the real lowdown." She gave Joan her profile. "We on the same page?"

"Umm," Joan replied, her mouth full of fries. She crushed the McDonald's bag and dropped it on the floor between her pumps.

They reached the high school auditorium, a plain brick structure with a row of metal doors. "This is crazy," Justin said as he turned into the overflowing parking lot. At the entrance, a twenty-something man with a nose ring carried a sign and shouted something unintelligible. His lustrous beard flowed over the suspenders of his high-water pants. Behind him, a young woman with a mass of dreadlocks shot through with mirrored spangles waved her own sign above her head.

"They must have a hundred pounds of hair between the two of them," Joan said with a chuckle, elbowing Tara.

"They're here because of you, Mama." Tara pointed and read aloud, "'Justice for Joan. Occupy Terrefine.'"

Lydia craned her neck and tapped the windshield. "You'd better take us right up to the entrance." Justin nosed the SUV past a solemn group of men and women in army fatigues bearing a finely stenciled banner: *Joan Saint-Romain lost her home. Who's the next victim of eminent domain?*

"Whoa!" Justin slammed the brakes. A man on stilts wearing a Guy Fawkes mask collapsed on the hood. He raised a middle finger before righting himself and loping off. "What's his deal?"

"Anonymous," Chase replied. "The secretive network of hacktivists. Or someone pretending to be. Either way, everyone seems to be hitching their star to Joan's." He clacked away at his laptop, then aimed his cellphone at the passing crowd. "Left, right, and in between. You'd win the presidency in a sweep if you were to run today, my dear."

"Let's do it," Joan said, lighting up a cigarette.

Justin eased past a gathering of women in black habits and blue jeans. Joan recognized Sisters Clara and Martha, who'd offered their help on the steps of the CYO after the first community meeting. Their mint green T-shirts read *Catholics for Social and Environmental Justice* above an image of the globe.

As they neared the steps of the auditorium, Lydia shook her head.

"What?" Justin asked.

"You were supposed to time it so that we'd get here first." She pointed to a gaggle of reporters and photographers surrounding Mrs. Honoré and Ricky Delray.

"There's Lew," Tara said, as a flurry of white flashed behind Mrs. Honoré and disappeared into the auditorium. "And the Thevenots," she added, as the teacher and her husband ducked inside.

Sheriff Grady stood at the bottom of the steps, surveying the parking lot alongside the Leittville sheriff. Justin braked in front of him and Lydia lowered her window. "We could use some help getting Joan through this crowd."

"You betcha," Sheriff Grady replied, opening Joan's door and offering up his hand. Joan registered his double take as her tan leather pump touched the ground. She squeezed his fingers and smiled as he tried not to linger on her dove-gray contours. Cameras flashed and the reporters pressed toward Joan, abandoning Mrs. Honoré and Ricky Delray.

"Joan! Mid-South has hinted at a new plan. Will you support it? What can we expect from you in there?"

Lydia's arm encircled Joan's waist, nudging her forward. "We'll be happy to take a few questions after the meeting."

Joan lifted her chin and called past Lydia. "You can bet I'll be listening hard to every word," she said, "just in case they try something dirty." The reporters squirmed closer, pelting Joan with requests for specifics. Several asked if she'd be pressing charges against Billy Fontaine. But Lydia and Sheriff Grady managed to wrangle her toward the auditorium entrance. "I won't forget y'all!" Joan yelled over her shoulder before disappearing into the lobby.

Once inside, an officer approached her with a short metal wand. "I'm not driving," she protested, covering her mouth.

"Not a breathalyzer," the officer said, scanning the front of her body. "A metal detector."

"Apparently Mid-South has received death threats," Lydia said, lifting her arms as the officer turned to her.

Joan was ready with a crack about issuing her own threat but stopped herself when Lydia's entire face seemed to rise up in a sharp, silent rebuke.

Inside the auditorium, the residents of Terrefine swarmed the lower sections of the bleachers, calling to each other as they took their seats, their chattering echoing throughout the gym. In the middle of the basketball court, a handful of Mid-South and DNR representatives milled around a table and presentation screen. The few reporters who weren't stationed outside crouched on the floor nearby.

The upper reaches of the bleachers flashed with banners and signs. A band of green-shirted PETA activists hunkered beneath an enormous photo of Lightning bearing the epitaph, *Not-Forgotten—Ethical Treatment for the Displaced Animals of Terrefine.*

A small Greenpeace contingent stared open-mouthed from behind their drooping standard, stunned by their close proximity to local militia representatives whose signs decried the police state and the death of individual rights.

There was a regiment of fiery young women, fists in the air, vociferously equating Billy's attack on Joan with the patriarchy's aggression toward women and the environment. The most prominent sign, in huge neon-pink lettering, was displayed by a lone figure at the top of the bleachers. *Chem-Trails: Stop Geo-engineered Weather.*

When Joan appeared, the auditorium exploded with cheers along with a smattering of supportive shouts for Mid-South. She flashed a thumbs-up as Lydia and the sheriff guided her to the seats Justin had secured near the front.

"Where's Tara?" Justin asked, when they were seated and able to hear themselves again.

"She was behind me," Joan said. "Did you hear all the clapping? My lord."

People continued to stream in long after the bleachers were full. A pair of Leittville policemen directed them to sit on the floor, forming rows that started at half court. When the last row settled beneath the basketball hoop, admission to the meeting was closed.

"Testing, one two three." A voice boomed through the speakers. "Can everybody hear me?" A man in dark glasses with short, wooly hair raised a hand above his head. "I'm Ron Carville, Mid-South's new community liaison. Thanks to Eddy Ledroit for acting as temporary liaison. He's now Head of Emergency Ops. You'll hear from him later."

Joan perked up, scanning the floor until she spotted Eddy in dark jeans and a button-down shirt, striding toward the Mid-South reps at the front of the room.

"Should I find Tara?" Justin whispered.

"Whatever tickles your fancy," Joan murmured, trying to catch Eddy's eye. "But she's fine. She likes to go off on her own sometimes."

"We're here," Ron Carville continued, "to give you an update on the sinkhole, what we know and what we don't know, and our strategy for moving forward. But first I want to address the elephant in the room, the events that transpired between a Mid-South employee and Mrs. Joan Saint-Romain."

A chant erupted from the upper bleachers and quickly ignited the entire auditorium. "Justice for Joan! Justice for Joan!"

"Please!" Ron tightened his grip on the mike. "Your attention!" Failing to quell the thunderous voices, he drew closer to Joan. When he was directly in front of her, the room grew calm. "Mid-South has already spoken with Mrs. Saint-Romain through her counsel. But we want to take it a step further and issue a formal, public apology in front of the whole community." Ron widened his stance and swayed his hips, as if prepping for a golf swing. "Mrs. Saint-Romain, we deeply, deeply regret the missteps that led to the terrible encounter between you and Billy Fontaine. That is not who we are." He bowed his head and rested one hand on his chest before slowly returning his moist gaze to Joan. "We hope you'll accept our heartfelt apology so we can unite and move forward together, as partners."

Joan shifted away from the delicate force of Lydia's nails on her waist. All around her, she could feel the residents of Terrefine, and the gallery of activists above them, frozen with the intensity of their listening.

She glanced at Eddy. As their eyes met, it seemed to her that a secret flew between them, that his lips drew aside in a faint smirk, that he allowed his eyes to roll the tiniest bit at Ron Carville's teary speech.

"We thank you for accepting our apology, Mrs. Saint-Romain." Ron smiled, the corners of his mouth downturned. He cocked back his hands to applaud.

"I could care less about Billy Fontaine. His screw has always been loose. You wanna get right with me and everybody else here who's been put out by that hole?" Her raised voice echoed to the topmost bleachers. "Forget the flowery words and crocodile tears. Figure this thing out and get us back to our homes!"

Ron clutched the mike to his belly as he waited out another swell of cheers. "That's our plan," he said, when the noise had quieted. "I hope this meeting will give you some assurance of that."

As the meeting got underway, the crowd was presented with dozens of intricate graphs and charts. A geologist was introduced who droned on for a half an hour, his presentation laden with complex terminology. When a scuffle broke out between a Greenpeace activist and a Citizen-Survivalist, Joan was thankful for the stimulation. She marked the rest of the time with a steady stream of Nicorette and by admiring Eddy during his presentation on containment berms, how the soft set of his lips played against the sharpness of his jaw.

"Psst." Justin halted his note-taking and prodded Joan, pointing to the gym's upper deck where Tara had appeared with Eddy's oldest son, Gerard. They were joined a moment later by Louis.

"Get her," Lydia mouthed to Justin.

"What's the big deal?" Joan whispered as Justin departed. "She's probably bored to death." Lydia remained silent, a tiny spasm dancing in the corner of one eye.

An outraged voice rose from the bleachers above Joan. "You expect us to let you plant explosives on our property?" It was Lew, standing tall, one hand buried in the pocket of his overalls. "That's your brilliant new plan? I have livestock. And my house is still standing, for now. I want to keep it that way."

"The explosives are no larger than firecrackers," Ron said, taking the mike from the geologist. "We'll also be using air guns and other vibrating devices to generate the signals needed for the 3D seismic survey. It's Lew, right?" Ron continued. "Lew, this is a carefully controlled process. The explosives are small and perfectly calibrated. The resulting sound waves will give us an accurate picture of what's going on underground so we can determine the cause of the sinkhole."

"Don't you think," Sister Clara said, springing from her seat, "that you've disturbed the earth enough without sending, what did you say, 3,000 of these devices thumping through the ground?" She flung her arms wide and shrugged. "Over and over you've called this sinkhole unprecedented. How can you know this won't make things worse?"

"Friends, this sinkhole has grown to nine acres." Ron aimed a laser pointer at the projector screen. "We lost two full acres just yesterday. The tremors continue. We haven't ruled out the theory of a storage cavern collapse as the cause. We're dealing with a host of unknowns. Including whether other storage caverns in the salt dome could be affected. The largest of those caverns from top to bottom measures twice the height of the Empire State Building."

The first drops of the advancing thunderstorm bulleted the auditorium roof, forcing Ron to raise his voice. "Seismic imaging is the only way we can get ahead of this thing. Work with us on this, please. Let these contractors on your property so we can get you back in your homes."

"You keep talking about our homes." Mrs. Honoré's voice rumbled from across the gym floor, where she was seated next to Ricky Delray. She rose to her feet. "But I suspect it's Mid-South's desire to preserve its own investment, those caverns and their valuable contents, that's behind this survey, more than any good intention to get us back in our homes."

Mrs. Honoré gestured toward the projector screen, which now featured a slide depicting Terrefine's subsurface in cross section. A dozen cocoon-shaped renderings of the enormous underground storage caverns were displayed, each with a thin strand protruding from its top, scattered across the flank of the salt dome. At the top of the slide, sitting on the ground surface above the salt dome, were tiny squares representing Terrefine's homes and businesses.

"And maybe that's not a bad thing," Mrs. Honoré continued. "At least you've got some real skin in the game. I've no desire to prolong what's becoming a media circus for the rest of the country. I'm going to let them on to my land. I suggest you all do the same." The auditorium was quiet as Mrs. Honoré swept her gaze across the crowd, making sure to take in every section.

Joan narrowed her eyes at Mrs. Honoré. She was something else. Swaying in the bleachers, like Moses himself come down the mountain, pronouncing the truth for one and all. Her truth, her way, her knowing what was best for everybody else. Even Eddy, hands resting on his leather belt, was nodding his agreement as he stared up at Mrs. Honoré.

And that sucker punch she threw, calling all the press attention Joan had drummed up for Terrefine a circus. Did Mrs. Honoré think she was too dumb to pick up on that? Joan clutched her temples as a crown of rage encircled her skull.

Ned Elder, the representative for the Louisiana DNR spoke up for the first time. "For the record, the state fully supports this plan and will be monitoring the activity. We urge you all to cooperate with Mid-South on this. Two months from now we'll have a near-perfect picture of what's happening down there."

"Two months!" Joan cried as she leapt to her feet. "That's too long. We need better!"

The short-lived calm dissolved into a pulsing repetition of "We need better! We need better!" Joan watched with satisfaction as Mrs. Honoré tried repeatedly to silence the chanting with her raised hand.

Joan raised her own hand, and quiet was restored. "Like I said, we need better."

Mrs. Honoré rushed to speak. "It doesn't matter. If we don't sign off, the state eventually pulls eminent domain. All we accomplish is prolonging this mess. That's just a fact."

"Let's see 'em pull eminent domain while I'm sitting on my front porch with a shotgun!" Lew growled.

Everyone began speaking out of turn, including the meeting's presenters. In the ensuing chaos, the bleachers emptied, with people cursing and casting angry looks at Ron Carville, the geologist, and Ned Elder as they left. Chase trailed after the agitated crowd while dictating into a small recorder.

Lydia dialed Justin as she spotted him descending the bleachers with Tara. "Bring the car to the side exit." She guided Joan beneath the stands, skirting the knot of reporters who'd crowded around the meeting organizers.

"Wait! I told 'em I'd be back," Joan protested as they neared the side exit. "They wanted to hear from me."

"They'll follow us to Rudy's," Lydia replied. "And we'll know what we want to say by then."

"I already know what I want to say."

Reporters and protestors teemed around the side exit as well. When Joan tried to field their questions through the hissing downpour, Lydia draped her jacket over Joan's head, as if trying to shield her from the rain.

Justin braked the SUV at the auditorium's side entrance. Lydia balked, noticing Tara in the front seat, then tumbled into the back with Joan in tow. "Go!" she barked, then slammed and locked the door on the phalanx of reporters closing in.

"What about Chase?" Justin asked as he pulled away, edging through the sheets of rain, past fleeing vehicles and protestors in search of cover.

"Forget him. He'll find a ride," Lydia said, then scooped her vibrating cellphone from her blazer pocket. "Lydia Desaurus." As she listened to the caller, an icy calm forced its way across her features. After several minutes she spoke, her clipped monotone even more controlled than usual. "We'd be open to a preliminary meeting to hear your terms. Tuesday should be fine, but I'll need to confirm. Is this a good number to call back? One sec."

Lydia hissed at Justin for pen and paper, and after a brief scramble and a near collision, he fumbled the items to the backseat. She scribbled the number and hung up.

Joan scanned Lydia's face and chuckled. "Either someone died or you won the lotto."

Lydia balanced the paper on her knee while programming the phone number into her cell. "That was GP," she said, tapping the screen. "Calling with an offer."

"Don't you mean GQ? That magazine that wants me on the cover?" Joan asked.

"I think she means Global Petrol, Mama," Tara said. "The parent company." She glanced at Justin who nodded.

"They want to settle the lawsuit this early on?" Justin asked.

"Not exactly," Lydia replied. "This offer is specific to Joan."

"Now we're talking. The big mama wants to meet with me." Joan jerked forward and tugged off her suit jacket. "I ain't wearing this monkey suit to the meeting, though. I'll tell you that right now."

"You won't have to," Lydia responded with a terse smile. "We won't need you at this initial meeting."

"Won't need me? Seems like I'm the only one you really do need. You said the offer was specific to me."

"That doesn't mean it's appropriate. Or ethical. It's my job to make that determination. And, to be frank, this is a whole different level of negotiation, requiring my full expertise and that of the firm's. Your presence would be counterproductive." Lydia's nostrils flared delicately as she crushed the phone number in her fist and turned to stare through the foggy window.

As Joan studied the back of Lydia's head, with its perfect French twist, her throat filled with molten rage. It was not until Justin turned into the parking lot of Rudy's Hotel-Motel that a coherent thought broke through her all-consuming fury. Lydia must be cut down.

20.

Bright fog drifted along the narrow road in front of Rudy's Hotel-Motel, invading the surrounding woods and shrouding the world in mist. A bird cry pierced the predawn stillness, echoing from all directions at once.

Joan and Tara stood alone in the road in front of Rudy's, hands resting on the lifeless little white truck they'd silently pushed from the parking lot, fearful that the clattering muffler might awaken someone. Joan was escaping—from Lydia, from the reporters, and from the latest wave of activists who'd flocked here after yesterday's turbulent community meeting.

The truck had lodged in a pothole. Joan eyed Tara, a finger to her lips, then gripped the tailgate. She threw her weight forward repeatedly, until the tire popped out. The truck lurched forward, almost nicking a school bus of sleeping activists parked across the road. A ragged snore escaped from the bus's second story, the cannibalized body of a 1970s VW van which had been welded to the roof.

Tara glanced back at her mother and mimed turning the keys in the ignition. *Now?* she mouthed. Joan shook her head and waved Tara forward, before again gripping the tailgate and heaving the truck into motion.

As they rolled the truck away from Rudy's, a train of RVs and news vans emerged from the fog, haphazardly parked along the rain-swollen ditch that bordered the road. Further on, the woods fell away and a ring of tents appeared around the remains of a campfire.

"Drive!" Joan hissed, when the tents were behind them. She gave the truck one last shove and then darted to the passenger side. Tara hopped into the truck and slammed the door. She turned the keys and revved the engine. "Anybody behind?" she asked, checking the rearview mirror.

"Nope," Joan said, twisting in her seat to gaze at the road. "We're good, but don't use the headlights. And head for town." She lit a cigarette and exhaled deeply as a slash of pink appeared at the edge of the sky.

"Where are we going?" Tara rubbed her eyes and yawned. Joan had given her minutes to dress before hustling her out to the parking lot. "Wherever it is, we gotta stop for gas. We're on empty."

"To meet with Global Petrol."

Tara froze mid-yawn. "Lydia said the meeting was Tuesday."

"It was. Until I changed it. Global Petrol wants to meet with me. Not Lydia. And last night she got on my last nerve."

"You can't go without Lydia, Mama!" Tara slammed the brakes and faced her mother. "Justin spent half the night explaining what a big deal Global Petrol is. He says they crush people like bugs. They own a hundred companies just like Mid-South all over the world."

"I ain't no fucking bug. And unless you want me to drive, you better get this truck moving."

Tara exhaled sharply. "I don't like it," she said as the truck regained speed.

Joan fumed. "Lydia has been acting like a boil on my butt." She plucked a tobacco shred from her tongue. "Last night, she wouldn't pay for my drinks unless I took 'em in my room. She's jumping all over everything I say to the reporters, cutting me off, twisting my words."

The final straw was when she'd followed Lydia from the lounge back to her room, insisting that she wanted to meet with GP alone. No lawyers. Lydia, cool as a cucumber, had replied, "Let's discuss it when you're sober," before shutting the door in Joan's face.

Joan leaned back into the truck's worn vinyl and glanced at Tara. "And muscling me outta some big important meeting that never would have happened without me in the first place? That shit's ending. I got my own plan."

The plan had been revealed to her in the late evening, inspired by the crystal meth the sallow boy had slipped beneath her door. It had initially presented itself as a harsh truth, one that Joan would never admit to another soul—Mrs. Honoré was right. This was all a circus. And she, Joan Saint-Romain, was the circus animal, trotting and tricking and shitting whenever Lydia snapped her fingers. Or Chase, or even Justin. The people of Terrefine, too. They had her jumping, calling her at all hours with their messages and requests. She may as well still be living under her daddy's fist or the old man's boot.

"So what is it?" Tara asked. "Your plan?"

"You heard what Chase said in the car yesterday? About me being president?"

Tara again slammed on the brakes. "Mama! He wasn't serious!"

Her daughter's eyes flashed sea green in the breaking daylight.

"Damn it, Tara. You're gonna give us both whiplash." Joan gestured to the road ahead. "Go! I'm not gonna tell you again."

As they accelerated, Joan addressed her daughter's sullen profile. "Chase's point, little miss, was that everybody would vote for me. Maybe not for president—yet." She waggled her brows at her daughter. "But I have their attention and their respect. And that includes bug-squashin' Global Petrol."

As Joan spoke, her mind felt clear and lively, like the silver pools of rain water flashing past and the woods writhing with escaping light and fog. She'd never felt friendly toward the future, but now it unspooled before her, bright and beckoning.

Tara slowed at a stop sign. "You just called up Global Petrol and said you wanted to meet sooner? Just like that?"

"Just like that." Joan leaned through the open window and spit into a puddle.

After a thoughtful silence, Tara pointed to the roadside sign of an approaching gas station. The plastic lettering read *We got your back, Joan!* "You could run for Mayor of Terrefine. That's realistic."

"You mean it?" Joan lowered her lashes, scrutinizing her daughter as they pulled into the station behind a mud-covered pickup truck with a small tractor in tow.

"You couldn't do worse than what's-his-face."

"I'll take that." Joan grinned, then ran her tongue across her inflamed lips. She threw open the truck door. "You got any cash, hon?"

"Four bucks. That's it." Tara handed over the bills.

"Two will get us where we're going. That leaves two for the lottery. I'm feeling lucky." She winked and slammed the door on Tara's protest.

After they'd gassed up, Tara steered them back on the highway, and Joan watched the roadside message of support for her recede in the side-view mirror. "You're right. I couldn't do worse than a lot of these so-called educated people." She grunted softly. "Lydia acts so tough, but I'll bet she never had to work for a damn thing. And Justin! That boy missed the boat on common sense." A pulse of jawbone appeared in the smooth plane of Tara's cheek. "Oh, come on, baby. He's sweet as pie, but you know what I mean. How many squirrels has he run over?"

"Two. That's just bad luck."

"And that armadillo yesterday? He could of missed that one."

"Lydia makes him nervous."

"True. But he seems jumpy by nature. Good thing he's got you looking out for him in these rough parts." Joan leaned over to pinch Tara's cheek, dropping a long ash on the seat between them.

"Quit it!" Tara shrugged Joan off.

Joan shifted her gaze from her daughter to the windshield and the delicate, gold-tinged clouds above. "So we're on the same team? You trust me to handle the big britches at Global Petrol?"

"Just answer one question." Tara gripped the steering wheel and stole a glance at her mother. "The truth." Joan nodded. "Are you high?"

Joan's heart walloped against her ribcage. Quickly the necessary lie blossomed, even as a fierce love for her daughter took hold. The girl had a keen gut, and more courage than all the men in Terrefine roped together.

"I'm as sober as Sister Clara," Joan said. "I've never been so clear-headed in my life."

Tara's rigid posture softened. "I'm sorry, Mama. I had to make sure."

"I know. I've given you reason. But today ain't one of them days, baby. I promise."

A raw, tender silence hung between them until the Terrefine city limits sign appeared. "The meeting's in the evacuation zone?" Tara asked.

"Nope. We're not going into town. Go right. On the bridge."

As Tara sped across the bridge, Eddy Ledroit's house came into view. In the front yard, a helicopter sparkled in the morning sun.

"Mama, you can't be seen with him." But Tara's gaze remained riveted on the helicopter as she turned into Eddy's drive.

"Why? He's just another one of Mid-South's hired hands. Getting us to our destination."

"We're flying?"

"Yes, ma'am." Joan winked at her daughter, then turned her gaze to Eddy who'd stepped from behind the helicopter. His usual jeans were replaced by dark slacks and a dress shirt. She took in his trim waist and sturdy thighs, and the cut of his chest beneath his navy tie. She braced for the usual surge of desire but, instead, encountered a flat void inside herself. Her hand flew to her jeans, palpating the coin pocket as she reassured herself that she had the remainder of the meth.

"Morning," Eddy called, when he reached the truck.

"Morning!" She slipped on the new pumps, having decided the extra height was worth the chaffing, and rose from the truck to stand an inch above Eddy. She slid her fingers into her back pockets and performed a languorous stretch.

"You sure clean up nice," she said, slamming the truck door behind her. "Mind if I pee before we leave?"

"Be my guest."

When she returned from the house, her mind and spirit freshly sharpened, Eddy was strapping Tara into the front seat of the helicopter.

"Sorry, hon. I'm riding up front this time."

"What about your fear of flying?" Eddy asked as Tara retreated to the rear of the helicopter.

"I think you got me cured," she murmured. As he buckled her in, she snatched a tube of Chapstick peeking from his pant's pocket and smoothed it along her lips.

"My entire career," he began in a soft voice as he gave her seatbelt a final tug, "I've never spoken one word to an exec at Global Petrol, much less one so high up the food chain." He stepped back, rubbing his clean-shaven chin, his eyes wide and bewildered. He leaned against the helicopter door. "It's not my business. But are you sure you don't want some kind of legal advocate to go along?"

"You're right." Joan grabbed a headset from the dashboard and fitted it over the bright fuzz of her scalp. "Not your business." She studied his face for a moment, enjoying their reversal of roles—her, the decision-maker, and him, clueless as a baby. She grinned and reached for the door handle. "We probably better get a move on, huh?"

Eddy powered up the helicopter and spoke into the radio. "GP base, Eddy Ledroit reporting in at 06:12 hours. We are ready for take-off, please provide destination coordinates."

"Roger, Eddy," replied the staticky voice. "Head east to New Orleans. Report in when you are ten minutes from downtown and we'll provide final coordinates."

As they took flight, Joan marveled at the blue splendor of the morning, which seemed to perfectly mirror the glow she felt inside. "Goddamn it's a beautiful day. Especially up here. I bet you forget how nice it is 'cause you do it all the time."

"I sure haven't noticed it lately," he responded. "My every waking thought is focused down there these days." He nodded toward the sinkhole which had appeared below them. It had quadrupled in size, devouring the road in front of her house and several feet of the yard. The helicopter was high enough that the ragged edges of the hole seemed smooth, leaving the impression of a small, placid lake. The sunlight glinted on the water and the oily surface cast a rainbow sheen. If it weren't for the assemblage of large machines at the far end, and the bright orange containment floats on the water, someone might mistake her home for lakefront property.

"We'll be able to row a boat right off the front porch soon, Tara." When her daughter remained quiet, Joan glanced back to find her staring at the earth, her lips a thin line. "You sad?"

Tara shot a look at the back of Eddy's head. "I'm pissed. It's not fair. Stuff like this never happens to rich people."

"I hear you," Joan said. "It's the smelliest kind of horseshit."

Joan did not give voice to the part of her that, at this moment, was celebrating the collapse, urging the hole to grow, to consume the yard, the house, the furniture and with it every dark corner of the past. She closed her eyes, overcome by the sense of liberation, the weightlessness of it. Let all that sadness, the shards of her broken life, sink into darkness to be buried in salt and mud for all eternity.

When she opened her eyes, the hole was gone. They'd gained altitude and the world spread out below her in a tapestry of rivers, forests, and fields. She glanced at Eddy and felt the lushness of him. She yearned to touch him, to taste his skin, to grip his body with hers. But she also read the burden of these days on his face, worn and weary despite the fresh shave.

"Hey," she said. "We'll have a good laugh about this in a few years."

His eyebrows shot up. "I'll probably be dead by then. I think I've aged twenty years in the past few weeks."

"What about your boys? I saw them at the meeting yesterday."

"Louis is hanging in there. Gerard has become intolerable. We can barely be in the same room together."

"Sounds like normal teenager stuff."

"No." He squinted at his control panel before meeting her gaze. "It's you. He drank the Joan Saint-Romain Kool-Aid. Got a T-shirt with your face on it. Now Mid-South is the devil, and, by extension, me. He's holding me single-handedly responsible for climate change, economic inequality, and corporate greed. I feel like I'm living with my archenemy. Only good thing that's come out of it is that he reads the news now. Before, all he used the computer for was games."

"You should see Tara." Joan nodded toward the back. "Going on about social media and all my views and likes and tweets. She went from zero to a hundred with all that. Now she's the one giving the lawyers ideas about where to post my videos instead of the other way round."

"Mama." Tara's voice cut in. "That's not his business."

"Relax. We're just two parents shooting the shit about our pain-in-the-ass kids." Joan popped a Nicorette into her mouth, then placed a cigarette between her lips. "Don't worry," she said, addressing Eddy. "I won't light it."

The helicopter followed the path of the Mississippi, massive, muddy, and serpentine. The few houses and buildings that dotted the banks became denser communities interspersed with the white silos and smokestacks of industry.

"Eddy Ledroit to GP base." Eddy tapped the mouthpiece to his lips. "We're approximately ten minutes from downtown New Orleans. Awaiting final coordinates. Over."

"Roger, Eddy. Touch down at latitude twenty-nine point five four eight five nine north, longitude ninety point zero four six four six west."

"Copy that."

Eddy guided the helicopter over slow-moving tankers and tugboats, past long lines of barges laden with rust-colored shipping containers anchored along each side of the river. An immaculate white riverboat with a ruby-red paddlewheel bobbed in the wake of a towering cruise ship.

As the helicopter descended, Eddy frowned and spoke again into the headset. "GP base, your coordinates appear to be over the river. Please correct. Over."

"Roger, Eddy. Confirming coordinates latitude. Twenty-nine point five four eight five nine north, longitude ninety point zero four six four six west."

"What the hell?" Eddy hovered above a three-story passenger boat far from shore. "Unless you want me to land on top of a yacht, I suggest you revise your coordinates."

"Roger. We see you." Two figures in bright orange vests appeared on the yacht's top deck which bore the painted circle of a helipad. "You are clear to land."

Eddy cursed, then lowered the helicopter gently onto the deck. As he powered down, Joan watched him struggle to contain his fury.

"What's the matter?" she asked as the two orange-vested attendants approached.

"I've never done that before. They didn't even bother to ask."

Joan's door swung open. "Stay low," cautioned one of the attendants.

They ducked from beneath the helicopter blades and were ushered into an enormous room lined with windows. A fountain stood in the center, its water cascading over a sculpture of cut stone. Low couches bordered glass coffee tables laden with fresh berries, cream, and French pastries. Joan looked away from the smoked meats and fish, feeling vaguely nauseous.

A tall man in a crisp white jacket approached with a silver coffee pot. "Cafe for madame?"

"I'll have an OJ," Joan replied, deciding against a screwdriver for the moment. She strode toward an elaborately carved, high-backed chair with a gold embroidered cushion and matching footrest.

"Mama!" Tara's insistent whisper followed Joan as she plunked down and stroked the scrolled arms of the chair.

"What, hon?" Joan asked.

Tara hurried over, her flip-flops thwacking on the polished wood. "Right shoe," she hissed.

Joan swung her foot to the opposite thigh and examined it. A bloody glaze covered the tan leather at the back of her pump, fed by a deep, oozing blister on her heel. "Huh. I must've done that last night. Didn't even feel it." She licked her thumb and rubbed the shoe clean.

A door at the far end of the room opened, and a tiny woman in a dark dress and low-heeled shoes entered.

"Bonjour," she said as she approached. "You must be Joan Saint-Romain." She smiled, speaking carefully through her French accent. "You have eaten some breakfast?"

"Sure have," Joan said, thrusting her juice in the air. "You the head guy's mama? I brought family, too. My daughter."

The woman accepted a bone-china coffee cup from the tall man, then extended her empty hand to Joan. "I am Sophie Alaoui. Chairman of Global Petrol. The head guy. *Enchanté.*"

For a moment Joan held the woman's gaze, noting the mum-colored scarf at her neck. Then she threw back her head and laughed.

21.

Joan rose from the gold-cushioned chair and shook the hand of the small sharp-featured woman with the silver helmet of hair.

"You were expecting someone different. You would not be the first," Sophie Alaoui said, her lips drawing into a bemused smile. "And this is your daughter?"

Joan felt Tara's gaze boring into the back of her skull. "Tell the lady hi, hon," she said, turning from Sophie to Tara.

"Hi," Tara said. "Mama, I need to talk to you."

"Looks like you are, darlin'."

"I mean alone. It's about what I asked you in the truck."

"We'll talk later, baby," Joan replied, widening her eyes at her daughter. What did it matter now if Tara thought she was high? They were here, with the most important person at Global Petrol. Game time. Tara was going to have to cool her jets. "Besides, we got a meeting to attend. Right, Sophie?"

"It is true. You will perhaps be bored, Tara. Would you prefer to stay here with Ben? My grandnieces and grandnephews find him quite entertaining."

Tara narrowed her eyes at the man, who watched her from beneath raised ebony brows. The curl of his smile deepened. "No, thanks," she replied.

"Before we meet," Sophie said, "I must ask for one final confirmation that we are both in agreement to meet without our lawyers present."

"Lord, yes," Joan said.

"*Bon.*" Sophie directed a burst of lively, unintelligible words to Ben then ushered Joan and Tara to a heavy double door of dark oak.

Joan cracked her knuckles as she strode into the room, pumping herself up for a face off with a table of stern-faced Global Petrol executives. Instead, she stepped onto an oriental carpet in a room lined with tapestries and artwork. Leather-bound books stretched floor to ceiling on the opposite wall, a few feet from another smaller door. There was no one else around.

Tara moved toward the books, examining the strange characters embossed on the spines. She started as Sophie's wizened hand reached past her and brushed across several volumes. "Farsi. Persian. It is a beautiful language," Sophie said. "French *aussi*. But I am perhaps too fond of the languages of my parents."

"We got Cajun French in Terrefine," Joan called as she collapsed onto a silk-brocade couch. "But mostly old folks use it." She whipped the lid off a porcelain vase with delicate tracings of gold leaf and peered inside.

Ben entered and made his way toward an ornate copper urn with a silver-spouted teapot resting on top. He carried the teapot and three small glasses to the low table in front of Joan and Tara and poured the steaming brew. Joan guffawed as he performed a dramatic dip of the teapot high above each glass.

"Mama," Tara protested, in a low voice.

But Ben seemed to appreciate Joan's reaction, adding flourish to each successive pour. "I'll be damned," she remarked when he was done.

"*Merci*," Sophie called as Ben pulled the door closed, sealing them in the room's protective quiet.

"You will be offended if I smoke?" Sophie asked, opening a small rosewood box and extracting a tuft of tobacco.

Joan brandished her Winstons. "Not if I can join you."

"*Bien sur.*" Sophie's sing-song voice curled around them as she sprinkled tobacco onto a creased paper. "But you should try one of mine. You will not encounter a finer tobacco in the world, I assure you."

"Thanks, but no thanks. These get me where I wanna go just fine. And they're the best bang for your buck." Joan fired up a Winston then took an extra-long drag to prove her point.

"And your transportation here. It was satisfactory?" Sophie tucked the expertly rolled cylinder between her lips, then relaxed into the couch. She seemed in no hurry, her yellow-flecked eyes drifting to the ivory lighter, carved in the shape of a dragon, hovering at her cigarette tip. They could have been fishing the bayou for bass on a Sunday afternoon.

Fine then. Joan could play the waiting game, too, and no way was she going to let a hundred-year-old granny beat her at it. She draped her arm across the back of the couch. "Eddy Ledroit did real good. Y'all need to give him a raise. And flying," Joan shrugged. "Tara's the one likes to fly. Personally, you give me a truck and a full tank o' gas and I'll drive all day, with a smile on my face. My longest drive in one shot was—"

"You got something to tell us, Mrs. Alaoui?" Tara blurted.

Joan froze, her arms in mid-gesture. Her eyes swung skyward, momentarily vacant. "Dammit, Tara." She let her arms fall. "I lost my train of thought. Thanks a lot."

"Enough of the small talk, eh?" Sophie chuckled, her gnarled fingers delicately stirring the air with her cigarette. "You are a good American, Tara. Okay. *On va commencer.*"

"Where's the rest of the honchos?" Joan asked, glancing around as if someone might emerge from behind a tapestry.

"There is no need for anyone else, Mrs. Saint-Romain. Though many of our officers would have gladly joined. Especially of the male persuasion." She waited for Joan's pleased grin, then plucked a small bell from the end table and rang it vigorously. "I am vested by Global Petrol with the power to make you a non-negotiable offer."

Joan's smile faded. She rubbed her nose and sniffed. "What if I don't like it?"

"Oh, I think you will like it. Very much," Sophie replied as Ben entered, bearing a stack of two dozen newspapers. He gingerly shifted the glasses aside and placed the papers on the table as Sophie continued. "If you were able to read five languages, you would see the reaction of the world financial experts to our declining stock price on the U.S. exchanges, triggered by the negative publicity from Mid-South. From you." The creases of her lids lengthened as she smiled at Joan. "Everyone is watching to see if other global exchanges will be affected as well. Some are betting on it."

Sophie's bony middle finger drummed the headline of one of the papers. "But this isn't what concerns me. Investors will forget, next month or next year. The stock price will rebound on its own."

Smoke trailed from her nostrils. "Instantaneous information, then instantaneous forgetting. More relevant are the coming state and local elections and the ability of popular outrage to influence the politicians. They, in turn, can interfere with our current and developing projects along the Gulf. This can have long-term effects on our strategy, our resource deployment, ultimately the continued growth of Global Petrol. You understand?"

"I understand interference," Joan said. "How about having your home and your whole life interfered with?"

Smoke spilled over Sophie bottom lip as she nodded. "I believe I have a way for you to benefit from our *interference* and for us to benefit from your popularity."

"How?" Joan asked. "Want me to take over your job?"

"Ha!" Sophie slapped her thigh. "Perhaps that is where this will all end. But for now, we'd like to draw upon your vitality to shore up our public image across the board. We have had other incidents in the past decade that have damaged our credibility. Fueling the world is a messy business." She turned her gaze to Tara. "Perhaps when you are my age, the full truth of what we have done to power the earth will be known." Sophie shook open a newspaper and grimaced. "I hate the computer. You will have to endure my old-fashioned journals."

"I hate it too," Joan said. "Gives me a headache staring at all those screens, especially the little ones."

"Yes, you have the migraines."

Joan gave Sophie a puzzled look. "How do you know about that?"

"We did a little background research. Our people have the ability to find out many things." Sophie mashed her cigarette in a heavy green glass ashtray. "Those things that are on record, that is. So, you have a prescription, we know about it. You get a speeding ticket, we know about it. You make a near-perfect score on the state school exam, we know about it." She let her gaze linger on Tara.

"Not me," Joan said. "I got better ways to spend my time."

"Your daughter."

"That's right. That's right," Joan said hurriedly to hide her confusion. Had Tara taken some test that she was supposed to know about? She tried to catch Tara's eye, but her daughter's gaze was on the carpet, tracing the profusion of mysterious flowers and vines.

"It's good to have such a powerful friend, no?" Sophie continued. "A friend who wishes to pay you a lot of money in return for a simple request."

"How much?" Joan propped her elbows on her thighs and leaned forward.

"Five million U.S. dollars." Sophie brought her glass to her lips, eyeing Joan over the rim.

Joan felt the impulse to pelt Sophie with a hundred and one questions about when, where, and how she would get her hands on that money. She was tempted, also, to jump up and dance, to whoop and holler and shower Sophie with thanks. But something in the old woman's look stopped her, something smug and knowing, as if she had Joan all figured out before she even set foot on the boat. As if her answer was a foregone conclusion.

Joan summoned her maximum poker face, which involved deadening her eyes and freezing her mouth in a half-smirk, a challenge since for the past several minutes she'd been fighting the urge to grind her teeth. She stroked the small lump in her coin pocket.

"Five million," Joan said, tuning her voice to match her muted look. "That about how much the president gets paid?"

"It is more. Enough to enable Tara to have a good education, for you to buy or build a new home, to go on holiday every year. If you are wise, you may never need to work again."

"You gonna run all this through Lydia?"

"If you'd like us to. But consider this—if you work directly with us, you can avoid giving Lydia and her firm almost half of the money in legal fees. At this stage, it's still possible to opt out of the lawsuit. If you wish, we will present you with a letter of notification for you to sign and send to your attorneys."

"What does she have to do?" Tara asked, wavelets appearing on her brow. "For the money?"

"Enter into a lifelong friendship with Global Petrol," Sophie answered. "Your mother will join us for a brief press conference tomorrow afternoon in Houston where she will read a prepared statement describing her change of heart toward Global Petrol and Mid-South. There is no need to publicly divulge all the details of what we've discussed here today. However, your mother will make clear her new understanding of GP's good intent toward the many small communities with whom we come into contact across the globe. She will urge those who have agitated on her behalf to stand down and declare her support of Mid-South's crisis response efforts, the full scope of which she had been unaware of until recently. Finally, after a little training, she will star in a series of advertisements for Global Petrol, applauding our environmental and social initiatives." Sophie pursed her worn lips as she gazed at Joan. "Your mother's beauty and charisma will be appreciated all over this country, perhaps all over the world."

As Joan imagined some fur-clad family on the other side of the globe, crouched in their icehouse, watching her on TV, the whole room wobbled. Tara's hand shot out and clutched the edge of the couch.

"The helicopter." Sophie patted Tara's arm. "We sent it away."

"You see that," Joan said. "She's still jumpy from the hole. Probably will be like that all her life."

Tara glowered at her mother, then asked Sophie, "Why'd you send Eddy away?"

"He is no longer needed. We have you booked in the penthouse at a hotel in the French Quarter tonight. We will send your mother some papers there and tomorrow morning we will fly together to Houston. Your first jet airplane ride, *oui?*"

"Wham, bam, thank you, ma'am." Joan shot up from the couch and rounded the coffee table to loom over Sophie. "You're mighty sure of yourself there, Mrs. A."

"You are not pleased?" Sophie asked, her eyes mild.

"I don't know. I'm gonna to take five in the bathroom. Decide whether or not to trust you."

"There is no need to trust me. In fact, it is ill-advised. Trust the cashier's check I will put before you after the press conference."

Joan strode toward the double door, and Tara leapt up to follow.

"Other way," Sophie said. "There." She gestured to the small wooden door, next to the bookcase.

"You stay, Tara. Keep an eye on this one." She winked at Sophie, who responded with a dry laugh. Tara frowned and returned to the couch, her cheeks flushing.

Locked in the bathroom, Joan bypassed the toilet and dropped to a plush divan, adjacent to the marble sink. As she tore the plastic baggie of meth from her pocket, a square of paper popped out and floated to the floor. She snatched it up and rolled it into a make-shift straw. As she laid out two thin lines of powder, the smell of Sophie's heavily perfumed tobacco drifted into the bathroom, as did her voice.

"I have a grandniece your age, but she is a dummy," Sophie droned. "Her head taken up with boys and clothes. Her face in the cellphone all the time. Soft. Lacking curiosity. But you are *très intelligente. Très forte.*"

Joan flushed the toilet, then quickly snorted the meth, while the water rushed noisily down the bowl. As a bright buoyancy crept across her blood-brain barrier, she fell back into the divan's velvet. The five million flickered enticingly through her mind, followed by a thousand permutations of Sophie's hawkish face. There was no way in hell that old bird was doing them any favors.

Yet, aside from bridling against the old woman's thinly veiled arrogance, Joan couldn't think of a reason not to race back in there right now and accept the offer, before Sophie changed her mind. Lydia would crap her pants when she heard how Joan, with her tenth-grade education, had walked away with five million, all on her own.

And Mrs. Honoré. Well. This might shut her up for good.

"What do you think your mother should do, Tara?" Sophie's murmur intruded on Joan's thoughts. She leaned forward, straining to hear her daughter's answer.

But Tara dodged Sophie by lobbing a question of her own. "What did you mean earlier, about me knowing the full truth of what you've done to power the earth? When I'm old like you?"

"I said *we*, meaning the human race. The internal combustion engine has altered the world in ways we could never have imagined. Now we can imagine, but it is too late. Our sin is that we've known for a long time. So you should enjoy your money. Take a lover. Exhaust the pleasures that remain. There is a freedom in it, *non*? Just be able to quit this life when you are ready."

Freedom is right, Joan thought as she stood at the wide marble sink and ran her pinky along each nostril, catching stray crumbs of meth. She was done living by everybody else's rules.

"Is that how you live?" Tara's muffled voice reached Joan as she examined an array of soaps, lotions, and cosmetics neatly displayed on the bathroom counter. "No offense, but that's kinda sad. And kinda conceited."

Joan broke the seal on a lipstick and unfurled a creamy coral, wiping away Eddy's Chapstick and smoothing color on her lips. She touched the high bones of her cheeks and flashed herself a dazzling grin. "You're rich, bitch," she whispered. She turned to exit the bathroom, ready to agree to Sophie's terms, when her eyes landed on the rolled-up paper she'd used to snort the meth.

"There could be something that you don't know," Tara continued. "Something that will make things right. Even with all your power to find things out, you can't know it all. That would make you God."

You tell her baby, Joan thought as she peeled open the square of paper. It was the lottery ticket she'd purchased at the gas station, boasting an estimated jackpot of ten million dollars, twice the amount of Sophie's offer.

"Don't tell me you believe in God?" Sophie's scorn was apparent, even through the bathroom door. "I thought you were a smart girl."

As Joan studied the ticket, she heard the whiskey-singed voice of an old drunk, a gambler. The last time she'd cocktailed at the casino, he'd tottered after her all night, spouting his philosophy on winning: *When the angel on your shoulder says it's time to cash in, it's a sure sign to goddamn double down.* At the time, his words had struck her as half-senile mutterings, but now, with her mind alight and her heart a warm drum, beating out a joyous rhythm for her quickening thoughts, the memory of his words took on a staggering significance.

"I don't know if I do believe in God." Tara's voice rose as Joan spun from the mirror. "But I'm not going to run around saying there isn't one. How could I ever be one hundred percent sure?"

Joan burst into the room, slamming the door into the wall. Ben rushed in, looking startled. He crossed over to the wall near the bookcase and examined the fresh indentation in the cream-colored paint.

"Sorry 'bout that," Joan said. "But I got my answer."

"*Tout va bien*," Sophie said, waving Ben away. "What do you say, Joan?"

Joan planted herself on the rug, inside a concentric pattern of flowered vines. "I thought about it, everything me and Tara have gone through and what our home and our lives are worth. All of it. I came up with ten million and not a cent less. Otherwise you can hire that talking lizard to do your commercials."

Smoke snaked along the deep creases that lined Sophie's mouth. "Ben?" she called, her gaze fixed on Joan. "What do you think?"

"Oh, that's not for me to say," Ben replied, with a melodic growl. "It is a lot of money, but of course we hope for Mrs. Saint-Romain and her daughter to be happy."

"Your daughter." Sophie tilted her head back and tugged at her earring, a knot of gold. "I will agree, if you allocate half to a trust, a kind of safe-keeping account, for her and her alone."

"You'll write the check for her tomorrow?" Joan asked. "Same as mine?"

"*Bon.* We will make arrangements. You have a deal."

Joan clasped Sophie's outstretched hand, clenching her teeth to maintain her blasé exterior, as silent laughter bubbled through her. "Come, baby." She nodded to Tara, whose eyes were wide, her mouth half-open.

After they'd boarded the boat that was to take them to the French Quarter, Joan glanced back at Sophie's yacht, catching a name stenciled into the prow.

"What's *Fortuna?*" she asked Ben, who was escorting them to shore.

"Today, she is you," he replied with a wink.

22

The French Quarter was just beginning to stir as the taxi bearing Joan and Tara crept along the narrow streets. Sour gusts wafted from the blackness of bars that never closed, their names displayed in flickering neon: Paradise, The Blue Door, and Daddy's Home. Stray trumpet notes drifted from a side street. A few tourists breakfasted on beignets and café au lait in a small outdoor plaza.

Upfront with the driver, Joan lowered her window to peer at the wrought-iron balconies draped in faded plastic beads. As the taxi braked for a sluggish horse and buggy, a ragged voice sounded from a nearby darkened doorway where a man lay sprawled, one foot in a filthy cast. "Hey, baby." A smile broke across his grime-smeared face as he met Joan's gaze and rattled the fist he'd shoved down his pants.

"Sad," Joan said, shaking her head. "That's where the hard booze'll get you. Me, I'll go two weeks with nothing but beer."

"You got some willpower, dawlin'. More than me," the driver said.

Tara mumbled something from the backseat, and Joan spun around. Her daughter looked as if she had a mouth full of firecrackers ready to blow.

"You better tell your face to cheer up," Joan said. "I heard they got a ban on sourpusses on the plane tomorrow morning."

Tara remained silent and shifted her gaze to the sidewalk where a woman in pigtails maneuvered her enormous stand-up bass past the cab.

"Tomorrow? Y'all leaving already?" the driver asked. "I hope you get to see some of the city first."

"We'll probably do a little something." Joan slung a long arm across the front seat. "They still got those Mardi Gras Indians?"

"Yeah, but they so commercialized now." The driver adjusted his battered fedora. "Like everything in New Orleans. It's all gettin' gentrified with the young hipsters that moved in after Katrina."

"You mean the ones with the big beards? I had some of them come to my protests. You mighta heard of me?"

"Come on, Mama," Tara said.

"What? This nice man might want to know who he's driving around."

"You somebody, darlin'?" the driver asked, with a chuckle. "Aside from a drop-dead beauty?"

"I'm Joan Saint-Romain." She shot the driver a coy glance, awaiting his delighted look of recognition.

"Saint-Romain. Saint-Romain. I think I have a third cousin who's a Saint-Romain…"

"The Terrefine sinkhole?" Joan prodded. "Almost killed my daughter? 'Bout to swallow up my house?"

"Uh-huh. I mighta heard something about that," the driver said, avoiding Joan's gaze. "All right, Mrs. Joan Saint-Romain. Here's your hotel. I'm gonna put y'all right in front. Be careful. We got a few of them sinkholes in the Quarter!"

Joan nearly collided with a red-coated doorman as she emerged from the taxi in front of a set of sparkling leaded-glass doors, capped by an elegant transom window. "Welcome to the Hotel Orleans," he said as he ushered Tara from the taxi. He stepped briskly to the rear and rapped the trunk.

"No luggage, bro!" the driver called through his window.

In the lobby, huge stone vases bristled with vivid long-stemmed roses, and heavy statues jutted from the walls, bearing trays of glass grapes. Joan halted, hotel guests streaming around her, to gawk at a massive chandelier high above, dripping with hundreds of crystal strands.

"Mama." Tara's voice bounced off the marble walls as she nudged Joan toward the hotel's front desk. But a dark-haired man in a gray suit and egg-yolk tie intercepted them first.

"Mrs. Saint-Romain? We've been expecting you. I'm Renaldo, your personal concierge. And you must be Tara."

"Just a second, 'Naldo," Joan said, drawn to a colorful display of brochures near a bank of ornate bronze elevators. Renaldo hovered at her side as she plucked a dozen different pamphlets promoting street cars, creole restaurants, the French Market, and a host of city parks.

When the rack was almost empty, she paused, then swiped the remaining brochures. "No harm in having backups."

"Of course," Renaldo replied smoothly. "Shall I take you to your room?" He escorted Joan and Tara to a private elevator. "I hope the penthouse suite will suffice," he remarked as they were whisked upwards.

The elevator doors opened onto a large living room filled with dark antiques and tall portraits of men in military garb. Two crystal liquor decanters gleamed atop a polished credenza, next to a bronze vase of magnificent blood-red roses. A plush couch stretched behind a low coffee-table, beneath a tall ficus tree in an embossed ceramic planter.

"This'll do just fine, 'Naldo," Joan said, kicking off her pumps and strutting barefoot through the remaining rooms. She rapped her knuckles against the edge of the indoor hot tub, tested the remote control of the plasma TV, and riffled the keys of the baby grand piano. "I'm not a fan of gold," she said, glancing at the gleaming fixtures in the spacious pink-stone bathroom. "But y'all managed to make it look okay in here."

With Renaldo at her heels, Joan returned to the living room where Tara waited, propped against the credenza, her rangy arms entwined around the waist of her worn cut-off shorts. As the concierge explained the mechanics of the card keys, the tinkle of laughter drifted through the French doors of the room's balcony, which overlooked the azure waters of the rooftop pool.

"Ladies, enjoy your stay." He passed the keys to Joan and Tara. "You're all set for a seven a.m. wake up call. A car will be waiting to take you to the airport. Can I get you anything else before I go?"

"Yes," Joan said. "Underwear. And some clothes."

Tara started to object, but Renaldo smiled warmly. "We have a small in-house boutique. I'll have a few things sent up." He lifted his brows. "I'm guessing you're a six?"

"Sounds about right."

Renaldo shot Tara a questioning glance, but she shook her head.

"Her, too," Joan said, rolling her eyes. "And shoes for us both." As Renaldo stepped onto the elevator, Joan called out, "And put it on the room bill!"

"Of course," he replied as the doors slid shut.

"I might have to go skinny dipping!" Joan chirped, sidling over to the balcony.

"Better wear goggles. I haven't seen you blink once since we left Rudy's."

Joan glanced over her shoulder, winked deliberately at Tara, then returned her gaze to the pool. Beyond the rooftop lay the brick buildings of the French Quarter with their tall wooden shutters. Farther still, the Mississippi River's brown churn pressed against the horizon.

Poolside, beneath a vine-covered gazebo, a jazz quartet launched into its opening number. Joan shut her eyes, letting the music caress her skin and penetrate her bones. "You lied to me." Her daughter's sullen voice interrupted Joan's carefree shimmy.

"What are you talking about?" Joan asked, continuing her dance.

"In the truck. You looked me in the eye and said you were as sober as Sister Clara. But you were high. And you still are."

Joan slowly turned to face Tara, her shapely silhouette thrust against the thick blue New Orleans sky. She stood tall, unburdened by any further need to lie or make excuses, to justify her words, her actions, her very being.

"I was protecting you. I knew you'd turn yourself inside out with worrying. Over nothing." She stepped inside and grabbed her cigarettes, placing a hand on her hip as she lit up. "This stuff I'm on now, it's just a super strong version of coffee. Lew told me that professional truck drivers use it to get across the country in one day. It's not really a party kind of drug. It's for working harder and thinking faster. Hell, he says even the college kids use it to study all night."

"It's not possible to drive across the country in one day. And that dropout gave it to you, not Lew. The one who's been creeping around Rudy's, staring in our windows. I threw a stick at him last night." Tara's nostrils flared as she pounded a fist into her palm. "I would have run him over with the truck if I'd known he was giving you drugs."

"Leave that poor boy alone. He's just got a little crush on me and not much else to his name. And you're wrong. This stuff came from Lew. I just wanted to make sure I had all my pistons firing for this meeting." An impish grin spread from Joan's eyes to her lips. "And tell me I didn't! Ten million dollars, Tara. Come on! Even you have to admit I did good."

"You did a great job. An amazing job. But you were lucky too, Mama. Just a hair from getting crazy and blowing this whole thing up. You couldn't see it, but I could."

"If there was any crazy in there, it was Sophie Al-hoo-whee, not me. You *know* that Ben fella is really her boyfriend. I bet they do it all over that big boat." Joan searched in vain for an ashtray and instead crushed her cigarette in the ficus pot. A heavy whiff of whiskey arose from the soil. Joan's eyes flew to the polished sideboard and the two crystal decanters, now emptied of their contents. "You poured all that booze into this plant?" She straightened up, a blade of raw hurt puncturing her golden mood.

In a flash, Joan saw herself in the mossy depths of her daughter's weary gaze. In Tara's eyes, she was a reckless and irresponsible mess, someone to be corralled and protected from herself and others. "You really think I'm good for nothin', don't you? That without you babysitting me, I'd go right off the rails." Her daughter's frown deepened, and her long fingers braided the fringes of her cutoffs.

"I'm not even worth telling about your big test score. A one hundred percent stranger knew about it, but not me, your own flesh and blood." Joan paused as a shriek and then a splash sounded from the pool. She shook her head. "Showboatin' around like you're one of them, a little lawyer. I don't understand half of what you're saying lately. But I don't need to! All I need to know is who I am." She jabbed her finger to her heart. "I am the mother, Tara. Me!" Again, she jabbed her heart. "I made a plan. I got us on that boat. I bargained with the big boss. And I got a goddamned huge settlement!" She threw up her arms and glanced around the room. "I made this happen, Tara! For us! Ain't that enough?"

Joan collapsed on the couch and clasped her hands between her knees. "Here's the rest of my plan." She pulled the plastic baggy from her pocket. A lump of powder was webbed in one corner. "Lew said it's best to stay up through the day, until dark. So I'm gonna finish this. Then I'm gonna enjoy this room, and this city, and this day, come back for a steak dinner and fall asleep in that huge goddamned bed." She scooped up a brochure for the Audubon Zoo, then tossed it back on the coffee table. "I thought we'd do it together, but that's for you to decide."

She rose from the couch and shut herself in the bathroom. As water rushed into the pink stone tub, she hunched above the counter. With two gritty snorts, she reduced her meth by half.

When Joan emerged a half-hour later, bound in soft white towels, Renaldo and a trim young woman had taken over the master bedroom. Shopping bags swung from their elbows and garments draped over their outstretched arms. Wordlessly, they arranged the clothing on the bed and neatly stacked shoe boxes by the full-length mirror.

"Casual and dressy in sixes, sevens, and eights," Renaldo explained when they were done. "Let me know if you need different sizes, colors, or styles." He turned to leave, motioning for the young woman to exit before him.

"Wait," Tara said. "How do we get to the zoo?"

For the first time in Joan's life, doors opened with breathless ease and the world revealed itself with the slightest touch—from the hotel's café whose chef appeared tableside to confirm that the French toast was to their liking; to the dark car with leather seats that ferried them to the Audubon Zoo; to the all-access pass Renaldo arranged entitling them to their own guide, unlimited concessions, and a Polaroid photo in front of the elephant house. And throughout it all, her daughter was by her side, witnessing every glorious moment.

At the zoo, Joan buzzed between the exhibits, her rose-colored sleeveless silk shirt and white linen shorts lending her a casual glamour. Renaldo had even thrown in a chunky bracelet and flashy white and gold sunglasses. Tara opted for slim olive-colored pedal pushers and a billowy cotton blouse. Joan was shocked when, after a pair of preteens mistook her for a celebrity, Tara gave her a sly look and offered to snap a group photo.

Only once did Tara refer to the next morning's press conference, to say she'd probably wear the pedal pushers again, and she refrained from trailing after Joan into the women's restroom.

Joan did her best to contain her torrential enthusiasm, dropping only a tiny hint to the zoo guide about her sinkhole fame and immediately letting it go when he failed to pick up on it. Instead, she channeled her energy into lavishing praise on the animals.

"He's smarter than half of Terrefine," she remarked, after watching a glistening sea otter zip through the water then leap from the pool to perform clownish poses for the crowd. She insisted on matching baby blue T-shirts with sea otter designs from the gift shop.

They left the zoo when it was late afternoon, Joan clutching a draft beer in one hand, and their photo from the elephant house and a bag stuffed with souvenirs in the other. At the zoo guide's suggestion, they made their way to the Fly, a neighboring park overlooking the Mississippi.

As they ambled past picnickers and circles of college kids playing hacky-sack, a sandy-haired young man with watery blue eyes caught Joan's attention. Her lips twitched into a smile as a hot gust rolled off the river and jerked the photo from her fingers.

The young man dropped his Frisbee and chased after the photo, batting the air until he'd snatched it. "I have this same picture with my family," he said, presenting the polaroid to Joan. "It's a classic shot."

"Thanks," Joan said. "Nice moves."

"I'm Carl, by the way." He gestured toward three young women picnicking beneath a tree and invited Joan and Tara to join. They were all students at nearby Tulane. "I could use a Frisbee partner," he grinned. "The girls all bailed on me." His eyes fell to Joan's beer. "And I've got lots more of those."

"One hundred percent up to Tara," Joan said, awaiting her daughter's immediate no. She wouldn't mind closing out the day basking in the affections of a honey-pie like Carl, but she also had no problem if Tara decided to call it quits. She'd finished the last of the meth in the ladies' room next to the swamp exhibit, and though she still felt alert, the drug's radiant hum was fading.

"We got a while before our ride comes," Tara said with a shrug, surprising her. "Sure."

Carl introduced Joan to Ivy, Beth, and Hannah, then launched the Frisbee to Tara, who'd positioned herself on a small mound of grass. She tracked its trajectory then leapt high, plucking the disc from the air.

"All right, baby!" Joan called as she ducked into the pool of tree shade where the girls munched green grapes and cheese cubes from paper plates. Ivy and Hannah admired the Polaroid picture, while Beth fluffed her soft brown bob and quizzed Joan about the zoo. As Joan described the sea otter saluting its trainer, Carl yelled that it was her turn to throw.

"Not me," Joan said. "Only sport I play is softball. And poker."

"Come on." Tara waggled the Frisbee. "You'll pick it right up."

Joan finished the last of her beer and shook the stiffness from her limbs. She strode to the middle of the green, where she hurled the Frisbee into a wobbly arc that somehow managed to reach Carl. She laughed as a spicy river wind swirled around her.

"That was almost perfect," Carl said, jogging over to Joan.

Behind him, Joan saw Tara tentatively approach the girls. Ivy patted a spot next to her. "Are you here to tour Tulane?" Joan heard the girl ask as Tara plopped cross-legged on the blanket. "Or Loyola?"

Carl placed the Frisbee in Joan's right hand. "Can I walk you through a throw?"

"Yes, indeed," Joan breathed, as he moved behind her.

"As you wind up the backhand, you want to keep the Frisbee horizontal. Then flick the wrist, which you did really well on your last throw." Carl's hands clasped hers and she relaxed against him, the solid feel of his chest guiding her through the release. "Now you try," he said, gently stepping away.

Joan wound up and lunged, and the Frisbee sailed into the late summer sky. "That was epic!" Carl yelled as he loped to the far side of the green.

After a few more of Carl's hands-on lessons, Joan collapsed on the blanket next to Tara. Sweat lacquered the edges of her buzz cut. "Mercy buckets," she exclaimed, accepting a fresh beer from Carl.

"Joan, we've had a brainstorm," Ivy said with a grin, revealing a wire retainer. "We are going to give y'all a quick tour of Tulane. What do you think?" She crossed her fingers and winked at Tara.

"Let's do it," Joan said, a yawn overtaking her smile. "Tara's the smartest person I know. They'll want her over there."

"You sure?" Tara asked. "What's the time? Our ride's picking us up at five."

Carl muffled a beer burp with his fist, while glancing at his phone. "That's an hour from now. The campus is a short walk through the park." He chucked his can against Joan's. "I'll get you guys back here in plenty of time."

They traversed Audubon Park on a bridle path that ran along a placid lagoon, Tara and the young women in front and Joan and Carl lagging behind. A canopy of hoary oak trees draped in delicate Spanish moss bathed them in cool shadows. Bicycles and joggers whizzed past, as well as dogs of all shapes and sizes tugging their owners along. A saxophonist planted himself in the middle of the bridle path and serenaded the passersby.

The park fell away, opening onto Tulane's campus and a row of stately, rough-hewn stone buildings with arched doorways and high rounded windows. Azalea bushes dotted the landscape, their fuchsia petals trembling in the hot breeze. The girls cheerfully talked over each other, pointing out departments, dormitories, and lecture halls.

"You'll love Tulane," Hannah said as she paused to massage a long scar on her kneecap. "ACL surgery. Lacrosse," she added, following Tara's gaze. "You ever play?" Tara shook her head. "Tulane has a rec team. You should try it. You know what you want to study?"

"I'm not sure. Maybe some kind of law," Tara muttered, her eyes cutting to Joan. "For the environment."

"That's right," Joan said. "She already knows more than most of those egg heads. She'll probably study flying helicopters, too. Right, hon?"

"Brilliant." Ivy nodded. "Augmenting your university education with military training will look great on your resume. Actually"—she shot a wide-eyed stare at Beth and Hannah—"our sorority would welcome a sister like you. It's not too soon for you to start considering your options."

When they reached the campus quad, an expanse of diamond-shaped patches of grass beneath tall shade trees, Joan begged off, plopping against a tree trunk and crossing her outstretched legs. "Y'all finish the tour without me." She waved. "I'll be right here."

"I'll keep her company," Carl said, tossing his long bangs aside with a jerk of his head.

As Tara mounted the steps, Carl dropped next to Joan on the grass. "Tulane is a pretty diverse campus." He plucked a clover flower and tucked it behind her ear, fingers brushing against the soft fuzz of her scalp. "There's all kinds of students here, from all over the world, serious scholars, activists, historians, future politicians. And a bunch of folks who are here to have fun. Partiers." He lowered his lashes, dragged his finger along the grass, then shot her a knowing glance.

"Is that right?" Joan glanced up at her daughter, who'd reached the topmost step of the library. Tara gazed across campus, her face illuminated by the late day sun. "Which kind of student are you?"

"I'm a journalism major," he replied, with a smile. "But I'm also a partier. And I'd guess by that restless jaw and those bonfire blue eyes that you are too."

"Mama!" Tara waved from the steps. "Ivy says I can go into the library. Mind if I check it out for five minutes?"

Joan waved her daughter on, then draped her head languidly toward Carl.

Tara

23.

An icy sliver pierced Tara's heart as she studied the gnarled oak tree were her mother had lounged. She shaded her eyes and glanced around the quad. There was no sign of her mother. Beth, Ivy, and Hannah were at the foot of the library steps, chatting with a student who'd waved them down.

"Hey," Tara said, interrupting them. "Where's your friend Carl?"

The girls looked confused. "Our friend? Not really. We just met him."

Ivy ran her tongue across her retainer wire. "After his Frisbee whacked me in the head, he came over, full of apologies, with a cooler of beer."

Tara tried to swallow through the sandpaper dryness of her throat. "But he said you were his friends." *Hadn't he?* She thought back to the moment Carl had appeared, just as they'd left the zoo, when he'd made a big show of chasing down the photo. With his long yellow bangs and broad grin, he'd seemed harmless, like someone from a toothpaste commercial.

"I knew that guy was creepy," Beth scowled. "Who throws the Frisbee to themselves?"

"Beth!" Hannah said, tugging the drawstring of her running shorts. "You said he was cute!"

"Well, he was." Beth tucked her bob behind one ear. "Is."

"And funny," Ivy added, turning back to Tara. "A journalism major. He said he was waiting for some friends. I'm embarrassed to say I was hoping they'd also be cute. And male."

"It's like an episode of SVU," Beth said, her voice quavering. "Wait. Are we accomplices to a kidnapping?"

"Jesus, Beth!" Ivy said, glancing at Tara. "Don't freak. It's broad daylight. We're on campus. I'm sure there's a perfectly logical explanation. Guys scheme their way into conversations with women all the time."

Beth shook her head. "Carl, or whatever his name is, lied to us all. Who knows if he's even a Tulane student."

"Why don't you just call her, Tara?" Ivy asked. "I bet she'll pick right up."

Tara pictured her mother's flip phone on the floor back at the Hotel Orleans, forced over the edge of the coffee table by the furious vibrations of Lydia's many calls. "She left it at the hotel."

"I think we should tell campus police," Beth said, her arms tightening around her narrow waist.

Tara spun around, sweeping her gaze across the quad, hunting for her mother's tall frame or a flash of close-cropped, white-blonde hair. Was she really going to report her mother, still high, to the cops? What if she hadn't yet finished the drugs? What if she again attacked an officer? Tara was already responsible for one arrest, having foolishly given her mother the Vicodin. She wasn't about to set her up for another.

As Ivy, Beth, and Hannah huddled together searching their phones for the campus police, Tara slowly began her retreat. She'd almost regained the sidewalk when Beth waved to her. "We've got the number! Ivy's calling."

"I'm so dumb!" Tara yelled, muscling a smile to her face. "I know where she is. With our ride at the zoo!" She whirled around, calling over her shoulder. "Nice meeting you! Thanks for everything!"

She bolted from the campus into Audubon Park, outpacing every jogger on the bridle path. The lazy charm of the park had vanished. The parade of dogs and their owners, the serenading trumpet player only magnified the reality of her mother's disappearance. And Tara's aloneness. She ran harder, pumping her arms, her lungs burning, until she reached the entrance to the zoo. She spotted the sedan with the Hotel Orleans sign tucked in the window and hurried over. Her heart sank when she spied the empty back seat.

The driver sat with her, uncomplaining, as she waited another hour in the parking lot for her mother to return. "I bet she's back at the hotel," he said, catching her eye in the rearview mirror as they merged onto Magazine Street. She nodded as if she believed him, even though he had already called twice to check.

"Mama!" Tara hollered into the hotel room as soon as the elevator doors opened. The living room and master bedroom were empty, the new clothes still strewn all over the bed. She lapped the suite, poking her head into the cavernous bathroom, then checking the second bedroom and the sitting room with its baby grand piano. Lastly, she emerged on the balcony overlooking the rooftop pool.

The sky was awash in smoky twilight. Guests held their cocktails aloft as they waded through the water, illuminated for the approaching night. A gas lamp cast its trembling glow on a couple, their limbs entangled, as they confided in low tones on a lounge chair. A tall figure near the bar waved and she felt a surge of relief. But the woman who smiled up at her wasn't her mother.

"I'm sorry, Tara. I haven't heard from her," Renaldo said when she reached him on the hotel phone.

"You didn't send somebody named Carl to get her? Take her somewhere?" She paused as a dark possibility formed itself. "She didn't ask you to get...something for her?" She recalled her mother gallivanting through the suite. Renaldo hadn't batted an eye when her mother ordered the new clothes. Who knows what else you could get at these fancy places?

He assured her the clothes were the only items he'd obtained for Mrs. Saint-Romain. "I promise I'll let you know if I hear anything."

"You swear you're telling the truth?"

"I swear. And I'm sure she'll show up soon on her own. Guests get separated from each other all the time."

Tara took refuge on the couch, her arms sealed around her bent legs. She veered from anger to terror and back again until panic usurped them both. As darkness gathered between the heavy antiques and in the plush corners of the room, her lungs tightened and a band of pressure encircled her head. Her throat felt clogged with oily water. She'd long ago pushed the memory of her near-drowning from her mind, but now the stink of the churning water, the chill, and the moment she'd gone under came rushing back.

She shot up from the couch and began sifting through the possibilities of her mother's whereabouts, searching for a fragment of steady ground. Her mother was strong. She'd killed the rattler. She'd even given Eddy a black eye. But she'd had a shovel then. What if Carl had a partner? Or several?

She lunged for the phone, convinced that she had to call the police. But then her gaze fell on the balcony where her mother had performed her victory dance, a mischievous glint in her eye, ready to party at ten a.m. Maybe she was the one who'd lured Carl away, to plunge into the nightlife of New Orleans, not the other way around. But why had Carl lied to the Tulane girls? Before ambushing her mother outside the zoo? *Because*, she answered herself, *he's a cold-blooded kidnapper.*

She scooped up the phone from the floor and flicked it open, clearing the alert for twenty-one missed calls from Lydia.

"Tara?" Mrs. Honoré's voice sounded wet and husky as she answered the phone. "You weren't at school today."

"I know, I'm sorry. I'll explain—"

"They can fail you for missing too many days."

Tara pulled the phone from her ear as Mrs. Honoré was overtaken by a spasm of coughing. "You gunning to join the town dropouts?" she added, when the fit finally passed. "You made a promise to get to class, girl. This is serious."

She dissolved into another long bout of coughing. Tara listened, alarmed at the severity of the hacking. The next voice she heard was not Mrs. Honoré's. "This is Nurse David. I'm sorry but you'll have to call back. Loretta's having trouble catching her breath."

Tara stared at the phone, the glow of the keypad in the darkened room staining her fingers red. Mrs. Honoré was back in the hospital. And Tara's call had probably aggravated her illness.

The phone display flashed and Tara's thumb hovered, ready to send Lydia's call to voicemail. But it was Justin's name that appeared.

"Joan!" he said as Tara picked up. "Thank God. Is this a good time? What the heck's going on?" He forced a chuckle. "Lydia's pretty upset."

"It's Tara." She paused to master the tremor in her voice. "Justin, everything's all screwed up."

"What do you mean? And where are you? Lydia's had me searching all afternoon."

"I don't know where Mama is. I need your help. I'm in New Orleans. At the Hotel Orleans."

"The Hotel Orleans?" He paused. "Are you sure about that?"

"I'm sure. Will you come? Please?"

"I'll be there in an hour and a half, tops. Don't move."

"Justin!" Tara yelled before he could hang up. "Don't tell Lydia."

Tara stationed herself in the hotel lobby to wait for Justin. She was too anxious to remain in the suite, alone with her mutating thoughts. Surveying the guests as they came and went at least made her feel like she was doing something. She noticed Justin the moment he arrived, as did everyone else. His loafer caught the edge of the rug at the entrance and he narrowly avoided face-planting into a huge bouquet of bright orange poppies. She jumped up and ran to him, abandoning the Coke and french fries sent over by Renaldo.

"Hey!" He roped her into a brotherly hug. "You okay?"

She burrowed into his armpit, ignoring the faint whiff of BO, feeling guilty for enjoying this contact when she should be mobilizing them to search for her mother.

Justin gently pried her away. "I'm sorry, Tara, but I gotta eat. Blood sugar." She nodded her understanding. She'd watched him grow faint once before when Lydia domineered a meeting long past lunch. "But I want you to tell me everything. We can hit the po-boy stand around the corner."

Inside Nicky Po's, they found stools near the front window. Justin worked on his catfish po-boy while Tara tried to choke down a plate of fried oysters.

"Thanks," Justin said, tossing his napkin on his plate and falling against the wall with a heavy sigh. "Now. What happened?" He raised his voice as a roving brass band marched past the window. The trumpeter, his cheeks ballooned past all reckoning, raised his cap to Tara as he slid by.

She took a deep breath and launched into her recounting of the past twenty-four hours. When she reached the point at which blood gushed over the back of her mother's shoe, when she finally admitted to herself that her mother was high, she paused to meet Justin's eyes, afraid to go on.

She recalled their many quiet conversations near the empty pool at Rudy's, beneath the twinkling web of the night sky, mostly about

law or science, sometimes about whatever random thoughts materialized. Philosophizing, Justin called it. She'd been surgically precise in
avoiding all but the most general details of her home life, fearing the
conclusions he might draw from her mother's drinking and drug use.
Justin on the other hand was generous and rambling, describing what
to her seemed a magical, pampered childhood without a moment's
loneliness or distress.

She had no choice now but to trust him, to reveal at least some of
the truth about herself and her mother, so he could help them. She
tried to read her fortune in his eyes, which regarded her now with
warmth and patience. But she knew a person's eyes could lie. The only
way to test someone's trust was to hand them something fragile and
hope they didn't break it.

She scooted her stool back and filled her lungs, firing off the words
before she lost her nerve. "I first realized that my mother was high on
drugs when we were on Global Petrol's boat."

For the remainder of her story, Justin listened quietly, with no sign
of shock or scorn. The only time he became animated was when Tara
described her mother's ten-million-dollar counteroffer.

"You gonna catch a fly," she remarked, reaching across her oysters
and tapping him beneath the chin.

"Unbelievable. No wonder Lydia shattered her phone against the
wall." He ran his fingers through his dark curls. "She still hasn't told
me your mom opted out of the lawsuit." He removed his wallet and
dropped a few bills on the table. "And you're sure there were no lawyers present for Global Petrol?"

Tara shook her head. "Just Sophie Alaoui and a waiter. And one of
those notary guys, right before we left. So they could get Mama's letter
to Lydia right away."

"So no apparent violation of any ABA rules of conduct," he mused
as they rose from the table. "The defendant directly tenders relief to
the individual plaintiff. No harm, no foul." He held open Nicky Po's
front door for Tara. "But expect Lydia to come after y'all for your
Rudy's bill. And whatever other expenses she incurred." He continued
holding the door as two women with shaved heads and dressed in black
leather passed through. "But that shouldn't be a problem with your
millions in the bank." He whistled. "Well-played, Joan Saint-Romain."

"We still have to make it to the Global Petrol press conference tomorrow," Tara said, suddenly aware that she'd been lulled from her sense of urgency while in Justin's company.

She grabbed the cuff of his blazer and pulled him beneath a streetlamp, away from the sidewalk stream of French Quarter revelers. "Did you know anyone named Carl when you were at Tulane?" She described Carl and how they'd met him, the visit to Tulane with Ivy, Beth, and Hannah, and her mother's disappearance.

When she was done, she waited to see her own panic mirrored in his face. Instead, he was thoughtful, rocking back on his heels as he stared into an oily puddle laced with confetti.

"Well?" she asked, when her patience had expired.

"Why do you assume Carl was waiting for you guys specifically? Maybe he really was waiting for his friends, but he got more interested in your mom." He lifted his eyebrows and shrugged. "She's very attractive. Gorgeous, actually. I can see some college guy jumping at the chance to spend time with her."

Tara picked at an imaginary hangnail to mask her discomfort at hearing Justin's reflections on her mother's looks. Was he speaking from experience? Would he jump at the chance to spend time with her?

"Even if she was a drug addict?" She felt the prickle of her own spite across her lips. "Who left her daughter with a bunch of strangers?"

"That's the other thing. You said your mom was tired, maybe even a little out of it. She'd been up for hours. It's totally possible they wandered off for some legitimate reason, to use the bathroom or get water. Maybe they start talking, or even making out. Sorry." She swatted away the hand he tried to place on her head. "Next thing you know a half hour goes by. It sounds like you kinda bolted out of there. Who knows? She might have shown up five minutes later looking for you."

"But that was three hours ago. Why hasn't she called?" She yanked the phone from her jeans pocket and froze. "Crap."

A voicemail had come in thirty minutes ago from an unknown number. "It's her," she breathed, huddling against a brick wall with the phone to her ear. She strained to hear her mother's message over the barroom cacophony in the background. She pressed replay and handed the phone to Justin. The only words either of them could make out were "Frenchmen Street."

"Sounds like she's having fun."

"That's no good either," Tara said. "She's gotta be ready to fly in the morning."

"Agreed." Justin glanced at his watch. "I was supposed to join Lydia in an hour for a conference call with a partner at the firm. But don't worry," he said, noticing Tara's stricken face, "I'll text her. Tell her I'm following up with one of the locals who claims to know Joan's whereabouts. That'll buy me a little time."

"Lydia will kill you if she finds out you helped us," Tara whispered, terrified that this reminder would send Justin running.

"Kill me and then fire me." He grinned, but his eyes clouded with worry. He flicked his wrist nervously, again checking his watch. "I'm going to pop into some of my old haunts on Frenchmen. Cab'll get me down there in ten minutes. If your mother calls you again, get a bar name, or better yet an address. And text it to me immediately."

"I'm going with you."

"That's not really practical. You're too young to get into the bars."

She pinned him with her gaze, remaining silent as he rattled off the reasons she should stay behind. When he'd finished, she threw out her arm to hail a cab, as she'd seen the tourists do.

"Fine," he said as a cab squealed to a stop and she tumbled into the back seat. "But you need to be careful. And vigilant. Keep your phone in your pocket. Ignore people who ask you for money. Or the time. Anyone loud and drunk coming your way, step behind me."

As the cab carried them from the French Quarter to the Marigny, and Frenchmen Street, Justin composed his text to Lydia, accepting several of Tara's wording suggestions before hitting *Send*.

Frenchmen Street was an endless river of music. It flowed from the bars, poured from the balconies above, and swirled at street corners and in doorways where small bands of musicians plucked out every style of music imaginable. Some even featured dancers. They flipped and twirled on tiny sections of sidewalk, delighting the crowd who stuffed their tin pails with dollar bills.

Every now and then Justin fumbled for her wrist and pulled her closer. At one point, they merged with a crowd standing enthralled as a tuba player soloed, his bandmates holding their instruments against their bodies as they, like everyone else, reveled in the dense notes of the big horn. Lights were strewn from balconies and laced through the branches of trees. Every inch of the street, every brightly painted door and window, seemed devoted to a grand, never-ending celebration. But the festive atmosphere only magnified Tara's angst. Her mother could easily be swept away for days, or even weeks, into this raucous merriment.

Justin checked all the spots he knew, describing her mother and Carl to the doormen, who summarily shook their heads. At times, Justin cut an odd figure, halting abruptly in the midst of the street partying, his face lined with concentration as he spun another elaborate excuse for his absence to Lydia via text.

Tara diligently checked her mother's phone every few minutes, then buried it in her pocket as Justin had instructed her to do. "We'll never find her," she lamented as midnight came and went.

As she slumped against a streetlamp, watching a thin-boned girl coax music from a piece of wax paper and a comb, Justin sprinted from a nearby bar, grinning. "Someone recognized her description. She was with a group on their way to the Music Box."

24.

The revelry of Frenchmen Street faded as the cab entered the Bywater neighborhood. Resurrected homes painted in lively tones of teal and aquamarine, orange sherbet and lemon bordered tumble-down shotgun houses whose weathered gray exteriors seemed to merge with the night. Streetlights were few, casting half-formed shadows on the broken sidewalks which were buckled by decades of relentless root-creep from the overhanging trees.

"You sure this is right?" Justin asked as the taxi crept down a road that dead-ended at a small wooded lot. A dark levee rose beyond the wood and hunkered against the moonless sky.

"Uh-huh," the driver said, rolling to a stop. "They do their thing in those trees up there. I ain't going further. This road'll eat up my hydraulics."

As Justin paid the driver, Tara listened to the darkness, trying to identify the series of clanks and whirs resonating from the direction of the trees. Justin jumped as a dark shape materialized from the shadows and sped past them. "Bicycle," Tara said.

Justin's phone chimed and he whipped it from his pocket, his pinched face illuminated in the screen's bleak glow as he read the incoming text aloud. "'You are a fucking moron. Call Triple A and get your ass back here. ASAP.'"

As he muttered about hypothetical wait times for AAA in the rural south, Tara hurried toward the trees. The strange sounds grew louder, and the road brightened. The path narrowed as they passed beneath a leafy canopy and rounded a sharp curve, ending at a tall, uneven wooden fence topped with a halogen lamp of twisted bronze. A scatter shot of holes had been drilled into the wood beneath a red-lettered invitation: *The cheap seats! Have a look!*

Tara put her eye to the fence. Inside was what looked like a miniature town, comprised of a dozen small wooden shacks cobbled together with corrugated tin, cast-off window frames, copper wire, and old pipe. Whirring propellers, fog horns, and flapping panels sat atop the roofs, operated by one or two people inside each little house, the source she now realized of the mysterious sounds. In the center, a phone booth of hammered tin housed a cowboy accordion player. At the prompting of a woman balanced atop a milk crate, the cowboy struck up a mournful tune. The crowd, gathered on overlapping picnic blankets, seemed mesmerized by the spectacle.

"What is it?" Tara asked.

"No idea," Justin answered. "Some kind of hipster performance art show or something."

Tara nodded, pretending she knew what he meant.

"Y'all came all the way here without even knowing what this is?" The low voice drifted from an opening further down the fence. Tara and Justin stepped back to peer at a girl in striped leggings and a lace slip perched on a stool. A silver stud nested between her bottom lip and her chin. Her hair leapt from her scalp in glittering black flames.

"We know it's called the Music Box," Justin replied. "That's it."

"Cool!" The girl smiled, her dark eyes crinkling against her darker skin. "It's an interactive sound sculpture. Or habitable music. Or found instrumentation. Or a perpetually emerging DIY soundscape." She threw up her hands. "Sorry. My first week here. I'm still working out the language. Anyway, you can go in, no charge. The performance is almost over."

"We're meeting a friend," Justin said. "A woman. Tall. Big blue eyes. Super-short blonde hair. Have you seen her?"

"Not since I've been on. But you can ask Uli. He worked the door until eleven." She pointed to a short muscular man in overalls, his goatee twisted and greased to a point.

Tara and Justin entered quietly, afraid to disturb the wonder and reverence that lay heavy over the listening crowd. To Tara, the sounds arising from the topsy-turvy little village weren't quite music but more like the frayed edges of music, windswept whistles and howls, beats from a fragment of spiral staircase, the plink-plank of floorboards as a white-haired girl hopscotched across them. Another player worked a set of ropes hinged to the ceiling of one of the shacks, like the riggings of a boat. The resulting tones triggered images of the field behind

Tara's house before a thunderstorm, when the wind was just coming up.

As she studied the crowd at the Music Box, she thought of yesterday's taxi ride to the hotel, and the driver's claim that New Orleans was being ruined by the hipsters. These people were a jumble of color and texture, sparkly and ragged, playful and mysterious. There were top hats and petticoats, colored pinwheels and even a unicycle.

"I like the hipsters," she whispered. Justin nodded and gave her a knowing smile.

Soon every house in the tiny village was strumming, thumping, and whirring, layering sound upon sound. A panel of the wooden fence nearest the crowd began to flicker and glow with projected light, accompanied by a persistent clattering, like a playing card in the spokes of a bicycle. The moldy splotches on the fence faded, and a series of shifting shadows sharpened into sepia-toned film footage. The jerky images and the dark fuzz squiggling in the corners of the frame mimicked an old movie, but Tara soon recognized the Music Box village as it must have been early that night. Shots of the audience milling around the shacks and interacting with the cranks, pulleys, and levers were followed by a close up of Uli stroking his pointed goatee.

A woman's face appeared, her wide eyes staring down the camera, then vanished as the footage jumped. When she reappeared her neck was exposed, pale and amphibious, her head thrown back in explosive laughter.

"It's her!" Justin said, as her mother's image dissolved, and the film looped back to the beginning.

Tara rose to her tiptoes, craning her neck to scan the whistling, clapping audience as the musicians emerged from the little shacks. When none of the beaming faces turned out to be her mother, or Carl, they pushed their way to Uli who was guiding people toward the exit.

"The footage covers the whole evening, since eight o'clock," Uli said when Justin asked about the film. "Lots of people have come and gone. I do remember that lady though." He raised his eyebrows. "I got the impression we were too mellow for her and her friends."

"Her friends?"

"The three of them kept talking during the performance."

"Did she seem…" Tara began, unsure of how to phrase her question.

"Like she was okay?" Justin finished. "Friendly with the other two?"

"I guess," he said with a shrug. "She wasn't okay when I asked them to leave," Uli added drily. "What a mouth." His eyes jumped to someone in the distance and he gave a thumbs-up. "Sorry, y'all. Duty calls."

Uli hurried away, stepping through the film projection as he did so. Her mother's face, then the flash of her throat, danced across his body.

"Hallelujah," Justin remarked, after reading Lydia's latest text. Mercifully, she'd relented because of the hour. "Though she did say she expects me tomorrow at nine a.m., on pain of death."

Tara reached down to slap a mosquito feasting on her ankle. "Okay," she said, straightening up.

"Okay, what?"

"You're about to say we should go back to the hotel."

"It's not a bad idea. Otherwise we could be wandering in circles all night. Plus she might even…"

"… be there," Tara finished.

Tara awoke to the dawn chill creeping through the open terrace door of the penthouse suite. She was curled in one corner of the huge couch. Justin was asleep on the opposite end, his arms folded into his chest, his legs resting on the coffee table amid the remains of their late-night BLTs and french fries.

She rose quietly and closed the terrace doors, then padded through the rooms of the suite. No sign of her mother. She returned to the couch and checked the flip phone. There was a new message from Lydia but nothing else. She drew her knees to her chest and studied Justin's face as his features materialized in the watery light.

She thought of Sophie Alaoui and the noon flight. She imagined the press conference filled with reporters who would happily broadcast her mother's no-show to all of America, or even the world. She squeezed her knees tighter, bracing herself for a renewed burst of panic.

But as she regarded Justin, his tousled curls and his dark lashes against his cheeks, the panic petered out. A certainty arose that her mother would eventually limp back to the hotel. They would probably miss the flight and Sophie would learn the truth—that her mother was unreliable and broken; that she didn't fit into the world beyond

Terrefine and never would. Justin would drive them back to Terrefine later today. He would help Tara beg Lydia to take them back. She either would or she wouldn't.

Last night, while they were waiting for room service, Justin had asked Tara what she would do with her share of the ten million. She'd admitted that she wanted to go to Tulane and be a lawyer, like him. Then, she waited for him to laugh. Instead, he described the various types of law, and the classes and professors at Tulane he liked the most. "You might want to consider shooting for the Ivy league though," he'd concluded, a fry dangling from his mouth. "You're much smarter than me."

Tara was silent as she ate the rest of her sandwich, stunned by the realization that Justin saw her, and her fate, as separate from her mother's. He'd rushed to New Orleans to help her, not her mother. He was on her side.

She knew Mrs. Honoré cared for her, but somehow Mrs. Honoré's advice about school failed to inspire Tara in the same way. Over the years, she'd stopped hearing her.

Justin nuzzled deeper into the couch and mumbled. In sleep, he looked younger than Gerard, whose face she'd seen snarling with a kind of meanness Justin would never display. He was so different from the men and boys of Terrefine. At times, he seemed impossibly innocent, even fragile. She often felt protective of him as he approached the townsfolk about the lawsuit or socialized at the gatherings around the pool at Rudy's.

A wave of tenderness washed over her as she studied all the details of him that had grown familiar over the past five weeks—his plump bottom lip; the indentation at the tip of his nose, as if pinched between a thumb and forefinger; the small, moon-shaped scar on his cheek, noticeable because the rest of his face was pink and smooth.

She smiled as her gaze fell upon his right ear, which formed a funny point at its peak. She slid closer to study the long fingers that gripped his outer arm, and closer still to hold her fingertips next to his, fascinated by his neat cuticles compared to her scourge of hangnails.

The urge to wrap him in her arms overtook her, to snuggle him like a baby, to squeeze him tight. She steadied herself on the back of the couch and eased one leg across his lap. She froze as he swatted the air, waiting until his hand dropped again to his side. When his breathing deepened, she gently laid her chest on his and nestled her face into his neck.

It was delicious to rest against him, a cozy closeness that was mostly absent from her life. She held still, breathing him in, letting his curls tickle her nose. She relaxed her body, feeling it grow heavier. A current of warmth, of pleasure, of comfort flowed from the base of her spine, filling the space between her belly and his.

She tried to remain motionless, not wanting to wake him, but she could feel her hips making tiny adjustments, pressing down on him. She nuzzled further into his neck, barely touching her lips to his skin. A noise bubbled out of her, like the cooing of a dove.

A hardness pushed up against her. She clung to Justin as his lashes fluttered open. His body stiffened as he reared back to look at her. "Tara?" His eyes dropped to where her thighs gripped his hips. "Whoa! This is not okay!"

He leapt to his feet and Tara flew backwards. Her head collided with the corner of the coffee table and pain splintered the base of her skull.

"Oh shit. I'm sorry!" Justin fell to his knees, cradling her bleeding head. A rush of relief broke through her pain. At least he wasn't so disgusted with her that he'd let her bleed to death.

A flash of metal was followed by a dull thump. The life drained from Justin's face. Water and roses streamed over Tara as he slumped to the floor at her side. A coarse voice sounded from above.

"Get off my daughter, mother fucker."

25.

Her mother's face swam into view, her eyes glinting, her lips drained of color. "Fucking pervert," she said, spitting on Justin's motionless body. "Just like your daddy."

"No..." Tara struggled to prop herself on her elbows but collapsed as fresh blossoms of pain filled her skull. A rancid gust of alcohol and cigarettes enveloped her as her mother crouched next to her, plucking the roses from her face and neck. Tara yelped as her mother probed her scalp where she'd hit the corner of the coffee table.

"Bastard got you good. But it's more bump than blood."

Her mother lowered Tara's head to the carpet, unleashing a wave of nausea.

"Lydia must have sent him. Lydia and Loretta Honoré. They know about Sophie." Her mother's gaze jerked around the room. "They been following me all night. They got cameras everywhere." She poked her head through the terrace doors before shutting them and drawing the drapes. "Can you believe they had the balls to film me and put me up on a screen tonight, in front of a whole crowd of people?"

She'd somehow held on to the Audubon Zoo shopping bag, and now she rummaged through it, bringing forth a plastic flamingo, then her cigarettes. "You can bet they're gonna try to keep us from getting on that plane."

"Justin." Tara shut her eyes but quickly realized her mistake as another wave of nausea set her spinning. She turned her head and heaved, and a swarm of stars erupted behind her eyes. She lay gasping as her mother mopped the vomit from her chin with a room service napkin.

"Puking make you feel better, baby?"

Tara tried to answer, but the effort sent bright flares pin-wheeling through her head. "Hurts," she managed to croak.

Her mother plunged her arm into the zoo bag until she withdrew a plastic baggy with a handful of pills. "This will kill the pain." She slipped a pill through Tara's parted lips then held a stale can of Coke to her mouth. "You'll feel better real soon. I promise."

Tara hesitated, afraid of what her mother might be giving her. She tried to sit up, but the pinwheels reformed into a single, throbbing dagger so insistent that she decided she didn't care what the pill was, as long as it made the pain go away.

"Good girl." Her mother patted her arm and returned the soda to the table.

The hotel phone sounded, a series of muted, underwater blips. At first her mother only stared, her body rigid, as if she expected the phone to launch an attack. Then she lunged for the receiver, ripping it from the cradle. "Loretta Honoré, you better stay away from what's mine. You hear me?" She gnawed the inside of her cheek, pressing the handset to her ear. "Do I sound like I'm asleep? I already told you, I'm awake. You don't have to keep repeating yourself!" She slammed down the phone.

Her mother stormed out of the room and soon the patter of the shower drifted from the bathroom. Tara shifted her torso so she could see Justin. He was on his back, his legs splayed in a figure four. His head was turned away from her, dark curls tufted against the oriental rug. The bronze vase lay nearby, a few remaining roses spilling from the neck.

"Mama!" she cried out, her voice ricocheting through her skull.

The gush of the shower continued uninterrupted. She waited, counting each rise and fall of Justin's chest as her head beat out a harsh tune and a trickle of tears pooled in one ear. "Mama!" she tried again as soon as the shower was silent. "It's all my fault! We need to help Justin."

"Your fault?" her mother yelled through the open bathroom door. She emerged seconds later, naked and dripping, to loom above Tara. "He messed with your head, didn't he? Made you think it was your fault for getting him horny?"

"It was my fault. I swear. He was trying to help me."

"Trying to help you?" Her mother drew a breath and lifted her gaze to the ceiling. Her breasts were stark half-moons, her nipples sharp, pink stones jutting above the slope of her ribcage. A fresh welt snaked above the glistening thatch between her legs. When she returned her gaze to Tara, she wore a look of rage so severe that Tara's breath caught.

Her mother leaned over Justin, as if she were going to spit on him again. "What kind of sick shit did you put in my child's head?" She slammed her toes into his ribs.

Tara stifled her cry of alarm and threw one arm in the air. "Take my hand, Mama! Help me up."

Her mother turned toward her, the animal fury in her eyes flickering. "You want to kick him too?"

"No need." Tara pushed herself to a sitting position. "You got him good."

"You said he was trying to help you."

"I didn't mean it. I was confused from the pain. He was trying to hurt me. But he didn't. Thanks to you, he's out cold."

Her mother's lip curled as she threw a last glance at Justin. She squatted, then looped her arms through Tara's. "Next time," she said, grunting softly as she lifted Tara to her feet, "when he pulls it out, you got to grab him down there. Twist it." Her breasts trembled as she demonstrated the motion. "I never taught you that?"

A cottony film began to wind its way around the inside of Tara's head, shielding her from the sharper edges of her pain and her anguish over Justin. But the stark certainty remained that she had to do everything in her power to get her mother, and herself, as far away from Justin as possible, so they couldn't hurt him anymore. And she had to get him help.

She searched her mother's face. Exhaustion frayed the corners of her mouth. Her skin seemed stretched to its limits, the sharp bones in danger of breaking through. She probably hadn't eaten since the fish fry at Rudy's two nights ago. Yet her eyes pulsed with brutal energy.

"Mama, do you remember the press conference? With Sophie?"

"Of course. What do you think I been doing all night?" She dipped back into the zoo bag, stirring the contents. "I worked on my speech with Carl and Night. Carl's going to school for newspaper writing, knows every word Chase ever crapped out. Night's just a dealer, but she had some good ideas too." She withdrew her hand and dumped the bag onto the floor, her fingers crawling across loose cigarettes, a lighter, key chains, T-shirts, and crumpled papers.

She snatched a vinyl coin purse, imprinted with the face of a grinning dolphin, and snapped it open. Tara glimpsed a baggy filled with powder before her mother resealed it and shoved it out of sight. "Here it is." She plucked a neatly folded paper from the mess. "I got the whole plan written out here. It's a hundred times better than anything Lydia did for me." The paper quivered as she held it out to Tara.

"You can show me on the way to the airport, Mama. You should get dressed. The car will be here soon. You don't want to miss your big moment."

Palming the coin purse, her mother left the room. As soon as she heard the bathroom door click, Tara retrieved the flip phone from her pocket. It was eight-forty a.m. Renaldo had scheduled the car pick up at nine.

"911 operator." The man answered on the first ring. "What is your emergency?"

"We need an ambulance. My friend…" her voice broke as she glanced at Justin's unmoving body.

"Take a deep breath. Give it another try."

"My friend got hit in the head. He's unconscious."

"I understand. Where are you?"

"Dammit!" Her mother's voice rang out from the next room.

"Hold on, please," Tara whispered, dropping to the couch and hiding the phone under her thigh.

"I had an accident," her mother said as she entered the room. Her head was thrown back, a wad of tissue trailed from one nostril. "Is this too Miss Pris looking?" She gestured toward her clothing, the second of the outfits brought up yesterday by Renaldo, a navy skirt and a crisp cotton blouse. From beneath the tissue, a bright red drop escaped, splashing her breast then plopping on the bottom edge of the blouse.

"It looks good. But you got blood on it. You better rinse it quick or it won't come out."

Her mother started for the bathroom but froze when the hotel phone sputtered to life. "I'll get it." Tara waved her on. "The car should be here now. I'll bet that's it."

"Good morning," Renaldo's voice flowed across the line as her mother left the room. "The driver is downstairs, ready to get you to the airport in plenty of time."

"Thanks," Tara replied, a small sob escaping.

"Is everything all right?"

She wanted to tear through the silk of Renaldo's voice, to scream at him to get help. But he'd probably come straight up to the room himself and try to stop them from leaving. She couldn't risk another explosion from her mother. Her plan to reach the airport was the only straight line in her mother's jumbled thinking.

"We gotta get a move on," Tara said to Renaldo, holding her voice steady.

"Of course. I won't keep you. Just be sure to check in at the United Airlines counter when you get to the airport. They'll issue your tickets."

She hung up and retrieved the flip phone. "Are you there, mister?"

"Yes, ma'am. Are you hurt?"

"Not me. My friend…"

"You ready?" Her mother's rustling in the next room grew louder.

"He's at the Hotel Orleans," Tara said to the operator, keeping her voice low. "In the penthouse suite. Hurry, please. It's bad."

"I'm dispatching an ambulance right now. What is your…"

She clicked the phone shut, switched it to silent, and returned it to her pocket. She promised herself that when they reached the airport, she'd slip away from her mother and call again to make sure Justin had been picked up.

"Let's get," her mother called from the doorway, trim in the navy skirt and cotton blouse. The blood spots were reduced to moist pink blotches. The zoo bag hung from one wrist. In the other hand, she gripped a half-full laundry bag bearing the Hotel Orleans logo.

"Ready." Tara touched the gooey knot at the back of her head and winced. She leaned forward, careful to keep her head level, and slipped on her shoes, not bothering with the laces.

As her mother passed Justin, she paused. Tara hurried forward, ignoring her thudding head, afraid that her mother might strike him again.

Her mother dropped her bags and crouched at his side. "Dumbass boy." She shifted his head so that his face was visible. His eyelids twitched with activity, as if he were having a bad dream. His brow furrowed and for a moment Tara felt certain he was going to wake up and explain some legal complexity.

"If it makes you feel any better," her mother said, pivoting to look at Tara,"he had me fooled too. I thought he was a good egg. A real good egg." She dabbed a tissue to her nostril, then drew it away to examine it. "You never know," she said, straightening up. "Maybe we did him a favor. Knocked some sense into him."

"Mama," Tara called out as her mother reached for the elevator button. A mass of conflicting words rose to her throat. She wanted to rage at her mother for hurting Justin, to thank her for coming to her defense, but most of all Tara wanted to lay her shame at her mother's feet for setting this whole disaster into motion. She also wanted to throw her arms around her mother, to hold her restless, flickering figure still. "Maybe we should just go home," Tara said, at last. "Forget about the thing with Sophie."

"Home?" her mother replied. "Tara, we got no home."

26.

The morning sun blazed through the tall windows at the front entrance of the hotel lobby, dousing the marble floor in a fiery pool of light through which arriving and departing guests dragged their quivering shadows. Tara stepped into the glare as she exited the elevator, her mother at her side. The brightness stabbed at her eyes, inflaming her aching head. She squinted, peering across the lobby at the front windows and the street beyond. A sedan waited at the curb. There was no sign of Justin's ambulance. From the far side of the lobby, came the measured click of Renaldo's shiny shoes. He greeted them as her mother dropped to one knee to dig through her Audubon Zoo bag, her skirt drifting high up her thighs.

"I hope you found your stay satisfactory?" His eyes sought Joan's downturned face.

"I'm looking for those sunglasses you gave me, 'Naldo," her mother replied, without looking up. "You're killing my eyes with all the light you got in here."

A slender woman in a robin's egg-blue suit and her thick-jawed husband stepped from the elevator, then slowed their pace to gawk at her mother and her rattling paper bag. Tara threw the couple a dark look, then crouched down to aid the search. "Here, Mama," she said, pulling out the sunglasses.

"I knew your mother would get back to the hotel just fine." Renaldo offered Tara a crisp smile as they followed her mother's rapid strides through the lobby. Tara remained silent. Again the urgency arose to tell him everything, to send him to Justin, to beg him to call for help regardless of the chaos that her mother might unleash. But as they stepped outside, Renaldo cocked his head, listening. A siren, faint but unmistakable, broke though the morning quiet. "Never a dull moment in the Quarter," he said.

Tara released a long sigh and gripped his hand. "Thank you."

"Of course! You're always welcome at the Hotel Orleans."

She turned from Renaldo in time to glimpse her mother in a brief tug-of-war with the white-gloved doorman who'd tried to load the plastic laundry sack into the trunk. He released it, offering a flustered apology and scrambled to open the car door.

"Good morning," the driver greeted them as they slid into the back seat. "Louie Armstrong International?"

"The airport," Tara replied. Careful of her still-throbbing head, she turned to watch the receding wrought-iron splendor of the Hotel Orleans. The siren had swelled to a shriek, prompting her mother to plug her ears. When they were several blocks away, the ambulance appeared, whipping around the corner and braking at the entrance.

She leaned her head against the window, her body slack with relief. As the driver turned onto Rampart Street, her gaze fell on the steps where yesterday morning, the drunken man with the filthy cast had leered at her. Today the doorway was empty, except for a scrawny kitten who followed the passing car with unblinking emerald eyes.

"Traffic's not too bad. I should have y'all there in a half-hour." The driver glanced in the rearview mirror, adjusted her neat braid, then returned her eyes to the road. Her lips continued to move as she resumed her cellphone conversation.

Soon the maze of the French Quarter was behind them, and they merged onto the interstate. Tara glanced at her mother. One arm hugged the zoo bag to her chest as she tugged at her eyebrows. Her jaw slid relentlessly from side to side.

"You look like a cow chewing its cud," Tara said. "Stop it."

"Can't help it." She dipped into her bag and pulled out her cigarettes. "When I smoke it's better."

"We're not supposed to let people smoke in here," the driver said, overhearing. "But I'll make an exception this once. Only 'cause I'm jonesing for one too. But I gotta keep all the windows down."

Tara rested her arm in the open window and thrust her face into the wind. Tears slid to the corners of her eyes and broke off in the torrent of air. *Let him be okay. Let him be okay. Let him be okay.* Her silent chant joined with the rhythmic throbbing of her head. She squeezed her eyes shut as the car slowed to a crawl and the gathering exhaust fumes threatened her with nausea.

"Looks like somebody wrecked," the driver said. "Nothing's moving as far as I can see. But we still got plenty of time."

Tara slumped against the leather headrest, her eyes still closed. Every few minutes, the car would inch forward. Drowsiness overtook her despite the mild racket of her mother rooting through her bag. When the stink of a new cigarette filled the backseat, she turned her head away, before again drifting into a shallow slumber.

"Hey!' Tara's eyes flew open. She jerked her arm out of the closing window.

"Sorry," her mother said in a low voice, her fingers on Tara's window toggle. "That car..." she pointed to a boxy blue car one lane over. "They started taking pictures of me."

Tara felt the prickle of unease. She'd never been to an airport, but she knew there would be crowds of people, some of them curious and staring, especially if her mother's behavior worsened.

"You brought the cellphone?" her mother asked.

Tara fished the phone from her pocket, erasing a new voicemail from Lydia before handing it over. Her head, which had quieted during her nap, sprouted fresh tendrils of pain.

Her mother punched the keypad and brought the phone to her ear. "Hi, Eddy." She cleared her throat. "This is a message from Joan Saint-Romain." Her eyes slid to Tara. "Do I sound funny?" she whispered.

"You're fine."

"Anyway, I'm a rich person now. You'll hear about it on TV soon enough. And on the computer. I was thinking about you last night. Or maybe the day before. Tara probably knows when." She squeezed Tara's knee. "I just wanted you to know that even though you've been slippery about some things, you and me are okay. You saved my daughter and..." Her mother halted, pulling the phone away. "The beep went off."

"That's okay. It recorded."

They passed a knot of emergency vehicles and a car flattened against a concrete divider. "Uh. That's nasty," the driver said, then tapped her phone to take an incoming call.

The flow of traffic accelerated and soon they were speeding beneath a sign for Louis Armstrong International. The car swayed as the driver broke out of her lane and steered toward an exit ramp. Tara straightened up for her first glimpse of the airport, but instead caught sight of a Global Petrol gas station. "Apologies," the driver said, after ending her phone call. Her eyes remained fixed on the road. "I miscalculated my fuel. I'm going to have to get gas."

"Thank God," Joan breathed. "I'm about to jump out of my skin cooped up in here."

"What are you gonna do during the flight?" Tara asked as the driver eased in next to a gas pump wrapped in Global Petrol's red and black logo. "You can't get out and walk around."

"Got that covered. I just took a couple of those pills I gave you," she replied. "So I can nap on the plane." She threw open the door and leapt out, the zoo bag dangling from her wrist.

Enclosed in the stillness of the car, Tara watched her mother round the diesel pump and head for the restroom. A man exiting the toilet held open the grimy door for her, tipping his baseball cap as she passed.

Tara reached for a folded paper that had fallen from the zoo bag onto her mother's seat, expecting to find Carl's press conference ideas. Instead she discovered an ink drawing. Beneath numerous cross outs, a house was clearly etched, its two stories covering most of the paper. She identified her room and her mother's, the bathroom, kitchen, and living room. It was a replica of the house they'd just abandoned.

But a smaller square, situated behind the house was new. Her mother had drawn two stick figures, an animal and a person, beneath her thick scrawl—*horse and barn for Tara.* The drawing was followed by a sequence of numbers, which she guessed were estimates of the building costs.

She refolded the paper, a weary tenderness invading her heart. She knew that her mother wanted good things for her, to shield her from the kind of harshness she'd had to endure growing up. But she always managed to tangle what should have been a straight line.

Even Justin. Her mother had meant well, was trying to protect her, but if she'd stopped to think about it, about who Justin was, then she would have known he would never attack Tara. She would have given him a chance to explain. But the part of her that was responsible for seeing past the storm of her own emotions was broken or dried up from non-use. The drugs and the alcohol didn't help, but they weren't entirely to blame either.

But then again, the attack on Justin wasn't really her mother's fault; it was Tara's. She'd set the whole disaster in motion. "I'm so stupid," she whispered aloud. Why couldn't she have stayed on her side of the couch instead of throwing herself at Justin? She smeared her wet nose on her forearm, then searched her pocket for the phone, hoping to sneak in a call to check on him. But her pocket was empty. The phone was with her mother, probably buried in the bottomless zoo bag. She glanced at the closed bathroom door, then scanned the rest of the gas station. The pumps were deserted. She spotted the driver chatting with two men in dark uniforms. One of them tossed his paper coffee cup away and glanced toward the car. She closed her eyes. The pain seemed to be migrating to the sides of her skull. How long had they been here? They were going to be late for their flight. She tried to care, but it was easier to give in to the softness of the leather headrest.

A door slammed nearby and her eyes fluttered open. Their driver had disappeared. The two uniformed gas station workers had grown to four and were facing the weed-lined building and the bathroom jutting from its side. One of them spoke into a walkie-talkie.

The bathroom door swung open and her mother emerged, sunlight illuminating the soft spikes of her hair. She walked quickly, her eyes downturned as she scrutinized the contents of the zoo bag. All at once, the four uniformed men fell to their knees, and for a moment Tara wondered if they were going to prank her mother with a group marriage proposal.

"Joan Saint-Romain, you are under arrest." The booming voice came from one of the kneeling figures. "Drop the bag and put your hands above your head."

"Mama!" Tara threw open the door as her mother plunged her arm into her bag.

A cascade of clicks arose from the officers. "Hands up! Where we can see them!"

Her mother looked up, her brows peaked with annoyance. She said something too low for Tara to hear, then snapped her fisted hand from the bag. A shot rang out. Tara roared and lunged forward. Arms encircled her from behind, immobilizing her as she witnessed her mother's collapse, the cellphone spilling from her limp hand.

27.

Tara fought to free herself from the stranger's arms, driving her heels into shinbones and slamming her head against a broad chest. Wetness spread along her scalp as her wound reopened. "You killed her!" she screamed across the pavement at the four dark uniforms closing in on her mother's splayed figure. Overhead the sky rumbled as an airplane took flight out of Louis Armstrong International.

"Get your hands where I can see them!" a police officer yelled, cleaving the air with his gun and taking a cautious step forward. The zoo bag had tumbled within a few inches of her mother. The officer lunged for it, jerking it out of her reach. The plastic flamingo went cartwheeling across the concrete.

"She dead! She's dead!" Tara yelled, continuing to thrash.

"Young lady, stop fighting me or I'll be forced to restrain you." The woman's voice belonged to the powerful arms encircling Tara.

Tara craned her neck, straining to see her mother through the cluster of officers. The white cotton covering one of her shoulders was soaked in red, but she was moving, tilting her head toward an officer who'd begun speaking to her in a low voice. Relief crashed through Tara's body.

A second officer drew near and reached for her mother's cellphone that lay on the pavement near her foot. A bright, slender leg scissored upward and caught him on the chin. The expensive sandal supplied by Renaldo took flight.

The rest of the officers descended on her mother in a frenzied pack. An enraged shrieking erupted from their midst. When they fell back, her mother's hands were cuffed and her feet bound.

"You're hurting her!" Tara again threw all her strength into escaping the woman's hold. "Let me go!"

"Just cuff her." A man's voice sounded from somewhere behind Tara. "That girl's a danger to herself and us."

"You hear that." The woman's breath was hot in Tara's ear. "Is that what you want? I cuff you and put you in the cruiser?"

"No!" Tara cried, terrified of losing sight of her mother. "I'll be still."

"Good. Now place your hands on the vehicle." Her eyes still riveted on her mother, Tara barely registered the hands sliding down the sides of her body, then the front and back of her shorts. "Turn around please."

The officer towered above her, her deep brown eyes boring into Tara's. A single plait had escaped the thick gathering of braids behind her head and stuck to the gloss covering her full lower lip. Her bronze nameplate read *K. Johnson.* "Your name and address?"

A string of ear-splitting curses poured forth and the officer's eyes darted from Tara to her mother who was still on the ground, her head bobbing as she shouted at the officers milling around her. Two more police cruisers had arrived, their sirens flashing dully in the noonday sun.

"Tara Saint-Romain. That's my mother, Joan." She raised a trembling finger.

"Hands at your side. Address?"

"Terrefine. We're staying at Rudy's Hotel-Motel now. But we used to live at 28 Horseshoe Drive."

"Date of birth?"

"October fourth."

"Happy birthday to you," said the male officer. Officer Johnson threw him a heavy frown and he fell silent, dropping his squat arms to his sides.

"Year?" Officer Johnson asked Tara.

Her mother's voice sounded again, thundering above the confusion. "You're real tough taking down an unarmed lady! You proud?" The blood stain now covered half of her shirt, yet she continued to lob insults at the police. A flash of light near the entrance of the bathroom caught Tara's eye. A lanky figure was tucked in the shadow of the awning, a camera obscuring his face.

Officer Johnson jotted down Tara's answers, then returned to her squad car, leaving Tara under the watch of her partner. "You gotta bionic mama," her partner said, with a wry grin. Tara fixed him with a stony stare, then turned to watch the arrival of the ambulance, followed closely by the bulky black van of a local news station.

Her mother's screams continued as the EMTs cut open her shirt and staunched the wound. "Call Sophie Alaoui. She owns this whole goddamn place!" she screeched as she was strapped to the gurney and fed into the ambulance's dark interior. The steel doors slammed shut on her final ragged cry. "Where's Tara? Where's my daughter?"

A shadow enveloped Tara. She glanced up to find Officer Johnson, her great chest widening as she took in a full breath. "We are going to bring you in to ask some questions in relation to an assault that happened early this morning at the Hotel Orleans."

"Is Justin okay?" Tara's head fell forward as she hid her tears. Drops appeared on the pavement at her feet. "It's my fault."

"Excuse me?"

"Justin getting hurt. It was because of me. I'm the one to blame, not my mama."

From the corner of her eye, Tara watched Officer Johnson exchange a long glance with her partner. The ambulance sped by, sirens blaring, flanked by two police cars. A reporter, speaking into a news camera near the station entrance, leapt aside as the flashing caravan drove past.

"Tara, you have the right to remain silent." Officer Johnson clasped her arm and directed her toward the cruiser. "Anything you say can and will be used against you in a court of law…"

As the officer droned on, Tara recalled the last time she'd heard these same words, as her mother was dragged from their living room through the front yard and paraded before a crowd of emergency workers. Her mother had fought, yelling and screaming, same as she'd done today.

But Tara had no reason to fight. She was being arrested. That's what happened when you hurt someone. As she crossed the parking lot, she kept her eyes on the flickering lights until they vanished into the sea of interstate traffic.

"Are we going with her?" she said as Officer Johnson nudged her into the back of a police cruiser.

"Not possible. We're taking you to Juvenile Intake for booking."

At the New Orleans Juvenile Intake center, Officer Johnson gave Tara a final lingering gaze before turning her over to an officer who shunted her through the booking process. A woman typed her information into a computer, pausing frequently to blow her nose. A man with a neat horseshoe of brown hair aimed a camera at her, directing her to "look up, look up!" Afterward, he rolled her fingers across a glass scanner, collecting the panel of loops and swirls that was supposed to belong only to her.

No one seemed particularly impressed by her arrival, though during fingerprinting she overheard a voice behind a partition mention "that sinkhole lady from Terrefine." Her numerous requests for information about her mother and Justin were ignored.

When the fact of her fatherlessness was recorded, she was asked if there was a relative or friend of the family who would act as her guardian. She thought back to her call last night with Mrs. Honoré, her spell of coughing and the nurse who'd gotten on the line to explain the pneumonia relapse. She shuffled through other possibilities—Lydia, Sheriff Grady, various townsfolk of Terrefine—each time butting up against the invisible wall surrounding her and her mother. She concluded that even sick, Mrs. Honoré was the only person she could rely upon with certainty.

"Loretta Honoré," Tara told the Juvenile Officer awaiting her answer. "She's at the hospital in Leittville."

When her booking was complete, a guard led her to a holding cell where she was told she would wait until Mrs. Honoré arrived. After that, a detective would question her.

"Let me know what you hear about my mama. Please!" she called as the heavy door swung closed. "And Justin!"

The cinderblock walls of the cell were coated a flat pink. It took her a moment to realize that the hunk of dull metal at the back of the room was a toilet. Two benches faced each other, bolted into opposite walls. She lowered herself gingerly on to one of them, her fingers gripping the cold edge. No one knew she was hurt. Her tangled curls camouflaged her wound and she'd managed to hide her stabbing headache and wooziness. But now, behind the locked door with its small glass window, she gave in to the violent throbbing.

Heavy disinfectant permeated the cell and the image of Sophie Alaoui, brushing her fingers along the gold-embossed titles of her yacht library, flashed in her mind. A grimace forced open her dry lips.

The oriental rug, the elaborate vases, the scented tea, all seemed like bits of a fairy tale concocted for little kids to fool them into feeling safe.

No detail was more fanciful than the ten million dollars. Her grimace widened as she forced her teeth into her bottom lip. How stupid that for a few hours she'd let herself believe that life had changed its mind about them, that she and her mother might not be doomed to struggle and scrape to the end of their days. When would she learn that her place, and her mother's, was at the bottom and always would be?

She spat on the floor, accelerating the drumbeat in her head. Even worse were her dreams of law school. Her cheeks flamed thinking of how she'd shared them with Justin; and how she'd pulled him down into the dirt and mess of her life, and her mother's. She knew that sometimes people lost their memories when they got hit on the head. Maybe when he woke up he would have no memory of her. She wished that for him.

She glanced up to find a pair of eyes filling the small window of the door. The guard rapped on the glass and pointed at the floor where her glob of spit had congealed, then frowned and shook her head.

"Where's my mama?" Tara called.

The eyes were replaced by an ear, a chin, a uniformed shoulder. The grinding of the lock propelled Tara to her feet.

"Against the wall," the guard ordered as the door swung open. "Hands at your side."

"Where is my mother?" Tara called as a beanpole of a girl slipped in, her thin frame all but lost in her huge black NFL T-shirt, her eyes restless and amused.

"Baton Rouge? Africa? The moon?" The girl scratched her forearm, which was flecked with thin scars. "You gonna give me a clue?"

"I ain't talking to you," Tara growled as the guard left, clanging the door shut. Tara balled her fists and locked her knees. She was relieved to find that she was taller than the girl, if only slightly.

"It's cool, it's cool," the girl replied, tugging the crotch of her red sweatpants and dropping onto the opposite bench.

Tara sniffed, threw a menacing glace at the girl, then slumped down onto her bench, her knees wide. She fixed her gaze on the floor where

Tylee luvz Cherone was chipped into the paint, framed by the shaky outline of a heart.

The room's sickly light wavered as again the guard stood at the window. Tara threw out her arm. "Hey!" she screamed, pain lashing her scalp. But the face was gone.

"You ain't been here before have you?" The girl grinned, exposing a front tooth the color of mop water. "They gotta do that. Visual check every fifteen." She scooted forward and cocked her head. "You hurt?"

Tara leveled her gaze at the girl, pouring the sharpness of her pain and the turmoil of her thoughts into her stare.

"All right. You ain't hurt." The girl scuttled to the back of her bench, then lapsed into silence. She folded one leg into her chest and began shaping her coarse hair into knots and braids. When she finished one half of her scalp, she began the other, muttering to herself as she worked.

Tara's lids grew heavy, her slouch deepened. She fought sleep but kept dropping off, her head tipping to the brink of imbalance, then jerking back again. Finally, after she nearly spilled onto the floor, her eyes flew open. The girl was watching her, a faint smile on her lips. Her hands were in her lap and her hair restored to its original rust-colored cloud.

"What are you looking at?" Tara asked, wiping a wet slick from her chin and squinting up at a lighting panel.

"I bet it's a hour you been sleeping. Me, I don't close my eyes when I come here. I'm too wired."

Tara studied the girl's bony face, her watery eyes, the stamp of ringworm on one cheek. A sudden flare of anger overtook her. "Why would anybody keep coming here?"

The girl shrugged. "I'm a runner."

"What the hell is that?"

"I run away. Cops pick me up. Bring me here till my fosters come for me. I stay for a while. Then I run again." The girl paused, then lifted her palm from the bench, leaving a moist handprint. "This is number five."

"That's just stupid."

"I ain't the only stupid in here," the girl shot back. "And you gonna be back. I know it. You got lizard eyes, like me." The girl widened her eyes maniacally, revealing their green-yellow depths. "When I was little, my mama used to say us lizard eyes are doomed to devil's work."

"I'm here because of an accident." Tara shivered and wrapped her arms around her chest.

"Yeah, me too." The girl smiled. "I accidentally stole a car."

The girl's hard laugh clattered against the pink walls, and Tara's shivering intensified. A kernel of panic pushed its way into her gut and began to flower. Had the police really called Mrs. Honoré? Or anyone? She tensed, trying to control her trembling, but the girl noticed and rose from her bench.

"They'll give you a blanket. Watch." The girl sidled to the door and banged her palm on the glass. Moments later, a narrow panel slid open. The girl's head drooped as she eyed the guard through the slit. "Officer D., we need some blankets. It's cold. Please."

"You see that," the girl said after the guard tossed two rough gray blankets on the floor before sealing them up again. "They bring you sandwiches, too, if you stay long enough."

She shuffled to the back of the cell and squatted over the toilet. Tara caught a glimpse of her skeletal legs before turning away. A melodic patter echoed from the bowl. "I heard 'em out there. The police. Talking about your *accident*." The cloud of hair wobbled. The gray tooth flashed. "And that boy."

"What boy?" Tara could barely push out the words. Her throat felt encased in cement.

"The one you and your mama killed."

"You're a damn liar." Tara shut her eyes and prodded the lump at the back of her head again and again, letting the molten pain beat back her hunch that the girl spoke the truth.

"Let's go, Saint-Romain." The guard's booming voice broke through the stale quiet of the cell.

Tara sat up, the scratchy blanket falling from her shoulders. The chill clamped down on her. On the opposite bench, the girl cracked open a fevered eye from beneath a lump of blanket. "Yeah, we gonna be seeing you, Saint-Romain," she murmured. "Saint. That's good." Her hollow cackle sounded as the door clanged shut.

The guard escorted Tara down a hall lined with barred windows, dead-ending at a set of reinforced metal doors. Beyond her own dim reflection, she could make out a parking lot and the sweep of early morning sky. When they reached the metal doors, the guard spoke into an intercom. "Coming through, Mixon." They were buzzed into a corridor facing a half dozen doors. The guard ushered Tara toward the nearest one.

The small, windowless room smelled of vinyl. A mirror stretched across one wall, overlooking three identical chairs. A fourth chair was occupied by Mrs. Honoré who stared at the gray carpet, her thick fingers gripping her knees. A small cylindrical tank on wheels was parked at her side, feeding a thin tube beneath her nostrils.

The door clicked behind Tara and Mrs. Honoré glanced up, her eyes quickly searching Tara's face and scanning her body. Coughing wetly, she seized the handle of the oxygen tank and rose to her feet, striding across the floor with surprising speed. Tara opened her mouth to ask about Justin, but the truth revealed itself in the mournful gaze that fell on her like a dark wing.

"Justin passed this morning, Tara. I'm so sorry."

Tara slumped as the breath sucked from her was then painfully thrust back into her, shattering the thin filaments of her nerves as it reentered. Her body began to shudder. Some part of her registered Mrs. Honoré's arms surrounding her in gentle strength, even as her mind spun away from itself, again and again, in a futile attempt to deny the horrible words Mrs. Honoré had spoken.

"I'm right here, girl. I'm right here," Mrs. Honoré repeated through her own bouts of coughing as waves of grief tore through Tara.

Mrs. Honoré's cotton work shirt was soaked when Tara finally pulled away, her choked sobs dissolving into emptiness. "I'm sorry it took me so long to get here, Tara. I had to go through all kinds of rigmarole to prove I could be your legal guardian. They got a court-appointed lawyer coming to see you soon. I got Ricky Delray checking to see if he's any good."

Mrs. Honoré withdrew a handkerchief and tucked it in Tara's hand. "Your mama got out of surgery a couple of hours ago. They'll talk to her when she wakes up and shows she's in her right mind." She brushed a calloused finger beneath Tara's chin and searched her eyes. "The police are saying you told them this was your fault. I know you didn't knock that boy in the head. You need to tell me what really happened so I can help you."

"It was…is…my fault." Tara felt the dull edge of her own voice. "Justin's dead because of me."

"It's not your fault unless you hit him. Did you?"

"He was at the hotel because of me. If I had just kept my mouth shut and waited for Mama to come back to the room instead of whining to him.…" Her voice trailed off.

Anger flashed in the depths of Mrs. Honoré's dark eyes, deepening them to jet. "Forgive me, Tara. I'm your friend. I care for you. But like hell will I entertain your self-pity right now. Or your habit of blaming yourself for everything that goes wrong with you and your mama. There's too much at stake. I want the truth. The facts. Did you hit Justin or do anything to hurt him physically? With your own hands?"

A clot of grief and shame gathered in Tara's chest. She tried to speak but her voice caught. She swallowed hard and balled her fists. "I snuck into his lap, while he was sleeping," she started, her words half-strangled. "I pushed myself, my body, against him." She squeezed her eyes shut. "Like some kind of pervert. When he woke up, he was so disgusted. He threw me off. And then…" Her eyes flew open and her arms jerked wide. "You have to believe me. It's my fault. I caused it!"

Mrs. Honoré took hold of Tara's shoulders and shook her. "I'm not gonna stand by and let you hang yourself." The effort dredged up a deep, racking cough, robbing Mrs. Honoré of breath. Her face sagged and she stumbled.

Alarmed, Tara grabbed Mrs. Honoré beneath the arms and led her, still gasping, to a chair. As she watched her only friend struggle to regain her breath, an aching weariness settled over her. This was the second time in as many days that Mrs. Honoré's pneumonia had been aggravated because of Tara. The first time was in the darkening hotel room, when she'd phoned Mrs. Honoré, frantic because of her mother's disappearance. Maybe she'd been wrong to call both Mrs. Honoré and Justin. But how was she supposed to know what to do? She was alone.

Tara imagined her mother, freed because of her own confession of guilt, returning to Terrefine by herself, while Tara was sent to prison.

Even in jail, Tara knew her days would be marked by constant worry and vigilance as, from a distance, she tried to keep her mother from tumbling over life's edge, from hurting herself or others.

As Mrs. Honoré adjusted the plastic tube beneath her nose, her breath slowly returning to normal, Tara saw the true nature of her own guilt with crystal clarity. Her crime was thinking that she was enough to soothe her mother's innumerable wounds, to keep their lives in some kind of balance, to pick up the pieces whenever her mother broke apart.

She leaned forward, covering her face, bowed beneath the weight of her failure. "I can't do it anymore. I can't make her better."

"I know, Tara," Mrs. Honoré replied, her voice thick, meeting Tara's sorrow with her own. "I've thought so many times that if it could be done, you'd do it. Your heart holds so much. And she loves you. She does."

"It was her, Mrs. Honoré." Tara's hands fell to her lap. She stared into her open palms. "Mama killed Justin."

Tara's voice was steady as she related the story of Justin's last moments, and everything leading up to them, to Mrs. Honoré. Soon after, Detective Harper, a slender man with large square hands recited Tara's Miranda rights once again, this time to both Tara and Mrs. Honoré. He then asked if Tara would be willing to waive her right to silence so she could answer his questions about Justin's death.

After a long call with Ricky Delray, and a harried visit from Tara's appointed lawyer, Mrs. Honoré encouraged Tara to speak to the detectives. "I'll be listening in. By law they got to let me. Just tell the truth. And don't let anybody mess with your facts."

With Mrs. Honoré observing behind a mirrored glass, Tara faced Detective Harper and his bushy-browed partner, Officer McCann. Her headache had dulled and her thoughts rose with fluid clarity. She described the whiff of bacon from the late night BLTs as she snuggled Justin while he slept on the couch, the thud of the vase hitting his skull, her mother's words thundering through the hotel room as she accused him of a thing he did not do.

The detectives let her tell her story in her own way, stopping her only to affirm the order of events, until at last she described her mother's shooting at the Global Petrol station. And her own arrest. "When I said it was my fault, I was thinking about how me climbing on top of Justin started everything." Tara looked up from her entwined fingers. "Like dominos, you know?"

"I think I do, Tara. But would you tell me in your own words?" Detective Harper tugged at his tie and leaned back into his chair.

"The first domino, I sit on Justin's lap, while he's sleeping. The second, he freaks out and jumps up. The third, I hit my head on the coffee table. The fourth, he tries to help me. The fifth, my mama…" Her voice quavered. "…rescues me. But I didn't need to be rescued. Not from him."

After a brief silence, Detective McCann tapped his pen on the table. "One last thing I'd like to circle back to before we give you a break, Tara." He consulted his pad, his snowy brows lifting. "How is it you weren't hurt when Justin pushed you into the coffee table? It seems like he thought you were injured. Your mother seems to have thought that too."

Tara wordlessly spun in her chair and parted her curls.

"Christ."

A chair creaked, followed by Detective Harper barking into the phone. "Get an EMT to Room 120. Now."

28.

Tara winced as the needle penetrated her scalp. She was seated on a gurney, separated from the coughs and sighs of the rest of the ER by a thin green curtain. She and Mrs. Honoré had waited almost three hours in the crowded waiting room before they were seen. A guard from Juvenile Intake had remained with them the entire time, attracting stares from those well enough to be curious.

"That should get you good and numb," the ER doctor said, his face fixed in a bland smile. He tossed the syringe onto a metal tray held by a nurse, her eyes enormous behind thick eyeglasses. "Go ahead and lie back so I can irrigate the wound."

Tara eased herself onto the table, anchoring her gaze to a metal bar in the ceiling tiles that formed a cross. A series of clicks sounded at the base of her skull.

"You're being released," Mrs. Honoré announced as she drew the curtain aside and then sealed it behind her. "Your mama woke up."

Tara tried to sit upright, but the doctor clasped her shoulders. "Hold 'em, tiger. I'm not quite done here."

"She's got a busted shoulder, but they removed the bullet and stitched her up." Mrs. Honoré neared the gurney, the wheels of her oxygen tank emitting a faint squeak. "The important thing is she told the detectives what happened. And you're free to go." She tilted her head and threw her voice beyond the curtain to the guard who was stationed there. "I would imagine that means you too, Officer."

"Ma'am, I'll depart as soon as I'm directed to do so by my supervisor."

"Last staple's the charm," the doctor said. Tara registered a final mild pop at the top of her wound.

"Is she okay to travel?" Mrs. Honoré asked. "I figure we'll get on the next Greyhound."

"As long as you bring a big bottle of water." He pushed his stool away from the gurney. "Keep chugging water, Tara. Today and tomorrow. You'll want to see your primary care physician if you get dizzy or nauseous. And to get the staples out."

Tara considered telling him she had no primary care physician but decided she didn't care. She slid to the floor, ready to get as far away as possible from this hospital, from New Orleans, and from the nightmare of Justin's death. She followed Mrs. Honoré down a corridor bathed in florescent light, past a trembling man in a wheelchair, and back through the swinging doors that led to the waiting area.

"Hey," a voice called as they neared the sliding glass doors of the entrance. Tara tensed as the Juvenile Intake guard strode toward them. "I've received the okay to drop you at the bus stop."

Two hours later, they were hunkered in the front row of a Greyhound, the city of New Orleans falling away behind them. Mrs. Honoré's head rested on Tara's shoulder. She'd fallen asleep before they'd even left the city.

Tara leaned her forehead against the window, feeling the vibrations of the engine through the glass. As green and brown earth rippled past, beneath the lengthening shadows of the setting sun, memories of Justin punctured her heart in an unending stream; his kindness, his openness, the fact that when he looked at her, she felt like she mattered. Justin alone had managed to break through the loneliness that lay thick across her life for as long as she could remember. He'd trusted in her ability to chart a way out.

She shuddered as the pure, physical sense of him washed over her. How was it that the most alive person she'd ever met was gone forever? The impossibility of it threatened to split her head in two. But that was the destructive force that was her mother, a force that crippled goodness and suffocated love and life.

The bus slowed, then swung onto the highway that skimmed the outskirts of Terrefine. The engine moaned as it accelerated, plunging them into a stretch of empty brown fields that merged with the darkening horizon. Nothing living stirred in the lightless landscape except a lone flame, a pure, radiant pink, floating in the distance. She stared, transfixed by the otherworldly beauty of it. "Flare stack," Mrs. Honoré said, triggering a hairy cough. "From a vent well. Mid-South will install twenty-six of them when all is said and done."

"What for?" Tara asked, her gaze remaining on the undulating light.

"To burn off all kinds of dangerous gases the sinkhole released underground, like the methane that killed Lightning. And would have killed me, if your mama hadn't pulled me from the barn." The flare slipped away, shrinking to a bright pinprick that was swallowed by the night. "Tara, I know you probably have all kinds of feelings about your mama right now—"

"I don't," Tara interrupted. "I don't have any feelings about her at all."

Mrs. Honoré pressed her lips together and settled back into her seat. Tara returned her gaze to the window until the driver announced the stop for Terrefine.

The bus slowed in front of the gas station where two days before they'd filled up the little white truck and her mother had purchased a lottery ticket. Mrs. Honoré's Chevy was near the entrance, half-blocking the sign declaring support for her mother. It was a short drive to Rudy's and as they neared the motel, Tara caught sight of the usual crowd drinking beer outside the lounge. As the Chevy's headlights swept across them, they ticked their heads toward the truck like a flock of curious birds.

Tara helped Mrs. Honoré unload her oxygen tank and maneuver it through the crushed shells of the parking lot to her room. The faint music drifting from the lounge only magnified the stilted quiet of the onlookers. As Mrs. Honoré jiggled her key in the doorknob, a grizzled voice flew through the evening shadows. "Is it true about your mama?"

Mrs. Honoré paused, then peered into the cluster of silhouettes. "Mind your business, Lew," she said, her voice calm.

"It's all our business, Loretta."

Mrs. Honoré swung around. "Hen-pecking this girl is not your business."

When Lew remained silent, Mrs. Honoré swung the door open and ushered Tara inside. "It's lucky most of those reporters took off for New Orleans," she murmured, when the door had closed. "Otherwise they'd be trying to gobble you up the way they did your mama."

Mrs. Honoré disappeared into the bathroom. When she returned, she held out a towel to Tara. "Go ahead and wash that jail off you, Tara. I'm going to see what Rudy's got left from dinner."

Tara awoke long after midnight, dragged from sleep by Mrs. Honoré's hacking. She pulled on her shorts and quietly shut the door behind her.

It was easy to break into her mother's room by jimmying open the window and slipping through the narrow gap. There were cigarettes and matches in the drawer of the bedside table.

She slipped through the shadows to the back of the motel. The ladder was still leaning against the wall of the cooking shed, from when she and Justin had climbed up with her mother to watch the fireworks.

Sitting cross-legged on the roof, she exhaled smoke into the moonless night, beneath a sky choked with stars. She closed her eyes, focusing on the familiar sounds—small creatures stirring in the surrounding woods, a plane droning high above, footsteps swishing though the wet weeds. Her eyes flew open. The ladder creaked as someone mounted the lower rung.

Quietly, Tara crab-walked to the back edge of the roof. She peered down, hoping for a nearby tree, but there was nothing but a pile of bricks. She jerked her gaze back to the ladder. A dark head hovered above the roof.

"*Le pauvre…*" the man's voice drifted softly through the damp night.

Tara remained still, unsure if the man had seen her or was speaking to himself. The ladder groaned and he stepped onto the roof. "I always wondered where you and Justin disappeared to on your little jaunts."

"Chase." Tara released a gust of air.

"In the flesh." His tongue tripped on his words.

"I didn't know you were a drinker," she said, scooting back to the middle of the roof. She tugged her last cigarette from the pack and struck a match.

"Nor did I know you were a smoker." Chase leaned in, his eyes glittering in the match's glow. "I guess we've each learned something completely trivial about the other." He hiccupped. "*Pardonez-moi.*"

"Mrs. Honoré said the press all went to New Orleans."

"The press," Chase sputtered in the darkness. "I've been reduced to *the press* by a thirteen-year-old urchin from nowhere, Louisiana." He released an airless burst of laughter.

"Fourteen."

"Splendid. Now you can legally marry in many parts of the world."

His hand brushed against Tara's as he plucked the cigarette from her fingers and brought it to his lips. "And a few places in these United States. With parental consent." Smoke slid past Tara's face. "This *press* man is here to capture the reactions of the residents of Terrefine tomorrow when hints of the true nature of your mother's trip to New Orleans surface. I predict anger, feelings of betrayal, and calls for a good old-fashioned tarring and feathering." He leaned away from her, his body jerking. The red glow of her cigarette arced beyond the edge of the roof and disappeared. "No offense, dear. It's just human nature."

"As if they don't already hate her."

"Justin's death, if not welcomed, was at least palatable. He's a Yank, not one of their own. And everybody knows your mama has a predilection for hotheadedness and occasional misfires." He collapsed back on the roof, his arms flopping at his sides. Tara gripped the hand that landed in her lap and tossed it back at him.

"The idea that she was protecting you," Chase continued, "could be viewed as noble, an extension of her righteousness. A quality that I exaggerated enormously in my reporting, by the way." He hiccupped and crossed his arms beneath his head. "But abandoning the troops before the battle has been won? And allying with the enemy?" He sighed heavily. "They'll be inconsolable."

Chase fell silent for several minutes and Tara wondered if he'd passed out. But he fluttered his lips and then clambered to all fours. "But don't let your mother's shortcomings stop you from pursuing your dreams of higher education. By the bootstraps and whatnot. Though Tulane is overrated."

"How do you know about that?" she stammered as he shuffled over to the ladder.

"Elementary, my dear Tara. Your intelligence is unmistakable to the keen observer, of which there are few in these parts. And as Tulane is upheld as our little state's academic bastion, it makes sense that you'd set your sights there. Though as I said. Highly overrated."

She moved to the ledge to watch his clumsy descent. "How did you know I was up here?"

"I've taken up temporary residence in my car. I've got a front row seat to all the nocturnal happenings at Rudy's. You wouldn't believe who's diddling who."

"You're sleeping in your car?"

"Mmm," he replied, his face submerged in darkness. "I await Lydia's emergence from her room. She hasn't come out since Justin's death."

The next morning, Mrs. Honoré surprised Tara, shaking her awake with coffee milk and the news that she'd rented a shotgun house in Golden Bayou, a small town a half hour from Terrefine. The revelation budged the stone from Tara's heart, if only by an inch or two. An hour later, the stone fell back in place as a flock of reporters descended on Rudy's.

Standing near the window in Mrs. Honoré's room, Tara pulled aside the dusty curtain to peer at the crowd assembled by the pool. Chase's stakeout had been rewarded. Lydia was there, impeccable in her black suit. A young woman stood a few steps behind her, also in black, her fingers flying over her phone as she took notes. Justin's replacement, Tara realized, her belly twisting with bitterness.

The motel's rooms had emptied and the remaining residents of Terrefine crowded around Lydia, their faces tense with listening. A fringe of reporters and cameras rippled around the gathering, agitating for a better shot or to launch a question. No one took notice of the grass snake slithering helplessly against the steep walls of the empty pool.

Tara raised the window an inch and Lydia's voice carried into the room. "Joan Saint-Romain's situation has no bearing whatsoever on this lawsuit. It was never about one person. The only thing that has changed is that we've lost a valued member of our team. Our hearts go out to Justin's family."

"But did she really do it? Try to finagle her own deal with GP?" Tara caught sight of Lew. His beard couldn't hide his ashen pallor, or the sharp downturn of his mouth. "It can't be true. It's gotta be Mid-South spreading fake news."

"All I can confirm is that two days ago, Joan Saint-Romain requested removal from the lawsuit. As far as the speculations leaked to the media this morning, you know as much as I do."

Mrs. Honoré's voice pulled Tara from the window. "You got everything from your mama's room?"

Tara nodded. The Hefty bag she'd filled with her clothes and her mother's stood next to the door. Mrs. Honoré zipped her duffel bag, wheezing as she bent low to shoulder it. "I'll get it," Tara said, tugging the bag from Mrs. Honoré's hand.

As soon as they opened the door, a clutch of reporters pounded across the parking lot to meet them. Tara kept close to Mrs. Honoré as they were pelted with questions. She swung her garbage bag protectively, feeling spurts of satisfaction whenever she "accidentally" made contact. When a camera bobbed in front of them, blocking their path, Mrs. Honoré wielded the oxygen tank like a battering ram.

When they were finally in the truck, Mrs. Honoré revved the old engine and peeled out of the lot. The road in front of the motel was still lined with a few of the car-campers who'd descended on Rudy's in support of Joan. As the Chevy squeezed past the school bus with the VW van welded to the roof, a carton of milk splattered on the windshield.

"Your mother's a backstabbing cunt!" a voice bellowed.

Tara spun around and caught sight of the full-bearded young man and his dreadlocked girlfriend who'd cheered Joan on at the last community meeting. Their faces were now twisted with rage.

The rented house smelled of mildew. For its entire length, the walls spanned less than two lengths of Tara's outstretched arms. But it was quiet. And when she felt creeped out by the cramped little bedroom, Mrs. Honoré agreed to let her throw down the mattress from the rickety twin bed on the back porch.

She'd just slipped between the thin sheets, borrowed from Rudy's until they could run to Walmart, when Mrs. Honoré's hacking sounded in the doorway. She stepped onto the porch, her face illuminated by a single birthday candle drilled into a Snickers bar.

"Happy birthday, girl. One day late." She lowered herself onto a cane rocker and held out the candy bar.

"Thanks." Tara propped herself on one elbow and blew out the flame. "You didn't have to go to any trouble. Lord knows I've caused you enough already."

"Go look in the kitchen."

When Tara poked her head into the kitchen, she found a laptop in the middle of the table. She ran her fingers across the keyboard, afraid to ask if it was meant for her.

"It's yours," Mrs. Honoré called from the porch. "It's used, but they tell me it's a good one."

"I can't believe it," Tara breathed as she stepped back outside. "It's too much."

"It's just enough, Tara. Put it to good use. Especially when you get back to school on Monday."

Tara felt her stomach drop.

29.

The whispers and sideward glances began on the school bus and carried forth to the treeless front lawn of Leittville High. With the sound of the morning recess bell, the buzz continued, flowing into the hallways and the classrooms. As Tara went through the motions of being a ninth grader, an electric aura followed her, but at a distance. No one seemed to want to heckle her up close.

It was only at lunch as she sat alone, hacking through a square of cold macaroni, that it dawned on her that the other kids were taking pains to avoid her. To test her theory, she picked out a senior, a football player, and caught his gaze. His eyes widened, then cut away at once.

It made sense. After all, she was the daughter of a murderer and, for all she knew, the first ever at Leittville High. Living with Mrs. Honoré, who for years had been at the center of her own cosmos of dark rumors, could only inflame the speculation.

She parked her fork upright in the macaroni and leaned back in her seat, feeling deeply relieved at the thought of being left alone. Perhaps she could cruise through the next four years with this bubble of isolation intact. A plan took form in her mind. She'd draw upon what she learned from Chase and Lydia and create a public persona, the strange and dangerous child of a killer. They'd spun her mother into a hero. She could just as easily paint herself as a villain.

Meanwhile, she'd begin the process of learning to fly helicopters, planes—whatever she could learn about on the internet. By the time she graduated, she'd be primed to leave this place behind forever. As she fed her tray into the dishwasher window, she felt almost peaceful.

"Hey!" The voice reached her as she stepped from beneath the cafeteria catwalk to the hard-packed grass. She looked up to find Gerard striding toward her, a careful smile on his face. His hair was freshly cut and he wore dark jeans and un-scuffed Nikes. A trace of dark fuzz had appeared above his lip. "Heard you were here."

"What else did you hear?" She crossed her arms and leaned into one hip.

His smile wavered as he searched her face. "Not much."

"Come on. I'd like to know. Really."

His fingers slid into his pockets and his honey-colored eyes darkened. "Just the stuff from the news, about what your mother did."

"You mean killed a man?"

"Yeah. And that you spent the night in jail."

"That's the truth."

Gerard rubbed the back of his neck. An explosion of spastic laughter reached them from far across the lawn. "A few are saying you helped. But the police let you go 'cause you're a minor."

"Is that so?" Tara paused to consider this new piece of disinformation. It might be helpful in keeping the rest of the school at bay.

"I told them no way," Gerard added, hurrying to catch her as she plunged into the crowded schoolyard. On each side, clusters of boisterous students fell silent as Tara walked by.

"Do me a favor, Gerard. Let them think what they want."

The recess bell sounded, and Gerard stepped in front of her, forcing her to stop.

"That's not right, Tara. People need to know the truth about you."

"No. They don't. As long as they leave me be, they can think whatever they want." She shifted her gaze to the raucous stream of kids pouring into the school building. "It's how I want it. I swear."

They walked the remaining stretch of lawn in silence. As she waved goodbye, Gerard asked, "Bike ride this weekend?"

"On what? You set fire to mine, remember?"

His face became a kaleidoscope of pinks and reds. "You can borrow mine. I'll use Louis's and double him."

"I'll think about it."

The school day mercifully ended, and the bus dropped her at the scraggly front yard of their new house. She found Mrs. Honoré in the kitchen, a large pot simmering on the stove. The dense sweetness of roast beef hung in the air.

"I see you made it home alive," Mrs. Honoré said as Tara shrugged off her backpack and gravitated to the stove. "How was it?"

"It was fine. I didn't miss much." She lifted the lid and leaned into the blast of savory steam. "You went to the Piggly Wiggly by yourself?"

"Just for a few things. They helped me load up."

"Mrs. Honoré." Tara turned to gaze at her friend. "I don't know how yet, but I'll pay you back for everything. The bus ticket, the groceries, the gas. All of it. I promise."

"Listen." Mrs. Honoré rocked back in her chair. "The state of my health right now, if you weren't here I'd probably have to pay somebody to stay with me. Like Mrs. Adelaide has to do with that home health care aide. That costs a fortune. Plus having a stranger in the house? No thank you. Tara, you're saving my behind."

"I can clean," Tara said, opening up the succession of cabinets and peering inside. "Scrub these down, if you want me to."

"Maybe so. I'm making my to-do list. Now come sit." Tara fussed a moment longer with a broken cabinet latch before joining Mrs. Honoré at the table. "She called," Mrs. Honoré said, her voice soft. "Collect from the jail."

"Collect call. What a surprise."

"I told her to try back tomorrow, a little later, when you're sure to be home."

"I won't talk to her."

"That's your right. Nobody's going to force you. Least of all me." Mrs. Honoré traced a burn mark on the table with her fingertip. "Just know that you're allowed to change your mind. Next week, next year, ten years from now."

"Thanks, but I doubt it."

"One more thing," Mrs. Honoré said as Tara rose from the table to stir the roast beef. "I wanted you to hear this from me. They got your mama an attorney. He told her they found that boy who gave her the drugs. The boy swears that snake in the grass Chase Robichaux put him up to it. You got any idea why he would do such a thing?"

Tara thought back to Chase's drunken visit on the roof, his tossed off comment about Tulane. Carl must have reported everything they'd said to Chase, including the details her mother was sure to have bragged about of their meeting with Sophie.

Tara shrugged. "Maybe to get back at her? He thinks he did all this extra work to get her in the news and she broke off to go with Sophie Alaoui. Or maybe he wanted to make a crazy woman even crazier so he could write about it."

Mrs. Honoré had witnessed Tara's interrogation, so she knew many of the details of the trip to New Orleans but not all. As they spooned hunks of roast beef from chipped ceramic bowls, dusk coloring the windows above the kitchen sink, Tara filled in the gaps. She related the helicopter flight from Eddy's front yard to the massive yacht anchored in the Mississippi. When she spoke of Sophie's five-million-dollar offer, Mrs. Honoré's spoon became still. When she revealed her mother's ten-million-dollar counteroffer, she watched the soft creases of Mrs. Honoré's face harden, her calloused fingers forming a fist on the tablecloth.

"It's true. Chase is a snake," Tara finished. "They're all snakes—Lydia, Sophie Alaoui, Mid-South, all those press people. But nobody forced Joan to shove anything up her nose. Or drink herself into the ground. That's all on her."

Over the next two weeks, other school events arose to distract from Tara's notoriety. There was a student expelled for being drunk on campus and homecoming preparations got underway, with the student body engrossed in the prospects of their Bulldogs, winners of last year's 3A division championship.

Tara still received the occasional stare or smirk, and she once overheard a stocky girl in the locker room after PE murmuring, "My daddy says that bitch Joan Saint-Romain cut the settlement in half. There's no pressure on the company 'cause nobody gives a shit about us anymore."

Tara ventured onto social media only once, setting up her laptop in a corner of the school library to scan the avalanche of comments directed at her mother. The once-admiring posts had turned hateful as the rumor of the deal with GP grew, mutating into versions that only faintly resembled Sophie's actual offer. There were theories that her mother had conspired with Mid-South and GP from the very beginning, that all along she had been a spy. A faction of posters suggested that the arrest at the house, when the police dragged her mother through the front yard, had been faked. Another theorized that Justin had discovered evidence of her betrayal, and she'd killed him for it.

The most recent article from Chase included a video of Billy Fontaine, the guard who'd been suspended by Mid-South for attacking her mother. He stood with his arm slung across his wife's shoulder as Chase asked him for his thoughts on Joan's arrest for murder. "Just deserts from the good Lord," Billy replied. "My family and I have been praying that the truth would come out about this unclean woman. We had faith. And our faith has been rewarded."

#TraitorJoan, #Shesnosaint, #GPsbitch were popular tags, but most horrifying was a pile on of violent comments to her mother's Facebook page suggesting that she be raped and mutilated. Her mother's story had become a vortex for everything about people that was ugly and vicious. As Tara deleted her mother's social media accounts, she felt like she was cutting out something cancerous.

30.

On her second Friday back at school, Gerard caught up with Tara in the hallway and repeated his invitation to bike ride over the weekend. "I got a surprise. Something I think you'll wanna see."

"Can't. I got stuff to do around the house for Mrs. Honoré."

But the next morning, as Tara dug the nose of the push mower into a thicket of browning grass, Mrs. Honoré flagged her from the back porch.

"You're done here," Mrs. Honoré said, once the roar of the mower died. "Those Ledroit boys are out front. And they have bicycles. Go!"

Tara parked the mower beneath the slip of corrugated tin that served as a shed, then threaded her way through the house, pausing to help Mrs. Honoré pack away the oxygen tank she no longer needed.

Outside, she found Gerard and Louis beneath a dogwood tree that overhung the narrow dirt driveway. Gerard wordlessly offered his bike to Tara, then wedged himself in front of his brother. Louis clasped his brother's waist as Gerard heaved the bike into motion, accelerating onto the thinly paved road.

Tara mounted Gerard's bike and fell in alongside the boys. Soon they were cruising past wide-open fields trimmed with clusters of trees fluttering gold and rust. They passed ramshackle houses with tire-less cars perched on blocks. Eventually, Gerard veered off the road onto a faint trail that disappeared into the trees. Branches scraped their forearms and tugged at their clothes as they wound through the woods. At times, they were forced to dismount and plow their front tires over bulging tree roots that blocked the path.

"How much longer?" Louis asked as they stopped to munch the sleeve of graham crackers that Gerard had brought along. Nearby, a mosquito hawk perched on the surface of a puddle, its micro-thin legs bowing the water.

"We're here," Gerard replied, gesturing toward the swollen trunk of an oak tree, reachable through a mire of rotting leaves. "After we climb up, I mean."

They slapped the rough trunk with their palms, giving any hiding creatures the chance to slither off, then began to climb, Gerard leading the way, grasping branches and balancing on knots. He halted in the crook of a wide branch and scooted aside, making room for Tara.

When she was settled, straddling the branch, she leaned forward to scan for Louis below. The height triggered a tickle deep within her gut as she peered down at his small bright face, tucked against the base of the tree.

"Come up!" she called.

"No way! Y'all are crazy," he yelled. "I'm staying down here."

"All right, punk. We'll be down in a few," Gerard called to his brother, then touched Tara's shoulder. "Look."

She followed his gaze beyond the edge of the wood, across a field of sugar cane, to where a house stood on the jagged bank of a shimmering lake. The water's surface was streaked with strange, pearlescent hues. Bright orange tubing cordoned off segments of the water and a small army of earthmovers and emergency vehicles was parked on a leveled square of land, directly across the water from the house.

Her house. Teetering on the edge of the oil-slicked waters of the sinkhole. She made out the remnants of the exploratory well in her backyard and the bashed-in corner of her room where the crane had gone wide. The grassy lot next door had been trampled flat from the relocation of her mother's backyard junk collection and the forceful gusts of the helicopter landings. She felt Gerard's eyes on her.

"We're inside the evacuation area. I used Google Earth and found a way I guess even you didn't know." He grinned. "My dad says they've got these seismic sensors planted everywhere, so they can tell hours ahead if a new collapse is coming. That means we could sneak into your house one night. As long as the sensors that afternoon were clear."

"Why?" Tara asked, pressing her palms into the rough bark. "I don't want to go back there."

"Isn't there anything you want? Stuff you left behind?"

"Like what? The bucket Joan used to vomit in? Old pictures of my black-hearted daddy? Can of red beans? There ain't nothing there for me."

"What about the iron pyrite I gave you?"

Tara looked down, letting her gaze tumble from branch to branch, the tingle igniting again in the pit of her belly. "Some things got left behind, Gerard," she answered, pushing herself upright. "I can't do anything about that."

"Hurry up, y'all!" Louis's cry echoed through the woods. "This is boring!"

"Relax!" Gerard yelled, then squeezed his eyes shut, his lashes delicate against his pale skin. "Tara, my dad had me start seeing this lady. Because of what we did. What I did. Burning your bike. I'm supposed to tell you that I lied to you about where we went the weekend before. We weren't fishing. We were at a one-year memorial with my mom's relatives. For her death."

The branch swayed, stirred by the wind, sending the dry leaves chattering. "They don't say it out loud," he continued, his eyes opening to take in the wide crown of the oak. "But they all blame my dad for her getting sick, for working at all these oil and chemical plants and dragging her with him." He rolled an acorn between his fingers, then stretched out his arm, letting the acorn drop. "I guess part of me does too."

"I'm taking a bike and leaving in sixty seconds!" Louis screamed. "I mean it!"

"Chill out, you turd! We're coming!" Gerard called, then turned back to Tara. "Anyway, the lady put me on this medication. It's supposed to help me with my mood."

"Seems like it's working real good." Tara smiled, sliding her eyes in Louis's direction. "Mr. Turd."

"Brothers don't count," he said, offering her a sheepish grin. "Best you can do is try not to kill each other."

As Tara slid toward the tree trunk to begin her descent, she was hit with a blast of an oily, noxious odor. On the branch behind her, Gerard began to cough.

"I smell something!" Louis's panicked voice sounded from below.

Tara gripped the branch with her thighs as vibrations rippled through the tree. Instinctively, she glanced toward the sinkhole. A flashing beacon had erupted in the midst of the emergency vehicles. From across the field, a faint tidal murmur reached her ears. Frothy cross-currents appeared on the water's surface as a thick rim of earth on each side of the house broke off into the sinkhole.

She felt another violent tremble through the tree trunk as a fissure crept down the back wall of her house. Seconds later, the entire front half of the home slaked off into the roiling waters.

31.

Gerard bribed Louis to keep quiet about trespassing inside the evacuation zone, promising him first dibs on their video game collection for the next month. But the following day, when Eddy Ledroit backed his truck up to the shotgun house, Tara wondered if maybe Louis had ratted them out.

"Got something for you," Eddy said, when Mrs. Honoré joined Tara on the porch. He rolled back the tarp covering the bed of his truck to reveal a regiment of feathered creatures, their shining eyes fixed on the ruptured storm clouds above, wings, claws and beaks frozen lifelike in various postures of rest, flight, and feeding. At the center of the flock, cushioned by a stained blue quilt, lay the majestic snowy egret, the last project of Mrs. Honoré's before the sinkhole drained Terrefine of inhabitants.

"We better move quick. Rain's coming," Eddy responded to Mrs. Honoré's look of surprise. "Got your CB radio, too."

Tara hurried to take up a barred owl, cradling the bit of dried wood upon which it was perched and delivering it to Mrs. Honoré on the porch steps. Eddy followed closely behind with a red-shouldered hawk. Next came a purple finch, then a roseate spoonbill. Soon, over half of Mrs. Honoré's original taxidermy collection had migrated to the little house. Owls, ducks, pelicans, and birds of prey occupied every available space, including the kitchen table where the snowy egret crooked its wings in pursuit of invisible prey.

When the last bird had been transferred and the CB stowed in Mrs. Honoré's bedroom, Eddy planted himself awkwardly on the porch steps, his fingers finding refuge in his jeans pockets. The sky had opened up and chill sheets of water crashed down behind him.

"I hope you don't mind that I went in your home without asking," he began, raising his voice above the pounding rain. "We were doing some methane sampling on your property. Back door was open." He tapped a muddy boot against the porch railing, releasing chunks of creamy dirt, then swept the mess over the edge.

"I'd given up on seeing these birds again. And my tools," Mrs. Honoré said, examining the open toolbox on her lap. "I can get working again."

"How did you know about her taxidermy?" Tara asked, folding her arms and leaning against the house.

"Most folks do. Plus, your mama talked to me about it a couple days back."

Light blazed across the yard, followed by a deep rumble that shook the porch.

"You're talking to her?" Tara asked. "Why?"

"I feel like I'm to blame for some of this mess. I could've handled things better. From the beginning." He released a long, low breath and bowed his head. "Tara, you were more suspicious about those bubbles than I was. You had a good gut. I wanted to see what I wanted to see and it almost got you drowned. And then the forced evacuation, and your mother's arrest… Horrible."

"It was you that bailed Joan out, wasn't it?" Mrs. Honoré asked. "When she got arrested by the state police."

He nodded as lightning pulsed overhead. "Everything spun so far out of control. And I guessed Tara and her mama didn't have many resources. I didn't know what would happen to Tara. Posting bail anonymously and getting Joan out quick was the only thing I could think to do."

Thunder rolled out to the smoky gray horizon. "And somehow," Eddy continued when quiet was restored. "Even with everything that's happened, Joan and I have become friends. There are things about her I admire. What happened with Justin was just terrible. But even still, Tara, your mama got people to pay attention, the governor included. He can't look away now. Word has it he's planning a visit. My bosses are scrambling to finalize their remediation plan."

"Remediation?" asked Mrs. Honoré. "The land is altered forever. There's no remediation. There's just helping people start over and get on with their lives."

"You're right. At this weekend's community meeting Mid-South will announce the start of the evacuation assistance checks. I hope you'll be there."

Tara scooped up a sandpiper whose wing had been damaged on the ride over and turned to go in the house.

"Tara, one sec," Eddy called.

She paused, fingers on the screen door handle.

"Your mama wonders if you're getting her letters."

Tara blew a leaf fragment from the sandpiper's back, then met Eddy's gaze. "I'm glad you got a friend, but please don't come around here messing in my business just so you don't have to feel bad." She yanked open the door and disappeared into the house.

For days after Eddy's visit, hard rains continued, flooding the roads and turning the earth to mush. The water rose, creeping toward the house, and at one point Tara donned the too-big galoshes she'd found in a corner of the back porch and sloshed through the yard to check the outflow of the drainage ditch. A squirming raft of tens of thousands of fire ants, the color of dried blood, drifted past her boots, each creature intent on keeping the whole afloat.

The day the rain finally let up, Tara returned home from school to discover that the soaked earth around the sinkhole had caved again, taking with it the rest of her childhood home.

"Eddy Ledroit called to tell us," Mrs. Honoré explained, setting a cup of steaming coffee milk on the kitchen table for Tara.

Tara blew on the scalding liquid, picturing the house, and all its contents—the water-stained couch, the claw-foot tub, the gritty rooftop where she'd learned to smoke—in a slow motion tumble through 750 feet of chilled waters, coming to rest like a wrecked ship on the floor of the sinkhole. Below these remains of her former life, the salt dome endured, extending thousands of feet into the earth, an underground monument to an ancient sea and a world when people did not exist.

"What're you thinking, Tara?" Mrs. Honoré's voice was soft as she poured her own cup of coffee from the dented silver pot on the burner.

"Just whether one day people will die off. The way the dinosaurs did."

"It's possible. The way we've been carrying on."

"Or maybe, we'll become something else." Tara paused to stroke the wing of the snowy egret. "Like the dinosaurs became birds."

"Maybe so. Life does seem to want to keep living, wherever it may find itself."

Mrs. Honoré and Tara met Ricky Delray at the Fry Palace in Leittville. He'd arrived first, securing a twelve-piece box of chicken and a booth near the window.

As Tara and Mrs. Honoré slid into the booth, Ricky waved a greeting, while continuing to gnaw his fried drumstick. A napkin was draped beneath his neck, his chin and mouth shiny with grease. He gulped from a paper Coca-Cola cup, then bunched the napkin against his lips.

"Sorry, first time I've eaten today." His eyes cut to the edge of the table where a manila envelope had been placed safely beyond his feeding range. "My colleague in family law says these are the papers you'll need to fill out to apply for permanent custody of Tara."

"Thank you." Mrs. Honoré peeked inside the envelope, then set it on the table next to her. "We'll look over this together tonight, Tara."

"I read them online," Tara replied, "so I can explain them to you."

"Good. Anything new on the suit, Ricky?"

"You probably heard that the governor publically threatened to sue Mid-South if they don't start offering everyone buyouts." He dropped the clean-picked drumstick into a paper tray filled with tiny bones. "Regardless of intent to participate in a lawsuit against Mid-South."

"I did hear something about that," Mrs. Honoré said. She plucked a napkin from the table dispenser and wiped a ketchup smear from the table. "Seems like a good sign."

"Maybe," Ricky replied. "Or it's the first stage of an audacious land grab." He pushed away his pile of bones. "Orchestrated between Mid-South and the state to clear out the residents of Terrefine and completely surrender the area to industry."

"Guess it depends on who you're asking," Mrs. Honoré replied, raising her brows. "Would the buyout include Tara's house?"

"Joan will get an offer, yes. But rumor has it Lydia's met several times with Justin's family about a possible wrongful death suit. That house was Joan's only asset." He popped a stray crumble into his mouth and met Mrs. Honoré's gaze. "Main thing is that you're going to have a buyout offer coming your way within the next few months that'll contain an agreement to release Mid-South from any future claims. I still hope to make this a high profile, precedent-setting case and hit Mid-South, GP, and ultimately all the oil and gas industry where it hurts. But it could take years." He glanced at Tara. "And it could get ugly."

Mrs. Honoré's deep sigh was interrupted by a spate of wet coughing. Tara plucked a napkin from the dispenser and tucked it in Mrs. Honoré's hand. "Your cold's coming back."

Mrs. Honoré nodded, then spat into the napkin. "I appreciate you being straight with me, Ricky. I got to think about all this. Things are different than when we started. I can't seem to find my righteousness."

"You have a look around, Loretta." Ricky's gaze drifted to the window and the highway that bordered the Fry Palace. A semi was roaring past, it's two-story trailer weighted down with new cars. "See if you can find it. And you let me know."

It was while shelling peas that Tara learned her mother had pleaded guilty to manslaughter. A petite newscaster on the small black and white TV informed viewers in her nasal monotone of the sentence.

Twenty years.

Tara's fingers continued to pry the green flesh from the pods as she listened to the Honorable Judge Patricia Long's statement that while Joan Saint-Romain may have believed she was acting in her daughter's defense, her reckless ingestion of prescription and illegal drugs and her abandonment of her child for many hours "…ran counter to any claims of the maternal instinct. A young man lost his life. That's what this sentencing hinges upon." There was a possibility for parole after ten years served. Tara would be twenty-four. Her mother would be almost forty.

Her mother's mug shot flashed on screen. Her blue eyes were empty of defiance. Sadness had etched itself into the corners of her mouth. For a moment, Tara felt a softening in her chest, but then the image of Justin sprawled on the hotel floor fell hard into her consciousness, as it did many times each day.

She switched off the TV and reached for the letter Mrs. Honoré had left for her on the kitchen table. Her mother's jumbled handwriting crowded the prison's return address into Tara's name. She set aside the bowl of peas and took up the envelope, padding into the next room, past Mrs. Honoré who was on the phone discussing the delivery of the snowy egret to LSU's ornithology collection.

It had grown too chilly to sleep on the porch, and Tara now slept in the second of the house's linear stack of rooms, between the living room and Mrs. Honoré's bedroom. Her room was sparsely furnished with a squeaky twin bed beneath the window, a wooden chair, and a low cabinet she'd found on the side of the road.

She wiggled her pinky into the keyhole of the cabinet door and pulled it open to reveal a stack of letters, weighted beneath the rattler skull. She slid the most recent letter on top, replaced the snakehead, then resealed the door.

As Tara left the room, the warped cabinet door popped open, leaving just a crack.

Acknowledgements

I'm grateful to so many folks who supported, loved, cajoled, and generally kept the faith for me as a I brought this book into existence.

I thank my husband, Gary Rabinowitz, for never doubting me as I began my writing journey in earnest (and for cheering me on the whole way!); my agent, Jeff Ourvan, for his wise counsel and belief in this book; Jaynie Royal and Pam Van Dyk for bringing me into the Regal House family and for their creative collaboration.

Much gratitude to Dawn Rebecky, Maxine Roel, and Nitza Wilon for giving me the courage to return to writing; the Wednesday night workshop (my early, early readers), Vicky Vidalaki, Heather Siegel, Judy Karp, Maureen Mehan, and Jeremy Goldstein for inspiration, camaraderie, and accountability; to my early readers (and beloved friends) Mary Minges, Sallie Sanborn, Steve Friedman and my lovely mom, Linda Bordelon.

Special thanks to Bill Stone for his generosity in sharing his geology expertise, brilliance, and time during countless phone calls. I would have been undone by the technical complexities of the sinkhole without him. And many thanks to William Murray who was kind enough to review and clarify some of the law enforcement details.

Much appreciation to my mom and my siblings, John Baum, Will Baum, Lily Harris, and Lance Bordelon for their love and support (also to Lance for his input on the legal aspects of the plot); to Perch Ducote for his treasured friendship and generous heart which buoyed my spirits and inspired me to stay the course (and for being an early reader); to my dear friend, Jamin London-Tinsel, whose devotion to art nurtures my own; to Brenda Mehl, sage and friend, for teaching me to allow all the parts; to the Witches for calling this book into being; and to the Sacred Circle for feeding my soul.

Lastly, for the folks of the real Bayou Corne sinkhole, and anyone who's had to endure displacement, may your fortitude lead you to solid ground.